THE COVENANT FIELD

ISBN 10: 0-923568-82-4
ISBN 13: 978-0923-56882-5

Cover Photo by Chris Zimmerman, late October, 2006. Isabella County wheat field.

Second Edition, published by Joker's Conundrum LLC
P.O. Box 180
Shepherd MI 48883

Electronic correspondence should be sent to:
setterindebtor@yahoo.com

For more information about the author, visit
www.authorchriszimmerman.com

Printed in the United States of America

THE COVENANT FIELD

CHRIS ZIMMERMAN

Also by Chris Zimmerman:

INTENTIONAL ACTS
THE SECRET-KEEPER

One

IT WAS NEARLY NOON Iowa time when we finally crossed the Mississippi River and into the rolling, corn-stubbled hills of America's breadbasket. Michigan's congested midriff was far in the rearview mirror as my dog and I rumbled over the land Lewis and Clark dubbed, "the great green sea." Once teeming with elk, buffalo, and prairie chickens, Iowa is now a testament to the destructive qualities of a hundred and fifty years of agricultural advancements. But they haven't destroyed all that was left of the prairies. In the fencerows and terraces, amidst the corn and beans, rivers and creeks, lay pockets of thick grass the color of butternut squash. It was in those weed-covered hills I made a horrible discovery one blustery December afternoon a year shy of our next presidential election.

Iowa has a wholesome innocence about it. The land lies before you like an open book. The farmhouses are sparsely landscaped, and the barns are brimming with purpose. There's very little clutter, and everyone—from implement dealers to the wait staff behind the counters at the coffee shops seem to have a hand in the business of farming. The land, the people, the pace of life is so different than what I was used to—it's like going back in time to when the inhabitants, the community, the entire nation had a connection to Mother Earth, to the cycle of life and the rebirth of the passing seasons.

When I finally exited the highway and pointed the old Suburban south towards the little town of What Cheer, I had polished off the last of the meatloaf sandwiches. What Cheer is the same as most other towns in Iowa. They're all about function. No flash or pizzazz. Necessity, necessity, necessity. The shops downtown are all about farming, eating, or growing things. They don't have any flower shops, or dog-grooming boutiques and, Lord forbid, fitness centers. The people in Iowa get their exercise the old fashioned way—by growing crops, tending the livestock, and eating food that was grown on the farm. Maybe that's why most folks who live there seem to be thin and healthy.

The hardware store across the train tracks hadn't changed since the last time I was there almost exactly one year ago. I recognized the weathered hardwood floors, the string of Swiss cow bells dangling from the back of the heavy, wide door, and the massive deer antlers fastened to a wooden border beneath the stained, false ceiling. The countertop was still a smooth sheet of ancient linoleum, with its center worn thin from decades of coins, currency, and paper sacks being pushed across its surface.

The man behind the counter was just as I remembered. He still had on a pair of denim painter's pants and an archaic, faded work shirt that could have had a name patch over the pocket. I asked for a non-resident hunting license and a box of shotgun shells.

The man behind the counter moved to a small, desktop computer and asked for my name.

"C. Derrick Twitchell…the second."

"First name?"

"Claude," I said, embarrassed.

"Oh yes," he nodded, smiling, as if I had conjured up pleasant childhood memories. "I remember you." Suddenly, I had made his day. "You're that reporter fella from Michigan, right?"

"That's correct."

"I recognized your name. We don't get too many 'Claudes' around these parts."

"I know. It's unusual."

He raised his eyebrows and continued.

"Especially those guys whose truck catches on fire in the middle of downtown What Cheer." He chuckled, and said 'What Cheer' as if it were one word.

"Don't remind me," I laughed half-heartedly along with him. "I almost lost my dog in that fire."

"Never mind your dog, that fire almost burned down the store, and damned near burned down the seed elevator next door."

"I'm sorry."

"You're sorry?" He looked at me.

"Yeah, I'm sorry."

"You shouldn't be sorry," he continued. "That was the biggest news in What Cheer for quite some time. I bet there was fifteen fire trucks here, from six different towns. Your story was printed in the papers, and on television." He was getting riled up, recanting the story. "That was something. I saw it on the news out of Des Moines. If it wasn't for your truck getting burned up in the process, it would really be funny."

I shook my head and peered beneath the counter at the boxes of shotshells festooned with ears of corn and fake leaves of red, yellow and orange.

"What started that fire, anyway?"

I looked up from the shotshell display.

"Catalytic converter, they think, but I really can't say for sure."

"Must have been the unleaded fuel in a leaded truck," he said, smugly. "What year was it anyway?"

"Eighty-seven."

"Oh sure," he said, raising an index finger to his lips. "Those catalytic converters turn cherry red if you run unleaded fuel through them. It's no big deal if you're just driving around town, but on long trips that baby will glow like a Christmas light."

"Guess I was lucky."

"What did you do, anyway?" His fingers scratched a small shrub of hair on the top of his head. "That will be ninety dollars for the license."

"Last year?" I asked, handing him a pair of well-earned fifties.

"Yeah."

"I walked to a motel, picked up a newspaper and the classified ads, and bought another truck the next morning. After that I went hunting. What else could I do?"

He laughed, affirmatively. "Here's your license, Mr. Twitchell, and your change. Need any shells?"

"Yes, I do. Sixteen gauge, for my new gun."

We finished our business. I was legal to hunt pheasants and quail in Iowa, now all I needed to do was get to the Emmert St. Peter farm in the waning hours of the day.

Iowa's shooting hours are from 8 A.M. to 4:30 P.M. The idea behind the limited hunting hours is that it protects the pheasants when they're still on the roost. It also keeps hunters hunting during the most daylight, where it is easier to tell the hens from the roosters. Only roosters are legal to kill.

At almost two, I pulled off the blacktop and onto one of the gravel roads that crisscrosses the countryside. My old Suburban was chugging along merrily, and I was proud of it. I loved the bench-style front seat, and the obnoxiously ugly seat cover I tied to it. It felt like a hunting truck, drove like a hunting truck, and even smelled like a hunting truck. I didn't pay much for it a year ago in Iowa, but I didn't get scalped, either. Even though I was desperate for a set of wheels, the folks who had it for sale didn't cheat me. That's what I've come to expect from the folks in Iowa: they're honest, fair, and willing to lend a hand or a leg up.

My English springer spaniel, Synch, recognized the uneven roads, the familiar chatter bumps, and awoke from a long nap in the backseat. She yawned, shook the cobwebs from her head and took a giant whiff of air from the passenger side window. Her tail wagged, sending the little curl of hair at the end into a dither. She smelled the intrigue, the adventure. She tasted the hint of corn, the mention of beans in the dusty, swine-filled breeze.

"What do you think?" I asked her. She yawned again, nervously. She was anxious. We both were.

At nearly two, we pulled into the long, gravel drive of the St. Peter farm. It hadn't changed a bit since last year, or since the first time I met them several years ago. The farmhouse and barnyard still sat on a round knob about halfway up a sloping, corn-studded hillside. The cellar still doubled as a pantry for homemade canned vegetables, and a place to hide when the storms of summer steamrolled the countryside. There were no cotton towels, linens or denim jeans dancing on the clothesline, but that's not to say that it wouldn't happen during the next warm spell, a basket of clothespins at the ready. I pulled right in, as if I owned the place, because that's what Emmert always said I should do. He's such a nice guy. He and his wife both are so pleasant, so kind. I always bring them a quart of Michigan's finest maple syrup and they seem to appreciate it. It's one of those things that I probably don't have to do, but it makes me feel better about the whole arrangement of hunting their farm without having to pay for the privilege. When I made it to the back door, there was a note taped to the sill. It read: "*Derrick, go ahead and hunt. We've gone over to the Amana Colonies for an auction and dinner. Mother made you some cookies, and there's soft drinks in the garage. We won't be home till late. Good luck and thanks for the syrup. Emmert.*

I laughed. Maybe it was a good idea that I brought along the maple syrup, after all. Until now, I never thought that anyone who let me hunt their farm really appreciated it. For years, syrup had been one of those goodwill gestures I gave to the farmers, but I really had no idea if they actually poured it over their morning pancakes or their homemade cornbread. I figured that some of them gave it away to their relatives, their neighbors, or the even the postman, for that matter.

After leaving the syrup on the doorstep, I drove the old Suburban out of the farmyard, down the lane and behind one of Emmert's old barns. Synch couldn't wait to get out of the truck. She bounced from the backseat to the front, shoving me out of the way.

"Okay, okay," I scolded her. "Let's go hunting."

In no time, I had donned my hunting chaps, a fleece pullover, and a comfortable pair of hunting boots. Synch had finished sniffing out the barnyard, sending a half-dozen semi-feral cats scrambling for the safety of a broken-out window or a rusty farm implement. They looked at my aging springer with either mild amusement, or curious disdain. It seemed that they hadn't remembered our visit to the farm a year ago.

I couldn't wait to get in a big walk after such a long drive. It felt good to stretch the legs, to handle a shotgun instead of the steering wheel. I couldn't wait to see how much the hill behind the barn had grown in the past year. With each visit, that hill somehow becomes harder and harder to tackle.

In either case, we had an excellent day for a pheasant hunt. The air was damp and moist- an excellent vehicle for carrying the scent of game. The skies were business-suit gray, flecked with the pleated shadows of potential snow. I put on my yellow shooting glasses and the countryside was bathed in a regal glow. Nut grass bunched in small, golden-brown pyramids in the gaps of sheep-wire fencing. They were neat and orderly, like the bundles of straw in an Amish wheat field.

Synch raced down the lane as I locked the Suburban and hid the keys in my vest next to my digital camera and a small handful of freshly purchased shotshells. I let her go, to burn off energy. After a couple days of hunting she'd forget about those frivolous escapades and stick to business. And when we'd stop for a break in the middle of a hunt, she'd be the one to curl up and take a mini-nap, if only for a moment or two.

The St. Peter farm is not unlike most of the farms in Iowa. The house is old, sturdy and big enough to accommodate a large family. Emmert and his wife, Carolyn raised three kids on the farm—two daughters and a son. The two daughters moved out of state after they were married. One of them married a railroad engineer, and now lives in Superior-Duluth. The other fell in love with a seed salesman who used to call on the elevator where she worked the summer months while attending school at Ames. The seed salesman eventually quit selling seeds, and now works for the pork industry as a lobbyist in Kansas City. Their son moved away too, to Iowa City, where he's in charge of the maintenance at the University of Iowa. Much like most farms in Iowa, the St. Peter farm is being farmed by folks who are in their seventies, with no children who want to take it over. As the farmers die off, and the farms go up for auction, much of the property gets scooped up by farming conglomerates, which put employees in the farmhouses, who in turn have little concern for upkeep of the grounds.

Little by little, Iowa is being overrun by big business.

The St. Peter farmhouse rests at the east end of the property, where a hundred and sixty acres stretches a half-mile wide by a half-mile long. When property values crashed during the farm crisis of the nineteen eighties, Emmert bought another forty at the northwest tip of his property. Carolyn despised the idea of spending more money for more property while their kitchen needed remodeling. Emmert listened to her wishes but bought the property anyway, knowing full well that the additional twenty-five acres of tillable ground would eventually pay for itself and a couple of new kitchens thereafter.

The forty wasn't really the best for farming, but then again Emmert probably didn't pay top dollar for it, either. It was in the middle of a broad valley, where the soil was black and rich, and in the intersection of a small river and two large creeks. It was one of those forties that had three workable fields, just big enough that a fair-sized tractor could get in there and take care of business.

My goal was to make it to the back forty before the end of shooting hours, not necessarily shoot a limit of pheasants.

Some guys want to shoot three roosters just as fast as they can. They measure their experience in the field by the heft of their game bag, rather than enjoying the magic that is pheasant hunting. The only thing I wanted to do was take my dog hunting, to watch her go and have the time of her life. If Synch happened to flush a rooster or two in range, and my shot was true, that would be just dandy.

When the farm lane snaked its way to the right, Synch and I marched up the left side of the hill. At first I thought that I hadn't worn enough clothes; December's talons cut right through me. But halfway up the hill, I was breathing hard and sweating like a riled thoroughbred. When we finally reached the summit, I was huffing and puffing, cursing the clothes I had worn and regretting the weight I hadn't lost.

But what a view from the top of that hill. I could see for miles. Iowa lay before me like a handcrafted quilt, a patchwork of bounty. With Synch sitting at my side, I decided on a plan. We'd take the second, thickest terrace around the back of the hill to the fence line. From there, we'd hike down the rest of the hill, through a piece of yellow grass and a stand of cottonwood with its carpet of bittersweet. We'd still have time to hit the forty, I hoped.

Synch was settling down now, and as long as we hunted into the wind, she stayed fairly close. When we hunted with the wind at our back, she would run far ahead and try to work her way towards me. Usually, though, the pheasants wouldn't stand for that intrusion, and flushed far out of range. It drove me mad, but I resisted the urge to yell at her, because that made the pheasants even more skittish. I learned a long time ago that it's better to realize that the dog will cost you a few birds, but they find more than they flush out of range.

Halfway through the second terrace, Synch jumped a couple of hens. They dashed away on those thick, lovely wings. Synch knew the sound, and followed the hens for a few fleeting seconds. She had struck gold. The smell of game.

Quickly now, we were covering the little strip of weeds that curled along the back of the hill. I could see the end of the weed strip a hundred yards ahead. The dog smelled more game and was marching along, tail a blur. I forgot all about my gun, my boots, my steps. Everything in the world was focused at the terrace end. The pheasants were ahead of me, no doubt, getting nervous, poised to flee. Synch was growing hotter too, her small, powerful legs gobbling up real estate.

When we closed the gap to fifty yards, they began their exodus. One hen. Two hens. Three hens, more. Synch heard the commotion and sprinted. I tried to keep up, watching the first rooster of the trip smash into the barbed wire fence at the end of the terrace, regroup, then fly away, unscathed.

Too far, I thought.

A dozen more steps and a second rooster made a low, right-to-left getaway. I was momentarily taken with its color, its size, the nimble way it covered so much territory with such little effort. It was the easiest of shots and one that I've made a hundred times. I threw the gun to my shoulder and found the bead at the end of the barrel. The rooster was making hay, getting away. I fired, but he kept smoking, miraculously. The rooster cackled, making the scene more urgent. I switched triggers and fired again, thinking full well that the rooster would be flailing dead in the yellow maize. He didn't miss a beat.

Nice. Drive all the way to Iowa, and miss.

I stood there for a second or two and watched him soar down the hill, to the west. Another hen distracted my attention, but I came back to the rooster, now a pepper speck on the horizon. He made it across the cornfield and at last settled into the heavy wood of the forty.

Synch didn't appear to be as disappointed as I was. She paraded down the cornfield, to where my shot whacked the corn. She's learned over the years that the smell of burnt gunpowder often leads to a dead bird. Or, a dead bird isn't far from the smell of burnt gunpowder. Whatever the case, there wasn't anything to find. And at least for her, it was no big deal.

On to the next.

We took the fence line down the rest of the hill, towards the valley and the piece of yellow grass without moving any more roosters. At almost four, we made it to the forty, where Emmert had planted three odd-shaped fields with beans. We were into the pheasants again. Synch smelled them, I just knew it. The little dog tags dangling from her collar were jingling to the beat of her footsteps. She drew me further and further down the edge of the creek.

Here we go again, I thought. Steadily we made our way, closer and closer towards the fence line, the property edge. Synch and I were herding them, driving them under the fence and off the property. There was nothing we could do. The ditch wriggled under the fence, and so did the pheasants. My little ditch bitch wasn't far behind.

When we made it to the fence, I stopped. Synch kept motoring, a fireplug on wheels. I felt like whistling her back, like calling off the deal. Twenty yards, she scurried ahead of me. Then thirty. I rolled my eyes and knew the outcome. She would follow the creek to an acre of grass near an old barn a hundred yards ahead.

I tugged at my sleeve. Four fifteen. There was no time to

reconvene. I stood at the fence and looked around. Iowa was all mine. Not a soul in sight, not a sign of life. Synch was now fifty yards out and, judging by her demeanor, was only a moment or two from scattering the masses.

This is not good.

I really wanted to follow. I wanted to tag along, but at the same time, knew the rules about trespassing.

It was just about that time that I heard the cackle. The rooster that I had missed along the fence line near the top of the hill was now thumbing his nose at me, daring me to cross. It was all I could take.

You're dead.

I leapfrogged the fence and started after the dog, quickly. Just as I knew she would, Synch left the ditch and plowed right into the acre of grass. Hustling still, I was with her in the abandoned farmyard when the mayhem began. The little acre of weeds erupted in the whir of wings. There were pheasants everywhere. My head snapped left, then right and left again. They all seemed to be hens. Finally though, I saw a rooster, and heard another. One right, one left.

Bang! The first tumbled in a heap, but I didn't have time to watch him fall. There was work to do. I spun to the left and found the second making his getaway near an old windmill. He was the mad cackler, the one with the Teflon feathers. I never really had time to savor the moment, to relish the flavor of revenge. He died as if he was hit with an iron skillet.

From a bird hunter's perspective, it was awesome. A double, in the waning hours of the day.

"Good girl," I cried. "Dead bird."

She gathered the first bird in her mouth and was trotting back to me.

"Good girl," I told her again. I don't know who was happier, the dog or me. After she delivered the first pheasant, she set her sights on the second. I followed along, but I really didn't need to. She found it, and I paused for a moment to take a few photos of my old dog, and our beautiful birds amidst the quaint yellow and orange bulbs of bittersweet. Years from now, when Synch was gone, I'd look at these photos and think that it was bittersweet, indeed.

"Let's go, girl," I told her, as I tucked my camera and my birds in my vest—tail feathers protruding from either side.

"Let's get out of here."

She snorted, and I patted her on the head.

Instead of following along, Synch spun around and headed for the barn.

"Come on, Synch-ie! This way!" She ignored me.

I whistled.

Twice.

I listened for her dog tags.

She was gone.

A gentle breeze captured the windmill behind me. It bellowed the metallic wail of neglect. The haunting, eerie noise carried into the valley, the hills, the lonesome cottonwoods along the edge of the creek. It sent a chill down my spine, as if it were nails on a chalkboard.

"Synchie, here," I yelled again, my heart beginning to race.

Nothing.

I walked towards the back of the barn—a hip-roofed, decrepit beast, built when Eisenhower was president. She must have found a few cats, I figured. Or raccoons. I tried to whistle, but couldn't. All of a sudden, my lips had turned to rubber.

I peered through the cracks in the wooden door and saw the front end of a tractor-trailer. No sign of the dog.

Several more steps along the back of the barn, and I smelled gas. Lots of it. A handful of pigeons must have been watching my approach, because they chose that instant to stretch their evening wings. I just about jumped out of my skin.

Quickly, I turned the corner of the barn, still smelling gas. Another gap in the wood siding and I saw that the tractor-trailer was connected to a tanker, the kind that I often see delivering fuel to gas stations.

"Synchie.... come on," I pleaded.

Another corner and I was in the front of the barn, where the two giant door handles meet. Slowly, I pulled them apart. The smell of gas was stronger now, obnoxiously so. It was everywhere. The gas stood in piles; it lay around in drums and five-gallon buckets, in plastic barrels, and gallon milk jugs.

Something is wrong, here.

I broke open the action on my little 16-gauge, reached in my vest and pulled out my camera.

Click.

I got the license plate.

Then the gas in all its piles.

After three or four shots, I inched my way to the front, to the tractor itself. Printed on the driver's side door were the words, "Parker Oil Company. Peoria, Illinois."

Click.

I closed the action on the gun, and set it against the front tire.

My foot found the little stirrup beneath the cab, my hand the handle at the bottom of the door. It opened slowly, and I couldn't believe my eyes. Strewn on the floorboard were the frozen, lifeless fingers of the driver, whose throat was slit from ear to ear. His blood was everywhere, caked and dried. I backed away in horror, regrouped frantically, and took three more shots of his pale white face, his fingers, his fingerless hands duct-taped to the steering wheel.

That was enough.

I slammed the door shut, in a panic.

My heart, a hammering mess.

I raced through the cans and barrels as if they were alive.

Run, man, run.

I was out of there as fast as my middle-aged legs could carry me.

Heck with the dog.

Hell with pheasant hunting.

I wanted to run, to hide, to erase the whole grisly nightmare.

In the blink of an eye, I was over the fence and back onto Emmert's property. I whistled for the dog, but couldn't. My mouth was a desert. I ran through the beans, the yellow grass, the cut corn. By the time I made it to the big hill, Synch caught up to me. At last.

We jumped in the old Suburban and raced for town, exhausted, relieved, and holding the evidence to something I knew was huge.

Really huge.

By the time we made it back to What Cheer, I was anything but cheerful. I was starving. The meatloaf sandwiches I had for lunch were long gone, and I knew that if I stopped at the police station, the cops would keep me there to all hours of the night. If the cops in Iowa were the same as the ones back in Michigan, they'd use food as a bargaining chip when it came to prying more information from someone in for questioning. I knew enough guys on the force to realize that they all have ways to coerce a confession.

As ghastly as the crime scene was, and as urgent as the situation was, I didn't want to call the police. At least not right away. As foolish as that sounds, I was in no particular rush. Besides, the dead body wasn't going anywhere.

I decided that before I called the cops, I'd check into a motel, grab a bite to eat, take care of my dog, and clean the birds.

That has always been my routine. Take care of business, then move on to the next project.

The body in the barn looked like it had been there for at least a day or two, another hour wouldn't hurt.

What could possibly go wrong in an hour? I thought.

Plenty, I thought again.

Knowing my luck, I probably left the cap to the camera on the lens, and all those great photos would be lost. I probably had dead batteries in the Kodak, anyway. I'm one of those guys who have the best intentions, but lack the follow through, or the attention to detail.

My ex-wife used to remind me that I was forgetful, but I can't remember why.

In either case, there were lots of reasons to wait, and very few reasons that prompted immediate action.

Twenty minutes later, Synch was curled up on the motel bed in a sleepy ball, twitching and whimpering that wonderful pheasant hunting scene on the St. Peter farm. She didn't even raise an eye when I came in from the cold with a pair of skinned birds. She didn't even flinch when I rinsed them off in the bathtub. Years ago, she'd roll up her sleeves and be right in there with me, gobbling down the pheasant hearts, and watching my every move until they were safely tucked away. Now she's lights out after a bowl of canned dog food and a long drink of cold water.

After ordering a pizza and taking a quick shower, I pulled out the digital camera and my laptop computer. The photos were all on the camera, thank goodness. They became powerful images when I converted them to the larger screen on the laptop computer. They captured the ghastly, horrible mess in gruesome detail. They were even worse when I moved them from the camera to the computer. The image of his blood-stained, bristly-haired fingers revealed a smallish gold ring with some sort of an engraved emblem on the front. It wasn't his initials, or a Jolly Roger, but something else. It burned a hole in my eyes, my mind, my conscience.

Call the police, Derrick. Don't be so heartless.

I reached for the telephone and picked up the receiver. Before I dialed nine-one-one, I clicked the computer one more time. The image of the dead man behind the wheel was insane, "worth a thousand words," as we say in the newspaper business. I zoomed in on his face: ghostly white, eyelids slightly open. It was horrible.

A knock at the door distracted my attention. I hung up the phone, paid for the pizza, and turned on the television. It was six o'clock, and the lead story on the news broadcast sent me reeling:

> *"The search for a missing Bettendorf man continues this weekend. Charles A. Cigan was driving a gasoline tanker truck, loaded with almost 13,000 gallons of unleaded fuel. He has been missing for ten days now after not showing up to deliver gasoline at an Iowa City distribution center. Excluding taxes, the gasoline had a value of over $26,000 and authorities report today that the internal global positioning system on board was deactivated, then reactivated, but attached to a different vehicle that eventually showed up in California."*

The picture on the screen was that of the California Highway Patrol and a disgruntled looking trucker in a white t-shirt.

> *"If you have any information at all on this case or any other crimes in Iowa, the Iowa State Police want you to call the Hawkeye Crime Line…"*

I looked away for a moment, just long enough to hear him say, *"If you see news happening dial pound seven-ten on your touchtone phone. We pay top dollar for news stories."*

All of a sudden, the gravity of the situation hit me. The police had no clues. Lord only knows, the FBI didn't either. Everyone wanted to know where that poor truck driver was, and his twenty-six thousand dollars worth of fuel. If the decision makers at the news station were smart, they would tell us more about the driver. Who was he? What's his story? They needed to tell us who Cigan was and why we should care about him. I thought that maybe I could help bring his story to light.

The news station had all the resources, all the money, and here a modest freelance reporter from three states away had all the answers. I felt like picking up the phone and calling the news station. And the cops. Cigan was right under their noses.

Then again, if I called the news station, I would become the story, instead of covering the story, and as much as I wanted to call the police—to do the right thing—that was no way to make any money.

I came to Iowa with an assignment to cover the presidential caucuses, to hunt pheasants, and have a good time. It wouldn't be that much fun sitting in a police station. The same could be said for the five minutes of fame I'd have on the television. I know that newspapers and news stations often pay big bucks for "exclusive" rights to news stories, and what I had was exclusive all right, very exclusive. It was worth a ton of money, probably more in my mind than in theirs, but somewhere in the middle would have been just fine.

And so, I dove into my pizza, hooked up my laptop to the Internet, and set up a bogus email account. Sure, I could have used my regular email account, but it didn't sound as salacious as the one I created. Besides, if they found out what my real name was, where I worked, and more importantly, didn't work, it may have compromised my bargaining position.

I wanted to make a great impression. A big splash. And so I wrote an email to the biggest paper in Iowa, the *Des Moines Register:*

"I know where Cigan is. Hire me to cover the story. I have tons of experience, and I'll give you the exclusive. See the photo attached. Hire me. Hire me. Hire me."

Instead of signing my own name, I made up an alias and sent it on its way.

I felt rather proud of myself sitting there in that Iowa motel room, having all the goodies to break the Cigan story. I pictured the editors in Des Moines getting a strange email and wondering what they should do with it. They'd scramble for direction from the publisher. Print the photo with a racy headline or quash it and turn my email over to the cops?

The Cigan story was a whopper, and I was already thinking about my own deadline. Even though the story would be easy to write, I had some time to make it perfect.

By then it was almost eight, Iowa time, and I was exhausted. I had been up since four-thirty in the morning, Michigan time. The long drive and the long walk took a lot out of me. Even though I was riled up just a few hours previously, I was beginning to unwind. I decided to lock up the Suburban, put on my pajamas, and spend a little time with the laptop, with my wonderful bird dog at my side.

When I made it outside to lock up the truck, I noticed a man smoking a cigarette on the grass easement across the street. He had on an orange hunting cap and was keeping a sharp eye on a pair of pointers who were gingerly walking through the motel's unofficial doggie dumping grounds. I nodded in his direction, then opened the back door of the Suburban.

I grabbed Synch's water jug, and reached for the handle on my gun case. When I did, I couldn't believe what an incredibly dumb move I had made.

The gun case was empty.

In my haste to get away from the crime scene, I had forgotten my gun in the middle of an Iowa cornfield.

Two

I COULDN'T BELIEVE MY EYES. The gun that my grandpa gave my dad and my dad gave to me, and I would give to my son if I ever had one, was gone. I had forgotten the family heirloom at the back of Emmert's farm.

I forgot it!

I set it against the tanker's front tire and left it there.

What a dope.

What a stoop.

Dad would be very disappointed.

So would Grandpa.

I barged into the Iowa motel room in a rage. I was so mad at myself. So disappointed. I kept thinking about Dad, lying there in his hospital bed, asking me to take care of the family treasure. He gave me the gun on the day he had a stroke, and I promised to take care of it.

The family shotgun was my responsibility, and now it was my responsibility to get it back.

But when?

And how?

It was now dark. Really dark. And as scary as the barn scene was in the twilight of late afternoon, it would be even scarier in the pitch black of night.

I weighed my options. I thought about racing out there and making the long walk across Emmert's farm. I thought about a flashlight, and whether or not I packed one. I didn't, but I could certainly buy one, if that's what I decided.

I could drive out there, too.

That would be my luck. I'd get stuck in the mud for sure and then I'd have to wander up to Emmert's house with my hat in my hand, a poor alibi, and a plea for help. And dear Emmert, he'd say it was no problem to fire up the tractor and drive back there, but I knew better. That would be the last thing he'd want to do after a relaxing day and a leisurely meal with his wife.

No, I couldn't drive across his property.

But I could drive across the neighbor's.

The tanker got to the barn somehow.

I went back to the truck and found the plat book that shows all the landowners in the county. Individuals own most of the land in Iowa, and it's listed that way. The names are as interesting, and as diverse as the European settlers who first tamed the earth in the eighteen hundreds. The Dolezals, and Paluskas from Bohemia, the DeBrowers, VerSteegs and the DeSmits from the Netherlands, and the Snoads and the St. Peters, from England. I found Emmert's farm in the plat book, and the little half arrows that connected the main part of the farm to the forty on the backside.

Beyond Emmert's forty was a chunk of land owned by MNM Inc. The barn, and the body of Charles Cigan, was located on a two-hundred-and-thirty-seven-acre parcel that was shaped like an oversized "C." I had driven by that parcel a number of times over the years, and it was just like all the other property in Iowa—rolling, amazingly fertile, and covered in row crops that produce a third more crops than the best land in Michigan. Nobody would have known there was a barn way in the back.

Nobody except someone affiliated with MNM.

MNM Inc. owned other parcels on the same page in the plat book. All were big, healthy chunks of land in several hundred-acre swaths.

When I turned to the directory in the back of the plat book, I discovered that MNM Inc. had many, many more parcels. They owned five pieces in Emmert's Columbia Township, three in Belle Plaine, six in Deep River, fourteen in Rolland, and five in Union. They owned thousands and thousands of acres. And that was in just one of Iowa's ninety-nine counties. Who knows how many acres they owned in the neighboring counties, the neighboring states?

All of a sudden, I was thrown into the story. I was a reporter again. Who is MNM Inc.? What's their story?

The plat book had no contact information.

The phone book had no listing.

I went back to the computer and searched the Internet. MNM had a wonderful website, full of proclamations about its excellent seeds, community involvement and humanitarian efforts. It donated corn to the Iraqi government and lab equipment to the local colleges across the Midwest. The website touted how its scientists crossed plain old rice with dandelions and called it "golden rice," which provided better nourishment to children in developing countries. There were pages and pages of press releases on their website, boasting of corporate responsibility, its "collective conscience," and commitment to providing America with the safest, most productive seeds available. It was such a nice, rosy outlook that I figured it all couldn't have been true. Every company in America has skeletons in its closet; and without being overly suspicious, I figured that MNM had its share.

I thought about calling Emmert and asking about his

neighbors, but that would only stir the pot. It would send up a red flag and that wouldn't be good.

The MNM angle would be one that I'd have to dig into during normal business hours.

I was tired. It had been a long day, a long journey. I left Michigan in the early hours of the day with a couple hundred dollars in my pocket and an assignment from the *Michigan Republican.* The editor wanted me to write a story about Iowa's presidential caucuses that were to begin in two days. Until now, it was the furthest thing from my mind. There were contacts to be made, sources to quote, the usual stuff that goes along with crafting a good story.

But for now, all I cared about was the Cigan story. It had been an hour or two since I wrote the *DesMoines Register*, and they still hadn't responded. Why not? What were they waiting for? Did they think I was a hoax? An amateur? Come on, man, the story is just waiting to be told!

My new email account just sat there. The inbox still virgin territory, the sent box still showing my inaugural message: *"hire me, hire me, hire me."*

I waited.

And waited.

Finally, I got one.

But it wasn't an email I was after. It was the dreaded junk mail everyone hates: *Improve your performance, buy viagra at half the cost.*

Lovely.

I set the alarm for an hour before daylight and drifted off to sleep.

Three

I OBTAINED THE FAMILY SHOTGUN under unusual circumstances, three and a half months before my trip to Iowa. It was the end of August, the day my mom called me at work and said that Dad had just had a stroke.

And really, he didn't look that bad when I first entered his hospital room and watched him sleep. By his lax posture, he could have been at home, taking a nap on the couch instead of being stuck in a hospital bed the way he was. His hands were at his side, and his jaw was slightly open. The look on his face appeared normal; his mouth didn't sag or droop, and neither did his eyelids. I watched him doze peacefully for a minute or two, listened to the beeps and buzzers from the equipment that monitored his bodily functions, and said a little prayer of thanksgiving.

Poor guy. I felt so sorry for him, but at the same time I wanted to know how it all happened, and how serious his condition was.

My sisters told me about their children and how great they were.

Mom was a little more helpful.

After I gave her a hug, and all that, she started in with all the details.

"We had a late lunch of egg salad sandwiches. You know, Derrick, mayonnaise, salt and pepper, a little yellow mustard. I always buy light mayonnaise, and even though eggs aren't the healthiest thing in the world, an egg salad sandwich really hits the spot from time to time. Oh, and it was on whole wheat bread, and dill pickle spears…"

Mom loves to cook, and takes pride in the way she prepares every meal. She gets excited over a new recipe, or a new cooking utensil, even when her husband of forty-seven years is in the hospital.

"Anyway…" I reeled her in.

"I'm in the other room sending a note and a birthday card to Aunt Florence, down in Boca Raton. You know she's going to be eighty next week?"

"Mom!"

"What?"

She looked confused, as if she was trying to remember something.

"Maybe she's only going to be seventy-nine." I raised my eyebrows and gave her the impatient look.

"Sorry," she said, apologetically. "Your father was in the den, on the computer, I think. He spends so much time in there. All at once he starts yelling my name."

Mom was very composed, very assured. There was no flutter in her voice.

"'Oh, God,' he said. 'I can't see. I can't see,' he kept saying. I went rushing in there and he's on his knees, his hands pressed against his eyes like this."

Mom gestured with her hands, her head, her whole body.

"I didn't know what to do, other than just call nine-one-one and get some help. I knew right away that he was having a stroke. I laid him down on the floor, covered him up with a blanket and held his hand."

Mom was starting to get choked up and she swallowed over

and over again. She fished a tissue out of her shirtsleeve and raised it to her nose. "'Oh, Chick,' I kept saying to him. 'It's going to be okay.' All he did was lie there, staring at the ceiling even though he said he couldn't see. The look on his face was terrifying. It was so blank, so horrible. I told him we should say a prayer, and that's what we did."

She dabbed her nose, folded the tissue, and clenched it like a rosary.

"We said the Lord's Prayer. I bet we said it five or six times before he starts smiling and saying 'It's working! It's working! It's working!'"

Mom blew her nose and smiled, tears rolling down each cheek.

"He says that he could see, not really well, but by the time we made it to the hospital he said that he could see the nurses and doctors leaning over him."

"I just saw him, Mom." I said. "He looks normal. He looks fine."

"I know it, Son. He looks okay, but he's really not."

"What is it?"

"It's everything. He's really confused, and gets words mixed up. Confrontational. He swears, he curses, Derrick."

"Dad? He's never sworn in his life."

"It's true. And he keeps commenting on the nurses and how cute they are."

I shook my head in disbelief.

"He calls them waitresses."

"My gosh."

"And he keeps praying to St. Martin DePorres."

"Who?" I asked.

"St. Martin DePorres," she said. "I can't figure it out. Why would he pay homage to the patron saint of interracial justice?"

I laughed, slightly. "Do you think that maybe it's St. Martin Island, where we went on vacation all those years?"

Mom had a blank look on her face.

"In the Caribbean?" She nodded. "Never thought of that, Derrick," she laughed along with me. "You're so smart."

Mom never could have seen Dad's stroke coming. Nobody could. For years, he struggled with high blood pressure, but he took his medicine, and was active on the hundred and twenty acre farm where he was born, raised, and brought up my two older sisters and me. High blood pressure may be called the "silent killer," but we lived with it for so long that the threat really lost its impact.

Dad had his own law practice in town but he embraced the farming way of life. He had a couple of tractors and a handful of implements that kept him puttering merrily throughout the year. In the dead of winter, Dad wore a pair of ratty-looking insulated overalls to the drive shed where he'd grease the bearings on the ten-bottom plow, or the fittings for the Allis Chalmers he called "Old Alice." In the heat of summer, he'd put new decking on the hay wagons, or sharpen the blades on the brush hog. There was always something to do on the farm and Dad was happy in his own little farming world.

Mom kept him on a regimen of low-fat foods and daily walks. They hardly ever had bacon from the local butcher shop, and Mom seldom made pies the way she did when I was growing up.

He had long since quit putting in regular hours at the law firm he started in Owosso, Michigan. Sure, he was still a partner, his name on the letterhead and the sign on the front of the building, but he didn't do much lawyering since his retirement ten years ago. When I was in high school and considering my career options, I asked him exactly what he did in his practice. He told me that he helped other farmers set up their wills and trusts, or buy property, or deal with government contracts.

On the surface, it seemed as if Dad had a straightforward general law practice.

Every once and a while, he had a client that would take him

out of town for a few nights. Those little business trips used to upset my mother. She never knew who the client was, where her husband was going, or what was the nature of the case. And Dad didn't volunteer any information, either. He kept his clients' names and cases confidential, and his out-of-town trips were one of the things that were sure to stir up an argument at home.

Over time, however, Dad learned that in order to smooth things over on the home front, he should bring home souvenirs for Mom. Dad started out small, with watches and earrings, but eventually he made his way up to pearl necklaces and the grand prize: a Ford Mustang, convertible.

In the community, Dad earned a reputation for being fair and honest, a good lawyer, and a hard worker. Sure, most of his clients were farmers, but they weren't *all* farmers. He gave Owosso's most prestigious businessmen just as much attention as the little guys down the street. Dad was confident, no matter what the social setting, no matter what he might have gained from their relationship. He was comfortable with a gin and tonic after a round of golf, or sipping coffee with the boys at the feedlot or the local diner. People enjoyed listening to what he had to say, and laughed when he laughed, even though there wasn't always humor in it. They took mild amusement in his theatrics, but at the same time admired his gentlemanly ways.

Dad didn't swear, tell off-color jokes, or make inappropriate remarks. His business suits were always sharply pressed, dark navy, gray flannel and the most subtle herringbones that Brooks Brothers produced. He kept a commercial trouser press in the corner of the bedroom, compliments of a dry cleaner who couldn't pay his legal bill. And he didn't pinch pennies when it came to shoes. He believed that a nice pair of Johnston & Murphy's was one way to tell the real businessmen from the amateurs. And he kept his shoes in spit-shine condition. Dad relished the thought of being a rural lawyer, of living in a small community, of making a name for himself by working hard, being a gentleman, and taking care of his clients.

And money was never an issue for my two older sisters and me when we were growing up. It's not as if we were flush with cash, but we weren't exactly scraping by, either. We all played sports in school, and went to camps in the summertime when we weren't taking care of our 4-H animals. Our clothes weren't designer brand names, but they weren't shabby, by any means. Dad worked hard at the office, and in the spring and fall there was always plenty of work to do around the farm. We had a rural upbringing, a decent, very typical American existence.

An hour after I had seen him sleeping in his hospital bed, I went back to his side. The man I admired was lying there in his thin, cotton gown, sipping water from a bent plastic straw. It was hard to see him like that. I wanted to give him a hug, to wave a magic wand and make him better. Our hands met—not with a typical handshake, but a palm-to-palm embrace—the kind of greeting used by brothers.

And in a quiet, almost brooding voice, he said, "Morning, Son."

His lips slivered into a crooked smile.

I smiled back, even though it was far from morning.

"Morning, Dad...."

"You don't feed to drive here." Dad's speech wasn't what it used to be. It was mixed up, slower than normal, like he plucked each syllable from a kettle of alphabet soup.

"It's only an hour or so from Alma to the hospital in Lansing, Dad."

He looked at me in disbelief.

"Asshole, I'm in Adrian."

I couldn't believe my ears! Dad never swore. Never cursed. He was confused. Mixed up. He wasn't sure where he was. Mom's family was from Adrian, not my dad. That mistake, along with vocabulary, made everything painfully clear: my dad was gone. He vanished. And in his place was the shell of a man I barely recognized. Physically he was there; mentally, he was in outer space.

"You, you, you shoulda sent a card."

He was smiling again, the right side slightly lower than the left.

"The kind that says 'get well soon' right, Dad?"

"You can write better something, Son. I'm just old man."

Dad didn't look that old. Sure, he had lots of gray hair, but it was the vibrant, silver kind of gray, not the drab, dishwater gray that everyone tries to hide. He was proud of his gray hair, and wore it longer than most men his age. I think he liked the way it curled on the back of his head under a seed cap in the barn, or his straw fedora on the golf course. And his hair wasn't too thin or too thick; it stayed in place when he convinced Mom to go for a Sunday afternoon drive in the old Mustang convertible.

"You're not an old man," I told him.

His smile withered into a grimace.

"These hoses. They're…they're…" His head turned left and right. They were everywhere. From his hands, his nose, his hairless, smooth chest.

"You're in need of a little maintenance, a little tinkering. That's all," I told him.

Dad wasn't buying it. He wore a blank look on his face.

I tried to cheer him up.

"Come on, Dad. You've just had a stroke. Think of yourself as one of those tractors in the drive shed. You need a little overhauling and you'll be ready for fall."

He rubbed his forearm with his hand, took a peek through the window at the late afternoon glow, and with a perfectly straight face said, "You'd see my waitress."

"What about her?"

"She wants to sleep me."

I didn't know how to react. It was so out of character for him. He would never say anything like that. In fact, he avoided everything that even whiffed of intimacy, or sexuality. That simply wasn't his style.

"Oh yea?" I asked, harmlessly. "Which nurse?"

"The nice figure, and blue size." He raised his eyebrows.

"Blue eyes, Dad?"

He nodded. For the first time in my life, I was patronizing him. I was telling him what he wanted to hear, although I couldn't believe what was taking place. The topic of our conversation would never have happened. Dad always controlled the topic of our discussions. What's worse, I never really stood up to him.

"Maybe she's married?" I suggested. "Did you ask her?"

"Of course not." He frowned, and I'm not sure if that meant that 'of course she wasn't married' or 'of course he didn't ask.' In either case, I let it go, just as I always did. This was no time to insert a spine and stand up to him.

Our conversation lingered. It bantered. He couldn't keep his train of thought. He told me that I should have sent a get-well card. And that card playing was fun. And I should write my own cards. He repeated things. I watched him reach for the Styrofoam cup of water on the tray. He took several swipes at it before he finally grabbed hold. The stroke had taken his depth perception.

It was about that time that we heard a tap at the hospital room door.

"Good evening, Mr. Twitchell." The voice belonged to a rather heavyset woman in a nurse's uniform. "Are you ready for your supper?"

Dad sat a little higher in his hospital bed and ran his fingers through his hair. The stroke may have affected a lot of things, but it had no bearing on the way he always tried to be impressive.

"Call me Chick," he crowed. "Call me Chick."

"All right, Chick," she said, tugging on the privacy sheet hanging from a metal track at the ceiling. "Are you ready for your supper?"

"Can I see menu?" he asked, loudly.

The nurse smiled.

"You already did, Chick," she countered. "You wanted the filet mignon, medium rare, and the Alaskan crab legs with melted butter, remember?"

She was talking his language.

Dad laughed, but could only come up with a very plain approval. "Yum-yum."

"I just delivered the last of the good stuff to your neighbor."

She rearranged the tray next to his bed. The Styrofoam cup stayed, but the flower arrangement from the men's club at church was moved to the windowsill.

I watched her move. For being such a large woman, she had a petite gracefulness about her. She was very businesslike. There was no wasted energy, no frivolity in the way she moved. Dad's meal was tucked in front of him, and his bed returned to an upright position.

"Would you like some fresh ice water to go along with your supper, Chick?"

"Montini..." He shook his head in frustration, but managed to regroup. "Martini out of question?"

"Doctor's orders, I'm afraid."

Her hands checked his IV, and the tube of oxygen under his nose. Her fingers were round and squat, sausage like. She was rather plump, and slightly older than me. I hoped that this wasn't the nurse that Dad was talking about. I hoped to avoid the whole situation all together.

"Son, Erik," he said.

"It's Derrick," I said. *So much for avoiding the whole situation.*

The nurse paused for a moment, and turned her head in my direction. I noticed her blue eyes framed by the apples of her cheeks. She reached across the tray of soggy vegetables and pressed meatloaf.

"He's available," Dad chipped in.

"Nice to meet you, Derrick" she countered.

I shook her hand but it really wasn't a "nice to meet you" kind of handshake. It was more of the polite kind of shake used by diplomats in a tense situation. In either case, it really didn't matter; instead of making eye contact with her, I glanced at my dad, who tried to wink at me.

"I'll have to ask my husband if his sister is still in the dating scene."

I grimaced, but managed a quick apology.

She took the whole situation in stride and left a moment later.

"Dad, what the heck are you doing, playing match maker?"

I was a little angry.

"W…w…what?" he sputtered.

"*'He's available?'*" I asked him.

"W…w…what?"

"Why did you say that?" I demanded.

His food sat there in a heap, but he paid no attention.

"You are…direct?"

"Yes, but she wasn't." I glared at him. "And besides, she wasn't even that cute."

He shook his head.

"I'm just frying to help you out, Erik."

I hate it when people call me by the wrong name, even when they have a great excuse, such as a stroke.

"Let's just leave my dating situation out of this, okay, Dad?"

I stood at the foot of his bed, arms crossed. Dad shrugged his shoulders, but still hadn't touched his dinner. "Why don't you eat?" I asked him.

He looked down at the tray with the silverware, the plate and the food. He sighed. He made a strange face. I watched him lift a hand, and raise a finger as if he was going to say something prophetic. Instead, he dipped his finger into his mashed potatoes, collecting a small dollop on the end.

"Dad!"

"W...w...what?" he asked. "You want to say the dressing?"

"The blessing? No, I want you to use a spoon."

"W...w...what spoon?"

I moved to the edge of his bed, sat down, and wiped the potatoes from his finger.

"Let me help you."

He smiled.

I picked up the spoon off the tray, dipped it in the mashed potatoes, and raised it to his mouth. He took a bite. Then another. It was an odd setting—the two of us sitting there together—the baby feeding the dad.

"Leave your mark on this world," he said, slowly, mouth full of food. "With children. Have kids. A wife. You need a wife."

I didn't want to interrupt him.

"I'm proud of you," he said.

He took a long drink, and I'm not sure if it was for a dramatic effect, or if he was really thirsty. "I'm in fall of my life, the first cue in church."

I listened to what he said, and fed him a bite of dinner.

"Dad, you don't have to get all sentimental."

"W...w...why not?"

"I don't know. It's not like you've just been delivered a death sentence or something." I searched for the right words, the right concoction of optimism and hope. "You've got a lot to look forward to, a lot of life left."

"I think that too, Son." His speech came to him as if it were strained through a coffee filter. "When I was in the second pew looking at my relatives in first r...r...row, I used to think same thing." The metaphor was right on the money and he knew it. He let it simmer on the front burner of our conversation.

"All those people gone. Thirty years have passed."

I nodded my head and listened to what he had said.

"What about Aunt Florence in Boca?" I asked him. "She's going to be eighty next week."

"She's mother's side…a quilt of nature. She'll see a hundred. Your mother send her two dollar birthday cards." He picked at the tape that held his IV against his hand. "Got good genes, Derrick. Her side of family tree."

"If it weren't for that accident, there's no telling how long Grandpa would have lived," I reminded him.

"Half the story, Derrick. Grandma died in her fifties."

Mom's mom died from bone cancer. A train accident killed her dad many years after.

"This stroke my wake up call. I should take care things. My affairs."

"Dad…" I offered him another bite of dinner, but he refused. The meal was over.

"What is it?" he asked. "Don't you like the thought of this? Someday it's going to happen."

I returned to my chair, and pulled it closer to the edge of the bed. He reached for the bank of bed adjustment buttons near the metal railings. Slowly the bed reclined, and Dad swallowed. He reached for my hand.

This is not good.

I sat down and put my hand through the metal bed railing-cold and harsh against my wrist. His hand was warm and firm, calloused on the inside of his knuckles, but his cuticles were smartly manicured. Dad swallowed. He looked up at the ceiling, then down at me like I was a child on his knee at story time.

"I w…w…want to discuss with you." He blinked several times. "Two things."

I pulled the chair a little closer.

"The first is you to t…t…take Grandpa's gun."

I had reason to pause.

"You do?"

He nodded slowly. Assuredly.

"Course I do," he told me. "Hardly hunt any more. They'll ever let me stumble around with a loaded shotgun."

"I know but..."

He let go of my hand, and swallowed. The hospital room air was thick and heavy, shrouded in cleansers and sterility and the beeps and buzzers of the equipment.

"You like the idea?" he asked.

"It's not that I don't like the idea, it's just that I always thought of Grandpa's gun as yours."

I didn't know what else to say. Grandpa's gun was a family heirloom, and I wasn't quite ready to be in charge of it. It was a big deal, all right. Dad inherited it after Grandpa died, and I remember how much pride he took in it.

"Who else am I going to give it to?" he asked. "Your sisters have never hunting, either do their husbands." He wasn't disappointed; he was simply relaying the facts. "Ask grandkids into hunting but they don't."

"You sure, Dad?"

"Yes, Son. You have it. Grandpa would be honored. Honor his memory, passing along a rum like his."

"I know, but I don't even have a gun safe."

His eyes fell back upon me. "K...k...keep it in gun safe until the season. You know where key is. Take it whenever you're ready."

I wasn't quite ready to believe that Dad wouldn't be in good enough health to use it anymore. I wasn't quite ready to take on the responsibility of taking over a family heirloom, either. Grandpa's gun was in excellent condition, and as rare as rare can be. Dad only took it pheasant hunting on sunny afternoons, when there was no chance that the morning dew could tarnish the pristine casing and the patina of seasons past. He never used today's heavy pheasant loads for fear that their increased power would stress the antiquated mechanics. Dad took it apart after every use and cleaned it with methodical attention to detail, even if he hadn't shot it.

When he did shoot, it took him twice as long, and I'm not sure if he did that to make sure the gun was like new, or if it was his wish to make his father-in-law proud.

I never asked Dad about his rationale for cleaning Grandpa's gun the way he did. When he broke out the cleaning solvents, oily cloths and gun-cleaning paraphernalia at the basement workbench, Dad never did much talking. He was lost in thought, lost in the memory, and the notion that Grandpa's gun had outlived Grandpa, and was possibly going to outlive him, too.

It was a sad day when Grandpa was killed on the railroad tracks, and the gun must have been a sweet-and-sour token of their relationship.

"You'll make the gun proud," he told me. "It's fun to bury…" He snapped his fingers in frustration. "Carry…and a dream to shoot."

"Thank you, Dad." I said. "I'm looking forward to pheasant season already."

"Good, be here adore you know it." He smiled at me proudly. Even though I was forty, and beyond the time when I needed a pat on the back, it still felt good to get approval from the old man.

"You'll have a good time with the gun, and care too of it." He smiled half-heartedly and fumbled his words.

Out of the sky blue he said, "I want you to be my trustee."

Our hands were no longer touching. "What do you mean?"

He stopped smiling. "A trust is a legal document, and a trustee is the person in charge of seeing it true," he explained. He hesitated.

"You can protect your ass, and avoid probate."

"I know, but I thought that was for when you die."

"M…m…most the time, Son. But you can take care now."

"Like what, Dad?"

"The gun."

"Oh, so the trust says that you want me to have your old shotgun?"

"Should be. Can't remember."

I listened to him speak, and the way he prodded his memory for tidbits of information.

"Carol always wanted that antique bathtub in the upstairs bathroom, and Allison wants the piano. Is it in there?"

"C…c…can't remember." He gazed my way, and for the first time in my life I noticed the spider veins forming a web across the bulb of his nose.

"Go look at it," he said, fumbling with his eyeglass case. "You'll see, Derrick."

I nodded my head and waited for more direction.

"It's summertime. Take Harley drive up to bank."

"What do you mean? What bank?"

"Isa..Isa..Isabella Bank and Lust."

I was still confused.

"You mean Isabella Bank and Trust, Dad?"

"Yes," he said. "Trust is in safe deposit box at bank at Mt. Pilot…"

"You mean Mt. Pleasant?"

"Yes. Mt. Pleasant," he said, nodding.

The beeps and buzzers distracted my attention, but Dad kept his train of thought.

"Grab my keys, Erik, would. In the closet."

I stood up, parted the privacy curtain, and opened the door on the little laminate closet near the entrance to his room. His shirt and trousers were neatly hung over a hanger, and his keys in a pile on the shelf, next to his wallet. I returned to the edge of his bed, and acknowledged his thanks.

"You're welcome, Dad."

He pulled his reading glasses from the case and dangled them on the bridge of his nose.

"That's b…b…bitter," he said, as he thumbed through each key.

I watched him fiddle with the entire set before looking up at the television with a puzzled look on his face. He kept more than twenty keys on the ring, and I never really thought about why he needed so many. He no longer had an office to secure, and we didn't lock the barn. The keys for the Harley, his pick-up, the Mustang, and mom's Buick were always kept on a small shelf near the back door, next to a box of wooden matches. Old Alice had a locking toolbox the size of a breadbasket on her flanks, but he never locked that, either. Regardless, I didn't ask him about the other keys on his key ring; there are some unexplained things about my dad's life that I needed to accept. Keys were one of them.

I hated to see him suffer. He couldn't remember which key was for what. His eyebrows made a funny shape as his forehead creased from the stress. And he smiled to himself at the whole scenario.

I thought about throwing him a life ring, about lending a hand. The guy never, ever had any trouble remembering things. Until now.

To break the tension, I got up from the corner of the bed and peered around the edge of the privacy curtain. Dad's mind and fingers were back on the keys. Finally, after a minute of deliberation, he found it.

"Here it is," he said, face beaming with pride. He held the key between his index finger and his thumb, as if it were a hook dangling from an impaled bluegill.

"This one you want, Derrick." His hand moved in my direction.

"Will take it off the ring, please? This….this…." He flexed

his fingers but couldn't find the right word. "I've got this damn..." He snapped his fingers, but couldn't come up with the right term. He was frustrated.

"Arthritis?" I questioned.

"Thank you," he said, relieved.

"No problem, Dad."

"Keep that key in your wallet," he told me. "Sign some papers when you get there." His voice was nearly a whisper and hard to understand. "Your name on the box's registry. We're the only two people who can access it."

He stopped speaking, and gestured with his hands to the privacy curtain. I stood up and peered through the crack again.

"They take you to the back of the bank, to a room with a row of safe deposit boxes. Understand?"

"I got it."

"The lady will open one lock, you open other."

"Got it, Dad. What number?"

My question threw him for a loop.

"What you mean, Son? There are two keys."

I shook my head. "No, no, Dad. What's the number on the box?"

He didn't flinch.

"The safe deposit box."

His eyes moved from mine to the television, and he furled his chin. I watched him think. And think. It was painful to watch. It was hard to see him founder in the sea of confusion. He was drawing a blank. A hollow, bottomless void. The poor guy. He put his fingers on his chin, and he raised his eyebrows.

"Never mind, Dad," I said, trying to console him. "They'll have it on file."

"N...n...no, you should know."

"It's not a big deal, Dad. I'll take care of it."

"One s...s...second," he languished. "I've had it for years."

Finally, dawn broke. "It's number thirty-four. The year I was born. Thirty four."

He took solace in small victories. The box number was one of them.

"Excellent."

"Yes," he smiled. "D…d…don't forget it. Thirty four."

"Oh, I won't forget it, Dad. You were born in nineteen thirty four, and that's the number on the box."

"Great."

"I'll get up to Mt. Pleasant soon."

"Soon?" he asked me.

"Next week," I told him, and judging by the look on his face, that wasn't the right answer.

"Right away," he said. "Read me trust. Tomorrow morning t…t…take care of business."

"What could be that important?"

Dad gave me the eye. He sighed.

"You okay this, Son?"

"Sure, Dad. I'm okay."

"Big job. I want you to do this for me."

"Okay, Dad. I'll take care of it for you. Whatever it is."

He nodded, and I put the key in my wallet, and my wallet in my hip pocket.

"You've never let me down, Son. Know that?"

He reached for my hand, mine for his. I sat on the edge of his bed, knee slightly bent. Amid the IVs and hoses, electronics and sterility, Dad waxed nostalgically.

"I always proud of you, Son." He cleared his throat. And blinked. And blinked. He had me blinking, too. We fought the tears in our eyes. "You okay this?"

"I'm okay, Dad. I can do this."

"You sure?" He smiled again.

"I'm your man. You can count on me. I'll go up to Mt. Pleasant tomorrow and take care of business."

"Thank you, Son."

Four

In the early years of my career, the newspaper I worked for sent me to an investigative reporting seminar hosted by Northwestern University near Chicago. The seminar was held at an old, ivy covered lecture hall during the middle of summer, when most of the students and faculty were on summer break. The list of instructors at the seminar was impressive, including Ed Bradley from "60 Minutes," a professor or two from the faculty, and a plaintiff's lawyer from the community who specialized in litigating libel and slander lawsuits. On day two, we'd have another lawyer who worked for the city of Chicago who planned on shedding some light on the Freedom of Information Act and exactly how to word our requests so they wouldn't be denied.

The lecture hall was packed with newspaper people from all over the country. Even though the building was made from stones the size of a small casket, half underground, and draped in the shade of a dozen or more handsome maple trees, it was quite warm inside. The moderators kept the double doors open on both sides of the auditorium, letting the sounds of summer mingle with a warm breeze; the only benefit was to keep the hall from feeling stagnant.

Most of the attendees were somewhat casual in their appearance. Some of the men wore faded khaki trousers and golf shirts, while others took full advantage of the time away from the office to wear shorts and t-shirts. Almost everyone seemed to have folded the thick, cardboard seminar cover into a small fan and waved it back and forth as if it were at a Baptist revival on a muggy Sunday morning.

I was single then, never married. Even though I was in my early thirties, I dated quite a bit, or at least went through the motions of dating. I never really found that perfect girl. Some of the women came close, and I probably could have been happy for a while being married to them, but there was always a reason to back away from that kind of commitment. I wanted a woman to sweep me off my feet. I wanted a woman to hold my attention, to be mysterious without being evasive. I wanted to look at her and think to myself that I'd never tire of looking at her.

And then all at once, it happened.

As we all waited for the first speaker to approach the podium, the prettiest woman waltzed down the aisle with the same drama as a passing thunderstorm. I'm sure that I was staring. I'm sure that if anyone saw me drooling at her the way I was, they would have known exactly what I was thinking. I couldn't help myself; it was love at first sight.

With just one look, just one glimmer, I could see the laughter in her voice; hear the joy in her smile. She captured me. She owned me.

I loved the way she walked, and the way her sundress beamed. Her blonde, fine hair made me forget about everything else in the world. And her pretty green eyes, they sparkled. She nearly took my breath away. I sat there blushing even though she ended up sitting three rows in front of me, and exactly five seats over.

Strange, what love, or lust, can do to a man. I was in awe. Or admiration. Not sure which. This beautiful woman seated in front of me did everything right. She had all the goodies I craved: a pretty face, and a gracious womanly figure. I like a woman that looks like a woman. I like breasts and round, scrumptious hips. I like healthy, strong legs and arms, too.

She had all that, plus a sharp image, and a confidence and poise that only comes north of thirty.

I knew that if I had the chance to talk to her, my cheeks really would have caught on fire.

Crazy, a guy in his thirties shouldn't blush when he meets a girl. A guy shouldn't feel his heart thrumming at the sight of a pretty woman.

Worse yet: *A guy shouldn't be wearing faded khakis and a stained golf shirt when the girl of his dreams strolls into view.*

I sat in my chair a little straighter. I raised a finger to my mouth, wetted it, and tried to remove the scuffs from my worn loafers. They were shabby.

You don't have a prayer, I thought. *You don't have a chance.*

For a while there, I really didn't have a chance. The seminar was under way and we were glued to our chairs.

When it was time for lunch, we all piled out of the auditorium and towards the commons about a block away. I struck up a conversation with an older, chubby gentleman from Cleveland who was closing in on retirement. All he could talk about was bobbing around Lake Erie in his sailboat, and visiting the islands scattered throughout.

People like to talk about themselves. Makes them feel important. By verbalizing their dreams, it must make them feel as if they are closer to achieving them. Whatever the case, the man from Cleveland was attached to my hip as we made our way through the buffet line and picked out our chicken roll-ups and fruit salad from a large metal bowl that had a pair of honey bees sipping nectar from the edge.

When we found our seats at the only vacant table, the man had to tell me about the time he got caught in a squall and had to hunker down in Put-in-Bay. I tried to act interested. When he stuffed a bite of food in his mouth I looked around the commons. No sign of the girl, but it was a beautiful summer day, with the sunlight sprinkling our table from the shade of ash trees overhead. House sparrows chirped at one another in the hedges, and I watched one hop to the front of a car and tweezer an insect from the grill.

A bird buffet line, I thought.

A couple of young men from the *Chicago Tribune* joined the table, wearing a set of purple Northwestern University ball caps. I assumed that they were still in college and doing their internships at the paper.

More people paraded by our table. There was laughter and idle chitchat. The help from the kitchen poured more fruit salad into the bowl and swished the bees away, but I watched them come right back.

And then, all at once, I heard a voice. "Is anyone sitting here?"

I looked up and it was the girl of my dreams.

"You are," I choked.

"Thank you," she said, placing her tray on the table next to mine. I couldn't help but notice the ring on her left hand as plain as day. "Come on ladies," she gestured. "Gather 'round."

A small entourage of women filled the remaining chairs at the table. The interns picked up their trays and left. The man from Cleveland was stuffing food into his face as if it were his last supper. He had it smeared all over his lips and part of his cheek.

Without an ounce of hesitation, Colleen tucked the flowered dress beneath her, sat down gracefully, and extended her hand.

"I'm Colleen Beyer," she said. Her smile was unbelievable, so friendly, more like a smirk. Her dimples weren't on her cheeks, but high, under her eyes. Before I could say a thing, she turned to the other women in her group, and recited their names. I looked around the table and nodded politely at each face, feeling the heat climb up the back of my neck. They all nodded, slightly snickering as if they could tell I was embarrassed.

"George from Cleveland," he butted in, reaching across my tray, taking her hand in his. "Really happy to meet you, Colleen," he said, mouth nearly full.

"Likewise, George" she said, looking somewhat surprised.

"Where are you from?" he asked.

"Milwaukee. *The Milwaukee Journal Sentinel.* How about you guys? Are you reporters, too?"

George liked to thump his chest. And stroke himself.

"Award winning, as a matter of fact. Won the Polk Award five times. Probably could be teaching the course today."

"Oh my," she smiled, and looked in my direction. "Good for you, George."

I smiled back, and blushed.

Her head turned to her plate, bowed slightly, and then she made the sign of the cross.

A religious woman.

"George likes to sail," I finally piped up.

Her face was in front of mine again, and my little statement piqued the most wonderful eye contact. As if she realized that I wasn't a coward after all.

"Is that right, George?" She asked without taking her eyes off mine. "What kind of sailboat do you have?"

"A Catalina."

One of the ladies seated on Colleen's right asked, "How big is it?"

George seemed to think that the question had something to do with his virility. He pumped out his chest, and in a deeper-than-normal voice stated, "Twenty-seven feet."

"Nice," one of the women nodded.

"It's really twenty-eight feet, including the swim platform."

"Makes sense."

George's attention quickly moved from Colleen to the woman seated across the table, which was fine. The guy was rather annoying, and nearly everyone at the table realized it.

"I'm Derrick, by the way. And it's really nice to meet you, Colleen."

She finished a bite of food and smiled again, her eyes searing a blaze right through me.

"Are you a reporter?"

"Yes, I am," I nodded affirmatively. "But I haven't won the Polk yet."

She snickered. "Good. I'd hate to feel intimidated. Neither have I."

George picked up his tray and moved across the table, to where the audience was a little more receptive.

"Where are you from, Derrick?"

"The middle of Michigan's mitten. A little town called Alma."

"That's neat. I like small towns." She seemed to be sizing me up.

"I work for the *Evening Journal,* but there's not much investigative reporting that goes on there, because there's hardly anything that needs investigating."

"That's the beauty of it though," she rebutted, raising a cloth, purple napkin to her curved lips, still belying a smirk. "You have the freedom to cover the stories you want."

I nodded in agreement.

"We've only had one murder in the last fifteen years, and outside of a few scandals, there's really not much that goes on in our part of the state."

"What about those scandals?" she asked.

"They happened before I got there, involving a sheriff from downstate who allegedly raped a female deputy in a hotel in Alma."

All of a sudden I was becoming more comfortable talking to her, and the longer I talked, the more time she had to eat.

"The trial went on for several weeks, I guess, with lots of testimony about the deputy and her sexual past. The defense argued that they couldn't get a fair trial in small-town Michigan because the sheriff was black. The judge took exception to the inference that we were racist, and chided the defense counsel on the steps of the courthouse. Everyone thought he did that because he was up for reelection, but the editors made it front-page news. Sold a lot of papers, that's for sure."

"A juicy story keeps the editors and bosses happy," she said.

"No kidding," I agreed. "What about you, Colleen?"

She placed her sandwich on her plate, took a sip from her water bottle, and asked, "What about me?"

My face was glowing warm again. Maybe I should have rephrased that question.

"Any scandals on your side of Lake Michigan?"

"Plenty," she smiled, apologetically.

I waited for more answers, but they never came. Colleen Beyer would play her cards close to the vest.

She had the barriers up, the defenses in place, but by the way she said "plenty," I knew there was something that she wanted to get off her chest. Whether or not she was going to tell me remained to be seen.

And really, I should have let it go. When I mentioned the "scandals on your side of Lake Michigan" I really wasn't prying into her personal business. I merely wanted to know about everything related to the newspaper in Milwaukee.

Throughout the rest of lunch and the walk back to the lecture hall, our conversation remained pleasant. I made her laugh a few times about George and his now infamous swim platform. She mentioned that the woman who took such an interest in his boat was a sailor herself, and was the type who would appreciate a man with George's sailing package. But we weren't the only ones laughing. George and the woman from Milwaukee were giggling and carrying on as if they were long-lost buddies. They waddled ahead of us and by the time we reached the lecture hall, George was in my seat, and she was in his.

"Why don't you sit with me?" Colleen suggested. "We're only about five rows down."

"Three.... I counted."

She blinked and stood in her tracks as if she couldn't believe that someone had taken an interest in her.

The story about her pending divorce, and the reasons why, would have to wait until after we all went out for pizza, when everyone else went back to their rooms. By then, she had a glass or two of merlot, a glass of beer from the pitcher, and a Bailey's with her coffee. While the rest of the bar swirled in the clouds of cigarette smoke, slurred conversations, and mindless laughter, Colleen and I chatted into the small hours of the morning.

She was fun to talk to, fun to watch. She had smooth, elegant wrists and fingers that fidgeted with the napkins, the glassware, her earrings. For the longest time, our conversation was light, and light-hearted. The bar was just noisy enough that we had to sit close to each other if we wanted to hear each other speak. At least that was the alibi I nursed as she told me all about her career as a college softball player.

Gradually, the topics of our conversation became more involved. For Colleen and her soon-to-be-ex-husband, the issue came down to children. She wanted them, and he didn't. While she felt that her biological clock was ticking, he became more and more content with the family he started with his first wife. Even though he told Colleen that he wanted to start a family while they were dating, he changed his mind a year or two after the nuptials were exchanged. She felt betrayed, and the issue served as a lever that drove the two of them apart.

But she didn't just throw in the towel. They did have some good times, especially in the early days of their engagement and marriage. For a guy in his early fifties, Colleen said her husband acted like a man half his age. He was passionate. He was fun. They took ballroom dancing classes together, and wore formal gowns and tuxedos for each event. He had a sixty-eight Corvette convertible painted cherry red, which was a favorite for their summer excursions to the orchards, fairs and balloon rides in upstate Wisconsin.

A couple of times, she even thought she was pregnant.

With each close call, with each sigh of relief from him, the disappointment became more and more acute. She said she prayed and prayed about it. She took her marriage vows seriously, but on the other hand, she knew that children were one of God's greatest gifts. By the end of her marriage, she quit praying for guidance; she was now praying for forgiveness.

Little by little, she was opening up to me. I'm not sure if I was just a listening ear, a friendly face, or a sounding board for all that was wrong in her world. I asked her questions, but didn't pry. She was fun to watch, and her life's story was interesting. I felt like a passenger in the Corvette, a dancer on the ballroom floor. I shared in her disappointment, and it must have showed, because all at once she started crying.

It was a little awkward.

Okay, more than just a little.

She was sharing some of the deepest secrets in her life, and we had only known each other a few hours. Maybe it was convenience that made her open up to me. Maybe she felt the same spark of chemistry that I did. Whatever the case, in the months after the seminar ended, Colleen and I kept in contact, mostly through email and telephone calls. She gave me the blow-by-blow account of her divorce proceedings, and the relief she felt when it was finalized. All I could do was listen, at least electronically, and lend moral support. When the ink dried on the divorce papers in late August, I sent her a little "relaxation care package," which included a tube of scented bubble bath crystals, mocha mix, a couple of romance novels, prepaid telephone cards, a handful of compact discs, and the *coup de grace*: a gift certificate for a one-hour massage from one of Milwaukee's health parks.

There's nothing quite like showing someone you care by sending her a thoughtful gift. My only wish was that I could have been there to see the look on her face when she opened it. It would have been fun to see her smile, hear her laugh, or say things like "Aw...."

Her phone call that evening was intense. She was so happy, I could tell, and keeping her happy became my ultimate goal.

There was no doubt that I was wearing down her defenses, getting inside her little world. And it was great. Even though we were far from being in a relationship, I still thought of Colleen every day, every minute. I took extra pride in the things I did around the house. The dishes were always clean. The place was vacuumed and dusted, and I organized my dresser drawers. I worked hard at the paper, too, taking on additional projects and making the extra effort for the stories the editors assigned. All at once I wanted to become a better man, a better reporter, a better person. I felt as if I was auditioning for Colleen even though a couple hundred miles and the breadth of Lake Michigan separated us. The seeds of love that were sown in Chicago were starting to germinate in Michigan and, I hoped, in Wisconsin, too.

And then, in early October, she invited me to spend the weekend in Milwaukee. Her email said it all,

> *"You could take the ferry across, or drive. Doesn't matter. There's an art-and-apples fair on the Door Penin-*

> *sula, or I can show you around town, if you'd rather do that. We can tour the paper, and I can show you my little cubicle, or, we can go for a long drive in the countryside. The colors should be perfect, the weatherman says it'll be decent, and there's bound to be a cow or two we could tip. Who knows? Maybe there will be a scandal or something we can put our investigative reporting skills to good use."*

I smiled. She made my day.

"*We'll make Ed Bradley proud.*" I typed in response. *"I'll be there."*

That was the thing about Colleen's emails, about mine, too; hers were rather lengthy, while mine were short and sweet. I didn't ramble on about my feelings or what was on my mind. In a humorous way, I boiled everything down to the least common denominator. Maybe it was the years of being a reporter—the economy of words—that made me correspond the way I did. Maybe it was my own manly way- keep your thoughts hidden, and you won't get hurt- that makes me deal with people the way I do. Either way, I always looked forward to her emails, and I think that Colleen enjoyed getting mine, too.

But that's not to say that the news copy she wrote for the paper was full of rambling, undisciplined discourses. That was hardly the case. Her leads were quick-hitting, punchy, and to the point, while the meat of the story was loaded with quotations, facts and relevant information. What's more, she had a knack for making complicated topics seem simple. She could cover the latest bankruptcy hearings, Milwaukee politics, or labor contracts without being intimidated. I enjoyed reading her stuff, and had a growing admiration for her abilities as a reporter.

Anyway, I couldn't wait to see her again. The emails were fine, and so were the packets of clippings she sent me, but a face-to-face visit was a big step. It's not like we were meeting for coffee or something innocuous. Our first official date would last a whole weekend, and considered a doozie in anyone's book.

I still remember the nervousness I experienced when I boarded the car ferry *The Badger* on a quiet harbor in Ludington, Michigan. Even though "the Badge" is enormous, and has made the long trek across Lake Michigan many times, it still is a bit intimidating putting your safety in someone else's hands. I was all wrapped up in the thrill of anticipation: of tackling Lake Michigan in a giant boat, of seeing the sights of a faraway state and, of course, seeing the woman who turned my heart to putty.

The ferry ride turned out to be no big deal. We putted our way through the pier heads, and the cluster of small-boat fishermen who were trolling for the season's last salmon. Lake Michigan was a welcome hostess: not exactly a sheet of glass, but then again, not a riled bully, either. When the Michigan horizon was just as distant as Wisconsin's, we were greeted by a low-riding freighter plodding its way north. Both captains exchanged pleasantries through the cryptic language of horn blasts.

The weekend was off to a good start, and got even better when I met Colleen late Friday afternoon in the lobby of the *Milwaukee Journal Sentinel.* She was all smiles—the toothy, wide grins that beam with sincerity. And hugs—they were so tight and firm that they nearly took my breath away.

Together, we made our way around the pressroom, and she introduced me to her bosses and colleagues, some of whom I recognized from the seminar in Chicago. Her little cubicle didn't exactly have a view of the Milwaukee skyline, but judging by the amount of clutter on her desk and pinned to the walls, she didn't have time for wistful musing anyway. The whole time we were together, she kept her hand under my elbow. It was as if she relished the thought of leading me around her world. Whatever the case, it felt right; it felt awesome.

And we had so much in common, at least when it came to our bosses' push for advertising dollars. The bosses on both sides of Lake Michigan wanted more dollars, more income, more advertising inches. The memos I read on her cubicle's walls could have been exchanged for the memos that were posted on my cubicle back in Michigan.

When the Saturday morning paper was put to bed and in the hands of the layout crew, Colleen introduced me to a Friday night tradition: pizza and beer with the gang across the street. I have since forgotten the name of the bar, but it really doesn't matter. It was a sports bar, with plenty of big screen televisions and memorabilia from Wisconsin's heroes. Colleen kept her hand on my knee under the table whenever she thought she could get away with it. By the time the second extra-cheese pizza was finished, we were holding hands under the table and it didn't really matter if her co-workers thought it was odd.

My tour of Milwaukee was just starting. We walked to her church, and she told me all about her priest, who gave the homily while standing on his tiptoes.

"Forgive me, Father," she said, and made the sign of the cross.

Several more blocks away, we entered a comedy club for a few laughs and a glass of sherry. She said she spent a lot of time covering politics at city hall when we walked past, but she was not one for going out on the town unless she had company. I felt a little awkward when we entered a dance bar near the Milwaukee campus of the University of Wisconsin. Most of the folks inside were younger than we were, but that didn't stop Colleen from pulling me on the dance floor whenever the disc jockey played one of her favorites.

And man, could she dance. It poured out of her. It transformed her. She pawed at her thighs, as if she were smearing them with suntan lotion. She threw her head back, spinning seductively as if she were courting a brass pole. It didn't bother her to see who was watching her, either. She didn't care about anything else in the world. All she did was let the music move her. It carried her away. She kept her eyes glued to mine, as she mouthed the words to each song.

She had plenty to watch, plenty to absorb. She was womanly all right. Plenty of hips. A great figure. I imagined the two of us, entwined and sweaty, in the ultimate dance of love.

If Colleen was that uninhibited on the dance floor, I had to wonder what she'd be like in the bedroom.

I couldn't wait to peel her clothes from her. I couldn't wait till my hands could touch her, my nose explore her, my ears hear her gasp.

And as it turns out, sleeping with Colleen would be like seducing a virgin. The first time I kissed her, she asked me what I was doing.

"I'm kissing you," I said.

She kissed me back.

The first time I reached for the buttons on her blouse, she asked if I had her permission for such clandestine advances.

"Of course not," I told her, but she didn't pull my hand away, or tell me to stop.

When my lips swept the length of her neck, the bulge of her collarbone, I didn't wait for her to ask me what I was doing. In fact, I *told* her what I was doing.

"I'm going to kiss your breasts," I whispered.

"You are?" she asked.

"Yes," I told her. "It's going to be great, Colleen. You're going to enjoy it."

I heard her gasp. "I will?"

"You will," I assured her.

I wasn't lying; she did enjoy herself.

We both did.

Colleen was a strong, confident woman, but she morphed into a timid minx any time we were making out. The sexiest thing about her was her mind. She knew how to flirt. She knew how to tease. But it was much more than that. She had a way about her that kept me intrigued. She kept me off balance with her wit, off-kilter with her charm. She was as unpredictable, and more determined than an all-day rain. I loved talking to her. I loved her quirky little smile, and those adorable dimples beneath her flirty eyes. I loved her for all the right reasons, and our time together was some of the happiest of my life.

We were married on a beautiful spring morning under a flowered gazebo on the stern of the *Badger*. Granted, it wasn't a church, but it wasn't a chapel in Las Vegas, either. The crew of the *Badge* relished taking part in our special day. They directed most of the vehicles to the front of the ferry, quarantined the stern, and set up enough chairs for our modest number of guests. I hired a string quartet, a caterer from Ludington, and had dozens and dozens of Colleen's favorite flowers, lilies, on the aisle, the gazebo, and the archway. When I raised the veil and gave her a kiss, the captain blew the horn as if I had just scored the winning goal in the Stanley Cup finals.

It was incredible.

Our big event didn't go unnoticed by the media. Both newspapers we worked for had photographers there, and they both published a shot of Colleen and me as we tossed rose petals over the railing and into the big, blue body of water. Our smiles were as sincere and honest as Lake Michigan was deep. We were so happy.

The story in the *Sentinel* was a kind of send-off for Colleen. After eight years on the job as a city-beat reporter, she notified management that she wanted to pursue other opportunities at the *Journal*. Granted, to go from a big-city paper with ninety-thousand subscribers to one a third that size took a lot of guts, not to mention a cut in pay. But, what the heck. She really didn't have any ties to Milwaukee, and Alma's cost of living was much less. I owned a quaint little house in town, not far from the elementary school where she had planned on taking our kids once they were out of diapers and old enough to attend.

Besides, working at the *Journal* really was a chance for her to shine in her career. She wanted to flourish. She wanted to thrive in a small-town setting and become a big fish in a small pond. Her experience in Milwaukee gave her tons of confidence as a reporter. She knew when to flex her muscles on a tough story, but she knew how to soft-pedal sensitive stories, too. She was thorough, so thorough, and dead-to-rights accurate. Even though the *Journal* didn't require its reporters to tape-record telephone conversations with sources, Colleen always did. And it paid off.

On more than one occasion she was accused of misquoting an influential attorney in town. But when she played the tape for him and her superiors at the paper, they all raised their eyebrows in surprise. Nobody at the *Journal* had ever gone to those lengths to make sure there weren't any mistakes.

She deserved the promotion to editor. She deserved the pay raise. She was good.

And I was lucky to work for her, to have her as my wife.

Within six months of our wedding, we both wanted to start a family. It became a mission. Sex became a means to an end. It went from magical to practical. There was no beating around the bush, so to speak. It was every pervert's fantasy: no playing footsy under the table at a romantic dinner, no wining and dining, no hand-holding, or furtive glances.

All we did was drop the drawers and go at it. We'd come home from work and get it on. We'd wake up on the weekends and make some noise before breakfast. With each passing month, with each disappointment, we became more and more serious. She bought an ovulation kit and monitored her temperature constantly. I used to tease her that the placard she posted on the refrigerator reminded me of a baseball schedule: the home games in green, the away games in red. She made me switch from briefs to boxers because she heard that my "twins" needed more space to breathe. The doctor said that I should try eating more fruits and vegetables, because a healthy diet leads to better sperm production. Colleen became a brood mare, and I was her stallion. Month after month, we tried. Month after month, we were disappointed.

It was about that time that we saw an ad in the paper for English springer spaniel puppies. Although neither one of us relished the thought of taking care of an animal, we had lots of love to give, a nice little home, and enough idle time that a dog seemed plausible. And the litter was adorable. They were all cute, all charming little fuzz balls. We could have been happy with any of them, but we decided on a harmless-looking female with a brown smear of color on her upper lip that looked like a mustache. We thought about calling her "Stash," because of her obvious characteristics, but then considered "Scoop," on account of our newspaper roots. Finally, we decided on "Synch," because that was name of Colleen's dog when she was growing up.

I was elated to have a dog, if for nothing else than she might help me find more pheasants. For years, I had walked around the farm fields near home and very, very seldom found any birds. It was pure luck when I did. When Synch entered our lives, I had a bird-finding machine, an instrument of joy, all wrapped up in a cute, furry package.

When you smell that innocent smell of a puppy, you can't help but think of what lies ahead. You see yourself as an innocent child when it licks your cheek or nibbles on your earlobe. You see the unbridled carelessness of youth, and the complacent reassurance of middle age when it's chasing squirrels or taking nap after nap. And when your puppy gets old, and barks for you to carry her up a flight of stairs because her hips are shot, you can't help but wonder who will be there to love you in that same manner. In a humble kind of way, a dog's life is just like our own—much too short, filled with joy and pain, uncertainty and, every once in a while, a delicious bone to fill our days.

Synch became our baby. She slept at the foot of our bed and got a bath at least once a week. We pampered her silly, and she became a source of joy while our baby-making tribulations continued to deteriorate.

And there were plenty of those. Colleen took the last of her divorce settlement money and together we visited a fertility clinic in Kalamazoo. On the way there, we passed Climax, Michigan. Of course, we had to make a joke every time we approached Climax. We made other jokes when we passed Climax, too. That whole joke thing helped ease the baby-making tension.

I don't like people poking and prodding me, even if they're a doctor. It's one thing if you're sick and need some medicine; it's another matter when it comes to discussing your most intimate bodily functions.

I probably shouldn't have been so concerned. Colleen had it much worse than I did. Her exam lasted almost an hour.

All I had to endure was a short exam of my own, answer two pages of questions about my health as a child, my diet, stress levels and whether or not the twins had experienced any trauma in their lifetime.

Of course, that left the sample.

My sample.

I knew it was coming, so to speak.

I dreaded it.

They told me to abstain from sex for two or three days prior to our appointment, so they could get an accurate sample.

The nurse directed me to a tiny room at the end of the hall.

"Place your sample in this container, and put the container back up here on the counter when you're finished."

I was nervous about the whole ordeal. Self-conscious. I was concerned about what the nurse would think if I was in and out of there in two minutes or a half-hour. I started thinking about the jokes they'd make around the water cooler. The quick guys must have been "slap-sticks" and the slow guys, "chap-sticks."

What's it going to be, Derrick?

Honestly, I don't remember how long I was in that room. The pornographic magazines they had stacked under the table were old and tattered, and ranged from raunchy to tame. They had catalogs from Victoria's Secret and JC Penney. It was embarrassing, to say the least.

I tried to act as if it was no big deal when I finally collected myself and walked back to the counter, about an hour later.

Maybe it was closer to five minutes later.

The nurse, now fully engaged in her work, hardly made eye contact. The only thing she said was "thank you."

All I could say was "my pleasure."

She didn't even flinch.

It didn't take the doctor long to diagnose that I was the one with the fertility problem. The proof was in the pudding: my little swimmers weren't very good swimmers after all. They had crooked tails. Or short tails. And there weren't very many of them, either.

The doctor sent us home to discuss our options: in vitro fertilization, and above all else, keep trying. It wasn't as if I was infertile, there simply weren't very good odds that conception would happen.

A year later we were back at the clinic with fifteen-thousand dollars at the ready. We poured our hopes and prayers into a test tube of fertilized eggs that were implanted inside Colleen. The next two weeks were emotionally charged. Colleen was a wreck from all the hormones she was taking, but it didn't stop her, and us, from praying about it 'round the clock. We wanted kids in the worst way. It was our hope and dream. Our last straw.

And when it didn't happen, the realization that we would be childless didn't sit very well with either one of us. It really hurt. Synchie could only do so much to cheer us up. When Colleen came down from her hormone high, she was an emotional basket case. All she did was cry, laugh, and rant about whatever came to her head. Her mood swings were off the chart.

On a warm Saturday morning several months later, I accidentally dropped a plate on the kitchen floor. It broke into a hundred pieces. That was the last straw for Colleen. She went off the deep end, flailing open the cupboard door and grabbing another plate. She raised the plate above her head then slammed it to the kitchen floor. And she didn't stop there. She yanked another one off the stack and did the same. The noise was intense.

"God damn it, you incompetent loser!" she screamed. "Can't you do *anything* right?"

I looked at her in disbelief, but she didn't miss a beat.

She reached for another plate and fired it over my head like a giant clay pigeon.

I ducked.

It smashed all over the kitchen floor.

Synchie ran behind the couch, stubby tail between her legs.

Colleen fired more. Insults. Glassware. Innuendo. Saucers. It was as if she was in college again, at the softball diamond. She was smashing them out of the park. Line drives. Towering blasts. It was horrible. The rage, the hurtful things.

That was it for me.

I'd had enough.

I stormed out of the house, and took Synch and drove to Ludington, the place where Colleen and I spent so many wonderful weekends. Instead of holding Colleen's hand, I held onto Synchie's leash. We walked the beach at sunset, and chatted with the fishermen along the pier. Our accommodations were less than glamorous. We slept in the back of my Suburban, and ate hamburgers cooked on a grill in a playground under the watchful eyes of passing seagulls.

There was no denying it: the infertility issue had become a fissure for Colleen and me. And it wasn't long before the fissure became a crack, the crack became a chasm, and the chasm became the wedge that drove us apart. The infertility issue spilled over into parts of our relationship. It was horrible.

We couldn't get over the disappointment. We couldn't move past the frustration. We tried counseling, and romantic getaways. Therapy with her priest. Anything. Everything. We prayed and prayed. Together. Alone. It was agonizing. I felt as if I'd never add up to what she wanted. I felt like a loser. And deep down, I knew that I could never really make her happy. I was the one who initiated a temporary separation. It was my guilt, and feelings of inferiority, that led to our parting ways. It was my biggest mistake.

We were divorced about two years later. Neither one of us hired a lawyer, or got petty about splitting our assets. She had her stuff and I had mine. We hadn't accumulated much, and since I owned the house we lived in before we were married, she really couldn't take that away from me. Bottom line, the two of us were agreeable about the ultimate disagreement.

And it was one of those things that we had to be cordial about. After all, we were still co-workers at the *Journal*, and we stuck to our pact not to air our dirty laundry at the office.

I really thought that Colleen would leave the paper in favor of greener pastures, but then again, our publisher was in the swansong of his career, and I think Colleen wanted his job. For any newspaper person, the title of "publisher" is the grand prize, the top of the ladder. Colleen had a great chance of getting it, especially with the *Journal's* reputation for hiring from within. There are plenty of qualified editors in the world; there are very few publishers. Once she got that title, she could move to whatever part of the country she wanted, and I think that was her ultimate goal.

She knew how to play the game. She dressed up when the corporate owners of the paper flew into town from Connecticut. She smiled a lot and laughed in the casual settings outside of the closed-door meetings. Behind closed doors, her presentations were always well-received by the big shots, I could tell. They hung around her office, and made nice talk among her framed shots of Truman Capote, Katie Couric, and Barbara Walters. Maybe they were enthralled with the same things that attracted me to her years ago in Chicago: her confidence, her flair, the way she crossed her arms across her womanly physique. But there was more to Colleen's appeal: she understood that the bean counters out East were concerned with money. Ad revenue drives the newspaper business, and even though Colleen didn't sell ads, she understood that good reporting, interesting features, and in-depth stories made the job of selling ads a lot easier.

Several more years passed. Our working relationship grew into a professional, productive arrangement. She'd hand out the assignments, and the staff of reporters would see it through. There were timely topics to report—house fires, bad car accidents, and small-town politics—but then she wanted to develop a historical perspective on the oil business in our little part of the state. "After all, gas is three-something a gallon," she explained. "People hardly remember what an important part of our town's history deals with the oil business."

It was true. Nobody really knew much about our area's oil business. Hardly anybody knows about it now. All they know is that gasoline is made from oil, and oil comes from the ground.

The technical aspects of how oil is pulled from the ground aren't very exciting.

It's the people involved—the characters in the process of getting that oil—that make the business so exciting. Over the course of four months—from the time Dad had his stroke in August, to my trip to Iowa in December—I learned all about those characters in our part of Michigan.

And therein lies the story.

Five

MOST OF THE OTHER REPORTERS in the *Journal's* stable rolled their eyes and put up a minor fuss when Colleen suggested that we cover the legends of the oil business. They were content to keep covering the same old stories, the same old house fires and car accidents.

But I liked the idea. I thought it was smart. The people who were influential in the oil business were dying off at an alarming clip, and they had first-hand accounts of the industry's history.

Besides, I was always one to stir the pot. I liked to investigate. I enjoyed sniffing out a story and seeing it through to completion.

And there was plenty to discover. The oil business is complicated, with its leases, mineral rights, drilling operations, not to mention the process of converting a barrel of oil into gasoline.

Our part of Michigan had lots of oil underneath it once upon a time, and the charge to procure it became a gold rush of sorts. There were lots of guys from all over the country willing to convert an investment of ten thousand dollars into monthly royalty checks of twice that amount. Legitimate businessmen poured into the area. Corporate leaders targeted Gratiot County as an area ripe with possibilities. They built a refinery in Alma, which became the backbone of the area's economy. When it closed years later, the abandoned equipment became a sorrowful reminder of the good old days of Michigan's oil business.

The oil rush from decades ago attracted a seedy element, too—as easy money often does. There were back-room dealings, laundered money, and deals ironed out with shady characters who were making hay in Las Vegas' infancy, and Havana's limelight. And there were celebrities, too: Dean Martin got in on the action. So did Frank Sinatra and baseball's Billy Martin.

But little old Alma had interesting characters, too. Floyd Clendenning was the son of a "tool dresser" who worked on one of the first successful oil wells near Muskegon. The year was nineteen twenty-five, when advancements in geology were almost laughable. So was the pay scale.

"My dad made about twenty-three hundred bucks a year during the thirties and forties. He taught me how to sharpen the drill bits, and maintain the wells," Floyd told me for a story in the *Journal.* "But back then, a new car cost five hundred, and a new house less than ten grand. Hell, a loaf of bread cost a dime." I changed "hell" to "heck" so it fit the paper's editorial criteria.

Today, Clendenning lives off his investments, his pension, and a few royalty checks from oil wells of which he was part of.

"Those checks weren't very big when oil was only ten bucks a barrel," he said, "but anything over sixty means that I'll keep my soup warm, and my gun powder dry."

Art Covington was a middleman between the guys that drilled the oil and the people who converted it to gasoline. He made a living by taking a tiny slice of what the producers produced, and what the buyers bought. It worked. He made a decent living by filling a niche in the market.

There were some not-so-pleasant sides to the business, too. Dick "Richie" Dawes' job was to drum up investors for wells in Isabella and Midland counties during the oil rush of the nineteen fifties.

"Back then it cost about a hundred grand to punch a hole

in the earth," he told me. "And I usually sold the shares in ten grand increments."

Richie became a little agitated recounting the story.

"But on one particular site, I had a guy from Chicago tell me that he wanted to buy five shares. Cripes, I never met this guy in my life, but I'm in the business, you know what I'm saying?"

He told me all about the Great Depression and how it affected his parents.

"I mean they had nothing. *I had nothing.* You know what I'm saying?"

Of course I knew what he was saying. There was nothing complicated about it.

"So we drill a hole," he continued, "and it turns out that it's dry, nothing down there."

I nodded.

"Maybe I should explain," he said. "All that money is gone."

"I got it, Richie," I told him. "It's an all-or-nothing proposition. If you hit oil or gas, you're in the money; if you don't, you lose your investment, right?"

"Right, but that didn't sit so well with the guy from Chicago."

"What happened?"

"He sent a couple of associates up I-94 to my parents' home in Remus. They were tough-looking guys. Real pushy. Never called first, but just rapped at the front door."

"Why didn't they talk to you?"

"All they wanted to do was deliver a message."

"What was that?" I asked him.

"'It's real simple,' they told them. 'If you want to ever see your son alive, you'll get our fifty grand back.' That's the kind of people we were dealing with. Thugs. These guys were thugs, and weren't afraid to use their muscles. My mom was bawling her eyes out, and Dad kept telling me that I should have been an accountant instead of an oilman. We couldn't go to the police—didn't dare to. They gave us about a week to come up with the dough. That was a lot of money back in the seventies. You could buy a new house for that kind of money."

The Dawes story was excellent, I must say. It was front page of section two—the local news. We had photographs and sidebars, quotations and a paragraph or two about the historical price of gasoline. I piled on the Chicago connection a little heavy, but Colleen didn't do much editing. We sold lots of newspapers.

When the dust settled on my story, and the town was abuzz with the prospect of mobsters in our midst, oilman Ira Kaminsky called the paper and set up an appointment with me. I was happy to cover his story, and as it turns out, he was one of the more interesting guys I had met. He was the grandson of a Russian immigrant who was raised on the east side of Detroit. His father worked in Ford's Rouge River plant during the nineteen twenties when more than a hundred-thousand workers toiled in a single plant. It was also the time of prohibition, when rumrunners and bootleggers transported liquor from Canada across narrow stretches of the Detroit River in boats during the summer, and ice bridges in the dead of winter.

"Those were tough times, as you could imagine," Kaminsky told me. "On one hand, you had the general public clamoring for booze, and willing to pay whatever it cost to get it. On the other hand, it was illegal, so there were lots of risks involved. Blind pigs and private, 'speak-easy' clubs popped up all over Detroit. People got roughed up—you had to if you were protecting your turf. There were always guys wanting a piece of the action."

I never asked Kaminsky why he knew so much about the Detroit area, or the blind pigs from almost a century ago. I figured that it was more of a history lesson than anything else. Some guys like to talk about what they know. Some guys like to beat their chests as a sign of their manliness.

Kaminsky had read my stories in the *Journal* about Clendenning, Covington, and Dawes. He saw their photos and complimented me over and over again about what a great job I had done. In reality, however, with each interview I had with the oilmen of mid-Michigan, the ante kept getting higher and higher. The latest guy wanted to outdo the previous. My stories became more and more entertaining, more salacious.

And the advertisers noticed. The independent gasoline dealers actually called the paper and took out ads. So did the propane dealers and natural gas conglomerates.

Colleen's idea was working.

Kaminsky was in his early seventies, retired, and in relatively poor health. His pack-a-day cigarette habit had finally caught up to him. He coughed and hacked constantly, and apologized for the interruptions. Still, he waved his hands in the air as he talked, fingers stained a morbid shade of yellow.

He seemed to relish the thought of having his own private audience, of being able to tell a reporter about his life in the oil business. Kaminsky's two-and-a-half-story Victorian was enormous and seated prominently on the fifteenth hole of the Alma Country Club. On Wednesday afternoons, he'd drive a golf cart or have his driver, Roger, take him to the clubhouse, where he and the rest of his cronies drank Bombay martinis, puffed their cigarettes, and monitored their stock club's holdings.

After almost forty years at the helm of Warmouth Oil Company, there was no doubt that Kaminsky had done very well for himself.

"I started out with nothing," he said. "Didn't have a pot to whiz in, or a window to throw it out of."

He raised his hands and waved, as if I needed an extra reason to believe him. "Moved up here after college, actually it was law school."

He cleared his throat, and coughed.

"That's where I met your dad."

"Oh yeah?"

"That's right. How is he, anyway?"

"He's great. Still got his hands into every…"

Kaminsky cut me off.

"From there I went on to become a permitting agent for the Shell Oil Company. It wasn't a hard job, after all," he told me. "When the mineral rights were secured, the investors in place, and the well testing completed, it was my job to get the permit approved by the government before we began drilling. The Department of Natural Resources split off the environmental side about fifteen years ago. The guys who handle the oil business are the Department of Environmental Quality, but back then it was the plain old Conservation Department."

He said that he spent a lot of time at the DNR headquarters in Lansing, rubbing elbows with the employees who would eventually approve his permits.

"Played a lot of golf back then. Those government guys were always treated like royalty when I took them out. Free golf at the finest courses, drinks, and clothing. You know, sweaters and cardigans with the club's insignia on the front?"

I nodded.

"They all had them," he said. "Tons of them. I'd think nothing of outfitting the entire department."

"Did it work?" I asked him.

"Sure it worked, I got a lot of permits issued in the three years I was there."

I scribbled my notes feverishly.

"But maybe I should have told you that off the record," he suggested.

I acknowledged what he said, and scratched what I had just written.

"What happened next?" I asked him.

"I scraped together a couple of investors and got in on an oil well over in Montcalm County. Our first well was a good one, and I got the taste of what it's like to pull Texas tea out of the ground." He coughed.

"It's fun," he said. "It gets in your blood."

"So how do you spend your days now?" I asked him.

"I still love it," he hacked. "Let me show you something."

He directed me to the back of his home office, where he kept a ledger the size of a narrow cookie sheet. "Look at this. This is all our holdings, all our wells in this book."

There were pages and pages in his ledger.

He coughed, and pulled a framed photo off the shelf. "Here it is, State Thirty-One." He held the photo up with such pride that it could have been one of his grandkids. I must have had a confused look on my face.

"We leased the mineral rights off the State of Michigan, that's how it got its name, and thirty-one is the township number in Isabella County."

I nodded.

"And here is what it has produced."

He flipped the green and white colored pages until he found State Thirty-One. "Look here." He pointed to a thin, squiggly pencil line at the far left side of the page. "When we drilled this thing in early eighty-one it was pumping three hundred barrels a week!"

"Wow," I said, not knowing if that was a lot or a little. But by his reaction, I figured 'wow' was a safe thing to say.

"Today it produces about four or five barrels a day which, at sixty bucks a barrel, ain't bad work if you can find it."

The line on the right side of the page was way below the line on the left. In between were the miniscule ups and downs as the well's production increased or decreased over the decades.

"If we work that well any harder, we get water in with the oil and that's no good." He said. "Oil and water don't mix. So we're just content to skim whatever Mother Nature can give us."

I nodded my head. He made it sound so fascinating.

Our interview lasted several hours. He showed me his photo album, and we picked out several shots to be used in the paper. There were few photos of him as a child, and I asked him about it. "Times were tough for our family. We didn't have much of anything, let alone money. People died at an early age. It was different then."

When I asked him about the guys drilling the oil wells and how dangerous it was, Kaminsky didn't deny it.

"Sure, guys died young in the old days, but that goes with the territory. The guys who ran the wells made lots of money."

"Anybody else die or get injured?"

Kaminsky coughed. Then apologized. He was thinking, but it didn't look like he was trying to remember something specific. By the look on his face, he was sizing me up, wondering if he should tell me another one of his war stories.

"I'll tell you, but it's off the record."

I nodded again, in agreement.

He raised his eyebrows, and gestured with his hands.

I set the pen on top of the pad of paper, and placed both on his cherry wood coffee table.

"My replacement, Max Hermes, was murdered, or at least that's what they think happened to him. They never found his body."

"What happened?" I asked him.

"You've got to understand, Derrick," he continued. "This is off the record, got it?"

It was the second time that he said it, so I knew it was something juicy.

"I got it. My lips are sealed."

He nodded, then pointed a yellow index finger at me.

"In the oil business, information is key to everything else," he said. "The Shell Oil Company used to spend millions of dollars each year searching for the next oil field. When Shell found it, everyone else wanted to know where it was. They wanted to use Shell's research, but they didn't want to pay for it. Once the permit application was at the DNR, it became a matter of public record. The cat was out of the bag about where they were drilling."

He drew a deep breath and coughed again.

"Shell's competitors didn't have to put all that money into research, all they had to do was pop their own well right next to them if they could lease the rights to it. "

"How did that get Max into trouble?"

"Hermes? He was selling information to Shell's competitors before he actually filed the permit."

"I don't get it."

Kaminsky wiped his lips with a handkerchief. I noticed the monogrammed "K" in the corner.

"The permit is approved by the government, and the government is formed by the people. Once the permit is public record, and everyone knows where Shell is drilling, the price on all the surrounding mineral rights goes higher and higher because of the competition. The land owner can lease the rights to the highest bidder."

"Oh, I see," I smiled. "But if there's only one bidder, the landowner doesn't know any better, the price is much less?" I asked.

"You got it." He smiled.

I nodded. "But what happened to that agent?"

"Word got out."

"What do you mean?"

"Two things, really. He got greedy and I think he had an axe to grind with Shell. He was ticked off that the company didn't make him vice president. You know how that goes; everyone thinks that they are more valuable than they really are. He couldn't stash a little money under the table and be happy with it. He wanted more and more. Word got out that he could be bought."

I watched him, and wondered how much of Max Hermes' story had to do with Kaminsky himself. It just didn't seem right.

"There are people out there that would do just about anything for the information Hermes had. We all figured that he double-crossed the wrong people. They never found his body. They never found any clues, but his wife eventually found fifty thousand dollars tucked away in the sump pump in the basement."

"How do you know that?"

He looked at me like I shouldn't have asked.

"Who did he double cross?"

The look became more intense.

That was the end of the interview.

Kaminsky was an interesting guy. He had lots of stories and a wealth of knowledge when it came to the oil business. When I left his estate, I noticed a rather gruff looking man with a thick neck vacuuming a shiny new Cadillac near the garage. It must have been Kaminsky's driver, Roger.

As I drove back to the paper, I thought about my story and what I should use for the lead. I had to boil Kaminsky's story down to one single paragraph, one clever sentence.

Strange, how you get lost in your thoughts—your own little world. I love to see a story through. I love to paint a picture with my words. The satisfaction of writing a really good story is akin to doing anything with pride and a commitment to doing your best. Kaminsky's story would be a really good one, I could almost see it in print.

I was back at the *Journal*, in my own little cubicle, my own little world. I opened my reporter's pad of paper, and gathered my thoughts. My fingers were poised to flail the keys. The computer screen was a blank canvas, a masterpiece in the making.

Just then the phone rang, and my whole world was turned upside down.

The quiver in Mom's voice said it all.

"Your father is in the hospital," she said sadly. "You'd better get down here right away. He's had a stroke, and he wants to see you."

Six

OUR FAMILY FARM is located on the paved road that runs between Owosso and Ovid, about forty minutes north and a little east of Lansing, and west of Flint. The road is straight and smooth, and the vehicles speed along in varying amounts over the limit. There is barely any contour to the land, and the county deputies and state troopers have really no place to set up a speed trap. Most times they fall in line with a row of traffic—behind a pickup truck or tractor-trailer for cover—then nab speeders who zoom past in the opposite direction.

The cops hand out lots of tickets on our little stretch of road because they say that speed is a factor in most traffic accidents.

If speed plays a factor, weather has a part, too.

We don't really get a lot of snow in our little part of the state. Oh sure, we get three or four good helpings during the typical winter, but when compared to Michigan's higher elevations farther north, we hardly get any snow at all. Then again, you don't need a lot of snow to create poor driving conditions. All that's needed is an inch or two and a blustery wind to sweep it across the pavement. In no time, a road transforms into an ice rink.

For years, Dad maintained a wire-and-wood slat snow fence on the stretch of acreage that bordered M-21. It was one of those chores he did between Halloween and Thanksgiving, when the land wasn't quite frozen, but the hint of winter was in the air. Dad believed in preventative measures, about taking extra steps to avert a calamity. He was afraid that if one of those speeders wiped out on a slippery road in front of the property, somehow he could be held responsible. Even though Dad was a lawyer himself, he had a general mistrust of other lawyers and their ability to make life miserable for those accused.

When I was in the eighth grade and my sisters were in high school, we talked him into giving up a few feet of tillable ground along the edge of the road so that we could plant a row of trees. The idea was that the trees would compliment the snow fence in the near future, eliminate the need for it altogether in the long term. But most important, it was good for the environment.

That was a big deal. Nobody in Shiawasee County took land out of production. The mindset among most property owners is that the land is meant to be cultivated. Every square inch.

My sisters and I decided on blue spruce. They were seedlings at first, and were barely visible once the grasses in May took hold. We planted them in rows three deep from the road, and staggered the rows so eventually the snow piled up around them instead of drifting across the road.

I remember the three lines of kite strings a third of a mile long that bordered the edge of M-21. They were ten feet apart and were our guide for planting the seedlings that were delivered to our house in moist little bundles. My sisters and I each had a row to plant, and Dad was the foreman who followed along on the tractor, where he kept the remaining seedlings on a hay wagon. It was important, Dad told us, not to plant the trees too close together, not to crowd them.

Dad told us that over time the bottoms would fill out and become nice and round. He liked big bottoms, and he wasn't afraid to admit it, even if it made my mother blush when he retold the story at dinnertime.

At first, the seedlings didn't do so well. A third of them never made it to June. We didn't water or fertilize them, which may have been part of the problem. We simply shoved them in the ground and hoped for the best. The following spring, we bought more seedlings to replace the ones that had died. In an effort to curb the grasses that were choking each seedling, we put a jot of straw around each one. It took a lot of straw, but it seemed to pay dividends. By the end of the third or fourth year, the seedlings were almost knee high, and were doing their part in the winter, too.

By then I was in high school and pursuing the most important things in life: girls and pheasants. My older sisters were popular in school and had a multitude of friends over to our house. The exposure to older women piqued my curiosity; it made the testosterone boil inside me. Even as a young man, I thought that older women had more confidence, more appeal, more independent charm. And for me, those traits were sexy then, and they still are today.

I really had better luck with pheasants than I did with girls. During the fall of the year, I used to walk the third-of-a-mile on the property as if I were a cat on the prowl. The grasses between each seedling were thick and tall, which made prime nesting conditions in the spring, and even better roosting cover in the winter. Since we didn't have a dog then, being stealthy and stopping often was the only way to get them to fly. Pheasants would rather run away from danger and hide in heavy cover when confronted with a perilous situation. Flying is a last resort. A stealthy walk through tight quarters such as the row of spruce—kept the pheasants guessing as to my location. By stopping often, and walking quietly, I unnerved them into flying.

Sometimes Dad took me hunting with his pals from the grain elevator, which was always fun. We never killed many birds, but the chance to hang out with the older men left an impression on me. I enjoyed that whole hunting experience. The camaraderie. The charm of a crisp October morning with the maple and oak woodlots draped in gold, and the corn a buttery shade of yellow.

During the first winter that my oldest sister was away at college, one of her pals, Judy Craigmyle, lost control of her vehicle where the stretch of clear road in front of our property met the adjacent iced-over patch. As is the case with most inexperienced drivers, she overcompensated once the car started to fishtail. And once that happened, she was at the mercy of oncoming traffic. Fortunately for Judy, she missed getting into a head-on collision. Unfortunately, the ditch on the opposite side of the road wasn't the greatest place for a crash landing. Especially when the driver's side door took the brunt of the collision.

Her left wrist was clearly broken when she managed to kick on our front door that dark winter evening. Mom and Dad recognized her as one of my sister's friends right away, and sat her down at the kitchen table. All Judy could do was cradle her bad wing with her good. She closed her eyes, stooped slightly forward and rocked gently. The pain of her arm, and who knew what else, must have been excruciating.

Mom wigged out. She was living every parent's nightmare even though it wasn't her child who was involved in the accident. She put on a pot of coffee, and poured Judy a glass of milk. After draping a blanket over Judy's shoulders, she turned the thermostat up to eighty. Dad calmly picked up the phone book, and dialed Judy's number, but the line was busy. He quickly walked outside to the car, and told Mom not to call an ambulance.

"Where are you going?" Mom screamed. "This is no time to monkey around with the snow fence!"

"No, no, no. I'm going to get her parents!" he yelled. "Their line was busy. I'll be right back."

Judy wasn't one of the more popular kids in school, but she wasn't one of the outcasts, either. She was smart, I knew, but I think she suffered from the "ugly duckling syndrome" throughout most of high school. Most of the boys didn't pay much attention to her until after high school, well after her car accident, and after Judy gained a great deal of confidence. It was about that time she ditched her glasses and bought contact lenses, which accented her wonderful blue eyes.

But she didn't look very pretty when she was sitting there at the kitchen table, a cup of coffee, a cup of hot chocolate, a glass of milk, and a plate of warmed leftovers within striking distance.

Mom had a generous heart when it came to company. And food. She wanted to make sure they felt welcome, even when they had broken limbs and were wilting in our eighty-degree hothouse.

The Shiawassee County deputies arrived at our house about the same time as Dad, and Judy's dad. They wanted to know if we knew whose car was in the ditch down the road. Dad invited them inside, just in time to see Judy's dad help her out of the chair. She was crying.

"I'm so sorry, Daddy," she said. He was crying, too; his little girl needed him like she never did before.

The cops wanted to see her driver's license, but Dad would hear nothing of it. He asked the cops to leave once they suggested that Judy might have been speeding.

One of the deputies had an axe to grind with Dad, after Dad sued the department and won. The patrolman, then a sergeant, responded to a bad traffic accident involving a drunk driver who had missed a stop sign in an unfamiliar stretch of road. The driver was Dad's client and suffered a broken shoulder as a result of the accident. The cop wouldn't let him receive medical attention until the following morning, when he posted bail. I forget how much money they settled for, but it was fairly substantial. Part of the settlement was that the sergeant was to be demoted, and the tree limbs that shielded the stop sign were to be trimmed by the county. And Dad's client, who was ticketed for drunk driving at the scene, didn't get charged with that, or the lesser charge of impaired driving. He didn't even get a ticket for reckless driving. All he got was careless driving.

Dad told them to conduct an interview once she had

treatment. If they wanted pictures of the car, it would be in front of our house. He told the cops and Judy's dad that he'd haul her car out of the ditch with the help of Old Alice, and bring it back to the farm.

Dad was a take-charge kind of guy, and a master at cutting deals.

And dear Mom, the eternal hostess, offered the two patrolmen a plate of warmed leftovers, as if it were a consolation prize on a game show.

"Have a seat, you fellas," she said. "You may be too late for the car crash, but you're not too late for some good eating."

Everyone rolled his eyes.

About a month after her car accident, and with her arm still in a cast, Judy brought Mom and Dad a homemade lemon meringue pie. It was her way of saying "thank you" for taking care of her during the accident.

Over the years, Judy kept in contact with my parents, more than she did with my older sisters. The car accident brought them together; the fact that she lived down the street made it convenient. Although Judy moved away after marrying a cop named Garza from Lansing, she moved back to a modest-sized ranch near a neighboring farm once she discovered what kind of a jerk he really was. When he wasn't on duty, the guy liked to drink; and when he drank, he liked to throw his weight around. Judy didn't want to raise her daughter in that environment. She knew that they'd be better off in a loving, one-parent household than a convulsing, two-parent war zone.

I always had a magnetic kind of attraction to Judy, although I never really asked her out. There was always a good reason why it didn't happen, and most of it had to do with proximity. She was off at college when I was finishing high school, and when I was off at college, she was in another town, starting her career. Dating never seemed to make much sense, but there was nothing wrong with admiring her when we both were in the neighborhood. We saw each other during the holidays, at the county fair, and virtually anytime I came back to the farm for a visit. She wasn't far from the farm, not far from Dad. We always had pleasant visits, and excellent conversations. Besides, she had those wonderful blue eyes, and a cute face that was dappled in freckles. The "ugly duckling" had blossomed into a beautiful lady. She had confidence to burn, and poise by the bushel. While the popular kids in her high school class put on weight, or grew bald after graduation, Judy took pride in her health, her career, and her family. She turned heads, no doubt, but she really didn't do much dating. There was hardly time for it, and since the divorce from the cop, the whole marriage thing left a bad taste in her mouth.

Dad handled her divorce, and the subsequent restraining order against Garza.

Judy liked to talk. And since she sold mortgages, I suppose those characteristics helped her in her career. Everyone- from her kid's soccer coaches, to the girls who had her cappuccino waiting for her at the coffee shop the same time every day- knew her name and what a nice person she was. Not surprisingly, nearly everyone in our little town had their houses financed through her company.

Judy plowed a lot of money back into her business, especially advertising. She bought space on the sides of busses, and her image was splashed on billboards near the edge of town. The local newspaper loved her, as did the radio station in town. She sponsored not only her daughter's soccer team, but the entire league as well. They all had Judy's little insignia emblazoned on their uniforms. Judy's likeness was everywhere, her logo imprinted in the minds, the thoughts, the souls of an entire community.

But Judy never got too big for her britches. Despite being incredibly busy with her career, her time on the city council, and her family, Judy still looked after my parents as a good neighbor would. She was sure to send a card at the holidays and on birthdays, and she hardly needed an excuse to drop off a batch of cookies or homemade brownies. Judy's daughter, Xochitl—Aztec for "flower"—thought of my folks as a set of surrogate grandparents. My folks loved Judy's daughter, and called her "Zoe-chee."

Xochitl enjoyed having my folks in her life, too. When most of the other kids had to scramble to get their grandparents to come to school functions, little Zoechee had multiple sets, including my folks. Not surprisingly, Xochitl's picture was on the refrigerator, with my older sister's kids as well.

And so, it was no big shock when the doorbell rang at our family farm at dusk the first night of Dad's stroke.

It was Judy Craigmyle.

In the flesh.

I recognized her right away, even though the curtains on the back door partially obscured my vision. There's no hiding a beautiful pair of blue eyes.

I had no time for gawking.

"Isn't this a pleasant surprise? Come in, come in," I told her, holding open the screen door at the rear of the old farmhouse.

"Thank you, Derrick. You know I just had to do something. I heard about Chick and had to find out more details." She swept past me, the scent of her perfume in her wake. I watched her go to the counter, a casserole dish cradled in one arm, and a bowl of fruit salad in the other.

"He's…" I searched for the right words, but didn't get far.

"Come here, Derrick."

Judy came to me in one welcome rush. She gathered me in, and held me close. There was no reluctance on her part. She squeezed me and wasn't the least bit shy about it, either. At first I withheld. I doubted her sincerity, but the longer we stood in that embrace, the more I realized that she needed a hug just as much as I did. And so, I hugged her back, not like a bear hug, but an old-fashioned hearty squeeze. I closed my eyes and lowered my head to hers. I felt the arm of her sunglasses, tucked behind her ears and framing her face like a bonnet, stiff and hard against my cheek. My hands were on her back, the madras plaid. It felt like summer, like a sundress should. I noticed her bra snugly pressed against her back, against the curve of her ribs. She had a hint of excess, a layer of love—just as I did.

It was just a hug. Just a hug, but I wished it would be the start of so much more. It was a wonderful sensation, the two of us dancing in the kitchen's ballroom: our bodies pressed together, our hearts beating to a common cause. I was incredibly lonely, anxious to find true love, and if it came from a friend of the family, I would embrace it.

The man we loved in similar ways had a brush with death, and it was a painful reminder of how treasured life is.

"It's going to be okay," I told her.

"Tell me, Derrick." She backed away, slightly, a half tear in each eye.

My hands left her side. Hers left mine. Our eyes never faltered.

"The good news is that he didn't appear to have any permanent damage to his arms and legs," I told her. "The bad news is that they're not sure of his mental situation."

Judy had a confused look on her face.

"They don't know yet if he's going to be okay," I continued. "I mean like..."

"If he's going to remember things?" she interrupted.

"Sure. That's what I'm getting at. He recognized me, but he called me Erik a few times. He recognized my sisters, too, but if all the grandkids or the sons-in-law would have been in the room, I don't know if he would have remembered their names. His speech is different. It's hard to explain."

"So what's going to happen?" she asked.

"He's going to be in the hospital for at least a week, they say."

Judy nodded her head.

"They want to make sure they get his medication straightened out and get him into physical therapy right away. I told Dad that I would look after the farm at least for a while."

She turned to the counter and picked up the fruit bowl, her freckled hands cupping each side.

"I brought a whole bunch of food. Where are Allison and Carol?" she asked, as she turned to the refrigerator.

"With Mom, in Lansing."

The refrigerator door swung wide, as she bent at the waist. I noticed the hem on her dress and the way it climbed slightly up the back of her thigh. All of a sudden I was the one with the speech problem.

"They figured that with the *thigh* price of gas it was just as cheap for them to stay in a hotel in Lansing as it is to drive from the farm every day."

Judy didn't catch it.

"That's probably true," she said, determined to find a proper resting spot for the dish in her hands. The pickles, the mayonnaise, the leftover egg salad needed rearranging.

"I thought I'd bring you guys a home-cooked meal, thinking that there would be somebody here to eat it."

"Let me help you, Judy."

I stooped over the open door and peered inside the refrigerator, Mom called "the icebox." The top row inside was loaded with low-fat milk, a giant container of spring water, catsup, a bottle of chardonnay way in the back, and a jar of Mom's raspberry jam. The door was just as cluttered, with a dozen eggs resting in their plastic dugouts, a stick of unopened butter, and cheese slices.

But the real view was happening at the foot of the refrigerator. Judy's hands were busy, but as she stooped there like a catcher at home plate, I couldn't help but marvel at the glimpse that was all mine. She wore a modest silver ring on her left foot, second toe from the right. It was bright and shiny, in contrast to her tan foot and white, slightly heeled sandals. Her calves swelled behind her silky, burnished shins, and knees, polished smooth. Where the back of her calf met the back of her thigh, the view kept getting better and better. Her legs were summer tanned, and slightly freckled with spots less frequent than the ones sprinkled across her hands and the bridge of her nose.

Farther and farther north I glanced. She was talking to herself; the bowl of fruit salad in one hand, a cluttered appliance occupying the other. Her dress was pulled halfway up her thigh, halfway to the promised land. Her thighs were strong and smooth, and as firm as the chilled butter sticks within my grasp. Her fruit salad passed my vision- the grapes so round and pert, the melon so ripe and satisfying. I couldn't help but imagine the taste, the tang, the temptation of the juice. It was wonderful.

"There, now," she said, standing up gracefully, and tugging at the sides of her dress. "Did you get a good view?" Her eyebrows were raised; her hands perched on her hip.

I was busted. My face started to burn.

"What do you mean?"

She snickered.

"You know what I'm talking about."

Her hands moved from her hips to each arm, crossed in front of her. I blushed even more.

"See how I made room in there for both the fruit salad and the tuna casserole?"

I smiled in relief. "Oh yes. It was wonderful."

"That's good, Derrick. Now, will you please hand me the tuna surprise behind you, or would you like to have it for dinner?"

"I was just thinking about dinner," I told her. "The day kinda got away from me."

I stood there in the kitchen, an unfamiliar casserole pan in my hands, a beautiful woman in my midst. "I had to feed the cattle, and take care of a few chores before I got in the shower a few minutes ago…"

"Aren't you hungry?"

"I'm starving, Judy."

"Well just sit down, Derrick," she said. "You've got a lot on your mind. Let me take care of you."

"That would be great, thanks."

I smiled.

"I'm going to have a beer, would you like one?"

Her head turned from the cupboard where all the plates were stored.

"Glass of chardonnay?" I asked.

"Sure," she said. "Why not."

Judy knew her way around my folks' kitchen. A second later she produced a graceful looking wine glass with a long stem and a cute little bottom.

She reached toward me, the long stem a short distance away. I reached for her, for the glass, for the notion of spending at least a few more minutes with a woman that I had never really pursued, but had always coveted.

"Thank you," she said.

Her eyes sizzled a hole right through me. There was magic in the air, sparks a'crackling.

"Let's see if you can't get that bottle out of the refrigerator without making a mess."

Now it was my turn to wrestle with the refrigerator.

And the bottle was buried way in the back.

Judy was busy with the dishes behind me. I heard the plates, the glasses, and the silverware. Her steps were quick and vibrant—her little toe ringlet as intriguing as buried treasure at the bottom of Lake Judy.

All my attention was on the bottle of chardonnay, tucked way in the back, halfway behind the plastic container of drinking water and the little knob that controls the temperature. I stretched, being careful not to spill the egg salad or upset the pickles. My hand found the bottle's neck, and I choked it tenderly. Steadily,

I tilted the bottle to the right, past the container of water. The wine inside the bottle sloshed toward the cork, but it didn't leak. I had the bottle nearly home free when Judy said something that threw me for a loop.

"Nice view, here."

The bottle of wine nearly fell from my hands.

I was still half-bent in front of the fridge, my posterior still facing the interior of the kitchen. For a second there I froze, thinking that if she really did like the view, I shouldn't ruin the image. I didn't say a thing; there was nothing to say until I stood up and assessed the situation.

Judy was behind me, at the kitchen sink, her hands splashing clean a ripe tomato from Mom's garden. Her eyes were gazing down the rows of spruce, now twenty feet tall, in the golden hour of the day.

"Yes, it is a nice view," I told her, again relieved. "I remember planting those trees with Dad and my sisters." My hand wiggled the cork free. Her glass was waiting on the counter near her elbow.

"Those were the days, right Derrick?" She had the tomato on a wooden cutting board, and was slicing it into smart little slices.

"What do you mean?" I asked her.

"I mean, when we were in high school, we hardly had a care in the world." Her hand held the glass as I filled it up, her eyes darted up and down. "The only thing we had to do was make good grades and stay out of trouble."

She thanked me for the wine, raised it to her lips and took a modest sip. Her lipstick left a crinkle of pink on the rim. She made it look so good, so tempting.

"At least for me, I used to think that our parents would be around forever."

Her wine glass was sweating. I watched the little beads of condensation gather, and eventually trace a long, sensual line down the outside edge.

Synch, who had been sprawled out on the welcome mat on the opposite side of the kitchen, drew a heavy sigh. In her younger days, she would have barked at the first signs of company, and would have nosed them silly until they acknowledged her presence. Now she relishes her time to snooze, and has all but given up on her territorial obligations.

"You're close to my parents, aren't you, Judy?"

She turned slightly towards me, one sandal slightly cocked over the other.

"Of course I am. They're like an aunt and uncle to me."

The microwave oven chimed, and it distracted her attention for a second. She lowered her nose to the plate, closed her eyes gently, and took a sniff. It wasn't quite ready, so she put it back inside. She opened the refrigerator door again, and pulled out the fruit salad.

"They've been like grandparents to Xochitl. They do lots of things together."

All I could do was watch her float around the kitchen, and think about what a great image it was. She was fun to watch, a dream to admire.

Dad must have had those same thoughts about Mom, once upon a time.

Maybe he still does.

Since his stroke a few hours before, nobody really knew for sure what was, or wasn't, going on inside his head.

"So are you going to stay here the rest of the week?" she asked.

"I'm going to try," I told her, and took a drink of beer.

"What's stopping you?"

"Work. I don't know how they're going to react to me taking so much time off."

The microwave chimed again, and this time there was no doubt that it was ready. The steam purled from the noodles, the tuna, the carrots and peas.

"I know... but it's your dad. They have to, don't they?"

I shook my head.

"Not really, Judy. I don't know what the laws are, but they certainly don't care much about them."

Judy pushed the tuna casserole onto the plate with the tomatoes, the scoop of cottage cheese, and a slice of wheat bread from the loaf she found in the fridge.

"All they care about is churning out a paper every day. That's what the advertisers expect and that's what they pay for."

The plate was now in front of me on the kitchen table.

"Thank you, Judy," I said, smiling. "This is wonderful."

"You're welcome, Derrick." She smiled back. "You've got a lot on your plate, if you'll pardon the pun."

I laughed. "Very clever...but aren't you going to eat?"

"Already did. I took Xochitl to summer camp this afternoon and we stopped for a bite to eat."

She sat down next to me and crossed one leg over the other. Behind her was the open window, and behind that, the barn and barnyard. Somewhere off in the distance, one of Dad's cows hollered in twilight's glimmer. Synch raised her eyelids slightly, but then lowered them once again.

"Where is summer camp?"

"It's up north a few hours," she said, swishing the wine in her hand. "It's a horse camp."

"That will be fun, won't it?"

"You bet it will," she said. "Those were the days weren't they?"

"Why do you say that?" I asked her, sprinkling salt and pepper on my cottage cheese and tomatoes.

"You're probably thinking that I'm some sort of sentimental fool the way I've been carrying on." She stood up from the table, opened the refrigerator and the bottle of wine. "First I start babbling about our childhood and now that my kid's off at summer camp. I want to be a kid again, too."

"Why's that?"

She poured more wine, and gathered her thoughts. She wasn't one to say things she didn't mean, but sometimes she didn't know exactly how to put it all into words.

"I feel like my life is half over now and I haven't had enough fun," she said.

I took a bite of tuna casserole, and wiped my lips. Judy was seated in front of the open window again, legs crossed, and her fingers toying with the glass' stem.

"What's fun for you, Judy?"

"That's the thing, Derrick, I can't remember anymore." She hesitated. "I make plenty of money, but almost everything I make goes back into the business."

She folded the corners of her napkin under her wine glass. They sprouted from the glass's rim like new sprouts in a May cornfield.

"How's that?"

Her hand moved from the wine glass to her head. She pulled the sunglasses from her hair, and laid them on the table. The frames were egg-shaped, and twinkled with tiny gold medallions at the corners.

"It takes a lot of money to keep my business going. I mean, I'm in direct competition with the banks that have huge advertising budgets and a staff of paid marketing professionals."

I took another bite of tuna. It was delicious.

"Yeah, but people finance their houses from Judy Craigmyle because of Judy Craigmyle. You're the best."

She nodded her head in agreement, modestly.

"That may be true, but if Judy Craigmyle stops spending all that money in advertising, they'll stop beating down my door."

I listened to her, but didn't offer any solutions. It was time to listen.

"I feel like most days I'm chasing my tail," she said.

"What are you going to do?" I asked her. "What do you want to do?" I rephrased it.

She sighed, and fidgeted with her sunglasses again.

"Probably nothing," she said. I've got too many bills to pay and a daughter to support to do anything rash. And I really have no reason to complain. I make good money, but I just wish it would come easier."

"Isn't that what we all want?"

"Easy money?" she asked, eyebrows furled.

"Sure," I answered.

"That's what I want..." She paused for a second. Her eyes turned from the sunglasses to the wine glass and the way her wine made laps around the sides when she swirled it between her fingers. "As long as it's legal."

"What about moral?"

"What about it?"

"Would you like to make a lot of money if it wasn't the most moral thing in the world?"

"I guess it would depend on what it was, and how immoral. Why are you asking me all these questions, anyway?"

I laughed, which was my way of wiggling out of a sticky situation.

"I'm sorry, Judy. I guess it's just the reporter in me, and I want to get to the bottom of your story."

"You never told me this was on the record, did you?"

"No."

"That's one of the cardinal rules of being a good reporter. You're always supposed to tell the interviewee that she's being interviewed."

"True enough. Will you accept my apology, Miss Craigmyle?"

She smirked in her cute little way and said, "Not before you answer your own question."

"*Where's summer camp*?" I asked, smirking just the same.

"No, no, silly. Would you like to make a lot of money even if it wasn't especially moral?"

She had me thinking.

"I don't know, Judy. That's a tough question. I think I would. It's one of those questions we used to laugh about in high school."

She was listening while the wheels churned in my head.

"Remember walking out to that big oak tree just off campus?"

She laughed. "The one behind the football field just off the school's property?"

"Oh yeah. You remember that?"

"Of course I do. I used to hang out there."

"You must have smoked cigarettes…" I suggested.

"Oh sure, everybody did, but I never really inhaled. They made me sick."

"Anything else?"

"What?"

"Did you smoke anything else under the big oak tree?" I asked her.

"Derrick, you seem to be forgetting something."

"What?" I asked.

"I'm the one who's asking the questions."

"Sorry," I said. She had me smiling. We both were.

"You want to tell me something about that big oak tree, don't you? Otherwise you wouldn't have asked."

"Are we on the record Miss Craigmyle?" I asked her.

She reached for my hand and slapped it.

"You're not going to tell me, are you?"

"Someday, maybe."

"Why won't you tell me now?"

I leaned toward her, lowered my chin, and stared into her bright, blue eyes. In my softest, sexiest voice, I said, "Because any good reporter knows that a good story doesn't come easily."

My move didn't fluster her in the slightest, even though our faces were only a dozen inches apart.

"Is that right, Derrick?" She called my bluff. Her hand

reached toward my face, and I thought that she was going to stroke my cheek, or pull me closer. Instead, she leaned in my direction, made a pointer with her index finger, and pushed me backwards by the lips.

"Some stories," she said, calmly, assuredly, and without hesitation, "are better off untold."

Her move put a damper on the situation. Or, more like it, *my move* put a damper on the situation. It was way too premature. It's one thing about being confident; it's another matter to be pushy. I was definitely pushy.

I backpedaled. She crossed her arms. *No way, Jose.*

"Dinner was delicious," I said. "Thank you."

"Are you finished?" she asked me, and I'm not sure if she meant, with the 'oak tree' line of questions, dinner, or the half-hearted attempt at kissing her.

"Yes I am. Thank you, Judy."

I stood. She stood. My dirty plate was between us like the blunder that I had just made.

"I should probably go. I promised Xochitl I'd send her an email after I found out about Chick. And besides, I've got a busy day tomorrow."

"Of course," I relented.

"Are you going to the hospital tomorrow?"

"Lunchtime."

"Good. Tell your dad and sisters I said hello. And Mom, too."

"Count on it, Judy. And thanks for dinner. It was a lot of fun catching up with you."

"Sure," she said. I waited for the same, something like 'yeah, it was,' but it never came. Instead, all she said was, "Okay, Derrick."

Judy turned, opened the back door of the old farmhouse, and took two steps across the porch. The springs on the screen door protested mildly as she opened it. It was a familiar sound.

It reminded me of home. The door slammed shut, as she skipped down the back stairs, past the tiger lilies and snapdragons in full bloom.

She turned to her car and I noticed the smile on her face. Her smile made me smile, too. She was proud of herself and the way she turned me down. It's nice to feel loved, to feel attractive, to know that you've still got what other people want.

And yes, it's fun to play hard to get, no matter what your situation is.

She was beautiful in her own unique way. I admired her looks, her personality as well. I liked the way she liked to work for a living, and the way she was strong and independent. She didn't rely on anyone, and that was appealing. She'd never be clingy. She had her own life, her own career, and didn't need anybody to make it complete.

As Judy drove away, Synch got up from her nap, and walked stiff-legged across the kitchen floor. It was her time for an evening stroll around the farmyard. I put the dinner plate in the sink, let her outside, and returned to the table. When I picked up my beer can, I noticed that Judy had forgotten her sunglasses.

They were there, plain as day, and I had to wonder if she left them there by accident or on purpose.

It must be an accident, I thought. *There's no way she would have done it on purpose. Either way, this was my chance to meet her again.*

She had a week off from the responsibilities of her daughter; I had a week off from the paper.

There's nothing like a week off to stir the soul, especially in late August in Michigan, when I knew that my father was out of the woods and was going to be okay.

I pictured Judy and me together, if not for a lifetime, a few hours.

The possibilities were endless.

Seven

THE COUNTRY MUSIC still blares when you turn on the house lights in Dad's old barn. The radio was either my dad's, or his grandfather's dad, who made his living by milking cows. The radio is hung from a barn rafter by a bungee cord, near the length of chain that dangles on a thin rope. When the door between the main part of the barn and the milk house is opened, the chain is raised; when the door closes, the chain goes down. The weight of the chain keeps the door from blowing open on a windy day, or being pushed open by one of the barn cats, or a wayward animal.

Leroy, the calf, could probably figure out how to open the door. He was always happy to have visitors, and the morning after Judy dropped off the casserole was no exception. Orphaned at birth three months ago, he's taken on a personality unlike any cow we've ever had. He almost wags his tail on our twice-daily visits to the barn. He bawls and prances around his little stall as if he were a puppy in a playpen, and I'm not sure if it's because he knows we'll let him run around the inside of the barn or if it's the prospect of fresh vittles. In either case, when I let him out of his stall, he runs down the alley behind the stanchions, throwing his head up and down, bucking and spinning wildly as if he had been watching championship rodeo.

Of course, he's always good for a blast of gas.

The barn cats look at Leroy incredulously. It's as if they can't really decide if Leroy is a threat to them, or if he's possessed by demons. Most cows are dumb. Really dumb. But Leroy is different. He's half-dog, I swear. He comes when I call him, and nudges his head under my arm just like Synch used to do when she was younger. I scratch him behind his big, floppy ears and under his scruffy chin.

If I had udders, Leroy's world would be complete.

I put his overgrown bottle of calf starter in its holder, pulled down a bale of straw from the mow, and noticed a pair of cats copulating near the grain bin. They made it look like fun. I love the way the tom bites her neck—for fun, or because he's into the whole domination thing? And the female—why does she howl and bare her teeth? Is she mad at herself for giving in, or is it because he's really hurting her?

It must have been the twang-like voice of the band "Lone Star" that made the whole cat courtship possible. Although I'm not one for country music, I can't argue with the unfiltered simplicity of it all. I should have been a songwriter. I mean, how hard can it be to write the lyrics: "*Bubble gum in the baby's hair, sweet potatoes in my lazy chair?*"

For the first time in several days, I had to write something that really mattered. I wanted to ask Judy out on a date, and at the same time, return her sunglasses to her. Even though it wasn't the most romantic prose in the world, I didn't think it was half bad.

Without your glasses you may not see,
What your tuna has done to me.
I'd like to see you, and it can't be too soon,

I've grown a beard, I howl at the moon.
Please be my guest at a table for two
At a cozy little place familiar to you.
Meet me at seven, under the big oak tree
And see what your tuna has done to me.

I wrote the invitation in my best handwriting, and buried it with her sunglasses in a small, padded envelope from Dad's roll-top desk. It was nearly seven a.m. when I tucked the envelope between my legs and started Dad's old Harley in the back of the garage. I knew that he hadn't ridden it in forever, but at the same time I was confident that it still worked.

When I made it close to Judy's house, I cut the engine and let the bike coast to an uneventful stop a hundred yards from her driveway. No sense in waking her up with the Harley's throaty rumble. Judy's lights were on, but her Dodge Durango was still in the driveway near the backdoor. I slid the envelope under a windshield wiper and tiptoed my way out of there as if I were the tooth fairy.

She'd get a kick out of my thoughtfulness. She'd snicker at my poem, I was sure. Whether or not she'd make it to my picnic was anybody's guess. I hoped she would. I couldn't wait to see her again, even though my thoughts were walking a tightrope between her and my dad in the hospital.

It was weird to see Dad as mortal. When I was growing up, Dad was my idol, and I thought that he'd live forever. He was always there for my sisters and me. Even when I was a teenager, and most of my friends were quarreling with their parents, I still thought my dad was a great guy. He made me want to be a better son, because I saw him trying to be a better man.

I had plenty of time to think about him as I made my way north to the Mt. Pleasant branch of Isabella Bank and Trust. Traffic was light that morning and the old Harley handled like a dream. I was cruising along, soaking up the summer scenery and August's foliage, which was the color of steamed broccoli. There was no need to hurry. It was just the bike and me, together. I had to be strong, and purposeful, just like the Harley. I had to be positive. Dad needed me. Mom needed me. They all did.

I kept thinking about Dad, and Judy, and my time away from the paper. I prayed that Dad would be okay, and at the same time was thankful that he wasn't worse than he was. I never did ask him why he kept a safe deposit box an hour away from the farm. It made no sense.

It didn't take long to notice the other motorcycles on the road, and how they all acknowledge each other with a little hand gesture. It's not a full-fledged wave, but something a little more subtle. I've noticed the folks in Iowa do the same thing when they pass a vehicle going the opposite direction. All they do is lift a couple fingers off the handlebar or the steering wheel and give them a little flex. It's not like they know you, or want to get to know you; it's simply a way to convey, "Happy trails."

Some of the bikes had women on the back. It takes a certain kind of woman to ride on the back of a motorcycle. She's got to be uninhibited, but at the same time she's got to trust the guy driving. She can't be afraid to get cozy, and wrap her legs around him, or be considered "bike candy." There has to be an adventurous side to her, and at the same time, a confidence in her sex appeal, too. A woman knows that people are looking at her, and when she's on the back of a bike it makes the spectacle all the more obvious. "If you've got it, flaunt it," I always say.

A few minutes later, I made it to the Mt. Pleasant branch of Isabella Bank and Trust just as it opened. A teller directed me towards the far end of the building, where a woman monitoring the safe deposit boxes behind a plain wooden counter asked for my identification. When I handed it to her, she had me sign a card, "just to make sure it matches your signature on file."

After examining my signature, she picked up the forms and

excused herself. I watched her walk across the length of the floor to a small cubicle at the far end of the bank. It must have been the signature that threw her off. I never remembered signing the card in the first place, and Dad must have signed my name for me. He was always pretty good at knowing how to get things done. After a moment, I saw an older woman step from the cubicle and wave in my direction.

I guess that meant we had the green light.

The vault wasn't as pretentious as I thought it would be. Sure, our voices echoed once we got inside, and the ancient tile was buffed to a pristine shine, but after all, it was just a place to store column after column of metal-clad boxes. They were lined up like something out of Goldilocks' nursery rhyme—there were momma-sized boxes, papa-sized boxes, and baby boxes.

Number thirty-four was papa-sized, which wasn't very big at all, considering that it was maybe eight inches wide, four inches tall, and nearly two feet deep. With box in hand, I was directed to a small, private room that reminded me of a confessional. I turned on the overhead florescent light, and closed the thick oak door behind me. The chair was comfortable enough: red velour, straight backed, and dressed in oak as well.

When I slid the metal cover open on Dad's safe deposit box, the first thing I noticed was the brown manila envelope on top. Folded in half lengthwise, Dad wrote my name on the front in his best handwriting. I pulled it out of the box, but there were lots of other things inside that distracted my attention: the deed to the farm, the titles to the pickup, Mom's Buick, the old Mustang, and the Harley. I hesitated. Dad sent me up here to look at his trust, not to rummage through his most personal documents. Still, I was curious. A rubber band held together a stack of envelopes from Raymond James, ripped opened at the end, the way Dad always did. I thumbed the stack and noticed another inscription, "college fund." On each envelope, he had written the names of his grandkids. What a great guy. He never told me about his plans for his grandkids, and my sisters never mentioned it, either.

Dad clung to the notion that the only way to get ahead in this world was through education and hard work. He instilled it into our upbringing. It was ingrained into our heads. He couldn't make his grandkids work hard, but at least he was making college a possibility for them.

Family was important to Dad. I always knew it, but now there were signs of it all over his safe deposit box. I found three small envelopes, the size of the ones used at wedding receptions. Each one had our names written on the front, with a date underneath. The dates were all on our second birthdays. Instead of opening the envelopes, I simply held them up to the florescent light and noticed a lock of hair in each one.

The back of the box had a two-inch stack of U.S. savings bonds. I never did look at the maturity date, but they were probably well past due. After all, there was a stack of currency too, earning no interest whatsoever. Hundreds all. A stack two or three inches tall.

I shook my head.

You're not getting a very good return on your money here, Dad.

Dad's belongings weren't all business. He had fun stuff, too. A program from the Tigers sixty-eight World Series. A signed duck hunting stamp from fifty-four, fifty-five and sixty-one. A lapel pin from a distant presidential election: "I like Ike."

He had stocks, as well. All blue chip, all well recognized companies with long histories and proven earning ability. General Electric. Coca-Cola Bottling. Dell. Dow Chemical. I love the look of genuine stock, with its fancy scrolling, and nostalgic font. Dad must have liked having the stocks themselves, too, rather than the statement that proved he owned them. He was into that—getting the genuine, the real McCoy.

He must have lived off the dividends, or maybe he just

cashed the dividends into hundred dollar bills and stuffed them into his safe deposit box.

I thought about counting the currency, but decided against it. It would have taken forever. I shook my head again, and rolled my eyes.

The little desk inside the booth was getting cluttered, but the box was still half full. He had newspaper clippings from a lifetime ago. His wedding announcement was there, tattered and yellow, complete with a picture of him and Mom standing hand-in-hand near the altar. Mom's dress spilled across the foreground; it formed a pool of satin at their feet. They looked so young, so innocent, and incredibly happy. Their smiles said it all. And the account by the paper—almost surreal in detail when compared to today's rushed summaries.

> *"The bride wore a white sheath with a scooped neckline and three-quarter-length sleeves. White gladiolas decorated the altar and the Virgin Mary bouquet was white snapdragons."*

Along came Allison, Carol, and me. Our announcements, all in a row.

Dad also kept some serious-looking documents too. They had boxy square fonts most often seen in the nineteen seventies and eighties. Across the top, in bold, underlined type: "Royalty Agreement." I skimmed the first paragraph, which was filled with lots of legal-sounding words such as "whereas" and "witnesseth." Each document had a lengthy description of an oil well. Its longitude and latitude. Its township, section and depth. And, in bold writing, it outlined Dad's interest in the proceeds. He was in line for a sixty-fourth or a thirty-second of the well's proceeds. He was in line for some sort of royalty on some sort of well that was drilled in a remote section of Northern Michigan.

It was very odd.

The guy never mentioned having a stake in an oil well, or wells. And it wasn't an isolated contract. He had lots of them. There must have been thirty royalty agreements in the stack, each one promising a portion of the profits.

I didn't know very much about oil wells, or how much money they produce. A sixty-forth didn't sound like much, but then again, Dad must have known what he was doing. Dad's business was always Dad's business, and I respected that. It appeared that his drilling interest was just another investment, and who knows, it could have been the risky side to his otherwise conservative portfolio.

Dad's oil royalties gave me reason to pause. The timing of it couldn't have been better—after all, we had just started covering the topic at the paper. How was Dad involved? Was he just an investor, or did he play a bigger role? I opened the door to my little cubicle and asked the woman at the desk outside to make some copies for me.

"No problem," she said.

When she disappeared, I turned my attention to an entire section of Lenawee County's *Daily Telegram*. The pages were wider than they are today, and there were several stories jammed across the yellowed front page. Michigan's U.S. Senator Alvin McNamarah was pictured stiff-armed, white-shirted and smiling the smiles of an election year. LaVern Philot used his connections at the local IGA to be elected president of the Adrian Chamber of Commerce. He seemed to have a wider smile than the good senator. I really didn't think anything of the paper until I found a story about a third of the way down the page. It was titled, "*Local man killed in early morning crash.*" The headline caught my attention, the story had a great lead: *Adrian's Karl McSkimming, 62, was killed early Saturday morning in what police are calling a "being in the wrong place at the wrong time."*

Karl McSkimming was my mom's dad, and Adrian is in extreme southeast Michigan. Grandpa's family was one of thousands who immigrated to the "Irish Hills" of Michigan to escape the potato famine in Ireland during the eighteen forties.

Grandpa Karl didn't die a slow, excruciating death. His was quick, and sure.

> *State police sergeant Dennis Whitford, from the Monroe Police Post, said that the investigation is ongoing, but it appears as if McSkimming's sedan had stalled on the Grand Trunk railroad crossing south of Blissfield.*
>
> *"There was no way I could stop," said train engineer, Benton Nartker from the Burlington National Railroad Company. "It was extremely dark, and by the time I saw the car, it was too late," Nartker said. The train was carrying a full compliment of grain and automobiles and was headed for Toledo, Ohio.*

The story had a picture of Grandpa's vehicle underneath the shot of Senator McNamarah and Mr. Philot. The pickup was a mangled heap, a charred, tangled mess. It was barely recognizable after the ensuing fire.

What a horrible, ghastly way to go.

Poor Grandpa.

> *McSkimming was pronounced dead at the scene. There were no witnesses, and the crossing didn't have an electronic warning system.*
>
> *It is the third fatal accident at that crossing in the last three years.*
>
> *He was preceded in death by his wife, Esther (Gates), and is survived by three grown daughters and nine grandchildren.*

The entire story was only about three inches long. It was short, but hardly sweet, and was written as if the reporter was in a hurry to finish it. Sure, he talked to the train engineer, and the trooper, but there was so much more he could have written. How does a car stall on the tracks? Why couldn't Grandpa push his vehicle out of the way? What caused the fire? What do you mean, '*no witnesses*'? Somebody saw something.

And what were the police investigating—why the train couldn't stop? Whether or not the engineer had alcohol in his system? Was Grandpa drinking?

Poor Grandpa.

What a way to go.

And Mom.

And all those grandkids.

I was one of those nine, and he died when I was in grade school.

His obituary on the inside of the front page offered no insight into what kind of man he was. The guy's life boiled down to a few short sentences, a few worldly accomplishments. The obituary never said anything about Grandpa's personality, or what his interests were, or how he shook your hand, or the way he laughed or stirred creamer into his coffee. There was so much more I wanted to know about the way he lived, and about the way he died.

And apparently Dad wanted to know more, too. Why else would he have saved the clipping?

I took a deep breath and tossed my hands in the air.

Enough was enough.

A knock on the cubicle's door distracted my attention. It was the woman with the photocopied royalty agreements.

I said "thank you," but was quickly swept back into the turmoil of doing Dad's bidding. I came to the bank to do a job, my first responsibility as his trustee. The big, thick manila envelope was waiting for me. I pierced the little metal clasps that held the flap in place. His trust was several pages long, and full of lots of important words. I skimmed through the legalese to where it outlined what he wanted me to do. The antique bathtub was mentioned. So were the piano and Grandpa's gun. There was also a note that the serial numbers on the gun were registered with the Federal Bureau of Alcohol, Tobacco and Firearms, and insured with Lloyd's of London. He put a lot of thought into his trust, which wasn't the least bit surprising. He always planned ahead. He was always one step ahead of the competition.

My first duty as trustee was to mail the contents of envelope number one. Ninety days after that, I was to mail the second. There were four envelopes in all, each with a number written on the outside. I had to open a larger manila envelope to find out what was on the letter inside. The suspense was right there, cloaked in all that secrecy.

Every time I mailed a letter, Dad said I was to take three hundred dollars for myself from the stack of currency. It was like a real-life game of Monopoly.

It didn't take long to find out to whom the first envelope should be mailed.

The Federal Bureau of Investigation.

Detroit, Michigan.

Nice, Dad.

And the return address. It was just as confusing.

A strange name and post office box in Alma.

What the heck, Dad?

What are you getting me into?

Eight

I WOKE UP WELL BEFORE DAWN on my second day in Iowa, and took Synch outside to do her business. She was a little sore from the previous day's hunting excursion, and walked stiff-legged through the damp grass. I gave her an aspirin when we returned to the motel room, to help ease the pain in her hips. She watched me fire up the computer and dial onto the Internet. The *Des Moines Register* must not have been impressed with my email, the photos, nor my invitation to cover the Cigan matter. They never bothered to email me.

But that was okay. I still might be able to scrape together a story for one of their competitors. And wouldn't that be sweet? I closed my computer, loaded my gear, the dog, my cell phone, the laptop, and everything else I could think of, and headed off to the local gas station for a newspaper and a flashlight. I was too early for today's *Des Moines Register*, and yesterday's was sold out. The selection of flashlights wasn't much better, but I did find one that looked like it would work for at least an hour.

The man behind the counter looked as if he had been up for hours. Maybe he had. I was probably too early for the day shift, and was at the tail end of the night shift. He rang up my items as if he were doing it in his sleep.

"What time does the paper get here?" I asked him.

"The *Register*?"

"Yes."

"Six or so."

I looked at my watch. I still had a half-hour.

"There should be a copy of yesterday's here, somewhere." He paused for a second. "Here it is."

The man behind the counter stood and proudly presented yesterday's paper. It was in a heap—the corners were bent and crooked, the fold a wrinkled mess.

"You can have it," he said.

"Thank you."

I handed him a ten-dollar bill and while I waited for my change, tried to find the front page. When I did, the man behind the counter said it all.

"Quite a deal, huh?"

"What?"

"That missing tanker driver."

I noticed the lead story: "*Bettendorf truck driver still missing.*"

Most of the article summarized the previous night's news broadcast. Cigan was supposed to be home days ago. The electronic transmitter was placed on a different vehicle and it led the authorities to California.

I bought a flashlight, batteries, and extra batteries for my tape recorder and my digital camera. My plan was to go to the barn, recover my gun, and call the authorities from there. I could tell them that I was out hunting and discovered the body. Happens all the time. Hunters find lots of stuff while they're out traipsing around the countryside. The police would have no idea that I left my gun out there overnight.

And so, in the gathering light of a snowy December dawn, and for the second time in two days, I drove south out of What

Cheer, Iowa. Past the old opera house and the grain elevator, over the railroad tracks, and into the rolling hills of corn and beans and innocent bliss.

I dreaded the thought of confronting that horrible scene again. The smell of all that gas. The vision of Charles Cigan, sitting there in his mobile tomb, his blood caked to his shirt, his neck, and the leather seat of his big Kenworth. It was a horrible thought, but one that I had to confront. I had to slide down Emmert's north fence line, zigzag across his forty, then make my way to the abandoned barn. I'd pick up my gun, wait a few minutes past legal hunting hours, and call the police. They'd all come racing out there in a cloud of dust and swirling snow. The sheriff and a deputy or two. The Iowa State Police. By mid-morning, I expected the FBI would show up in their plain-colored sedans from the offices in Des Moines, and lose their patience with the locals and the way they compromised the integrity of the crime scene. They'd shake their heads and think that the locals were incompetent. The little acre of weeds that held all those pheasants the night before would be a parking lot of cops. Some of them would get stuck in the black earth, made slippery from the falling snow.

I'd have to give my statement a dozen times throughout the day, but that would be okay. I had nothing to hide. I would tell the truth.

And, I would ask questions of my own.

I would be on the job. I would be getting the inside scoop. The very inside scoop.

Who was Charles Cigan, and why was he murdered? And what about MNM Inc? What's their story? The police didn't know that I was a reporter. They wouldn't realize that I was fishing for information, too.

At almost six-thirty, Synch and I drifted past Emmert's sleeping farmhouse. I parked the Suburban in the entryway to his cut cornfield at the north end of the property. Together, we waited for more daylight. Radio Iowa had the listing of commodities that mattered most: pork belly futures and corn prices. I listened intently to the information, and the excitement of the announcers' voices: both prices were up, which was good news for everybody in Iowa. It seemed odd to be concerned with the price of corn or hogs. In Michigan, and I suppose in a lot of other places in the country, hogs and corn are simply taken for granted. Bacon and cornflakes are as easy to obtain as hamburger and peanut butter.

We sat there for twenty minutes or so. I sipped my coffee, and Synch yawned nervously at the prospect of another day of mischief. Quarter-sized snowflakes floated out of the dawn and drifted harmlessly to the windshield. All was still. All was quiet. It was just another peaceful sunrise in the breadbasket of America's heartland.

At seven o'clock, I quietly opened the truck door, loaded my gear in my hunting jacket, and headed west. A dusting of snow insulated the sound of my footsteps and the galloping merriment of my wonderful dog. I heard the squeals and chatter from the farmyard across the street and down the road. It was the neighbor's hogs banging into their metal feeding bins in an effort to wake their owner. "Feed me, feed me, feed me," they seemed to say. It must be like an alarm clock. It must work, because the hogs always get fed.

Synch and I skirted the big hill behind Emmert's farmhouse, but there were no pheasants in the terraces. Hardly ever do you find pheasants in the same spot a day after you roust them from cover. Besides, it was too early in the day for them to be up in the corn, eating breakfast. Most of the pheasants I know would be still in bed, curled up, and waiting for the warmth of daylight to pry them from their overnight lairs.

And it's just as well we didn't find any pheasants. My mind was racing ahead to the barn, to the dead body, and my prized family shotgun.

When I made my way to the back of Emmert's forty, the wind was already beginning to stir. The snowflakes came down with a slant, and they puffed against my cheeks, my ear lobes, the brim of my hat.

It was nearly seven-thirty when I jumped the fence between Emmert's forty and the back of MNM property. I didn't even look around to see if anyone was watching. The back of the barn was just as I had left it—a fieldstone foundation, a sloping, gentle roofline, and ancient, weathered planks for a shell. The weeds around the barn stood tall on nimble stalks—their seedpods, and foxtails befitting of a crafter's collage. I heard the metallic wails from the windmill, and it sent a chill down my spine all over again.

Let's make short work of it, I thought.

Get the gun.

Make sure Cigan is there.

Call the cops.

It was the simplest of plans, a slam-dunk of an idea.

What could possibly go wrong?

Everything.

It always does.

I am a loser.

An utter imbecile.

An ignoramus.

Of course the gun wasn't there. Neither was the body. Or the tanker. Or any of the gas. It was all gone.

Whoever murdered Charles Cigan got rid of the evidence.

All of it.

And now my goose was cooked.

I pried open the massive barn doors and peeked inside. An old John Deere tractor sat in the same place where the tanker had been. I saw a mechanical hay rake parked in the corner, a hay baler near that. On the opposite side of the barn, I heard the pigs. The hogs. The pork bellies. Whatever you want to call them. They were oinking and squealing the way pigs do. They looked at me with those beady eyes and floppy, hapless ears. Someone went to great strides to cover up the mess that was there only a few hours previously. The barn no longer smelled like gas, but swine and pigs and hogs.

Even the floor was different. They covered it in fresh mulch, or sawdust, and groomed it birthday-cake smooth.

I looked for my gun, hopelessly. Of course it was gone. That was the thing that tipped them off. That was the item that sent Cigan's murderers reeling. They must have come to the barn to load up on gas, realized that they had a visitor, and dashed away in a panic.

And now I was the one to panic. My gun was gone, plain and simple.

I made it easy for them to find.

It was gone.

Long gone.

I was so disappointed. So mad at myself. My predicament. And the way I brought it on myself. How can I get ahead in this world if I keep doing dumb things over and over again? I shook my head in disgust. I sighed. I cursed. Neither worked. The disappointment coursed through my veins like venom. And it hurt.

The snow was coming down in sheets. Quiet, betraying sheets. It covered my boot prints; it buried the tanker's tire tracks. Even if I went to the police now, the evidence was either gone or buried by the snow. I stood at the threshold of the old barn and watched the snow boil over a nearby hill and settle into the barnyard. It came at me like the grief stirring in my head.

I failed.

I am a failure.

My gun was gone. It probably went in the cab of someone's pickup truck, then to the attic or the closet of that someone's house where he'd keep it for decades. He would never clean it, or pat it down with an oily rag. The metal would become pitted with the acne of tiny rust spots. And who knows, it might show up at an estate auction years from now. It might fetch two hundred dollars, when its value today was worth almost twenty times that figure. In Iowa, guns are nothing more than tools for killing. There's no sense in paying for the engraving, the gold inlays, or the beautifully textured wood, when a cheaper piece will kill pheasants just as well.

And the more I thought about it, the more it made sense that I could use that mentality to my advantage. The people that killed Charles Cigan would much rather have their freedom than a frilly shotgun.

We'd strike a deal: my silence in exchange for the family shotgun.

What could be better than that?

Sooner or later they'd return to feed the pigs, I thought to myself. *If they didn't, the neighbors would hear them squeal and that would cause a scene.*

And they could read my note.

I had a little reporter's pad in my hunting jacket. I had a pen. The words came to me with no problem at all, "*give me my gun and I'll keep quiet.*" It wasn't especially glamorous, but it was effective under those circumstances. It was plain and simple, but I needed more. How many chances does a writer have to write a ransom note? The page was still blank, so I added another line, in the same vein as the first: "*You have twenty-four hours or I'll squeal like a pig.*" I wrote my cell phone number at the bottom of the page, and rammed the note through the tines of a pitchfork. I must admit, it looked rather intimidating. And when I placed the pitchfork against the inside doors of the barn, I figured that there was no way that they could have missed it.

Maybe I could get the gun back. Maybe things could turn my way. I was hopeful. I'm always hopeful. In my own little way, I search for the best outcome in the worst situations.

Dad would never need to know that I had lost the gun.

Maybe I could salvage the hunting trip and actually do a little more hunting.

When I made it back to Emmert's property line, Synch came trotting at me with that smiling expression of hers. She didn't realize the gravity of the situation, the dire circumstances surrounding our walk to the barn.

The walk back to the truck was uneventful. It gave me the chance to work off some of the adrenaline from back at the barn. Synch jumped a hen or two out of the yellow grass at the bottom of the big hill, and we stopped to admire a nice buck that was sneaking its way down the creek bottom. The snow was piling up, and the wind was blowing it around the countryside. All things considered, it was a pretty, peaceful setting.

I kept thinking about the barn, and my little ransom note. *It was the right thing to do*, I kept telling myself. *It was the only way I'd get my gun back.*

By the time we made it back to the truck, the snow had inched its way under my hunting pants and over the tops of my hunting boots. I could feel its seeping cold against my ankles, my calves, my wool socks. I started the truck, cranked the heat to high, and took a moment to brush the snow out of my pant legs.

It was just about then that I heard the tap-tap-tap on the Suburban's side window.

Nine

IT WAS NEARLY FIVE by the time I pulled Dad's old Harley into the garage back at the farm on that warm, late summer day. It had been about twenty-four hours since his stroke, and I had put a couple of hundred miles on his motorcycle between Owosso and the bank in Mt. Pleasant. I took off my helmet, flicked a few bugs off the bike's windjammer, and noticed the way his bike seethed in the afternoon humidity. The engine, the muffler, the transmission- everything seemed to be catching its breath, through clenched teeth.

I had a lot of fun riding that bike.

I'm glad Dad suggested it.

But this was no time for relaxation. There was work to be done. I had to take care of the cattle, the cats, Leroy, and, of course, Synch. They were all happy to see me and, more important, the food I brought them. I was in a rush; my date with Judy was close at hand.

The wicker picnic basket was still in the front closet, above the topcoats and raincoats that smelled of mothballs and a dozen dresses Mom had yet to take to Goodwill. The games from my childhood were there too—Mousetrap, Monopoly, Battleship, and Operation—the boxes still duct taped at the corners, the corners still rounded off and worn thin.

The picnic basket was a beauty, and I think it must have been a wedding gift for Mom and Dad. It simply oozed with nostalgia, and its sturdy, square construction reminded me of an old DeSoto, or a Cadillac. The lining was checkered white and red, and puckered along the top edge of caramel-colored wood trim. A quaint thermos bottle was wedged in the corner with the help of a couple of weathered leather straps. Mom must have been the one to put the silverware and the cute, plastic plates in a plastic Ziploc bag. They were clean as a whistle, or at least clean enough for me.

Mom still kept the blankets in an old cedar chest near the flight of stairs. I picked out a red tartan, about the size of a queen size mattress. It smelled like a cedar swamp, like the north woods. It wasn't the softest blanket in the bunch, but its red and black color would be perfect for an August evening, when everything else in the world was a rich, summer green, or a parched, earthen brown.

I raced outside to the garden and raided Mom's carrot patch. They were small, pinky-sized, and although they weren't as sweet as they would be in October, they weren't bad, either. Mom's cherry tomatoes practically begged me to pick them. They hung on the bushes like the bulbs on a Christmas tree. Together with a small, round cantaloupe, they'd complement the other finger foods I had in my quiver of arrows.

I couldn't wait to see Judy again. I couldn't wait to see her smile, to hear her laugh, to watch her stroll to me under that big oak tree in the middle of that giant wheat field. It would be a special way to spend a few hours together in the waning hours of a warm, August day. It had been forever since I had cared for someone romantically. Seductively. Judy stirred something inside me. I felt my heart sing. I felt it race.

I kept telling myself to deny those feelings. That we should take our time. Take it slow. After all, we had known each other for years, why press it now?

It was nice having those thoughts, however wrong, however inappropriate. I couldn't help myself. Even when I was in high school twenty years ago, I always had a thing for Judy. We were always friendly, but never engaged. There was always something that kept us apart. There were always excuses why I didn't see her after she graduated: the miles between us at college, our careers, her engagement, her husband, my wife, her separation, my separation, more miles. They added up. They pulled us in different directions.

Until now.

Was it fate that brought us together, or just another one of life's quirky circumstances?

I'm one of those guys who is very impulsive. I dive, and then think about the depth of the water as I'm falling. I jump headlong into things without thinking them through. When I was younger, I used to be a compulsive buyer. I bought everything on a whim, and never really considered how I was going to pay for it. I got in trouble with credit cards, and stupid offers such as "No payments for six months." Finally, though, I wised up, and sold all the toys I bought on credit to pay for Colleen's engagement ring.

There were certainly worse ways to spend the money. Colleen meant the world to me then and I never regretted marrying her. From time to time, I still think about her as my wife. I wondered about what kind of mom she might have been, and what kinds of things our kids may have done after school. I pictured her in the stressful race to get our daughter to softball practice, our son to hockey games, while still being able to balance the checkbook and keep the household running like a well-oiled machine. And then I realized my whole impression was wrong.

Even if I could have kids, I'd be the one running the household errands, and she'd be he one to bring home the serious bacon. She was the one with the promising career, the room for advancement; I had reached the top of my career as a reporter, a writer, a teller of tales.

Would I ever get married again? Sure. Despite the soured way Colleen and I ended our marriage, I still would like to try it again. I like the thought of having a wife. Of having someone to talk to at the end of the day. Of sharing life. And death. And watching helplessly as our parents grow old, become ill, and test the limits of our love.

Judy's parents were in great health. Her dad still worked the family farm, and her mom was enjoying her retirement from the post office. Together, they puttered around the farm, their own vegetable garden, and as the first chilly winds of winter came, traveled to Arizona in their motor home. They were independent, healthy, and happy.

And so was Judy. She had a way about her. A flair. A confidence. She took charge of her life and offered no excuses for her failures, and no apologies for her achievements. I thought that maybe some of her success would wear off on me, the same way that her perfume left a smear of fragrance on my bicep from the night before. It was sweet and inviting. Uncomplicated. So was she. I must have smelled it a dozen times before I went to sleep that night. It was the only tangible reminder of the excellent hug she gave me earlier in the day.

One thing was for certain, after last evening's misguided attempt to kiss her, there was no way I was going to make the first move. Ever.

If I burned that bridge again, I might never get to cross it.

And Judy's bridge would be one worth crossing.

I skipped into the living room and tossed a Ray Charles record on Mom and Dad's old stereo. The quality wasn't very good, but I didn't let it spoil my mood. Ray always brings out the best in any situation, especially when it's blaring loud. I remember Mom and Dad used to listen to it when they were getting ready to go out on the town.

And now it was my turn. As I stood at the kitchen sink, cleaning the carrots and washing the cherry tomatoes, I thought about Judy and how much she turned me on. There's something sexy about a successful woman. She knows what she wants. And more importantly, she knows how to get it. I knew that there was something brewing between Judy and me. I knew that I made her laugh, that I made her smile. If she didn't care about me, she would have dropped off the food and left. No, she went beyond cordial. She was interested. She was sizing me up. She was playing hard to get.

I pictured the two of us under that lonesome, big oak tree in the middle of that big wheat field. All alone. At first, she would sit on the corner of the blanket, arms crossed. She would listen to her inner self, and would be demure, interested, but not overly so. She'd sip her glass of wine. She had a lot going for her, and she was a professional. A picnic would be appropriate. A picture of her on a picnic would look good on a billboard. It conjures images of a wholesome courtship, a delicious mingling. She was a hard worker, a successful executive, but she can make time to smell the roses. And what better way to smell the roses than under a big oak tree on a romantic picnic?

Still, I clung to the notion of something sexual between us. It could happen. Anything's possible. Under the oak tree would be adventuresome, and exciting, but it wouldn't be one of those long, lingering encounters. If she ever got caught having sex in a public place, it would be embarrassing, not to mention a blow to her career. How could she ever face her daughter again, knowing that she was caught red-handed just off the school's campus? How could she go to her daughter's parent-teacher conferences and not feel the world's glare upon her?

There were lots of reasons why it shouldn't happen, but the

reasons it could were enough to melt the strongest of resolves.

It would start so simple. We'd wait until well past sunset, when the dusk's orange melted into a honeydew balm. I'd tap her on the finger, and tell her how much I liked the way she painted her nails. I'd lie on the blanket and make a comment about her toe ring and ask why she wore it. I wouldn't let her answer me with an "I don't know," kind of response.

"Do you like your feet?" I'd pry. *"Like your toes?"*

People just love to talk about themselves.

"Do you wear it under your business shoes?"

"What else do you like about yourself?"

"'What are you most proud of in your life?"

"Tell me, Judy."

Of course, Judy would have a hard time answering some of those questions. Anyone would. She'd walk the tightrope of self-confidence and bragging. Her answers would be modest, and yet forthright. She'd think of what she'd want to say and what she said would stir other things to talk about. And what she said would make her smile. And laugh. And make her eyes twinkle.

I'd tell her that she had wonderful eyes. And that she was beautiful. And that I couldn't believe that she didn't have half the county's men asking for her company. I'd be sincere. Genuine. It might make her blush. Or relax. Some people soak up compliments like a sponge. They like to hear people say what they've been telling themselves for years when they look at themselves in the mirror, or when they slide hoops of silver on their toes.

Judy would like hearing my compliments. She'd lie on her side and prop her head on a hand. She'd dabble the end of a carrot in dip and drop it into her mouth. She'd take a sip of wine and it would spill down the side of her mouth, the edge of her cheek, the top of her neck, where all the perfume goes. I'd watch her dab it with a cloth napkin, and think to myself that the napkin would be another reminder of what a great evening we had.

I'd keep the napkin for days, and take a whiff at every chance.

And as the evening progressed, I envisioned Judy on her back, looking up at the sprawling limbs of oak, and the way they reached for the sun. We'd giggle when the flocks of starlings came to rest, and be thankful that they weren't Canada geese. I'd take her hand, across the bed of finger food, the glasses, and the empty baby bottles of wine. In my own little fantasy, her hand would squeeze mine. And then, in the quiet dim of twilight, when all the world was quiet, and the day's last rays of sun retired, she'd come to me with a hearty kiss. With lips as soft as satin. With the heat of a steamy August afternoon. God, I love the flavor, the feel, the flesh.

She kissed like a goddess.

Like the angels in heaven.

My hands moved to her face, her hair, her arms. They were soft, and smooth, and tan. Like summer in Michigan.

I kissed her cheek, her earlobe, her neck, before coming up for air.

I'd look around for any sign of danger, for any sign of intruders. If someone were to stumble upon us now, we'd be embarrassed, but not humiliated. We were just kissing, merely snorkeling in the sea of sensations.

But I wouldn't have long to look around. She'd pull me close. She'd yank me under water again, only this time she wouldn't let me come up for air. She unbuttoned a button on her blouse, exposing that fertile playground where her chest stops and her breasts begin. They spilled over the edge of her bra. I kissed her. Over and over. From the side. Backhanded, if that's possible. Her perfume filled the air, now chilled in the evening's pall. It smelled like a woman in heat. Like smoke from a battle. A love fest. I unbuttoned another button. With my teeth. Her bra lay before me like a Christmas present I always wanted. She had a pair, a set. They were round and beautiful, and full of wonderful toys. Wondrous joys. Fun, fun, fun.

She closed her eyes and bit her lip, now smeared with pink. I felt her hands rake my head; her nails, my scalp. She was directing me. Pulling me right, pushing me left. I obeyed her commands; I was a tool of delight. Her bra was a lacey little number, berry beige, and dressed with thin, velvety straps that crept up the sides of her freckled breasts. My mouth, my nose, my lips brushed the fabric. I felt the budding stem of her nipple pressing fast against her bra. I toyed with it. I nibbled her nipple. She gasped.

So did Synch.

On her food.

She's always had a difficult time eating dry dog food. She takes a mouthful and wanders with it across the room. Almost every day she gets a kernel stuck in her throat that causes her to have horrific bouts of coughing. I've thought about putting a little warm water on her food, but her teeth are badly decayed. The vet said that if I didn't want to spend the five hundred dollars to have her teeth cleaned, I should get her to chew on anything hard. Either way, she interrupted my little dream.

And it was just as well. The carrots were clean and trimmed. The cherry tomatoes were ready to go, and the softball-sized cantaloupe was getting hard in the freezer.

Upstairs I flew. To the shower. To the ironing board. To the stash of Dad's aftershave. I felt like a kid again. On a date. A very important date.

At six thirty, I threw everything into the Suburban. Synch gave me the evil eye as I headed out the door. And it worked. I stood there on the top step of the porch, thinking about the evening ahead, and whether or not she would cramp our style. No, old dogs have a way of making themselves small. They know that they're not allowed on the blanket, and that the only way they'll get any treats is if they sit on the sidelines and beg with their facial expressions. She was good at that.

Obviously.

A minute later, I had her bowl packed and a couple of water

bottles tucked under my arm. Sure, it was hot out, but Synch needed the exercise. And the attention. So did I.

We were off to the high school. To the back of the bleachers. To the cut wheat field and the giant oak tree. I think Synch thought we were going hunting. She always does. She thinks that every trip in the Suburban is an adventure. It's just as well. That sense of adventure is contagious.

When we made it to the field, Synch kicked her enthusiasm into overdrive. She dropped a gear, and her nose. Tail-a-blur, she trotted far ahead of me. I whistled for her, but she kept motoring. If I couldn't slow her down, the heat surely would. It must have been close to eighty degrees, and the humidity hung in the air like sheets on a clothesline. I watched her race—as fast as her little eleven-year-old legs could carry her—into a flock of starlings. There must have been a hundred in the bunch.

During puppy hood, she used to "spring" into the air when bounding through a field, or bumbling into a flock of birds. She was deadly. Deadly and gentle. On our first few trips to Iowa, she managed to catch a few pheasants out of mid-air. They were all hens, and still very much alive when she brought them back to me. That was always a fine line for me. Scold a dog for doing what evolution had taught it to do, or admire her talent?

In either case, I didn't feel that badly about her catching pheasants in Iowa. There are so many birds there that it seems that they'll never run out. For years, I thought that a hen-grabbing bird dog was the worst thing that would ever happen to me. I had no way to know that this year's trip would be filled with so much trouble, so much danger.

Anyway, Synch eventually made her way to me at the big oak tree. Just as I figured, she was out of breath and hotter than a pistol. She pawed at the earth, and lay on where she scratched. I poured her a drink and she nearly dove into the bowl. That would be it for her forays, her little sorties into enemy territory.

Just as well. Judy would be arriving soon, and I still didn't have the table set. I wanted the setting to be nearly perfect. I wanted her to think that I could put together a decent spread—a romantic coup. The grass under the old oak tree was stunted, except for a few sprigs that took advantage of the rain and the way it slithered down the tree trunk. Other than that, the grass was six inches tall, lopped like the ears on a rabbit, and thick enough that it didn't have any holes. In other words, just right for a blanket.

At ten after seven, I had the entire spread laid out as if Martha Stewart herself had orchestrated it. The cherry tomatoes and carrots were on one plate, a small container of dip resting in the center. The cantaloupe was still chilled when I whipped out my pocketknife and cut it into small cubes. It dripped the drops of summer's bounty, and would be in sharp contrast to the smoked liver pate and a mini-loaf of French bread. I laid out the crackers, the toothpicks for the melon, and a set of plastic glassware for the wine, still chilling in the cooler. It was pretty as a picture.

At a quarter after seven, I opened a bottle of beer and took a seat against the trunk of the oak tree. Synch lay next to me, still panting, but still ready to spring at a second's notice. I gave her a few pats on the head, an ice cube or two, then looked for Judy. She'd be along at any moment, I just knew it. She'd come waltzing over the hill in a flowing denim skirt and a wispy cotton blouse. She'd pull her hair up, and have it tucked beneath a mottled, straw hat. I pictured her with her sandals in her hand, instead of on her feet. The occasion, the setting, the atmosphere was carefree and wonderfully romantic.

All I needed was Judy.

At seven thirty, I whipped out my cell phone and checked my messages. Colleen called and said that she was sorry to hear about Dad. She also wanted to know when I was coming back to work. Apparently, the guy I interviewed before my departure—Ira Kaminsky—had called her office several times wanting to know when the story about him would be published.

No message from Judy, and it made me wonder if I included my cell phone number on the note I left her. I thought about calling her, but I didn't want to seem anxious. She'd be along at any moment, gushing with apologies. Guilt is a wonderful thing and I might even use it against her.

Five minutes later, I opened another beer and started after the pate. It was awesome on a cracker, even better with a gulp of beer. The melon was good, so were the cherry tomatoes. I was hungry, and so was Synch, who practically begged me to feed her the pate. It worked.

Finally, at nearly eight, just as the sun was starting its final approach on the horizon, she appeared. I brushed the crumbs off my golf shirt, set my beer down next to the empties, and stood up to watch the spectacle. Her figure appeared out of the early evening glow, like the vapor from a genie's bottle, like the image of a summer samba. She had the hat on all right, a cowboyish-looking number with a wide brim and puckered sides. And she didn't go with the skirt I imagined, but a pair of trousers. Closer and closer the image came to me. She was wearing a wide belt that held her handgun on her hip.

This is going to be fun, I imagined. *We're going to do a little role-playing, right out of the chute. I'm so naughty, Judy. Oh so naughty. Cuff me, baby.*

When she was fifty yards from me, I acknowledged her presence with a wave and a "Howdy, pardner."

Judy didn't answer.

"Punch any cowpokes?"

Still no answer. Closer and closer she came.

"High-oh, Silver, away." My voice tapered off as if I were surrendering to the notion that maybe it wasn't Judy after all.

The voice said it all. It was deep and scratchy. Masculine.

"That will be enough," the voice said. My world crashed. It was so embarrassing. It was a cop! With a mustache. And an attitude.

"Who gave you permission to be out here?" The guy was in my face. My heart raced. For all the wrong reasons.

I couldn't speak. My tongue tied in knots.

"Nobody."

"What's this?" He picked up a beer bottle, and the pocketknife.

I stuttered. "I was having a picnic."

The cop again looked down at the blanket.

"Just you and your dog…"

Synch, ever the opportunist, saw that I was engaged with the cop, and dove into the pate. She choked it down.

"It's against the law to have open intoxicants or weapons within a thousand feet of a school."

He asked for my identification. I dug it out of my wallet, and handed it to him. We stood there in the evening glow. He gave me the gimlet stare that all cops do.

"You're Chick Twichell's boy, aren't you?"

"Yes, I am. His son."

He nodded.

"I'm just having a picnic."

"Ever been on the sex offender's list?"

"No. Never."

"You're lucky. You exposed yourself."

"What?"

"See those cameras?" He pointed up the trunk of the tree to two small cameras angled right and left. I noticed the wires and the way they slithered further up the trunk. My heart sank. "They're powered by solar panels, activated by motion sensors, and transmitted to police headquarters. We just installed them this week. School starts in about ten days."

I was a wreck. "I had to pee, officer. That's all I was doing. I wasn't exposing myself."

"Mr. Twitchell, I suggest you pack up your picnic gear and get out of here."

Ten

After spending the last week of August in the hospital, Dad was sent home to the family farm. The doctors said that he would need plenty of speech and physical therapy, in addition to constant monitoring. They performed all sorts of cognitive tests on him, but they weren't exactly sure of his mental capacities.

Judy stopped by the day after the disastrous picnic, and apologized for her absence. She had a client come into her office after hours with a unique loan situation, and since the mortgage business had been so bad, she figured that she had better take all the business she could get.

"I'm sorry, Derrick," she said. "I really am. I used to close ten or fifteen deals a month. Now I'm lucky to do three or four."

I smiled, and took it all in. She acted sincere, and honest. I understood. She said we'd have to try again. I agreed, but figured that I wouldn't be the one to initiate it.

It was just as well the picnic didn't pan out; there was work to be done, back at the paper where the old saying is that "you never pick a fight with someone who buys ink by the barrel." A reporter can make your life miserable. A reporter can dig into your private affairs, print quotations from your neighbors, your preacher, your sixth- grade teacher, if it will make a good story. Give a reporter a reason to investigate you and he's liable to make your life a living hell. A reporter with an axe to grind is a lethal instrument.

For the most part, the reporters at the *Journal* were just regular people. We did our jobs—drum up a story, write it in a clean, descript style, and put it to bed. We all knew what the editors wanted: accuracy, facts, quotations and sources, and more accuracy. We were schooled to be accurate, and expected to be so. The editors hate it when they have to make a correction. They hate it when they have to admit they were wrong. It's a sign of failure, a blunder, which compromises the paper's credibility. And when that happens, advertisers bail.

It was the end of August, the official start of the high school football season. The *Journal* embraced high school sports, and for good reason. It unified the community. It created a buzz. Before the season started, every team in the area had the chance to be league champions. Every team had all those players, from all those families, who bought all those papers.

Our regular sports writer was on vacation the week before Labor Day. So was Colleen. The publisher asked me to pinch-hit for both of them. I was happy to do it.

The *Journal* featured a different high school football team in each of the weeks leading up to the start of the season. Our hometown team, the Alma Panthers, a perennial football powerhouse, was slated to be in the Sunday paper. It's really not a difficult story to write since most of the stuff for the paper comes directly from the school itself. They send us the photos, the stats from last year, the schedule, the players' positions, height and weight. All we have to do is call the coaches and get a few comments. The story practically writes itself.

The coaches are all the same. They say that they're excited about the season, and the prospects for a league championship. On the other hand, they show a great deal of respect for the other teams in the league. Their quotations are filled with hyperbole and clichés, such as "We're going to take it one game at a time," or "Barring any injuries, we should have a good team."

Friday was a busy day. The primary elections had just concluded a couple of weeks before, and the final two candidates in each race were bombarding us with press releases, phone calls and emails. We had to wade through them all and decide which ones deserved our attention. It was hectic. Chaotic. And fun. It was the frenetic pace I loved.

Our deadline is always three in the afternoon, even for the Sunday morning paper. The *Journal* is published five afternoons a week and Sunday morning. The deadline hangs over our heads like a black cloud. Put the paper to bed and the black cloud disappears. By noon that Friday, the Alma football piece was nearly finished. I talked to the coach and got the goods on the team, the players to watch, and what we could expect in the season opener.

They supplied me with a photo of the team captains, two on offense, two on defense. I entered the captains' names into the computer: Ronnie Leslie, Mark Skeith, and the Dickman boys: Dave and Earl. When I looked at the photo, however, there were five guys pictured, not four. It was the kind of stuff that really makes me mad. I mean, how incompetent? I called the Alma Athletic Department, and left a message for them to call.

"I'm sorry, but if you don't call me back by two forty-five Saturday afternoon, we'll have to pull the photo for Sunday's paper," I told them.

"Who was that?" I knew the voice anywhere. It was Colleen's boss and the publisher, Byron Hovey. We called him Mr. Potato Head because of his obvious physical characteristics. I hung up the phone and looked up at him. He had a chin like a baked potato. It stuck out of his throat like a giant, whiskered legume.

"The athletic department at Alma High School. They gave me this potato…" I shook my head and gathered myself. "…I mean photo that has five guys in it, but they only have four names for a caption." I handed him the photo, and he looked it over, flipping it one way then the other. After watching him fidget with it for several seconds, I thought he was practicing his magic tricks, as if at any second he'd pull a rabbit out of his sleeve.

"So they gave you this photo," he said, "with five guys pictured, but there's only four names on the back?"

"That's right."

"I don't see how we can use it if we don't get that fifth guy's name."

I nodded.

Byron placed the photo on the corner of my desk and walked away.

I thought that was the end of it.

I scanned the photo into the computer, then dropped it electronically onto the bottom of the second page of Sunday's sports section, right next to my story about the team. It was a nice shot of the guys. They all had those stiff, tough-looking expressions on their faces. Their shoulder pads made them look tougher yet, like gladiators. I came up with a caption for the shot, which I thought was rather clever:

*Leaders all, on both sides of the ball. Quarterback Ronnie Leslie and tackle Mark Skeith are offensive co-captains, while twin brothers Earl and Dave Dickman *and some other guy * are defensive captains.*

I highlighted the *some other guy* part so I wouldn't forget about it before Saturday afternoon's deadline.

The deadline for Friday's afternoon newspaper came and went.

And then things got really hectic. We got word that the former president of Alma College, James X. Berry, had died. He was an important man, too—generous, a former Citizen of the Year, one of those larger-than-life characters that every town adores. Of course, the timing couldn't have been worse. We were short-staffed. Somebody had to whip up a glorified obituary for the front page. Somebody had to take the bull by the horns. It was me.

I dove into the story, detailing his education and his professional accomplishments.

"Dr. Berry was a pillar in the community," said the current president, Laurie Robinson, "He put Alma College on the map as an academic powerhouse, and he helped cultivate a spirit of giving with the alumni. Endowment gifts grew from $375,000 to more than $11 million."

The story wasn't especially exciting, but it was a story and one worth covering. And then, at nearly five, an announcement came across the paper's police scanner: a judge had been shot outside the courthouse.

I was off in a flash. The courthouse was next door, while the state police and sheriff's departments were at the other end of town. If I hurried, I could get to the crime scene before the cops had a chance to secure the area, before the paramedics could wheel away the victim. I grabbed a camera, a pad of paper and my reporter's satchel. It was a mad dash. People were racing out of the courthouse parking lot. Women held tissues to their eyes and noses. They were hugging each other. The courthouse deputies were still on high alert. They busted out the shotguns and flack jackets. Sirens wailed from the other end of town, and were getting louder. My camera was in overdrive.

It was one of those rare stories that make a newspaperman's career, with enough tragedy to pique everyone's interest. It was going to sell a ton of newspapers; they'd all be reading my stories.

I circled the courthouse. Someone yelled, "He's gone. He's gone. He just took off."

Thank goodness. The judge was clinging to life just outside the threshold. Deputies huddled around her as if they were a herd of musk ox defending one of their own. They all wanted to help her. They all saw the blood, and the way it poured out of her. They scrambled for blankets, and something for a pillow. I was close enough to hear them talking to her.

"Come on Your Honor. Help is on the way. Hold on, Deborah."

A sergeant, kneeling at her head, pointed towards the parking lot with one hand while he held the judge's hand with the other.

"Get these cars out of the way," he yelled. "Make room for the ambulance." There were legs and feet in the camera's viewfinder, but I kept shooting. They'd add depth and perspective. The sergeant's face said it all: his rage, his compassion, his horror.

Judge Deborah Noyes just lay there. Deadly still. The woman who went to college on a soccer scholarship, and was saddled with an unfortunate name comprised of "no" and "yes," was heaped on the courthouse floor; her white blouse stained a crimson red. The color in her face was almost gone, her hands ghostly white.

"Hold on, Deborah," they said. "Jesus, please. Hold on. Help is on the way."

The sirens were on us now. So was the ambulance. They screeched to a halt on the street; they jumped the curb and drove on the lawn near the courthouse doors. The voices of men shouting filled the air. Central dispatch was everywhere. In stereo.

"White male, late twenties…five foot seven to five foot eleven…white t-shirt, blue jeans…driving a white Monte Carlo…license plate number: zebra, Wilma, fox trot, niner-eight-two."

The paramedics were quick and professional. They donned their blue rubber gloves and gently rolled the judge onto a stretcher. They buckled her in securely, and rolled her quickly down the stairs. A couple of state troopers held the rear door of the ambulance open as they loaded the gurney inside. Deborah didn't move, or flinch. She didn't give us the "thumbs up" gesture or anything. It looked bleak. And my camera caught it all.

The ambulance roared out of the parking lot. So did half the cop cars. Central dispatch said that the suspect was last seen headed west on M-46, toward Riverdale.

None of the officers, troopers or deputies would talk to me. They said it was too early in the investigation to go on the record. I turned my sights on the women who were hugging at the opposite end of the building. They had moved to the employee parking lot across the street. One woman, Margaret Jankovich, said that she had been a court reporter in Judge Noyes' courtroom for the last fifteen years. "She was the most wonderful boss in the world," she said, wiping the tears from her eyes with a shriveled tissue. "And she didn't really act like a boss. She was a friend." They spoke as if Judge Noyes had died.

"What happened?" I asked.

One of the other women piped up and said that the shooter ambushed her.

"She usually stays until six or seven o'clock, but today she had to leave early so she could take her grandson out for his birthday dinner." The woman took a deep breath and said sadly, "He's only eight years old."

Jankovich composed herself, slightly, and said that the judge "was only about ten steps in front of us. Just as we're leaving the building, this man runs out of nowhere and says, 'You were wrong, wrong, wrong! Now you're going to pay for it!'"

She shook her head and made a make-believe pistol with her hand.

"He just about jammed the gun in her side and shoots. He shot her. Poor Deborah, she just went limp. The smoke was everywhere. And the sound, it was like a firecracker. Only worse."

I was scribbling like mad. I spelled her name and asked if it was correct.

Jankovich nodded.

"What happened next?"

"The guy just couldn't believe it. He's like 'Whoa, what have I done?!' The expression on his face was a shock. Like he couldn't believe that a bullet would actually harm someone."

"So he just stood there?"

"Yeah."

"Then what?"

"He ran to his car, and takes off in a flash. I don't know

why, but I just thought to write down his license plate number even though I recognized his face."

"You know who it is?"

"Yeah, it was Ernie Peffers. He was in court a few weeks ago, maybe a month. His wife divorced him and got full custody of their kids."

"And Judge Noyes handled the case?"

"That's right. It was a no-brainer," Jankovich shook her head again. "The guy had a criminal record for dealing drugs, and the wife wanted no part of it. She had photos and video of her husband whipping up a huge batch of crystal meth."

"Really."

"I remember it because I was the one who had to catalog it all as evidence."

"What was Peffers' response at the divorce proceeding?"

"He went ballistic."

Jankovich had gathered her composure. She opened her car door and underhanded her purse onto the passenger side seat. The two other women she was talking to had already started their cars and left the parking lot.

"He was a hot head. Had all those tattoos and piercings. He kept saying 'You can't take my kids from me. You can't take my kids from me. This ain't over yet.' The court deputy had to throw him out."

"Was that unusual?"

"Yeah, it was. We don't see a lot of that."

She slid inside her car, buckled her seatbelt, and started the motor.

"I'm sorry, but I have to go. This whole thing has been horrible."

I waved goodbye, but just as quickly as I did, a police officer flagged her down. She stopped her vehicle and stepped out of the car. I heard her tell the officer the same things she told me, only it took twice as long. I went back to my notes.

"You can't take my kids from me. You can't take my kids from me. This ain't over yet." I had the makings of a good story—the action captured on film, the heartbreak of a fallen judge, and the rage of a psychotic defendant. Still, there was more to get. More to dig up.

I hustled back to the Suburban, and poured through the phone book. There was only one listing for Ernest Peffers. He was from Riverdale, west of Alma about ten minutes. I scratched his address in my reporter's pad of paper, and headed in that direction, as fast as my aging truck could carry me.

Riverdale is most noted for its deer hunting and tavern, aptly named the Riverdale Tavern, where they serve deep-fried fish dinners and cold beer. It's an establishment where all walks of life sit in the shadow of a massive lumber baron-era mirror, framed by a pair of mahogany-colored beams.

Riverdale is a half-rural, half bedroom community where the residents work in factories or at the surrounding universities in varying capacities. And, like many communities, Riverdale can also attract a coarse side of society—where outcasts from the surrounding cities can rent a mobile home, or a run-down farmhouse, on a desolate road for three hundred bucks a month. Including utilities. Pets are okay. Even rottweilers, or "rotties" as they call them. Some of them home-school their kids, and shoot deer out of season from the surrounding state-owned land just to keep food on the table.

In other words, it can be a rough neighborhood, where laws are followed, but only by a distant second to the latest Nascar standings.

Peffers' house was in the boonies—at least seven miles off the nearest pavement, and near the end of a dead-end road not especially high on the road commission's list of priorities. And really, there was no mistaking which house was his. The cops and ambulances were at the end of his driveway—a long, snaky trail through the woods.

At some point, Peffers' house must have made a pretty good hunting cabin because the neighboring property was owned by the state. Any time you buy property that borders state land, it's like getting more than you bargained for.

There was no way the cops would let me down the driveway; the only way I could get close to the action was if I drove to state land, and crossed onto Peffers' place.

It was a risky proposition, not to mention a dangerous one, but what the heck, most reporters would have hung out at the end of Peffers' driveway and tried to get a glimmer of what was going on. I wanted to get behind enemy lines. I wanted to document what was about to take place, if I wasn't too late.

This was the kind of story that only comes along once in a blue moon. A very rare blue moon.

And so, I nonchalantly rolled past the cops, who were talking to a couple of paramedics, and into the neighboring two-track. I was casual about it, as if I were a tourist on a mushroom-picking mission. They didn't suspect a thing. My old truck bounced and chugged its way around the dried-up mud holes and over the ruts. After about a quarter mile, I parked in a wide spot in the road and grabbed a green fleece pullover from the back seat. Nobody had followed me. It was all good. I quietly shut the door behind me and headed north, through the bush and forest towards the Peffers' house.

The mosquitoes weren't as bad as I thought they might be. They still buzzed around my ears, and my neck, but they weren't in swarms like they quite often are in May and June. After about ten or fifteen minutes of quiet stalking, I made my way under the single strand of wire, and several ancient "no trespassing" signs nailed ten feet up in the trees. Beyond that was the clearing where Ernie Peffers lived. It looked like the mobile home was dropped in the center of an acre of cleared forest.

At first, I was about a hundred yards from the action. It was hard to see with all the forest clutter in the way. I moved up a tree. Then another. And another. I moved left, towards the front door of the mobile home, where three or four patrol cars were staged. I spotted Peffers' white Monte Carlo and several cops crouched behind the trees in the back yard. They wore black camouflage, and had scoped rifles pointed at the home. There must have been more on the other side, where I couldn't see.

Peffers was surrounded.

So were the cops, by mid-Michigan's most opportunistic reporter.

I had a perfect spot to watch. It was just thick enough to conceal my movements, but close enough to have a great view of the action. And the action wasn't long from taking place.

I recognized the state police lieutenant crouched behind a squad car. He was in his early sixties, and groomed his graying mustache into a pair of anvils above his upper lip.

"Come out with your hands up, Peffers," his voice warned through a bullhorn. "We know you're in there."

Nothing happened, but the music inside the house became much louder. I recognized the song.

"*Hey, man. What a good shot, man.*" The song is about a despondent rock singer who calls a press conference to announce something very important. Once everyone is seated, and the cameras are rolling, the rock singer breaks out a loaded pistol, throws it to his temple and squeezes the trigger. He kills himself in front of all those people.

The song is intense. The voice is guttural, aggravated.

"*Those who were right there, have a new sense of fear.*"

Peffers was at the end of his rope.

Suicide by cops.

"Come out of there, Peffers, or we're going to open fire." The cops crouched behind their patrol cars and got a better grip on their handguns and rifles. They shifted their weight, and braced for the impending volley. "You have ten seconds."

Ten seconds came and went.

The lieutenant waited another ten seconds.

"Fire!"

"I wish I could have met you."

The forest erupted. Peffers' home was minced in the roar of gunfire. I ducked behind my tree and plugged my ears. It carried on for a minute. I heard glass breaking, and the gasp of Peffers' mobile home absorbing all those rounds, all that energy. It was intense. Beyond intense.

As quickly as it started, the shooting stopped. Smoke hung in the air like fog. The music was killed. It was deathly quiet. Spent shell casings rolled off the hoods and trunks, plinked off the bumpers, and onto the gravel driveway below.

The cops ducked behind their squad cars again, and reloaded their weapons.

Peffers appeared. At least part of him. He waved a white cloth, maybe a tee shirt, from behind a broken sill. "I'm coming out. Don't shoot. Don't shoot."

Everyone felt the tension. They repositioned themselves, but still kept their guns pointed in Peffers' direction.

The front door was riddled with bullet holes. At least a dozen. There were big holes and little holes, entry wounds and exit tears that looked like tiny starfish.

The door slowly opened and a beanpole of a man suddenly appeared. The back of a shirtless man. He started down the stairs. In reverse. Arms over his head. An enormous tattoo covered his back—a giant hand, a defiant fist, middle finger proudly erect. He backed down the stairs, exposing an inch of boxer shorts above his baggie blue jeans.

When he stepped off the front porch they told him to stop.

"Hold it right there, Peffers," they yelled.

Peffers kept coming.

Slowly.

He was taunting them, giving them all his giant middle finger.

Daring them to shoot.

"Hold it Peffers. Get on the ground."

A couple of cops holstered their guns. Peffers had closed the gap to forty yards, and it appeared that the cops were about to charge him. I was looking over the cops shoulders, down the barrel of their guns, in perfect position to see what was about to take place.

Then thirty-five yards.

He never had the chance to make it to thirty. A single clap of gunfire sounded. Peffers went down in a heap, his face a disaster.

"What a good shot, man."

"What the hell?!" I heard the lieutenant cry, angrily. "Who shot him?" he yelled. "Who the hell shot him?"

He tossed the bullhorn inside the patrol car, disgustedly, and reached for the microphone clipped on his white shoulder strap.

"Bring that ambulance up here, will you? The suspect is in need of medical attention."

That was an understatement.

Ernest Peffers was dead before he hit the ground.

A bullet in the back of your head has that effect on a person.

Some of the troopers rushed to Peffers' side—for their own curiosity, or to confirm the fact that he was dead. Other officers ran to the mobile home, I assumed to make sure that Peffers acted alone. They slipped inside, guns drawn and at the ready. A moment later, they returned with a bucket of empty Sudafed containers and a can of denatured alcohol—two ingredients for crystal meth. The coast was clear.

The cops opened the Monte Carlo, rummaged inside for a moment or two, and pulled out a handgun dangling by a pencil. It looked to be a thirty-eight or a forty-five.

Everyone sighed. The ambulance backed up the driveway-beeping, beeping, beeping. The lieutenant pulled everyone close. They huddled in the driveway, twenty yards from the paramedics. There were six or seven I estimated, dressed in their uniforms and black bullet-proof vests. I couldn't hear what was being said, but it reminded me of the dialog that takes place at the pitcher's mound during an important part of a baseball game. He pointed left, he pointed right, and he pointed at each and every one of them. But more importantly, he pointed to the ground, over and over. He gestured as if he was slamming a make-believe gavel on a judge's bench. They all nodded. They all agreed on the plan he concocted, whatever it was.

The paramedics loaded up the body and headed down the driveway.

I watched the cops. The lieutenant had seen enough. He whipped open the patrol car door, slid inside, and sped off. The remaining troopers put away their rifles and shotguns, and cataloged the drug paraphernalia. A couple of them took off their hats and tossed them inside their patrol cars. They swatted mosquitoes, now gathering in the dusky gloom. A large roll of yellow tape appeared, and they enclosed the mobile home in a daunting cocoon of plastic. A couple of other troopers appeared from the back of the mobile home. They were carrying the corpse of a dog; its tongue dangling lifelessly from the side of its open mouth. It was a rottweiler, and a big one at that. When they reached the back of the patrol car, they dropped it unceremoniously. One of the troopers, a female, let out a "Whew." The other flexed his hands as if his wrists ached.

They opened the trunk and pulled out a black bag. A body bag. They crouched there for a moment or two, unzipped the bag, and placed the corpse inside. They fought with the legs but managed to seal the deal. One last heave, and the dog was safely stowed away. Out of mind, out of sight.

And that was it.

Twenty minutes after they killed somebody, the police picked up most of their spent shell casings and were gone. The place was vacant, at least for now. I stepped from the woods and onto the driveway. It was hard to look at where Peffers died. His blood and tissue were everywhere, and flies wearing little green jackets buzzed and crawled over the mess.

I looked down the driveway. Grass grew down the center, despite being shadowed by the canopy of trees. Way at the end, around several gentle bends, they had strung up more yellow tape.

I was behind enemy lines all right. I got the whole story. The police had no idea I was there, with my mind racing, with my notes-a-scribbling, and most important, with my camera clicking.

I got it all. I got all the goodies. The lieutenant on the bullhorn. The eruption of gunfire. The surrender. And the most powerful image of all: Peffers' execution. It was deliciously satisfying. It was the kind of break I had hoped would come my way when I wanted to become a reporter many years ago.

The readers of the *Journal* were going to eat it up. So was the Associated Press. Who knows, maybe even the *Detroit Free Press*, or the *Detroit News*, or a host of other newspapers across the state?

Mr. Potato Head didn't share my enthusiasm. He was waiting for me back at the paper that Friday night and wanted to know what I came up with.

I told him about the judge, and Jankovich, and what a great source she would be for Sunday morning's paper. He smiled, as we made our way to my little cubicle.

"Excellent," he said.

Just as I was about to tell him about Peffers, he interrupted me, and said that he had already spoken to the state police lieutenant, and heard that Peffers was killed.

"That's right. He's dead." I agreed.

"He said that Peffers ran at them with a handgun. They're doing some ballistics testing on it now to see if it was the same one used on the judge."

I looked at Byron, just to make sure he was serious.

"Is that what he said?"

"Yeah. They had to shoot him, for their own safety."

I looked at Byron. He was serious.

So was the lieutenant.

"What else did he say?" I asked him.

By then we were back at my little cubicle, and Byron pulled up a swivel chair. He sat on it backwards, so the back of it was pressed against his chest.

"He said that the subject engaged them in a shootout, before charging them with the gun in his hand."

"Is that right? Do you believe him?"

"Well sure I do. I've known him for years. He's a great guy."

I nodded, pulling the digital camera from the satchel.

"You're not going to believe this Byron, but his statement couldn't be further from the truth."

I plugged the camera into the computer, and began the process of downloading everything from the camera into the computer. It would take a minute or two.

"What are you talking about?" he asked, angrily—like someone had sliced his ears into quaint little slices, fried them in hot vegetable oil, and sprinkled them with sour cream and onion powder. He propped his elbows on the back of the swivel chair, and I noticed the muscles in his jaw flexing.

"Just a minute. You'll see. How is the judge?"

"Still alive, apparently, but not doing so well. She's got a lacerated liver and spleen, and a whole bunch of other things. She's still in surgery. If she makes it through the night it'll be a miracle, they say."

"Who told you that?"

Byron bobbed his head, as if I shouldn't be asking him questions like that.

"Someone at the hospital, that's who."

We talked briefly about the layout for the front page of Sunday morning's paper.

And then the photos appeared, as if they were playing cards in a video game of high-stakes blackjack. Hit me. Hit me. Hit me. They were wonderfully poignant, a fabulous account of the biggest thing to hit Alma in years. I got Jankovich and her pals crying under the outstretched arms of a mountain ash. I got the deputy, torn between duty and compassion for the fallen judge, holding her hand, directing traffic.

Byron gasped when I showed him the three-dozen shots of Peffers' house.

"Holy, hell!" He put his hand to his mouth, and froze. "How did you get…?"

He bit his index finger between the first and second knuckle. It was a magnificent show. The shot of Peffers' fall was intense. We could clearly see that his back was to the line of cop cars in the foreground. The front of his head was a gaping cavity. It was gone.

More importantly, there was no weapon in Peffers' hand.

Hovey stood and slammed his chair under the desk next door. All of a sudden he was mad as a hornet.

"How the hell did you get in there to take those?"

I saved the images on the computer. All of them. He came back at me a second time, directing me to stop typing and pay attention to what he was saying.

"I said, how the hell did you get in there to take those photos?"

I looked up at him and couldn't decide if he was mad at me, the lieutenant for lying, or the fact that I might be forcing his hand so early in the developing story.

"You know," I bobbed my head the same way he did to me several seconds previously. He shouldn't have asked me that. "Someone let me in there."

"Who? Who let you in there?" He was yelling.

"Byron, please."

I looked down the row of cubicles, and several people from

advertising looked in our direction. They had never seen Byron this upset. None of us had.

"It doesn't matter, Byron," I told him, confidently. "Don't be pissed at me, I'm just the messenger. Let's just send these shots to graphics and let's have a closer look at them on the big screen, okay?"

He was pacing. He was wound up. A great story will do that to a newspaperman.

I fired up the office email, picked out seven or eight of the best images, and sent them on their way. Byron and Colleen got a set. Me, too.

Byron watched the whole thing. He crossed his arms and paced the pace of a man with too much on his mind. He was weighing the gravity of my photos, of the lieutenant's statement, and how it should all play out in the Sunday edition of the *Journal*. "Byron, please, it's late. Let's just sleep on this thing tonight. The deadline for Sunday isn't for another sixteen hours. We've got lots of time, and a red-hot story."

He wasn't listening. Or he pretended not to listen. I was jabbing him. Poking him. Rubbing his nose in the controversy.

"It's getting late," I said. "Let me dig up a photo of Judge Noyes. Let's see if she makes it out of surgery. I'll write these stories tonight, and we'll decide on a plan in the morning."

He stormed off, but before he conceded defeat, he said, "Okay, but I'll review the final copy. And I'll handle the statements from the cops."

I watched him go. He had a peculiar shape, and an odd gait.

It was just like him to get the final word, to request the final word, too. It was still his newspaper and he liked handling the reins; I knew it, he knew it, but he wanted to assert his authority any time he could. But with that said, I was certain that he'd want to avoid anything controversial. I'd have to soft pedal the execution of Ernie Peffers, that's for sure. The *Journal* had a reputation for staying a mile away from anything controversial, regardless of whether or not we were right. He always took the safe route, and took pride in the fact that the *Journal* had never been sued.

And so, I started in.

The leads are always the toughest to write, but this one came to me in a heartbeat:

> *As surgeons try to save the life of Judge Deborah Noyes in Gratiot County Hospital, police killed her alleged assailant, Ernest Peffers, 29, at his Riverdale mobile home late Friday afternoon.*

Not a bad start. I liked it.

> *Witnesses say that Peffers approached the judge with a firearm about 5 p.m. Friday afternoon at the north courthouse doors.*
>
> *"He just about jammed the gun in her side," said Margaret Jankovich, of Edmore. "I was only about ten feet behind her when this guy walks up to Deborah (Noyes) and says, 'You were wrong, wrong, wrong. Now you're going to pay for it.'"*
>
> *Jankovich said that Peffers shot Judge Noyes in the side of her abdomen, before dashing to his car and speeding off.*
>
> *Jankovich worked in Judge Noyes' courtroom as a court reporter, and said that Noyes handled Peffers' child custody case less than one month ago. Noyes ruled against Peffers, citing his drug habit as a reason to deny him full custody.*
>
> *Peffers' ex-wife testified against him at the hearing, and Jankovich said that she had photos of Peffers engaging in the manufacture of illicit drugs.*

> *After the shooting, state police found Peffers barricaded in his mobile home in the 7000 block of South Lumberjack, in Riverdale.*

That was about all I could write. Byron and I would have to decide what would be in the paper after that. He would have to believe me, and my photos, or the account Lieutenant Christofis told him.

There was more to the story that I could dig into.

I pulled up the plat book, to see who owned the property where Peffers' mobile home was located. It wasn't Peffers', but another man whose address was on Lumberjack Road. I looked him up in the phone book and gave him a call.

"Yeah, that was my mobile home," he said. "Used to be our hunting cabin." The voice sounded as if he was an older gentleman. "The cops called me up and asked me about Peffers."

"What do you mean?"

"They came right out and asked me what kind of guy he was."

"What did you tell them?"

"I told them that he was a son of a bitch, so help me God."

"Why's that?"

The voice on the phone languished for a second.

"It's late, Mr. Twitchell…"

"I know it is, but this poor judge has been shot."

I was pulling at his heartstrings, in an effort to get him to talk.

"Peffers is a jerk," he said. "One of my worst renters ever. He's six months behind on his rent, and he won't pay. I go down there to collect on it and he's got this friggin' dog the size of an angry farm animal…"

"What else did the cops say to you?"

The voice on the phone took a deep breath.

"They told me that they had the place surrounded, and that Peffers was locked inside. I told them, 'Good! Maybe you can collect my back rent while you're at it.'"

"Okay, but why would the cops call you?"

"They said they were going to use tear gas on him and if that didn't work they were going to shoot up my mobile home."

"So they asked you first about shooting it up?"

"Yeah. I told the cops 'No way, unless you want to waive the back taxes I owe.'"

"What did they say?"

"They really didn't say anything, but I figured it was worth a shot, so to speak."

I laughed. Then thanked him for his time. The guy had no idea what had taken place at his mobile home just down the street, and since he didn't ask, I really wasn't going to volunteer anything either. He'd have to buy a newspaper and find out all the juicy details along with everybody else.

It seemed odd, though. Why would someone with the state police call the owner of a house and ask permission to shoot it up, when they had the right to do that anyway, if a gunfight erupted? It simply didn't add up.

Saturday morning came and went and Byron had yet to make an appearance at the paper. I thought for sure he would have been in there Saturday morning, rattling his sabers the way he always does. It was now almost two in the afternoon, an hour before Sunday's deadline. I had to move on this thing. The Alma president's story was polished up, and moved from the headline to the bottom of the front page.

Across the top of the front page, I typed in big, bold letters: "*Judge slain, assailant killed by police.*"

My lead was changed to reflect Noyes' passing.

> *The people who worked in Judge Deborah Noyes' courtroom said that she will be remembered for being a wonderful person, a caring mother and grandmother, and a tough, but fair judge.*
>
> *The man who fired a .38 caliber handgun at her near the courthouse doors Friday afternoon, Ernest Peffers,*

29, of Riverdale, was shot and killed by police later that evening.

Noyes was 68, and had planned on retiring from the bench at year's end.

I thought about the rest of the story, and how I was going to work in Peffers' execution. Lieutenant Brian Christofis from the state police wouldn't return my calls. Neither would the post's commander, Stephan Wieczorek. I thought about emailing him, or dropping off a photograph with the hopes that maybe it would motivate them to call.

There was nothing left to write but the truth, so I let it fly.

Witnesses say that the police surrounded Peffers' mobile home, and instructed him to surrender. When Peffers refused, police opened fire. After a minute of constant shooting, Peffers waved a white cloth, and said, "Don't shoot. Don't shoot."

Peffers then backed down the front stairs of the mobile home, unarmed. When he failed to follow a police command to stop, he was shot in the head. Paramedics said that he was pronounced dead at the scene.

No tear gas was used in the process, but according to Alma College criminal justice professor David Vance, "It should have been in that situation. Any time you can flush out a suspect without shots being fired, it is better than the alternative."

The owner of the home, Kris Kobylarz from Riverdale, said that the state police called him before the incident happened.

"The police called and wanted to know if it was okay if they fired at the place. I thought they had the right to engage in that if they thought that their safety was in jeopardy."

> *Vance agreed.*
>
> *"Police departments don't typically call the property owner to ask permission to shoot up the home. If it happens during the course of a conflict, there isn't much a property owner can do about it."*
>
> *Witnesses at the scene say that the police found a handgun in Peffers' vehicle after he had already been shot.*
>
> *Lieutenant Brian Christofis at the Michigan State Police did not immediately return phone calls to the paper.*
>
> *Judge Noyes was endorsed by the State Police League, and the Federal Magistrate Judges Association. Her nephew, Arlan Scheperly, is a trooper at the Clare State Police post.*

I thought it was a pretty good story. It was fair. It was the truth.

Mr. Potato Head agreed.

He showed up at my cubicle at two forty-five. In typical fashion, he sat on a swivel chair, backwards. When I pulled up the front page on the computer screen, he squeezed in next to me. I watched him, and the peculiar way he raised his head to see through his bifocals. His hand had a small tremor and when he jockeyed the mouse, the cursor on the screen wiggled.

Sunday's front page was beautiful. The headline was a grabber. So was the photo of the deputy and the fallen judge next to him. My caption underneath the photo was just as powerful.

> *Split emotions. Deputy Wallace Reihl comforts judge Deborah Noyes with one hand while he directs traffic with the other.*

Set within the column, I had a smaller photo of Peffers, hands stretched over his head. The giant, inappropriate tattoo was gone; I deleted it.

"Okay," Byron said. "Let's go with color for the shot of the deputy. That's a good one."

"Thanks," I said.

He continued reading.

"This is good too," he said, when he got to the second story about Deborah Noyes and her law career, her involvement in the community, and the varied organizations she was a part of.

"Are you okay with what I wrote about Peffers and the way he was shot?"

Mr. Potato Head never looked in my direction, but said that it was fine.

"Thanks."

It felt good to get a compliment. It felt good to hear the words, "That's a good one." I was smiling, knowing that tomorrow morning, Gratiot County, along with parts of five other counties, would be reading my account of the horrible events.

I was confident. Almost cocky.

"That's a wrap, Byron. I've been over it a hundred times and I think it's super clean."

He nodded his head in agreement.

"Okay then. Why don't you head for the hills?"

"Don't you want me to send this off to the press room?"

"I'll take care of it," he said.

I never thought anything of it.

He seemed sincere enough. He never mentioned a thing about Lieutenant Christofis and all those holes in his story. Byron believed me and, more importantly, my story, rather than the lieutenant's. He had my back, so to speak, and it felt great. It went beyond that. It felt awesome.

And so, I left.

I could hardly wait for Sunday morning. It was going to be one of the greatest stories I had ever covered. A double murder. A judge, no less. With all that drama. With all that sizzle. What an unbelievable break.

What a great way to end the week.

I was just tickled.

Elated beyond words.

And unfortunately, I had nobody to celebrate it with.

Other than Synch. She was always up for a party, and since it was Labor Day weekend, that was all the excuse I needed. I dashed home, picked up my girl and loaded the old Suburban with goodies for a cookout. We stopped at a butcher shop in downtown Alma, and I picked out a big hunk of cow. I love the way steaks from a butcher shop come wrapped in white butcher's paper. Even though the meat is probably just the same as what you'd get from a giant retailer, I always think it must be better because of the way it's packaged. Styrofoam seems so sterile, so impersonal. White butcher's paper is like the wrapping on a Christmas present. It's delightful. It's a gift.

We made our way west again towards Riverdale, and the Peffers' home. I wanted to take another look at it; I wanted to relive what had happened. And when we arrived, it was just as I had left it. The yellow tape was still strung up at the end of the driveway, and the grass still grew long and spindly down the center. I opened the glove compartment and pulled out a pair of binoculars. Parked halfway down the driveway was a dark gray van, the words "MSP Crime Lab Unit" on the doors.

I didn't imagine the events that had happened. I saw it with my own two eyes.

The cops executed Peffers. Right, wrong, or indifferent. They killed him.

I only stayed there a minute or two. Just long enough to revisit the event in my head. It was time to move on. It was time to have some fun.

Synch and I made our way farther south and a little west to Crystal Lake, which is anything but crystal clear, especially on Labor Day weekend. The jet skis, water skiers, and pleasure boaters would have the lake riled to a creamy froth. But that was okay; it's what you've come to expect on a holiday weekend in Michigan. Jump in the water. Let your hair down. Have fun.

Synch loves the water. She trotted right in and swam amongst the children tossing foam footballs and plastic Frisbees. They pretended Synch was a shark, and screamed and scattered as if they were on the set of *Jaws*. Although the scene was loud and hectic, it made me smile. It made me laugh.

I gathered her in, and we made our way to an abandoned picnic table at the back of the park. She was happy and cool, and didn't mind that I had tied her leash to the leg of our table. She watched me pour the charcoal into the grill and spray it with lighter fluid. It roared into flames, but quickly settled down. All we had to do was wait for it all to turn a pleasant shade of gray.

That's one of the best things about using charcoal instead of a gas grill—it gives you time to unwind. And boy, did I unwind. I cracked a beer, opened a bag of pretzel rods, and sat down on the bench, near my beautiful dog. She panted slightly and took mild amusement in the fox squirrels that were loping from oak tree to oak tree in the day's lengthening shadows.

It had been a hectic week. Dad was going to be okay, it appeared. At least he could walk, and do things around the farm. It would have been torture to see him in a wheelchair or suffer from some sort of paralysis. Even though he couldn't communicate very well, it wouldn't be the end of the world. We would be okay.

I watched the scene in front of me. It was like a snapshot of life. About forty yards away, an entire family had two picnic tables pushed together and were having dinner. The grandparents were at the end, and it appeared as if the conversations were passing them by. They sat there, eating their corn-on-the-cob, coleslaw and chicken drumsticks. There were two sets of moms—both my age—who were nitpicking their children about reaching across the table, using a napkin instead of their shirts, and being nice to their siblings. The dads were sipping beer as I was, and were shamelessly admiring the fine broods they were raising.

I spotted a young couple seated on a park bench not far from the water's edge. They were perhaps in their mid-twenties. I saw her wedding ring as her hand scratched his back. She loved him. He loved her. I could see it in the way he looked at her. I could see it in the way she cupped his side with her hand. She enjoyed the feel of his body, the curve of his muscles, the firm, hardness of his skin beneath his thin shirt. They were still in that delightful time of their marriage, when each other's bodies were uncharted territory. When the thrill of each intimate encounter was a magical experience.

I remembered those times with Colleen. I remembered when sex with her was fun. When it didn't have a purpose, but if we wound up pregnant, that would be okay, too. When the only reason we did it was because she thought I was hot and I thought she was hotter yet. I remember when I could hold her by her belt loops, raise an eyebrow and she'd know exactly what I was thinking.

I remember the time I rented an old Chris-Craft the summer we were married. We got up early, drove to Ludington for the day with no other plans than to spend it near Lake Michigan. It was a spur-of-the-moment idea to rent a boat, a nice boat. But, what the heck, I've always been an impulsive kind of guy.

It was just after noon when we finally got the last of the instructions from the rental boat operator on the shores of Hamlin Lake. He told us to stay out of the marsh at the east end of the lake, where the fireworks were to be launched, and to be careful not to scratch the boat's finish when we threw out the anchor. Hamlin Lake isn't far from Lake Michigan, in fact, only a massive sand dune separates the two. It's on that sand dune, in the lee of the prevailing westerly winds, that everyone hangs out and spends the day.

It was on that sand dune that Colleen and I tossed out an

old bed sheet and spent the day reading books, smearing suntan lotion on each other, and barbequing steaks at suppertime. We took long, refreshing swims, which were always followed by more rounds of suntan oil. I loved the way her skin moved beneath my fingers. I loved the way she closed her eyes and reeled in the sensation. I loved untying her bikini top and watching the strings fall to the bed sheet beneath her. She always raised an eyebrow in mild protest. I consoled her with words of unsightly tan lines and the dangers of sun poisoning. She closed her eyes again, surrendering to my whims, submitting to the impending bliss.

After dinner and a bottle of merlot, we loaded up our stuff and went for an evening cruise around the lake. The boat made it special. It was in immaculate condition. The wood was nearly pristine, and the interior was trimmed in green leather. There was a smart metal plate at the bow that helped us slice through the diminishing waves. I felt important behind the wheel. I felt as if I were rich, that I was tasting the ritzier side of life.

And so did Colleen. She looked the part, with her oversized sunglasses, and her blonde mane pulled behind her ears. I reached to her, and placed my hand on her knee. She put her hand on mine and squeezed my fingers. We puttered past the cottages and waved to the water-skiers getting in the day's last ride.

She thought it would be great to have a place on the lake. To have a boat like the old Chris-Craft. To have kids and be happy forever. We were young and full of dreams. Full of hope.

By then it was nearly dark, and the fireworks at the far end of the lake were in view. I punched the accelerator and we were off in a flash. We were on plane, scooting across the lake at forty-five miles-an-hour.

Colleen let out a holler.

We both did.

Everyone raced to see the fireworks. There were maybe two dozen boats anchored near the mouth of the marsh. She told me not to get too close, so I backed off the throttle and eased to a pleasant stop a quarter-mile from the action. There was no need for an anchor. The wind had subsided and the lake was a sheet of inky, black glass. We sat there together on that comfortable bench seat, the bow lights as red and green as the fireworks on the horizon. She scooted closer to me, her elbow at my knee, her hand rubbing my shin. I put my arm around her shoulder, squeezing her bicep and tracing a line to her elbow. We were all alone. She reached for my hand. Her fingers clenched mine. They entangled. And then, slowly, she pulled my hand to her chest, to her bikini top now sheathed in a sleeveless cotton blouse. I cupped her in my palm, lifting slightly, while not taking my eyes off the fireworks. She had such wonderful breasts. They were so round and pleasant. They had a heft to them. A handful. A wholesome harvest. I fumbled with a button on her blouse—the one in the valley of her breasts. She helped me. She unbuttoned them all, when I only wanted one. Her defenses were distant smoke on the horizon. My hand moved to her side. I felt the curve of her hips, her waist. So nice. I watched her eyes and the way her lids drooped slightly. She was getting into it. She liked the feel of my hand on her bare breast, my fingers sensing the pebbled goodness of her nipple. I wondered if she could feel the grit of sand against her bare skin. I wanted to brush it off, but that would have spoiled the moment. After all, sand in the swimsuit is one of the souvenirs of a day at the beach. So is the taste of suntan oil. I love the flavor, the aroma, the silky smoothness of it all. I started in on her earlobe. Gently. Softly. The scent of coconut oil filled the air. Another souvenir. Her eyes closed, but she wedged her elbow further up my thigh. I felt it brush the outskirts of my swimsuit, now sporting life of its own. I sensed her breathing quicken. Her heart race. She bit the corner of her lip. She threw her head back against my arm, my lips, my embrace. It felt so wonderful. Her free hand lifted my shirt, and she toyed with the tuft of hair south of my belly button she had nicknamed, "the happy trail." We were getting riled up. Both of us.

The fireworks on the horizon couldn't hold a candle to the intensity that was burning in the cockpit of that old Chris-Craft. I thought about making a move, but she beat me to it. She rolled my way, straddling me, kissing me. She held my head between her hands and plowed her tongue into mine. It was warm and wet. So inviting. She raised herself so that her breasts were at eye level. They blinked at me in the glowing spasm of the fireworks. It was wonderful. And so was the grit, the sand, the remnants of a day at the beach. I didn't have time to relish in the excitement.

She stood, still above me, and tore the cotton blouse from her shoulders, her bikini from her chest. My hands brushed her knees, her thighs. It felt as if I were finger painting. I pulled at her skirt and it fell in a crumpled heap like a wisp of cotton gauze. Now all that remained was her string bikini bottom. It was right there, right in front of me. I kissed each thigh with my lips, each calf with my hands.

I looked up at the view—the way her breasts saluted my maneuvers. They stood at attention. I didn't languish in the image, however. There was work to be done. There were joys to be had, elation at hand. And I didn't waste a lot of time. As much as I wanted to make the moment last, I longed to steamroll the inevitable. I was all lips. And teeth. And tongue. I felt her blonde tress beneath my cheek and smelled the goodness of it all. I nosed my way underneath her suit, and sensed the heat pouring out of her. My fingers found the elastic ties of her suit. They nearly sprung when I set her free. She was all mine.

Or maybe not. Instead of straddling me again, Colleen sat on the edge of the boat, leaned backwards, and was gone with the subtlest of splashes.

It was such an erotic scene. I still remember seeing her beautiful face above the watery plane and the way the fireworks made everything glow. I could make out her hands, her arms, her limbs and the way they churned at the water. She flipped on her back and kicked her feet, scissors-like. Everything was right there in front of me, the whole package. The whole delicious view.

"Come on, jump in," she said.

I stood on the seat and pulled my shirt over my head.

"That's it," she begged. "Swim suits are not allowed."

I looked around. We were all alone. The fireworks were crackling and booming with great intensity now. The grand finale, or just the build up to it? Didn't matter. We were all alone. I untied the cord around my waist and let my suit fall to my ankles. I took a step up to the boat's gunwales and pretended it was a stage. So much for modesty.

"Welcome to Las Vegas, everyone! Our next guest has a bowl full of salads…I mean a soul full of ballads. How about a big hand for Derrick Twitchell and his swinging organ?"

Colleen laughed, and sputtered as if she had swallowed a teaspoon of lake water. "Will you come in here?"

"One more thing," I told her. "I never mentioned that I was an Olympic swimmer. "

"Tell me. Tell me."

"From the United States of America, breaststroke specialist Derrick Twitchell and his amazing short arm."

Colleen laughed.

I blew kisses to the applauding crowd, then encouraged the little guy to wave.

"Sorry folks, he can't wave. He can only bob his head."

Colleen howled with laughter.

"Come on," she said. "I want to pet him."

"Say it again, I can't hear you. The applause is too loud."

She was laughing.

"Can I pet him?"

"What?"

"Can I pet your dog, sir?" I looked down and saw one of the cutest-looking boys from the neighboring table standing at Synch's side, a can of soda pop in his hands.

It was all a dream, Colleen and me. I was so far lost in the daydream that I didn't hear the little waif with a red pop mustache standing in front of me.

"Of course you can. Her name is Synch." I watched him, and the way his small, dimpled fingers tapped her on the head. It made me smile. There's nothing quite like the trusting innocence of a child. Strangers are kind. Dogs don't bite, or growl, and the world is a loving, peaceful place.

He looked to be about four years old and wore a pair of denim overalls, shirtless. I reached for his head, and felt his hair. It was smooth and baby-fine, and it made me wonder what kind of hair my kids might have had.

An instant later, his mother came to rescue him and they toddled off together. Hand in hand.

I woke up early Sunday morning, and took Synch for a walk into downtown Alma. The sidewalks were still rolled up, the streetlights still on. A passing storm left the streets covered in a slick sheen of rainwater. Hardly anyone was up. Barely any cars stirred.

When Synch and I made it to the bakery, I tied her to a small ash tree near the newsstand in front of the building. I saw my headline looking back at me: "*Judge slain, assailant killed by police.*" It made me smile. It made me want to buy a paper right then and there and find out what had happened.

I skipped inside our local French bakery and smelled the yeast and the sugar and the coffee. It was wonderful. A group of men in their sixties and seventies were at the corner table, sipping their morning java and laughing about whatever it is that old men find humorous. I noticed the framed pictures on the walls—from France, I suspected—of a boy running down a brick-covered street, a loaf of French bread under his arm. There were other shots, too: of a couple having a candlelit dinner, a loaf of sliced Vienna in their round, wicker breadbasket. It looked like fun. I wished I were there. The pictures made bread look so healthy, as if it were the elixir of life. In a lot of ways, it is.

I ordered a medium coffee, and a pecan roll, heated, "*s'il vous plait.*" The woman behind the counter smiled, and disappeared into the back room with all the mixers and sacks of flour and square boxes the size of small cakes.

The men in the corner were still laughing. I looked in their direction and they were all glaring right at me.

"Hey, Twitchell!" one of them said, holding up the front page of the sports section. "Nice story!" They all laughed.

I smiled politely. Modestly. "Thank you."

The woman behind the counter reappeared a moment later, my pecan roll resting comfortably on a Styrofoam plate, a plastic fork and knife at the ready.

"That will be two-twenty-five," she said.

In my head, I was ten steps behind her- at the table with the men- wondering what they meant by all the laughter. Was there something I had written in the newspaper? Something I forgot to write in the story? What could it be? I dug a five-dollar bill from my wallet and laid it on the counter.

"I'd like some quarters if you have them."

"No problem," she said. "Buying a *Journal* this morning?"

"Yeah."

"You're in for a treat. They really messed up big this time."

My heart sank. *This couldn't be*, I thought. My pride took over. I thumped my chest. She had fired an insult my way and I wasn't going to stand by and let it happen.

"No they didn't."

"Oh yeah, they did," she said without hesitation, reaching under the counter and producing the front page of the sports section. "Look at the photo at the bottom."

She slid the paper my way, and there was the shot of the five guys in football pads.

Oh, no.

My heart sank further still.

The athletic department never called back.

I never pulled the photo.

And worse yet, I never changed the 'some other guy' part.

I forgot. I forgot. I forgot.

Now, everyone was laughing at me. The girl behind the counter. The men in the corner, having their morning coffee. Laughter. Laughter. Laughter. It was everywhere. They were all laughing at me. The boy on the brick-covered street pointed his baguette in my direction and howled with laughter. It was a nightmare. Even the couple with the basket of sliced Vienna took a break from their timeless fascination to humiliate me. It was horrible.

I read the caption.

Leaders all, on both sides of the ball.

So far, so good.

Quarterback Ronnie Leslie and tackle Mark Skeith are offensive co-captains.

Nothing wrong with that.

Twin brothers Earl and Dave Dickman.

Everything fine there.

I wrote *some other guy* for the fifth player, whose name I never obtained.

Only *some other guy* wasn't there.

It read **some other sucker.**

Only the paper didn't say *sucker.*

In fact, it started with an "F."

I couldn't believe it! Mr. Potato Head sold me out.

Very funny.

I was going to lose my job.

I was going to be fired.

What in God's green earth was I going to do now?

Eleven

A FEW MINUTES after I had written my one and only ransom note and rammed it down the tines of a pitchfork, I heard the knock on the Suburban's side window. The knock wasn't a wimpy tap-tap on the window, either—it was crisp and hard—a heartless, bitter interruption. My head snapped to the sound. It was Emmert St. Peter standing in the brisk, Iowa air. His coveralls another year faded, his hair another year thinner. I laughed nervously and opened the truck door.

"Good morning, Emmert."

We shook hands. And laughed about the snow. I noticed his Carhart jacket and the way the seams were beginning to fray.

"I was having breakfast this morning when I saw a nice buck working along the creek bottom," he said, proudly. "Watched him through the binoculars, when I spotted you and your dog."

Emmert's hands gestured. His fingers were thick and muscle-bound, calloused and yet soft to the touch. His wedding ring was thin and weathered from the years, and too small for his finger.

"You must have seen it, right?"

"Sure did. Looked like an eight-point, maybe a ten."

"It was a dandy." He nodded. "Why don't you come up to the house, Derrick? Mother put on a pot of coffee and she just took a pecan pie out of the oven."

I really didn't want to take the time. I really didn't want to visit. I had a story to write, phone calls to make. There was stuff to do. Jobs to be done. Go man, go.

"Sure," I said, merrily.

"Great, park behind the drive shed, will you? Just like you own the place."

I nodded, but I didn't have the courage to ask why he wanted me to park behind the drive shed. There must have been a reason.

After Carolyn poured the coffee, Emmert sat down across the table from me, the bottle of Michigan maple syrup between us. He didn't have to speak as loudly as he did in the blustering squall. He was all business.

"We thought that you might be interested in this," he said.

He reached under the table to the chair next to him and handed me a copy of today's *Des Moines Register*. I could hardly believe my eyes: "*Truck driver feared dead, Register hit with ransom note.*" Beneath the lead story was the sub-headline: "*Police search for Michigan man.*"

I buried my head in my hands and let out a groan. A deep, guttural groan.

Emmert and Carolyn didn't say a thing. They were watching me and my angst.

I hardly had the courage to read the story.

But I did.

I saw my photo. It was a really old one, I used in the *Evening Journal*, back home in Michigan. How did they get that?

It was easy.

> *Late Sunday afternoon, the* Des Moines Register *received an email from a Michigan man regarding the whereabouts of the missing Bettendorf truck driver, Charles Cigan. The email arrived with a digital photo showing what appeared to be Cigan's body. The* Register *turned the email and the photo over to police investigators.*
>
> *"We're not convinced that the person in the photograph is, in fact, Mr. Cigan," said Detective Sgt. Stanley Upah with the Iowa State Police. "There are lots of ways to digitally enhance photographs."*
>
> *The email came to the* Register's *office by an alias for the individual whom police are calling "a person of interest." That person, C. Derrick Twitchell is a freelance reporter from Alma, Michigan. Police say that emails have their own identifiable coding that allows law enforcement officials to track who sent them.*
>
> *"It works especially well with on-line predators," said Upah. "but this is the first time we've used it in a missing person situation."*
>
> *Anyone who has information about Twitchell's whereabouts is encouraged to contact the Iowa State Police.*

My heart sank. What a horrible situation. The police must have spent all night piecing together the puzzle. They'd figure out where I bought my license. They'd figure out where I spent the night. All they had to do was wait for the magistrate to okay the search warrant and they'd come barging into the motel room, guns drawn. They were probably there already.

All of a sudden, I was really glad that I had packed my laptop. At least they wouldn't have access to that.

I looked up at Emmert. Then Carolyn. They had worried expressions on their faces. Their kids may have abandoned the farming way of life, but they certainly were never in this kind of trouble. In a way, I felt like one of their kids, a long lost son who comes to visit much too infrequently.

I kept reading.

> *Twitchell worked as a reporter for the* Evening Journal *in Alma, but was recently terminated for editorial content.*

Oh, bull.

> *His former supervisor, publisher Byron Hovey said 'Twitchell's reporting techniques were less than accurate, and that he had a penchant for exaggerating the truth.'*

I shook my head. What a lie.

> *Hovey said that Twitchell frequently visited Iowa to hunt pheasants and wrote about it in the newspaper.*

I shook my head in disbelief. Hovey sold me out again.

"Looks like you've got yourself into a sticky situation, Derrick."

I looked up at Emmert and the way he raked several wisps of hair over the shiny dome on his head. His hands were on the bottle of syrup, and he seemed to be thumping it with his fingers.

> *Twitchell's ransom note arrived at the* Register *electronically shortly after six Sunday afternoon: 'I know where Cigan is. Hire me to cover the story. I have tons of experience, and I'll give you the exclusive. See the photo attached. Hire me. Hire me. Hire me.'*
>
> *"Although the* Register *does occasionally hire freelance reporters, the safety and well-being of the general public is always our top priority," said the* Register's *publisher, Harriet Ewoldt. "Mr. Twitchell sent us his*

resume several months ago, but we would have never hired a stranger to cover a story of this magnitude, especially when we're not sure of his credentials."

"We hope that the email and photo were a farce, and that Mr. Cigan will be found alive and well."

I shook my head again. The paper lay before me like a poor report card, like the results from a biopsy. It was horrible news. They were after me. The police. The cops. Everybody.

And after today's paper, and compliments of my ransom note at the barn, even Cigan's murderers were on my tail.

Carolyn St. Peter skated across the kitchen floor, a pecan pie between her oven-mitted hands. The crust was golden brown and inviting, each pecan suspended in the pool of corn syrup, eggs and Carolyn's secret—a quarter cup of brandy. It smelled just as good as it looked.

I looked outside the kitchen window and reeled in the view. We were on the side of the big hill, facing north. I saw where I had parked, and how Emmert must have been able to see the buck that was out for an early morning stroll. It was a peaceful setting with the rows and rows of corn stalks, and the snow piled at the foot of each one. Despite the cold outside, it was warm and homey inside. As warm as pecan pie and a smiling reunion from an old friend.

Emmert's words rang in my head. "*Looks like you've gotten yourself into a real mess.*"

I didn't know what to say.

It was a real mess.

And getting messier by the minute.

"What are you going to do, Derrick?"

I looked across the table. Emmert's face was sincere without being nosey. I knew that the next line of questions would deal with Cigan, and if I really knew where his body was. I didn't know what to do. I didn't know what to say.

It seemed that my life had hit rock bottom.

I came to Iowa to get away from the trouble in Michigan. My dad, his health, and his crazy trust. My ex-wife and my former employer. And all the stuff with Ernie Peffers and Judge Noyes.

My troubles in Michigan were the least of my worries. Now I was wanted by both sides of the law.

"What am I going to do, Emmert?" I asked him.

He sat up in his chair a little straighter, and leaned into the answer. Carolyn placed her hand on his shoulder and lolled her head in anticipation. They were anxious to hear my answer, but I had no idea how to respond. I hesitated for a second. Maybe two. My head was swirling with details, with the horrible mess that was taking place. I felt awful.

"What am I going to do, Emmert?" I asked, one more time.

"I'm going to have a piece of pecan pie, that's what."

Twelve

LABOR DAY SEEMED TO LAST a month. It was agonizing. I wanted Tuesday morning to hurry up and get here, but at the same time I wasn't sure what I should do. And it's probably just as well that I had time to think things through. Had I run into Byron Hovey in the bakery Sunday morning, I probably would have blown a head gasket and mashed him like a pot of boiled potatoes.

I was so upset.

So furious.

It's one matter to do things to get rid of an employee. It's another to print the mother-of-all swear words in order to get rid of a member of the staff.

I couldn't understand why he wanted to get rid of me. I am a good reporter, a good employee, and I have been for a long time.

It's strange how life can push you around. It can nudge you into uncomfortable places, unusual situations. For quite some time, I have been thinking about my career and the way I might be selling myself short. Even though it's good to have a job and steady pay, something inside of me said that I should be taking bigger strides, taking on bigger challenges. I was in the prime of my life, the most productive years of my career. Did I really want to spend them working in a small town newspaper, or should I be expanding my horizons to bigger cities, with larger circulations?

Maybe it's just as well that I was going to lose my job. That little voice inside my head was about to be set free. If I wanted to be the man, I certainly would have the chance.

Alma is a two-newspaper town: the *Evening Journal* and the *Gratiot County Recorder*. The *Journal* is published six times a week, and by everyone's account is "the" paper in town. Its circulation is over thirty thousand. It is well staffed, and aside from the occasional "f-bomb," puts out a respectable product every day. Byron Hovey took a big chance by printing that obscenity the way he did, but he did it because he knew he could get away with it.

When there's no competition, you can afford to have an off day.

The *Recorder* isn't much competition to the *Journal*. Printed once a week, the *Recorder* has long been considered "that other paper" in the community. The differences between the two papers are obvious. The *Recorder's* press is old. The photos are somewhat blurry, and the typeset isn't very crisp, either. They cover events that aren't necessarily "newsy," but rather "what's happening." You may not find out the blood alcohol level of a drunk driver accused of killing a pedestrian, but you can read all about the cook who serves a tender Swiss steak at the local senior citizen home.

The *Recorder* is old school; the *Evening Journal* is mainstream.

The *Recorder* is small town; the *Evening Journal* is big business.

The two papers don't compete against each other; the *Recorder* occupies a little niche within the community that the *Journal* thinks is irrelevant.

I spent Sunday afternoon on the computer, searching for ways I could make money as a writer. I thought about the *Recorder.* Even though they seldom hired reporters, they might entertain the thought of it, especially if I worked on straight commission off the ads I'd sell. It was a novel concept, but it was so unique that I thought they just might consider it. I had a hunch that the folks at the *Recorder* hated the staff at the *Journal*, because the *Journal* thought they were better than everybody else.

The *Lansing Daily Press* had a job posting for a city beat reporter. The *Oakland County Press,* the *Chicago Tribune* and the *Des Moines Register* all had openings for a reporter with at least five years experience. I had twice the experience they wanted, and I was willing to relocate.

There were plenty of travel magazines in Michigan that were always looking for clean stories with great photo support.

I could crank up my outdoor writing, too. The *Evening Journal* never really did appreciate the outdoorsy piece I contributed every once and a while. Mr. Potato Head had no interest in hunting or fishing, and was generally close-minded to anything other than bowling or horse racing. I wrote hunting and fishing articles for the fun of it, and people noticed them because they weren't written like news stories. I tried to capture the feeling, the sensations, the ethereal aspects of every hunting and fishing adventure. In other words, it wasn't your typical "hook and bullet" kind of story, where the writers explain how, when, and where to catch fish. My stories were all about the experience, rather than the outcome. And people enjoyed reading my stories. Men, women, sportsmen, and housewives all commented on how much they enjoyed reading my stuff. Perhaps I should have written more of those. But then again, I was comfortable in my role as a reporter at the *Journal.* I wasn't hungry enough to write those stories with more regularity.

Without a job, I was going to get hungry. Without a regular paycheck, I was going to have to scramble to make ends meet. But I was up for the challenge. I was going to make things happen, if nothing else than to prove Mr. Potato Head wrong.

For certain, the vengeance was boiling inside of me.

It was the revenge that fueled my motivation. In two hours time, I had my resume composed and polished to a glossy hue. A few minutes later, it was in cyber space, waiting in mailboxes of editors and personnel directors across Michigan, in Chicago, and in Iowa, the state where I hunted once a year.

Strange how your entire career can be summarized on one page; it makes it all seem so insignificant.

On Tuesday morning, I woke up early and put on my best wool suit, a white, ironed dress shirt, and a sharp necktie. I shined my shoes and took the old Suburban to a car wash. And then, at a little after eight, I walked into the paper with my head held high. Everyone stopped what they were doing and watched me. I was a marked man, a bull's eye painted squarely on my back. Byron tried to appear relaxed when I marched into his office, and pulled up a chair. I knew he was sweating just as much as I was. He wore a sport coat. Byron never wore a sport coat unless it was a special occasion.

It started out like an old fashion shootout. A stare down. Neither one of us wanted to go first. Or blink.

Finally, he started.

"We have a problem," he said.

I nodded.

"I'd say so."

He nodded back.

"Why didn't you pull the photo of the football players?" he asked.

"Why did you print the f-bomb?" I fired back.

"It was your job as temporary editor to catch that."

"You're not denying it, then?" I asked him.

All at once our voices were raised.

"For heaven's sake, Derrick, I didn't put that in there!"

"Who did it then? The same guy who changed my copy, my story, about the execution of Ernie Peffers?"

"I did that."

"Why? Are you covering for somebody?"

"Hell, no. I changed your story because I did."

"Byron, I was there. Peffers was unarmed! You changed my story to cover up the cops killing him. I was there. I saw it. They executed him."

"That's your story, Derrick, but I got the lieutenant and one of his troopers on the record stating that Peffers charged them. Had the gun in his hand. Now tell me, who am I going to believe, them, or somebody who was in there trespassing?"

"Me, damn it! I saw it with my own two eyes! I had the photos, and you pulled those, too."

He shook his head, no. Shamelessly.

There was no sense arguing with him. He was set in his ways and I wasn't going to change his mind. I could see the writing on the wall.

"Let's just make this official, shall we?" I asked. "Go ahead, fire me."

He stood up, leaned across the desk and uttered, "If that's what you want, I'll let you have it. You're fired."

"Thank you," I told him, standing just the same. "Someday, Byron, you are going to regret the way you handled this. If you wanted to fire me before, why didn't you go ahead and do it? That was a cowardly stunt you pulled, and someday you're going to regret it."

"Get out of here." He pointed at the door.

I started in that direction, but stopped short of the threshold.

"This time I get the last word. I'm going to expose you for the coward that you really are."

I slammed the door and headed towards my cubicle, my knees were a little wobbly, my hands a little jittery. Adrenaline has a powerful effect on a man.

Colleen was waiting for me at my cubicle. She sighed.

"I'm supposed to escort you out," she confessed.

I should have guessed that Byron would have had the whole thing choreographed.

"That's fine. Can I get some of my belongings before I go?"

"Sure," she said, in a conciliatory voice. "Take your time."

I sat down and looked for a tissue. The adrenaline had my nose running, and I sniffled.

"Here," she said, handing me a box from the neighboring cubicle.

"Thank you."

"You're welcome. I've never seen you cry, Derrick."

"I'm not crying. It's just my hay fever acting up." I blew my nose and wiped the corner of my eyes.

"I know," she said.

I looked in her direction, and saw her standing there, arms crossed across her navy blue blazer, hair drawn to a tidy flaxen bun on the back of her head. She wore her hair up almost every day of the workweek. It was so fine and smooth, so nice and blonde. I wanted to run my fingers through it, one last time.

"What do you know about the matter with Peffers?" I asked her.

"Derrick, please. It really doesn't matter now, does it?"

"You don't want to say, do you?"

"Not really," she said. Her hands were on her hips. "All I know is that we really messed up by printing that curse word. That's unheard of, you know that." I reached under my desk and found a box of copy paper that I used to collect recyclables. Colleen reached for the top of my little cubicle.

"I didn't do it though."

"I know you didn't, but I think Byron's hands were tied on this one. We're just hoping that Connecticut doesn't see it."

I was opening drawers, and grabbing everything I saw: floppy discs, ink pens, and wads of paper clips that had very little value. I'm not sure why I grabbed half the stuff I did; it just seemed like that's what's supposed to happen when you leave an employer. Colleen asked me what I was going to do for a job.

I looked up at her and the way she was trying to play both sides of the coin. She was trying to be sympathetic to me and yet not jeopardize her position at the paper.

"Not sure, Colleen. It's not like I can start over as an accountant or something. I'll land on my feet, somewhere, somehow."

She watched me pick up the photo of Synch, blow the dust from the frame, and put it in the box. "I told Byron I was going to get even with him."

"Why did you say that?"

"Because I am."

"Derrick!"

"Colleen, I've been a good employee for a lot of years. You can't just fire me for something I didn't do. Besides, he didn't believe that I was at the scene of Peffers' murder. I sent you the photos for heaven's sake. I sent them to you."

"I know you did. I got them. But you know what, I'm going to pray for you," she said. "Haven't you heard of turning the other cheek?"

I raised my eyebrows. "Haven't you ever heard of an eye for an eye?"

She shook her head. "This kind of attitude isn't healthy, Derrick, and I don't think your dad would approve."

"I get the feeling, Colleen that you really don't like the thought of me moving on."

"What do you mean?" she asked.

"I mean, I always had the feeling that you enjoyed being my boss, that you liked keeping tabs on me, and to some degree, being in control."

My statement didn't exactly throw her for a loop, but it didn't set really well with her, either. It was something I never would have never suggested while I was still employed, but now that I was fired, it felt like the shackles of self-restraint were gone.

"I'll miss working with you. You're a good reporter, I'll admit," she said. "But I don't think that I'm a control freak. We agreed to keep our dirty laundry out of the office."

She wasn't going to admit anything. She watched me load everything else into the cardboard box.

"I guess that's it. I got everything."

She nodded. "I'll walk you out."

"That would be fun, for old time's sake," I said, sarcastically.

She gestured with her head, "Come on, let's go for a walk."

We didn't really say anything as we walked through the paper, one last time. Everyone looked up from their work, just to watch the spectacle. I've never been fired from a job. Ever. Despite the shame of it all, I held my head high. I did my best for the paper, for the community. I had nothing left to give. No regrets.

When we made it to the parking lot, she followed me to the driver's side door of the Suburban. I opened it, tossed the box of goodies inside, and took off my suit coat. There was something else I had to get off my chest.

"I never told you how much I enjoyed working with you, too, Colleen. You were always fair, and thorough, and I think someday you'll make a fine publisher."

Colleen still had her arms crossed. I was making her uncomfortable.

"After our divorce, I was a little concerned that we were going to let some of the bad blood spill over into our working relationship. But it never happened. And I want to thank you for that. You were a wonderful boss."

She smiled. "Derrick, please. Don't say anything else." She raised her finger to her lips.

"I still care about you, Colleen. You know that."

"Derrick."

I don't know what took hold of me. I reached for her elbow. Both of them. I kissed her. On the lips. Quickly, but not that quickly. It was over in a second. Maybe two.

"Bye, Colleen. Pray for me."

There was no blushing.

There was no insecurity.

I was moving on.

The headquarters for the *Gratiot County Recorder* is located in the old, nostalgic part of downtown Alma, where flower shops, a French bakery, insurance agencies, bookstores, and law offices conduct business. The *Recorder's* building was in serious disrepair. Its stucco-façade was cracked and peeling, patched in places, and caulked in others. There wasn't any sign out front, but an ancient shingle that read, "Claety Printing" hung from a wrought iron stanchion. I swung open the thin aluminum door and walked inside. The gal behind the front counter was on the telephone, typing away at her keyboard. I noticed the bulletin board behind her and the announcements posted in random fashion. One notice caught my attention, because it looked like it had been up there for years: "Classified ads, three dollars. Obituaries, fifteen. Photos extra."

That was absurd. If the publisher knew what he was doing, he could get three times that amount. He must not have realized that people will pay for the stuff they want, regardless of the cost.

The counter was well worn, and cluttered with stacks of

business cards, a flyer from the local funeral home, and a box full of mints, packaged into quaint little rolls the size of a stack of coins. There was clutter everywhere.

A moment later, the woman on the phone directed me to the basement, where she said I'd find the publisher, Walter Claety. I had to weave my way around the garbage bags full of pop bottles. They were everywhere, and wherever they weren't, they had buckets and trashcans collecting water from the leaky fixtures that appointed the upstairs apartments. A gray cat with a long, swishing tail nibbled food from a Cool-Whip bowl and made me wonder where they kept its litter box.

On second thought, and whiff, maybe they didn't keep a litter box after all.

The place was a mess. I bet they had four hundred dollars worth of pop bottles lying around in garbage bags, and giant boxes. Diet Coke, regular Coke. And Vernor's ginger ale, lots of Vernor's.

Walter Claety wasn't especially excited to see me that morning. After all, I showed up unannounced, and had on a suit and tie. Nobody wears a suit and tie, especially not Walter Claety. It was Tuesday morning, and since the day before was a holiday, he was a day behind the Thursday deadline for Friday's paper. He wore a thermal jersey under a faded red chamois, which was rolled at the cuffs. A stained, vinyl apron hung around his neck that drifted nearly to his knees.

He was in the process of converting giant sheets of blank film into the negatives that would eventually turn into newsprint. The archaic machine he was babysitting was called a "plate maker," and was the size of a chest freezer. A bright light beneath the lid shined on the wall behind him where several women in scantily clad outfits promoted a brand of hand tools. It was a pleasant distraction. Beautiful women always are.

Walter Claety did it all. He wrote the stories. He cut the negatives. He took the negatives to the press upstairs and fed the paper through the machine. On Friday mornings, he delivered the papers to the newsstands around our little town, then sent stacks and stacks of them with the dozen or so delivery people he had hired. On Friday afternoons, he paid the bills, did the accounting, ordered supplies, and worked on the stories for the following week's paper. It must have been a monotonous exercise. If the three o'clock deadline was an albatross at the *Journal*, then Walter Claety's routine must have hung around his neck like an ostrich at the *Recorder.*

The last thing he wanted was another project, like me.

And so, I cut right to the chase: money. I explained to him that I didn't want any salary. I was to work on straight commission, split sixty-forty. He gets the sixty; I get the forty.

That got his attention.

Then I told him that I would design and write the copy for the ads, and handle any collection issues. He nodded.

There was nothing for him to lose. He had what I needed—a place to print my stories, and the opportunity to make some money—and I had something he wanted—someone who would give him a little more free time. It seemed like an excellent fit.

And just to be sure there wasn't any confusion; I put everything in writing on a document titled, "Memorandum of Understanding."

Walter Claety was impressed. His plate maker chimed with a solitary bell ring and he threw the latch on the front of the machine. The blaring light dimmed. I watched him flip the lid—a giant cookie sheet—and the blank sheets of film had magically morphed into the first four pages of Friday's *Recorder*. He pulled the film off the cookie sheet, held it to the florescent light bulb with both hands, and smiled a wide, nearly toothless grin.

Walter's pop-drinking habits had caught up to him.

"I'll tell you what, Derrick," he said. "I don't have much use for the *Evening Journal*, and anybody who gets fired from that place is okay with me." I smiled. "I've read your stuff before. It's good. And accurate. If you wanna write for us and sell ads too, that would be fine."

I was relieved. The very day I was fired from my job, someone else had hired me. Granted, it wasn't a very good job, but at least it was a job. Walter Claety gave me a chance, and that's all I ever wanted.

In keeping with the *Recorder's* editorial tradition, I kept my stories lighthearted, human interest, rather than hard news. I covered Alma College's football team as I've never done before. I went beyond what was expected of me at the *Journal.* For the first three weeks of our arrangement there, I didn't sell any ads at all. I didn't even try. All I did was make the *Recorder* a better paper with my writing, with my stories, with my outdoor column. If I was going to sell ads, I'd have to do it with a little ammunition, and that ammunition was the fact that our newspaper was more appealing than the *Evening Journal.*

And then, I formed a strategy. I took a look at who was spending money at the *Journal.* They had plenty of advertisers. Car dealerships. Insurance agencies. Chiropractors. The local hospital spent a ton.

I was gunning for the *Journal.* I was going to hit them right between both eyes: the stories they covered, and the money they earned. If they wrote about a house fire, I wrote about it, too. Only I did it better. I interviewed the people whose house had burned, and documented the trouble they were going through. I took photos of them at the store, buying necessities such as underwear and soap. I showed them rummaging through the charred remains of their house, looking for family keepsakes such as photo albums, and wedding pictures. I got quotations and photos of them and their insurance agents delivering claim checks and heartfelt hugs at a time when their clients needed them most. It was a great public relations coup for the *Recorder,* even better for the insurance agents.

And the agents responded. The first ad I sold was a half-page whopper that ran alongside the story about the house fire. Walter Claety said that the story and the ad together blurred the line of good journalism.

I told him that it crossed the line, but we should print it anyway.

After all, the agency agreed to run the ad four weeks in a row, and that was going to cost a lot of money.

Instead of charging the agency the ridiculously low amount that Walter suggested, we raised our rates to within twenty percent of the rates I used to see at the *Journal.* And it worked. They paid, and paid, happily.

Walter Claety was a nice guy, and was devoted to printing a decent newspaper, but he really had no concept of the paper's worth. He didn't realize that he could charge a lot more than he was. He didn't realize that price seldom gets in the way of a great idea.

Walter forgot the second rule about newspapers: they don't print news; they print money.

Bottom line, under Walter's old way of figuring ads, the insurance agency would have paid seventy-two dollars for a half-page ad. I got them to pay two hundred and seventy-five. And they didn't even blink. The companies that the agency represented shared the cost of the ad as long as the agency used the graphics approved by the companies.

And the best part about it all was that the ad spawned other ads from neighboring agencies. It became competitive.

I was working hard. I was constantly writing, constantly working the angles. I hung out at the courtroom and followed civil and criminal cases. I targeted the cases involving the lawyers who had the biggest ads in the *Journal.* I took photos of them in action—in the courtroom, in the hallways talking to their clients, on their cell phones, and looking impressive in front of the juries. I wrote flattering summaries of the cases, and after the story was printed, I clipped it out and sent it to the lawyers involved in an envelope with the words, "personal and confidential" printed on the front.

And then I probably crossed the line.

OK, I'll admit it. I did cross the line.

I called the lawyers' offices from a pay phone and pretended to be an accident victim. I told them that I read about them in the paper and was considering them to handle the case against the parties responsible. I questioned the lawyers' experience, and whether or not they had what it took to make sure justice was served. Even though I never talked to the lawyers themselves, it created the buzz around the office that every salesman covets. It made it much easier to sell an ad. Many ads.

By then it was the middle of October, and the governor appointed a temporary judge to replace Deborah Noyes. My story about her replacement didn't really present any chance for ad revenue, but that was okay. I was nearly up to the same level of pay that I was used to at the *Journal*. Granted, I didn't have any benefits, but at the same time I knew that it wouldn't be long before I could afford those, too. I never worked so hard. I never got so much satisfaction out of being a writer, out of being a man. I was so alive.

I was so clever, yet such a slut. There was nothing I wouldn't do to get the story, to sell the ads, to make the money, to keep a roof over my dog's head and mine. It was so much fun. I loved the confidence that was pouring out of me.

And I didn't put all my eggs into the *Recorder's* basket. I expanded my horizons to the *Michigan Republican* about covering the presidential caucuses in Iowa, and they loved the idea. I wrote a story right after the Noyes' murder for the *Detroit Free Press*, but they cut the section about Peffers' shooting, just like Byron Hovey did. Nobody wanted to believe me. Nobody wanted to hear the truth about what happened.

It would have been fruitless to contact Lt. Christofis at the state police post or even the commander, Wieczorek. Nobody was talking about it. Nobody cared. All my phone call would do is stir the pot. I didn't want to be a meddler, but at the same time, the cops did something wrong. Very wrong.

What they did would make a great story.

Somewhere.

Somehow.

And so, I decided to write a letter to the top dog at the state police in Lansing.

> *My name is Derrick Twitchell and I am a freelance reporter from Alma. On Labor Day weekend, I witnessed the surrender and execution of Ernest Peffers in Riverdale. Contrary to what may have been reported, or what state police investigators have concluded, Mr. Peffers was shot and killed even though he wasn't armed at the time. He made no gesture toward the troopers. I was there. I witnessed everything.*
>
> *Enclosed please find a photograph of Mr. Peffers just before he was fatally shot. Notice that his hands were over his head, his fingers outstretched. Again, I reiterate, there was no weapon.*
>
> *I would suggest that he was killed unnecessarily, and that members of your department handled the matter with lethal force, when it was not necessary. Neither Lt. Christofis, who was present at the time of the incident, nor the post commander, Stephan Wieczorek, would return my phone calls.*
>
> *Make no mistake, this situation is not going to go away.*
>
> *I encourage you to talk to the members of the force and get back to me at your earliest convenience.*
>
> *Sincerely yours,*
>
> *C. Derrick Twitchell.*

I was confident that the director of the state police must have known about the Peffers matter; he must know about every fatality at the hands of the department. They must conduct some sort of investigation whether or not deadly force was appropriate. My letter would raise some eyebrows. It would make the lieutenant and all those troopers at the scene uncomfortable. The great lie they cooked up for the betterment of the department was about to come unraveled.

Then again, maybe it wouldn't. Photographs can be tinkered with. Images can be doctored. I was just one voice against the people who were there. If they already concluded the investigation, then what was the sense of stirring things up again?

I sent the letter anyway, and hoped for the best.

And then I decided to steal a little more thunder from the *Journal*. Since the day of Dad's stroke, I had wanted to do the story about Ira Kaminsky, but never had the opportunity. I know that he called the *Journal* and inquired about the piece I was supposed to write. He seemed anxious to see the story when I conducted the initial interview, too.

I thought for sure that he would give me the go ahead to write the same story for the *Recorder*. I thought for sure that he would have thought of something else to add to the story to make it more interesting. I still had his photos. I still had his story fresh in my head.

I was half thinking that my piece about Kaminsky would generate a fresh round of advertisers that were connected to the oil business. It worked at the *Journal*. Surely it had a chance at the *Recorder*, too.

And so, I loaded up my leather-bound organizer, jumped in my old Suburban and drove to Kaminsky's small mansion on the fifteenth hole of the Alma Country Club. His house was just as I remembered it, with its circular drive, and those impressive ivory-colored pillars across the front. A new Cadillac STS was parked at the front door, engine purring quietly.

It was Wednesday afternoon, and I figured that Ira Kaminsky was on his way to the golf course for his stock club meeting. As I walked past the Cadillac, the front door opened and he appeared. I heard him yell, "Come on, Roger! Shake a leg, will you?"

I smiled.

"Mr. Kaminsky? Derrick Twitchell, newspaperman."

My announcement startled him. He looked at me and raised his eyebrows.

"Remember me? From the *Journal*?"

Ira Kaminsky slammed the massive front door to his house. He took several steps my way, as if he was going to shake my hand. I smiled again, expecting that his smoke-colored fingers would be wrapped around my palm. I moved my organizer from the right hand to the left, and outstretched my arm.

Ira Kaminsky walked right past, as if I wasn't there.

"Mr. Kaminsky?"

The whole thing startled me. I followed him to the rear door of the Cadillac, and watched him reach for the handle. He wheezed. I smelled the plume of smoke in his wake. It oozed out of his skin; it became the fabric of his wool suit. Kaminsky opened the door to the Cadillac and unbuttoned his sportcoat. I didn't want to let him leave. There was something wrong.

"I have your photographs, sir, the ones you gave me for the article in the *Journal*. I'm now with the *Gratiot County Recorder* and I want to run your story in that paper instead."

The front door to his house closed again, and the chunky man with nearly no neck at all walked toward the vehicle.

Kaminsky lowered himself into the backseat and said, "Roger, escort this slime bag to his vehicle, will you?"

"Wait a second," I said.

"He's got some photographs of mine."

"Here, take them."

I opened my organizer, but before I could hand them over,

Roger snapped them out of my midst. He was a big guy, and had a double chin that kept him from buttoning the top button of his dress shirt. The next thing I know, he's got his hand on my elbow, and is directing me down the driveway. I've never had anything like that happen to me. I've never been ushered out of anything, except for that one time in college when I was caught drinking peppermint schnapps at a football game.

Roger had a firm grip on that tender spot just above my elbow. I tried to break free, but he clenched me even harder. I didn't like it at all, but I still had something to say. I had to get the last word.

"Roger, this is no way to treat a lady."

Roger didn't speak. He wasn't paid to speak. When we made it to my truck, he gave me an extra push. He was good at that.

He returned to the Cadillac, arms slightly cocked to the side the way weightlifters do, sometimes. I watched him jump inside the car and speed away, down the circular driveway and off to wherever his boss wanted him to go.

I couldn't believe what had just happened. Kaminsky was a nice guy two months ago, but now he was anything but cordial. He was downright rude. He called me a "slime bag," of all things. That was uncalled for. I am a good guy. I am a hard worker, and aside from a few little sleazy shenanigans to pad my pockets around the paper, I was still basically a good person.

Maybe I wasn't a good person after all, but I certainly wasn't a "slime bag."

I didn't do anything wrong where Kaminsky was concerned.

I shrugged it off and drove away, thinking maybe that was the end of it.

Boy, was I wrong.

My trouble with Kaminsky was just beginning.

And there would be lots of it.

Thirteen

A MONTH BEFORE MY TRIP TO IOWA, Michigan had its first taste of winter. Early December has a way of making you forget about the beautiful leaves of mid-October. The sun's pale, thin light cast the family farm in a somber shade of gray. I hate December for the very same reason that I dislike March: both months give a taste of decent weather, but for the most part, they mean snow and cold and winter, winter, winter.

It had only been a week before my trip to the farm at Thanksgiving, but I was in the mood for a little time alone with my folks. And my dog. And all those acres. It was still pheasant season, and I really wanted to walk the family farm for old time's sake. If I could visit with my parents, and go hunting, it would feel like I killed two birds with one stone.

Early on a Saturday morning, Synch and I put together our overnight bags and pointed the Suburban south by southeast to Owosso. I nearly hit a deer near Ithaca. Then another near Ovid. Since deer season opened three weeks ago, deer had turned into nocturnal creatures.

Finally, though, I made it to the farm just as the eastern

horizon was beginning to stir. When I opened the truck door, I noticed how much the farm smelled like breakfast. I gathered a hint of Belgian waffles and Columbian coffee, and dawn in rural America. I loved the smell of it. I loved that time of day, when life was just starting to stir, when that painstaking list of things to do in the next sixteen hours was still in mental negotiation.

Mom was up, and in her housecoat and slippers. She had the table set and had little glasses of orange juice above each plate. She gave me a kiss and a hug, and told me to take off my hunting jacket. Before I knew it, I was seated at the kitchen table, a cup of warm coffee in my hands. She smiled at me, and placed her hand on the back of my head just as she used to do when I was younger. It was like I was seven years old again. I was glad I called her and announced my intentions to visit. She likes to put out a big spread of food, even if it's only her son that comes calling.

"Pheasant hunters need a big breakfast," she used to tell me. "You're going to burn a lot of energy out there."

I smiled.

"Thanks, Mom."

She smiled back.

"How's Dad?"

She quit smiling. She shook her head. "He hasn't been himself. You know that."

"What do you mean?"

"Since the stroke," she sighed. "There are many things different about him. He talks differently. He swears and curses, and rambles on about things that have nothing to do with what you asked. And he cries at the drop of a hat. My gosh, he never used to swear, but now he curses non-stop. And he gets so frustrated when he can't find the right words."

"I can see why. He's a lawyer, for heaven's sake; he had to master the language."

Mom turned away, and kept her head in the breakfast. She

sliced a melon in half and scooped the seeds and pulp into the drain for the garbage disposal. I watched her place each half of the melon onto a cutting board, then plunge a small filet knife through the rind. In no time at all, she had the honeydew cut into eighths, the rinds tossed in an ice cream pail for the mulch bin. She picked up each melon wedge, and cut it into chunks. It looked so good. Her hands cradled each piece as if it were Holy Communion. It was her way of showing reverence to the heavens; it was her way to acknowledge that the melon was made to replenish our bodies.

Who knows what was going on in Mom's head? She was a strong woman, and proud Christian. Cooking and baking were gifts from God, and hardly ever would she let a day go by without her getting the itch to whip up a pie or a batch of cookies or a pot roast for dinner.

And now that Dad was sick and needed a special diet, it presented a new set of cooking challenges for her. She embraced it. She took pride in it, and enjoyed feeding him reduced-fat oatmeal cookies, or a sugar-free strawberry pie.

I watched her squeeze a half lime over the top of the melon. It drizzled over everything. She flipped the lime peel onto the pile with the rind and yesterday's coffee grounds, and then brought the bowl to the table. The floor upstairs creaked, and I knew that Dad was afoot.

"How are you holding up, Mom?"

"What do you mean?"

"Dad's condition has to be hard on you. "

"It is."

I watched her wipe her hands on her apron. The simplicity of her statement said it all. It was so powerful, so out of character for a woman who enjoyed talking.

"It's like I have a kid in the house again." She rolled her eyes in frustration. "I should have enjoyed our time together. We should have made the most out of things when we were healthy. Now that he's not himself, I wish I would have never taken our time for granted."

"Are you getting any help?"

"You mean am I seeing a shrink or something?"

"No, no. I mean does anyone help you out with him?" I asked her.

"Yes, thank heavens." She raised her hands to her chin, then looked up to the ceiling. "For about a month we had a nurse and a physical therapist here one day a week. The pastor at the church comes out on Tuesdays, and Judy comes by every Wednesday after work just so I can get out of the house without him."

"Judy Craigmyle?"

"Yes. That's right."

"Why does she come out?"

"Just to help."

"Oh?" I asked, somewhat curious.

"She stays here for a few hours and has dinner with him while I get groceries and run some errands. I can't take your father to town with me because he's so hard to deal with."

"What do you mean?"

She paused.

"He's mad that he can't drive, and then he tries to tell you which way to turn, even though it's wrong. The other day I didn't turn where he wanted me to turn and he poured his bottle of water all over my skirt."

"Geez, Mom."

"I know it. That's just the start of it, Derrick."

"What else?"

"It ran all over the car seat."

I chuckled.

"No, no. What else about Dad?"

"Lots of things."

"Tell me some."

"Last week, he said that he wanted to sell the Harley. I

mean, he really wanted to sell the Harley. His reasoning skills are horrible."

I watched her race around the kitchen. She poured batter into the waffle maker, closed the lid, and continued.

"I told him that fall was no time to be selling it, but he just wouldn't let it go."

She moved back to the stove, and gently rotated the sausage links as if they were eggs in her nest of down.

"So finally, I tell him to put a 'for sale' sign on it, and to put it out near the end of the driveway."

"Then what?"

"When nobody called to buy it in the first hour, he went back outside again." She shook her head. "And next thing I know the police are here. Your father moved the Harley into the middle of the busy road out there. He said that 'it would have better visibility if it were parked in the middle of the road instead of at the end of the driveway.' Can you believe that?" The toaster popped, and she had the butter knife humming. "He could have killed somebody!"

"Holy cow, Mom."

"I know it. I've had to hide the car keys because I'm afraid he's going to drive somewhere and hurt somebody."

The noise upstairs was now downstairs. Dad was on his way.

"Speak of the devil, here's the man of the hour."

Dad stood in the entrance to the kitchen. Tears rolling down each cheek. He pointed in my direction, and said, "Morning, Son." Our reunion was a little more emotional for him than it was for me.

I noticed his outfit, which was remarkably child-like. His hair was combed in places, disheveled in others. He missed a button on the front of his forest green chamois shirt, so that one side hung lower than the other. And his boxer shorts. They were so cute and white, and big. They hung almost to the tops of his knees.

"How about some coffee, Dad?"

He nodded, then sat down at the table, next to me. Mom had his seven-day pill holder near his plate, and she reminded him that he needed to take his medicine.

"Today is Saturday, Chick."

I noticed his flannel shirt, and the way he forgot to button down the collar. Dad would never have let that happen. He never overlooked details like that. I smiled at him, but didn't want to believe that it could be happening. There were other details about him, too. He missed shaving a dime-sized portion of his face, under his jaw, about halfway towards his ear. The whiskers were three-days long and gray. It was way out of place.

"Looks like you're ready for a little pheasant hunt this morning?"

He nodded, "I'll go."

Mom opened the back door, ran downstairs, and returned a moment later with his canvas hunting pants.

"He's been talking about it all week, Derrick, ever since you called." She placed his pants on his lap, and helped button the button on his shirt collar.

"Great, Dad. This will be fun. Like old times."

He smiled, and pulled on his pants, one leg at a time.

"Have you seen many birds?" I asked him.

"Other day saw two hens and a…." He stopped dead in his tracks.

"And a rooster," I suggested.

He shook his head, no.

"Quail?"

"No," he said. "Oh geez. Can't think of it."

"No big deal, Dad. It'll be fun just getting out there, like old times."

He smiled, swallowed three or four pills, and chased them with a glass full of orange juice. Mom filled up the glass and he drank that, too.

She placed the plate of toast on the table, next to the melon and the jars of homemade preserves—sugar-free strawberry, peach, and currant.

"Hope you boys are hungry," she suggested. "There's nothing like a big breakfast to get the body going."

And what a big breakfast it was. She made sausage, scrambled eggs, corned beef hash, Belgian waffles, and if that wasn't enough, homemade cinnamon rolls. We could have stayed there eating until mid-morning. It had been quite a while since I had even seen a breakfast like that, let alone eaten it.

I rolled up my sleeves and started right in. It was wonderful. Mom's scrambled eggs are sprinkled with dill, a hint of cream cheese, and they tasted absolutely incredible.

Dad hardly wanted anything at all. He took a bite of eggs, and nibbled at the whole wheat toast, but that was about it.

"What's the matter, Dad? Aren't you hungry?"

He shook his head, no.

"Sometimes he eats like a man possessed, other times he just picks at his food," Mom said, pouring more coffee in our cups. "I don't know how much to cook half the time, because I never know if he's going to eat or not."

"You'd better eat, if you're going to keep up with Synch and me," I said.

Dad was getting mad, I could tell. He was never one to be bossed around, or analyzed. He got up from the kitchen table, and wandered towards the back door. He found his hunting boots, and returned to the table. We watched him kick off his house slippers, and noticed the color of his socks—one white, the other gray. It was a shame to see him slide the way he had.

"Wonderful breakfast, Mom." I said. "The honeydew is delicious. You always know how to pick them."

She smiled back, and drifted to the back of Dad's place setting. I watched her comb his hair with her fingers, and press her body against the back of his head.

"You're right, Derrick. I do know how to pick them."

Dad smirked, and snapped his fingers. "Son of a gun. It was a fox."

Mom slapped his shoulder.

"What's that supposed to mean? I still am a fox!"

Dad shook his head. "No, not that. The other day…"

We looked at him and the way he struggled to find the right words.

"I saw two hens and a fox when they were combining the corn."

"Oh wow! That's great, Dad. That's what you couldn't remember from a minute ago?"

He nodded. And smiled. So did Mom. "A red one. It was pretty."

"Great, Dad. I bet it was."

He nodded for a second, smiling the smiles from never-never land. We watched him bend at the waist and fidget with his bootlaces, but it was quickly becoming apparent that he couldn't figure it out. Mom said that the doctor told her that the stroke had affected his brain in many ways. Depth perception was one of the things that left him. She told me that he could no longer help her with the dishes because he drops everything off the edge of the cupboards and countertops.

"And it's not just the dishes," she said. "He stands way too close to people. Like he's lost that sense of personal space."

His condition was beginning to wear on her, I could tell.

When she finished lacing his boots, they disappeared to the other end of the house.

I finished breakfast by myself, then set my sights on clearing the table, but I didn't get far.

Mom had helped him open the gun safe, and retrieve her father's prized shotgun. Then she helped him with his scarf, and gloves, and hat. He was once again in the kitchen, only this time he was ready for day care, ready to catch the school bus of fun.

"This is yours now, Son."

Dad never remembered telling me about it in his hospital bed. He reached toward me; hand perched under the lever between the barrels and the stock of a family heirloom.

"Thank you, Dad."

I held it in my hands, and marveled once again at the fine engraving, the gold inlays, and sleek profile.

Mom looked on, approvingly, and handed me a box of shotshells, sixteen gauge.

"We had better go," he said, "if we're going to get at those birds before they wake up."

I smiled. The stroke may have affected his ability to do a lot of things, but it certainly hadn't quelled his enthusiasm for pheasant hunting.

In no time at all, we were outside again, in the barnyard. I let Synch out of the truck and directed her towards the opposite side of the house, where the long row of spruce still presented the best chance of finding birds. The key was going to be keeping her—and, more important, Dad—off the road, while still hoping that any birds we flushed would come my way.

Dad was into the hunt, I could tell. He wasn't thinking about being careful, or watching his steps. He volunteered to march through the center of the spruce, and suggested that I cover the edge, where the cornfield met the trees. Synch didn't need to be given directions. She zigzagged in front of us, crashing through the overhanging bows, tasting the wind for any sign of intrigue. I hung a small, Swiss bell on her collar so that we could keep tabs of her passage.

We didn't flush any pheasants from the spruce grove. Synch really never got birdy, until we neared the end and a cottontail rabbit made an appearance. That got her riled up and into the hunt.

Dad was disappointed with the results of our first pass through the farm, but he remained optimistic.

"You never know," he told me. "Could be birds down fence

line, or towards b…b…back, or along the…" He paused, and made that frustrating smirk.

"The ditch, right, Dad?"

He sighed, frustrated, and pulled a hanky out of his pants pocket. I watched him wipe a drop from his nose in the morning chill.

"I'd sure see like you kill one with that gun," he told me, confused.

"I'd like to see me kill one too, Dad."

He didn't exactly wink at me, but I knew the intent was there.

We walked the half-mile fence line nearly shoulder-to-shoulder, at a pace somewhat faster than a saunter. It was the perfect pace for a little chat. He told me the story again about the first rooster he ever killed, compliments of a beautiful point by the family's Irish setter, Sugar. His long-term recollection was superb; his short-term memory was a different matter.

It was nice to be walking in the corn with Dad. He always told the farmers who leased the land that there would be no fall plowing. He thought that fall plowing was a waste of fuel, and that a plowed field in the winter was an eyesore, not to mention a dearth to wildlife.

Dad had other ideas, too, that weren't especially popular with his farming friends, but certainly were ahead of his time. He believed in creating a little buffer strip of grass along the edge of the farm's ditch to prevent the chemicals used in the fields from entering the watercourse. The buffer strips helped stop erosion and created crops of a different kind—the kind of bounty that stirs the soul instead of padding the pocketbook. He took more joy in seeing a pair of hen pheasants and a red fox than he ever did from the checks he received from the farmers who worked the earth.

The government now pays farmers to plant filter strips when Dad was doing it all along.

By the time we reached the back of the farm—the end of the fence line—Dad said that he wanted to take a break. We weren't exactly carrying a torrid pace, but then again, I had forgotten that it had been a little over three months since his stroke.

A break was a good idea. Dad took the lead. He sat against a large beech tree where the fence line met the neighbor's woods. I took the shells out of Grandpa's shotgun, and placed the gun against a nearby fencepost. I sat near Dad, against another post. Synch seized the opportunity to pull on the season's last strings of grass. She choked, of course.

It was a nice morning for December. The wind hadn't picked up yet, and the sun carried a meek warmth. A solitary nuthatch drifted onto a leafless limb above us and probed the nooks and crannies for a breakfast morsel.

The farm lay before us like an old, familiar friend. We knew everything about it. The rows of corn, so straight and tidy. The acres. All those acres. Dad fed his family in part off the land, off the crops. He was a good steward of the land, a good man and father. It was torture to see him slip the way he had.

"Son, very important I want to d…d…discuss with you," he said.

I watched him, and figured that it must have been fairly important by the expression on his face.

"I appointed you as trustee."

He took off his hat and tucked the earflaps inside.

"Important job, Son," he said, placing his hat back on his head. "You're going to be in charge of my trust."

I looked at him and realized that he was serious. He didn't remember anything about telling me that same thing three months ago.

"I know, Dad."

He looked at me.

"We've already gone over this. I've already been to the bank, and opened your safe deposit box. Remember the number on the box, Dad? Thirty four?"

Confusion.

"I already mailed two envelopes from your trust. The first one was to the FBI in Detroit. Remember that?"

He furled his eyebrows.

"I don't know what you had written in the letter because I didn't open it."

He nodded, but quickly became distracted by the contents of his old hunting jacket.

"The second envelope was to the United States Attorney's Office. Remember that, Dad?"

He pulled a pair of shotshells out of his pocket, held them between his thumb and forefinger, but didn't answer my question. I let him sit there for a moment, not to make him feel bad, but hoping that the silence would stir some sort of recollection.

It almost worked.

"I remember, some things, Son. Saddest days of my life. I was only ten or twelve years old. Nibble of July- haying season- when Dad ran up to the house in a panic. He was so upset. Mom kept yelling at him, 'What's wrong? What's wrong?' but he really didn't answer. Dad took the twenty-two from the mud room, and headed back outside."

Dad had excellent clairvoyance. He remembered every detail. And for the first time in forever, it was a story that I had never heard.

"We didn't follow outside, because whatever Dad was up to couldn't be good. I called for Sugar, but she never came. I called her over and over, but it was Sugar who was in trouble."

"What happened to her?"

Dad snapped out of his nostalgic reverie, and turned in my direction.

"Farming is dangerous, you know that, Derrick."

I nodded in agreement.

"Part of the r…r…reason I went to law school. Safety isn't one of farming's strong suits."

"What happened, Dad?" I had to reel him back in. "With Sugar?"

"Oh, forgot." He corralled his thoughts. "Dad was hay c…c…cutting. Cutting hay, and Sugar was in wrong spot at wrong time. Cut all four of her legs off, above her ankles. N…n…nothing we could do but what was humane. She was the best hunting dog…"

He rambled on and on about Sugar in his choppy, mixed-up way of talking. He probably couldn't tell what we had for breakfast, but he could remember his bird dog from a half-century ago.

"She had some odd habits. Pooped under truck tires. Must have liked the smell of it, and spread it all over the countryside."

I tailored my line of questioning to Dad's long-term memory.

"What kind of legal work did you do for the oil and gas industry?"

It worked. It was like it happened yesterday.

"Lots of stuff. Plenty of tile work…."

"Title work?"

"Title work," he nodded, and gave Synch a pat on the head. She shook her head and pulled at a burr from her flanks. "Lots of title work, make sure whoever owned parcel of land, actually owned it."

Dad looked into the sun and closed his eyes.

"Leases, contacts, min…min…mineral lights and leases," he said, repeating himself. "Deals between landowners and the guys who wanted to drill for oil."

"Where, Dad?"

"Up north. Mt. Pleasant and Clare, northern Michigan-Gayling, Kal-aska…"

"Kalkaska?"

"Yep," he nodded. "Kal-aska, Gayling…. even Manistee."

Dad repeated himself over and over, and made up the name

of cities. There is no such town as "Gayling," but there are two towns called Gaylord and Grayling. I let it go.

"Why didn't you tell us that's where you were going? It's not like it was top secret, or anything."

"It is, Son. Oil business is notori…notori…notori…"

"Notoriously?"

"Yes. Secret. I worked for tough guys. If I don't keep their secrets safe I could have wind up dead."

I nodded my head in agreement. "It's not like you were doing anything illegal, right? The oil business is a legitimate business."

"Sure." He licked his lips. "Quick money att…att…attracts some people."

I nodded.

"Dad, why would you be sending letters to the U.S. Attorney's Office now if you say that the oil industry is filled with secrets and tough characters?"

He looked at me in disbelief. "I did?"

"You did, Dad. It was in your trust. And I'm your trustee." I hesitated. "You directed me to mail those letters, and there's more to be mailed." Dad looked up at the branches as if they would hold an answer. He didn't remember any letters, so I changed gears.

"What's up with all those oil and gas leases in your safe deposit box?"

Dad absorbed what I said, but he stopped short of recalling the information. I backed up further still.

"How did those oil men pay for your legal services? Did they just write you a check, or was there something else?"

He smiled.

"Some oil men didn't have money, other did," he laughed. "Came to their last play—their last drilling project. New guys didn't have money, but lured of striking it big." His eyes were no longer on the tree branches; they flickered with memories from long ago. "They want to cut expenses, reduce their overhead. That's what I did."

"What do you mean?"

"Took interest in the new wells."

"That makes sense. Instead of getting paid up front, you negotiated a slice of the pie."

He nodded his head. "Right."

"That explains why you had all those interests in the oil wells in Isabella County. Did it work?" I asked him.

"Not every…some wells dry, but some were real plushers."

"Gushers, Dad?"

"Gushers. The best were Isa…Isa…Isabella County, near Mt. Pleasant. Hotbed for drilling. A long time."

"Why there?"

He shrugged his shoulders. There was no hesitation in his voice. "Don't know why, Son. Fields are in pockets. Raisins in bowl of cereal." His hands flicked left and right, to illustrate their randomness. "Mt. Pleasant have a very good field, called the convent…"

Dad snapped his fingers.

"Convert, Dad?"

He shook his head, "No, no."

"Convent, Dad?"

"No, no. The covenant field."

"Okay." I said. "The Covenant Field. Why did they call it that?"

Dad scratched his chin, and remembered.

"The well was on state land, but in order to drill we had to give the ch…ch…church next door some of the action."

"What do you mean?"

Dad's recollection was decent, but I could tell that he really didn't like sharing everything about his involvement. For years and years, everyone in the family thought he was simply a small town lawyer; his revelation now seemed to be as startling for me as it was for him. He sighed.

"Regulator says you need two-hundred acres to drill. We leased one-eighty from the state, and extra twenty from a church. Forgot preacher's n...n…name. He said he would take the profits and do God's work."

"So the church got a percentage of the profits?"

He nodded. "Had everyone praying for oil, but wasn't the only one to get profits. Covenant Field in eastern Isabella County. State owned land. They gets a cut. They gets a percentage, too."

Dad flinched. He snapped his fingers, like he couldn't think of something, but I had no clue what it was.

"Erik, what the hell is it?"

I shrugged.

"What the hell. What's the dozen number? You know, nine, ten."

"Eleven?"

"No, no." He was getting mad.

"Twelve?"

"Thank you. State gets twelve pre-cent on everything that comes out of the ground."

I nodded. "I'm listening."

"Twelve pre-cent is a lot." I nodded my head, and waited for the next caveat. "Wells drilled on state land everything is public record. Everybody knows what's going on. The drilling guys can't give twelve pre-cent to the state, and make profit. Had to keep numbers secret."

"How did they do it?"

"Put counter valve on inside bend of pipeline."

"Why would that skew the numbers?"

"Easy, Son. Same as water flow in a cream." He shook his head. "I mean stream. Current is always faster on the outside bend in a river, than the inside."

"Yeah, but wouldn't the state catch that?"

"Not if r…r…regulators paid off. Had a guy on inside.

With the state. One of many secrets they kept. They floundering, I mean laundering money. Exporting…"

"Extorting, Dad?"

"Yep. Extorting landowners, the state people. Regulators."

"Those are some pretty heavy accusations."

"True."

I nodded my head in agreement, but the notion of dear old Dad having some dealings with shady people didn't exactly sit too well with me.

"But wouldn't there be some sort of checks and balances farther down the pipeline?"

"No," he said, matter-of-factly. "Started smoking pipes in high school. Dumbest moves ever made. Sick to stomach."

He laughed, and made a sound as if he were throwing up.

He got "pipeline" confused, so I had to readdress the question.

"I wasn't asking about that kind of pipe. I was asking about the oil pipeline and whether or not the state checked production numbers farther down the line.

"State never checked tankers hauled crude up to a branch of the Kalkaskan pipeline in Lewiston. "

"Dad, it's Kalkaska, or Alaska. Which one? It's one or the other."

"Alaska."

"The Alaskan pipeline? In the little northern Michigan town of Lewiston?"

He nodded.

"Kalkaskan pipeline comes south across the Canada, splits in North Kabota." He snapped his fingers. "I mean North Dakota. One branch goes across the Upper Peninsula. Environmen…environ…environ…"

"Tree huggers?"

"Yes," he smiled. "They have a field day if they knew every hour twenty thousand gallons of oil flowing under Mack Bridge."

He chuckled at the horrid possibility of an oil spill under Michigan's most noted landmark.

"Pipeline south to Lewiston," he said. "Collection place for fields in northern Michigan."

"What happens after that?"

"Pumped to re…re…refineries in Sarnia, Ontario. Made into gasoline, diesel fuel. A gasoline pipeline across southern Michigan, and Illinois. Gets delivered to stations by tanker trucks."

"How do you know so much about it, Dad?"

"Just do. How I made living, legal work."

"Why didn't you tell Mom what you were up to?"

He took a deep breath, like he didn't quite know how to answer my question.

"She didn't need to know. Have to keep my clients' secret."

"I know, but you could have let us know where you were going."

"Son," he paused. "What do you say we fish our hunt? Got to be few birds in the ditch ahead."

Synch quit scratching the fur around her ear and sprang to life, cocking her head the way attentive dogs do.

I stood up first, and offered him a boost. He took my gloved hand in his, and I gave him a gentle pull.

"Thank you," he grunted.

"No problem, Dad."

I watched him brush the leaves and clutter from the seat of his hunting trousers. He turned to me, and pulled at his leather gloves, belt high, right in front of me. I noticed the stain between the fly and the gusset of his trousers.

"You must have sat in something wet, Dad."

He looked down and shook his head, as if the stain wasn't a mystery after all. He was embarrassed.

I shouldn't have said what I did. As soon as I said it, I realized that Dad was struggling with incontinence issues, and it must have made him uncomfortable. Rather than apologize, or make a big deal out of it, I let it go. We both did. Besides, Synch had already started into the thick grass along the edge of the ditch, not far away.

We headed in her direction, not exactly at a quick pace, but certainly faster than a comfortable mosey. The day's only rooster could have erupted at any second, and even though Dad wasn't carrying a gun, neither one of us wanted to miss out on the opportunity.

"Son, just a second," he said, tugging at my sleeve. "One more thing to t…t…tell you."

I looked at him, somewhat confused. It seemed that maybe he would have said all that was important back at the tree.

"Two things. I app…app…appreciate what you're doing me." The words didn't come easily.

"I'm like old beech tree there. I'm fade away, Son. Decay. Doctors say I'm losing it."

Dad bit his lip, and swallowed.

"There's no turning back now."

He took off his hunting cap again and I saw him swallow, like he was getting choked up.

"I think we need to make covenant of own—promise me to take care of what's in trust, okay, Son?"

"I got it, Dad." I reached for his hand to shake it. And we did, although the handshake quickly turned into a hug. He squeezed me like a bear, and I felt the curl of his hair against my ear. I smelled his aftershave—so subtle, so man-like. I'm not sure how long we stood there, but it was a little longer than I would have liked.

"You can count on me, Dad," I finally said.

"Good, Derrick."

I looked towards Synch, whose tail was a blur as she made her way under the tall grass. There was no mistaking her body language, there was no mistaking the frenetic ring to her little Swiss bell—a pheasant was close at hand. I took a step, maybe two in her direction.

Dad reeled me back in.

"Son…second thing."

"Just a second, Dad. Synch has got one going, here." I trotted in her direction, not thinking about Dad, his trust, his shady clients in the oil business, or anything else in the world. My every attention was focused on my little dog, and the mayhem that was about to occur. She was hustling in the yellow grass, a fireplug on those short, stubby legs. I watched her dash right, then left. She lost the scent for a second, and doubled back in a rabid panic. Down the ditch she went, to where an immense clod of black earth fell to the creek's edge, and several mounds of grass that had enjoyed a bountiful summer. Synch plied them all, like the shell game at a carnival.

She sprang.

She sprung.

Eanie.

Meanie.

Miney.

Moe!

The ditch erupted with the colors of a circus clown. A pair of roosters, both cackling mad, tore out of the yellow grass, grabbing air with each powerful stroke of their wings. Despite the rush of adrenalin, the splash of color and the hurried getaway, I still had an excellent chance at getting one, or the other. Maybe both.

If only I hadn't forgotten the gun at the fencepost where Dad and I had our little chat.

It was another dumb move on my part.

I watched the roosters gain speed and velocity.

I couldn't believe they were getting…

Bang!

The first rooster somersaulted.

Bang!

The second crumpled in the autumn chill.

I looked at Dad and couldn't believe my eyes. He stood

there in the yellowing corn, pee-stained trousers and all, the family shotgun in his hands.

Smiling.

He was smiling.

"All right, Dad!" I howled. "That was awesome!"

He opened the action on the gun, sending the spent shotshells flinging in a baby puff of gun smoke.

"You, you forgot gun, Derrick. Second thing I was tell you."

"I know it." I laughed. "But you haven't forgotten how to use it." I walked in his direction, laughing, and admiring the man I admired my whole life. The guy bailed me out again. Only this time, the stakes weren't very high.

I gave him a high five.

And then I patted him on the back.

Hard.

Then it was me that wanted to hug.

So we did.

Probably longer than what he wanted.

It was a strangely ironic scene. I was gushing with pride. Even though Dad had probably killed hundreds of pheasants in his lifetime, these two were special for me because of his diminished mental capacity. The shots—both of them—were as pure and true as ever, despite his vision that lacked depth perception, and all the things wrong with his head. And poor Dad, dealing with his stroke-induced dementia, still had the wherewithal to remember the gun I had left behind.

In his younger days, he might have chided me for forgetting the gun. In his younger days, he might have reminded me that the gun was a family treasure, and I should be more responsible. Not today. He handed me the gun for the second time in several hours, and patted me on the back. And as Synch carefully gathered up the second rooster in her graying muzzle and trotted proudly to us, I looked at Dad in the early winter dim. His chin was a crinkled bulb; his lip flinching slightly.

Dad was crying.

So was I.

The scene was one I'll never forget.

We'd have to wait until nearly dinnertime to tell Mom all about our little adventure at the back of the farm. She left a note on the kitchen table that she had run to town.

"There's chili in the crock pot for lunch, and cold cuts are in the ice box," she wrote. *"Dad likes his sandwiches with mayonnaise on both sides of the bread, mustard on top of the cheese. We're all out of pumpernickel bread, but there's a loaf of rye thawing on the counter."*

It was just like Mom to look after the men in her life. She had everything planned for us, and the scent of her wonderful chili filled the old farmhouse and spilled into the air outside.

Dad took off his hunting pants in the laundry room, and came back to the kitchen table dressed in a bathrobe.

It was almost routine—as if he had gotten used to the bouts of incontinence and had planned for it accordingly.

The rye bread was thawed and nearly fresh-out-of-the-oven delicious. There's nothing like a hearty bread with a rich, chewy crust. It makes the best sandwiches, the best noontime meal. I think Dad was waiting for me to make his lunch for him, but I never made any gesture. If the guy could shoot two roosters lickity-split, he certainly could put together a ham and cheese sandwich.

Two of them, in fact, piled high with honey-baked ham, cheddar cheese wrapped in white butcher's paper, and sliced dill pickles. And two bowls of chili. And an apple he picked from the tree near the rear of the barnyard. And then, for dessert, he warmed a cinnamon roll he didn't have for breakfast.

I was beginning to understand what Mom meant by his episodes of compulsive eating. I think he would have stayed there at the kitchen table all afternoon, if I didn't suggest that he turn on the television to see who was playing football.

While he napped, I cleaned the gun and both pheasants. Synch balled up on the little throw rug near the sink. She twitched and fidgeted in her sleep, surely replaying the hunt that had just taken place. It must be fun for a dog to hunt, to smell birds and, in her case and for springer spaniels everywhere, to want to spring when the scent of game is near. It must be a satisfying sensation to scoop one up in your mouth and bring it lovingly back to your master's hand.

Synch looked as proud of those pheasants as Mom did of the bowl of melon or the pot of chili.

On the way home from church Sunday morning, we stopped for a paper. The *Lansing Daily Press* had a story that caught my eye. It showed up on the left side of the front page, in a long column, bordered by a small line that separated it from the rest of the stories. There was no by-line, but the Associated Press took credit for the piece. *Alma man implicated in 30-year mystery.*

I read the headline twice, just to make sure of what I was reading.

> *Alma man implicated in 30-year mystery.*
>
> *Ira G. Kaminsky, 70, from Alma, Michigan, is at the center of an investigation involving the disappearance of Max Hermes, who vanished in the summer of 1980. Police never found his body, but have reopened the case after receiving an anonymous tip.*
>
> *Law enforcement officials have begun excavating a small wooded area on the back of the abandoned Shell Oil Refinery on the outskirts of Alma. Hermes was Kaminsky's replacement at the Shell Oil Company during the 1970s.*

The story nearly blew me away.

No wonder Kaminsky was so upset! He told me about Hermes off the record, and now it appears as if I betrayed his confidence.

Granted, the story didn't say much, but then again, what's not said may be just as important as what is.

All of a sudden, I felt really lucky to have only been escorted to my vehicle. Roger seemed like the type of guy who could do a lot worse. And take pride in it.

It was time for me to tuck my tail between my legs and head for cover. It was time for me to set aside my journalistic impulses, and get out of Dodge.

It was time to pack my bags and head west—into that fertile prairie where people still lift a finger or two off the steering wheel when they pass a vehicle on the road; where the farms still have brushy pasture lanes, and grassy places that hide pheasants by the score. I needed to get away, if for no other reason than to clear my mind of Ira Kaminsky, my father, my ex-wife, and the story of Judge Deborah Noyes.

Iowa was calling me.

In her own quiet way, disguised by the scent of hogs and cattle, the dust from gravel roads, and the bustle of America at harvest time, Iowa was calling me. She invited me on the whim of a distant memory, where a long walk in a hearty, corn-filled land can make a man so thankful to be alive.

In my wildest dreams I never would have thought that the long walk would lead to madness—that a pleasing walk in an early winter cornfield could turn into the discovery of a dead body.

Just when I wanted to get away from my troubles in Michigan, my troubles followed me west to dear, innocent Iowa.

My life would never be the same.

Fourteen

CAROLYN ST. PETER wasn't the best housekeeper in the world. Her kitchen counters were covered in clutter: coupons, sale flyers, newspaper clippings and magazines opened to features that she must have started reading, but never got around to finishing. I noticed the plain, giant box of "clear plastic wrap" beneath the linoleum cupboards and how it appeared to be an unsightly fixture in her array.

Carolyn didn't let my request for a piece of pecan pie interrupt the tasks she had to accomplish. She went back to the kitchen counter, and weighed clumps of hamburger into one-third pound handfuls. She was halfway through the process of turning a ten-pound plastic bag of ground cow into a handsome stack of hamburgers, all individually packaged in clear plastic wrap.

Iowa is meat-and-potatoes land. Eat hearty. Live hearty. Hold dear the promise of a new day, and take solace in your accomplishments when it's all through. Package your hamburger into one-third pound portions so they'll always cook evenly, and thaw with the same regularity when it's time to whip up a meatloaf or a batch of sloppy Joes.

Carolyn and Emmert had a hard time digesting the notion that their neighbors may have been involved in some sort of wrongdoing. Almost everybody in rural Iowa is honest and hardworking. Murders are unheard of and white-collar crime is as rare as hen's teeth.

But that's not to say that they wouldn't take advantage of a situation if it happened to present itself. There was no telling who may have taken some of Cigan's free gas. At three-something a gallon, fuel has become a treasured commodity. And tractors burn a ton of it.

I wouldn't put it past Emmert—or any other farmer—to fill up his tractors and then call the police.

It's human nature, I think.

Even though Emmert and Carolyn seemed like really nice folks, I really didn't know them that well. If they were like the farmers in Michigan, they probably got a little aggressive on their taxes, and fudged the numbers on the government-sponsored crop subsidies.

I asked Emmert who could have killed Cigan.

He shook his head. They both did. The St. Peters were as confused as I was.

"I mean, there are always people out there in the summer," Emmert said. "Migrants. Lots of migrants."

Emmert got up from the table and walked across the ancient linoleum floor to the kitchen sink. He rinsed his coffee cup with cold water and knocked a pair of aspirin from the bottle on the sill.

"The property is owned by a seed company, MNM, out of Illinois. They bought the land, the farm, from the VanOsselears three years ago. It's happening all over the countryside," he said. "The little family farms are gone. It's turning into big business."

Emmert swallowed his aspirin, and chased them both with a gulp of water.

"Nobody wants to farm anymore in Iowa. There used to be four families to a square mile, now we're lucky to have one or two."

He shook his head.

"The average farmer is like me—in their seventies—with nobody to take over the farm. Watch the paper, Derrick. There's an estate auction every day, almost. Big business steps in and buys the land, bulldozes the farmhouse or uses it to house migrants. That's the end of it. They don't care about what happens next. All they want is money."

"What do the migrants do?"

He shook his head again. "They help with the seed corn in the summer. It's really quite interesting, but it's a lot of menial labor. In the spring, the combines plant six rows of female corn and two rows of male corn. When it starts to grow tassels, the migrants go in there and snip off the six rows of female corn, so that the genetically enhanced male corn fertilizes everything. It's labor intensive, but that's what they gotta do. There are mobs of migrants over there, each with hedge trimmers." He massaged the wrinkles on his forehead. "Sometimes we can hear them and their *bomb* fires in the summer. They like to party and have a good time, even when they've been out there working for fifteen or sixteen hours a day."

I had to wonder how he got 'bomb fires' mixed up with 'bonfires.'

"How do you know so much about it, Emmert?"

"Because my son-in-law..." Carolyn glared in his direction. "*Our* son-in-law used to work for that seed company before he went to work for the lobby in Kansas City."

"What else did he tell you?"

Emmert chuckled. "He was in sales, so he really didn't get into the nitty-gritty of how they produced this stuff, or the genetics of it all. All he knew was that MNM's brand of hybrid corn was resistant to drought and rootworm borer."

"Is that a big deal?" I asked him.

"Oh yeah, but even more important is the fact that you can spray MNM's brand of corn with weed killer and it still grows."

"How does that work?"

"It's all genetics, Derrick," he said, reserved. "It's mad scientist kind of stuff."

"Why did he leave the company?"

Emmert hesitated. "The official reason is because he got a better opportunity, but I think there were other reasons."

Carolyn didn't flinch, but I knew when to back off. I was bumping up against a family secret or an unpleasant topic. I decided to change gears.

"What about the gas? The tanker?"

"What about it?" he asked me.

"The tanker was from Illinois, and so was the seed company. Is that just a coincidence?"

"Beats me, Derrick. We mind our business. You know that."

"I know, Emmert, but doesn't it seem odd that of all the places they could have hidden a body, they hid it in a barn you can't even see from the road?"

"You're right, Derrick. Why here?"

"I'd like to ask them that."

Emmert rolled up the sleeves of his shirt. He was getting riled up. Like he wanted to see that justice was served.

"Let's go out there and wait for them. I'll get my gun. Carolyn, we'll need some sandwiches. Maybe a thermos of coffee. We may be a while."

Carolyn laughed, sarcastically.

"You're not going out there, Emmert."

"No, no, no, Emmert, Carolyn's right. I don't think that's a good idea."

I told him about my missing shotgun and the note I left behind.

"They'll call me," I told him. I took my cell phone out of my shirt pocket and laid it on the kitchen table.

"Besides, let's let the cops be the heroes. I think we should be smart about this. "

"What do you mean?"

"I mean, you only get so many chances to break a really big story. And I'm talking now as a reporter, understand?"

They nodded.

"Even though the paper blew my cover, it doesn't mean that I still can't look into Cigan and his disappearance, right?"

"Right."

Emmert sat at the table again. Carolyn put the hamburgers in the freezer, laid her wedding ring on the sill next to the aspirin and washed her hands repeatedly. That old-fashioned, corn-fed Iowa beef has a way of sticking to you. She disappeared into the living room and turned on the stereo. Christmas music.

"But isn't that what the police are supposed to do?"

"Of course it is," I said.

"Don't you think that they should be the ones to investigate?"

"If Cigan were alive, I would say so. But he's dead. I saw it with my own two eyes. They tortured him. They duct taped his hands to the steering wheel, and snipped his fingers off like horns on a steer."

He winced in pain, and cinched one hand over the other. "I know, but…"

"Emmert there's something I need to tell you."

I took a deep breath. And paused. They both sensed the urgency of the situation. The St. Peters huddled around the table and listened intently. It took five minutes or more to explain, but I told them all about Judge Noyes, and the way the cops covered up Peffers' murder.

"Besides," I said, "I told whoever killed Cigan that I would give them twenty-four hours to give me my gun back."

Emmert nodded. "Did you put a time on when the twenty four hours was up?"

His question was a legitimate one, a simple one, but it sent me reeling.

"No." I grimaced, then confessed, "I always thought it would be fun to write that, so I did."

Emmert shook his head. "How are they going to know when their time is up?"

I didn't know what to say. It appeared as if I dropped the ball again.

"They will figure it out."

Emmert shook his head, disappointedly. Just like my dad used to do on occasion.

"Tell me, Derrick. Is this what you mean by 'Let's be smart about this'?"

I laughed.

"Not exactly, Emmert."

"I don't like this, Derrick," he said, the smile quickly dashed from his face. "Not all cops are bad. There may be some in Michigan, but I don't think that's the case here." He rubbed the wrinkles over his eyebrows for emphasis. "Besides, you're putting our safety in jeopardy."

"What do you mean?"

"If you left your gun at the barn, they're going to realize that someone was out there hunting, and the only way to access their property is from one of the neighbors. That leaves us, and the Baackens down the road."

I frowned.

"They may be watching us right now."

Emmert got up from the table again and pulled the binoculars from the top of the refrigerator. He raised them to his eyes and looked north, towards the Baackens'. South was no better; his vision was swallowed by the harrowing snow.

Just then, my phone rang. It startled Emmert and Carolyn. Me, too, until I realized it was the *Evening Journal*, back home.

"Derrick, it's Colleen. What's going on out there?"

I got up from the table, and walked to the mudroom, with all its clutter. It was quiet, almost private.

"What do you mean?" I asked her.

"I mean, Byron's running this big story back here about you and the trouble you're in."

"He is?"

"Yeah, he is. *Former Journal reporter wanted in Iowa.* How does that grab you, Derrick?"

I didn't know what to say. I should have known that he would do something like that. It was almost expected.

"Let me guess. There's my photo in there, too, right?"

"I haven't seen the layout yet, just Byron's copy. He wrote the story all by himself." She was whispering, and she talked really fast. "It's going in tonight's paper, front page."

I let the image of me on the front page sink in.

"Well…"

"Well what, Derrick? He's quoted some state trooper named Upah out there. Do you need a lawyer?"

"No, no," I said. "If I do, I'll call Dad."

"I hate to see your career go down the tube."

"Don't worry."

Our conversation was a brief one. She had to go. I had to run. But between the lines, I knew that Colleen still cared about me. About my career. My well-being. I never thought to ask her about Kaminsky and whether or not they found the remains of Max Hermes.

All of a sudden I realized that there was just as much going on back home as there was in Iowa.

Before I could open the door from the mudroom my phone rang again. Walter Claety was riled up.

"I got a couple cops here from Lansing, Derrick," he said. I could hear the stress in his voice. "Some special assistants to the director at headquarters. They're here, at the paper, and they're asking me all sorts of questions about you."

His voice was muffled, as if he cupped his hand over the receiver.

"Like what?"

"Like 'where the hell are you?' that's what."

"What else?"

"Like what you know about that judge who died, and the guy who killed her. They want to see everything you've written, and want to access the computer system. They want to see everything we've published since Labor Day."

"Show 'em."

"I don't want to show them!" he shouted. "They've got two patrol cars in front of the building, with the lights on." He was rambling. "I got half the town poking their heads inside the shop, asking if everything is okay. You'd think I was handing out five-dollar bills."

"That's good, Walter. A little controversy will help sell newspapers."

"I don't want to hear that!"

"What?" I asked him.

"I don't like controversy. I don't like cops in my building, asking questions."

"Walter, just tell them that I am out of town, and I won't be back for a few days. Get their business cards and I will call them when I get back, okay?"

"Yeah, yeah."

"Oh, and Walter," I said. "I'll have a really good pheasant hunting piece for you by Thursday's deadline."

He didn't even say goodbye.

But Emmert did. To Carolyn.

"We're going to go for a drive," he said. "Not sure when we'll be home."

Emmert corralled me in the mudroom and looked me over. He sized me up. I looked too much like an out-of-towner, he told me. The blaze orange hunting cap would draw too much attention, as well. He directed me back to his cache of jackets, caps, coveralls and goulashes. He let me borrow a canvas jacket and a faded-green John Deere cap.

"Here," he said. "If you're going to blend in with the community, you're going to have to dress like one of us."

Fifteen

EMMERT CAME UP with the idea that I should follow him to his brother's farm three miles farther south and a half-mile east. As we neared the intersection of two brushy-looking fencelines—one on each side of the road—a rooster pheasant trotted across the gravel in front of us, his tail cocked high and his little feet scrambling a million miles-an-hour. I reached for my gun, as if it was an amputated appendage, but it was still gone. And it made me mad.

My forgetfulness still made me mad.

Emmert told me to park my Suburban in the drive shed, so that the rear bumper was against the back wall. That way, nobody could see that I was from Michigan. He didn't mention it, but I knew what he was thinking. He didn't want anyone to read my vanity plate I concocted on the day I graduated from college.

For a graduation present, Dad helped me with the financing for my new—well, almost new—pickup truck. It was one of those Ford Rangers. Manual transmission. No air. AM radio. Not a lot of truck, but not a lot of payment, either. And that was a good thing, too. Journalism majors fresh out of college aren't exactly in high demand, especially those with a mediocre grade point average and whose college career spanned three sitting presidents. But after all those years, the changed majors at two different universities, I finally graduated. I did it. I did it. And so, when I went to the Secretary of State's office to register my prized new pickup, "I did it" seemed like the vanity plate that was most appropriate.

Ten days later, when the padded envelope appeared in the mailbox, I was so excited to put it on my new truck. The excitement quickly faded however when I opened the envelope and "IDIDIT" somehow came back as "IDIOT."

When I went back to the Secretary of State's office, the lady behind the counter said that it wasn't their problem that they couldn't read my writing. It would cost another seventy-five bucks, and a special registration fee to get it corrected. I didn't have the money then, nor would I for a long time, so I decided to let it go. For years and years, I was an "idiot," but as the Iowa authorities looked for a Michigan man and his unusual license plate, I was thankful that the "IDIDIT" wouldn't give them any extra motivation.

Emmert has never noticed my license plate, or has chosen not to mention it. Just as well.

Carolyn said she'd keep an eye on Synch until we returned, just as long as she behaved herself.

Emmert said he wanted to help me with my investigation.

"If you want to be a reporter, I'll help you," he told me. "I'll show you around, but you just gotta leave us out of it, understand?"

I nodded.

"We had nothing to do with it, and we want to keep it that way."

We were bouncing along in Emmert's pickup truck, an early nineties Ford, with dust on the dashboard nearly an eighth-of-an-inch thick, and a cinnamon-scented air freshener dangling from the rearview mirror. Fords always make that odd-sounding whine when they turn the corner. I could hear it inside the cab and it reminded me of the times I spent with my dad, back on the farm. If it were twenty-five years ago, we could have been on our way to a baseball game, or a school function. Emmert made me feel comfortable, as if I was family.

When we drove past the same brushy fence lines, Emmert asked me if I spotted the rooster that dashed across the road in front of him.

"Of course I saw it," I told him. "How could I miss him?"

Emmert laughed. "I was waiting for you to slam on the brakes, but then I remembered that you don't have a gun."

He looked across the cab in my direction and smiled.

"You gotta come to Iowa with a spare. I got one behind the seat if we see another one. It's a four-ten, about that long."

He spread his hands so they were twenty inches apart—much too short for a real shotgun, but I think he did that to emphasize how short it really was.

"The shells are in the glove box."

"Why didn't you shoot it, Emmert?"

"I don't know."

"Don't you eat pheasant?"

"Of course. I've had hundreds of them. Thousands. When Leon and I were kids there were a lot more than there are now."

"Seriously?"

Emmert took off his work gloves and sat them on the seat near his right hip, next to the garage door opener that had a piece of duct tape stretched across the center.

"Things were different then. There was much more cover. More weedy areas. The corn wasn't as tall or as healthy as it is now, because they didn't have herbicides or fertilizers that they do today. There wasn't this genetically modified corn that can grow in the Mojave Desert. We had more pasture lanes and ponds and areas with cattails. We got birds today, but nothing like there was. My dad shot three hundred and sixty-five one season." Emmert was chuckling. "Said he wanted to have a pheasant for every day of the year."

"You had pheasant every day?"

"No, no, but that's only because there were ten kids. We needed five roosters just to feed us dinner. We ate it like chicken, and that was back in World War II, when shells were hard to come by. Dad was a good shot. Know how many shells it took him?"

"No," I said, anxiously.

"You're not going to believe this, three hundred and seventy five."

I laughed at the enormity of his father's success, if not the exaggeration.

"He only missed ten birds. He was a great shot. Great hand-eye coordination." Emmert laughed. "We used to tease him and say that if he enlisted in the infantry, the war would have been over in a matter of weeks. But even after the war, times were tough. When I started hunting by myself, Dad was frugal with his shells. He only gave me three shells at a time and would tell me, 'Here's three shells, now bring me back three of something.' And he was serious, too."

Emmert's story lasted the three miles back to the VanOsselear's place.

"Here's where those migrants lived," he gestured with his hand and pointed a finger. "Looks barren now."

The farmhouse wasn't exactly boarded up, but the shades were drawn, and the snow had drifted slightly against the front and side doors. Emmert slowed the truck to a crawl.

"Somebody's been here, though." He pointed down, to where the gravel road met the driveway. "See how the mud on their tires is now scattered on the road? Somebody's been here."

I looked down and saw what he was talking about. It wasn't much of a clue, considering the snow, but it was a clue, nonetheless.

"I think you're going to get your gun back before you know it."

His truck lurched ahead, compliments of a sticky clutch and a manual transmission. We were on our way again.

"Hand me your plat book. Let's go check out the other parcels of land that belong to MNM."

The second and third places we looked at were the same as the first: nearly boarded up, and shrouded in the season's first coating of snow.

"Maybe they went back to the homeland," he said. "I don't see them anywhere."

"What are we looking for?"

"Those migrants. They killed that driver and stole his gas."

I looked at Emmert and the way he leaned over the steering wheel. His eyes darted from the road, to me, to the ditches on either side. Emmert was looking for pheasants as we plodded along the snow-covered gravel roads. I watched him drive and the way there was no urgency in anything he did. He raised an index finger off the steering wheel when he passed an oncoming vehicle.

But Emmert seemed to be resigned to the fact that the migrants were the ones responsible for Cigan's murder.

"Emmert, you can't assume they did it. There's an old saying in the newspaper business about the word assume."

"What's that?"

"It makes an ass out of you and me. Get it? Ass, you, me..."

He smiled. "I get it, but who else could it be?"

"That's what we've got to find out," I said.

His truck lurched to a halt.

"What are you doing?" There was nobody around. No farmhouses. No MNM. No migrants. I looked in the rearview mirror. No cops or game wardens. Iowa lay before us in sections. A field of picked corn. Another of beans. No ditches or fencelines. Nothing, nothing, nothing, except for the weeds on either side of the road.

We were all alone.

"Get out."

I looked at Emmert. He clenched his teeth.

"What?"

"Jump out."

I reached for the door handle, expecting that he might pull a weapon and admit to Cigan's murder. It would be just like me to stumble onto his murder scene. No wonder he didn't want to call the police; he was the one who did it, and I was the one to foil his plans. I thought about running. About hiding. About using Emmert's truck for cover if he pulled a handgun.

It was hardly the case.

"Reach behind the seat and grab the gun."

I breathed a sigh of relief, opened the door, flicked the lever for the seat and found a remnant of a shotgun lying there. No gun case, no protective sock. It was lying in the dust with the vice grips and cotter pins and Phillips-head screwdrivers. It was only about two feet long, because it no longer had a stock, but a pistol grip instead.

"Grab some shells out of the glove box," he whispered. "Two poles back, corn side of the road. There's a rooster. Maybe two."

I glanced down the road. A hundred yards away, a telephone pole stood in silence, a clump of weeds sprouting at its feet. All I had to do was walk down the road, approach the pole and flush the birds, Synch-style. Perfectly legal. Perfectly Iowa.

Emmert's four-ten was a pump. As I walked down the road to the telephone pole, I sent one little shell up the magazine, racked it quietly into the chamber, then pushed two more into place. *Surely one shot out of three would be true,* I thought. I raised the gun awkwardly to my shoulder. It was nearly impossible to aim because it was so short. Emmert's gun was built for instinctual shooting. Don't even try to aim. Just let 'er fly.

Twenty seconds later I was at the pole. Down the ditch I went. I found my footing at the bottom, amongst the weeds and stalks of canary grass. All at once, the place erupted. A big, handsome rooster boiled out of the grass, its tail as long as a hockey stick. I raised the gun and fumbled for the safety. There was none, so I fired and fired and fired. I could hear each shot *whack* the corn stalks; each ounce of lead puff the snow. The first shot was behind and high, the second low and left. The third was nothing more than a Hail Mary—a prayer that went unanswered. The rooster soared across the corn. I watched him coast, flap his wings and coast again.

Emmert backed up to greet me. "I gave you three shells, now give me three of something." He laughed. "Dad would be very disappointed."

"Sorry, Emmert."

"Come on. You're probably not used to shooting a little gun like that."

"You mean without a stock? Or a safety?" I laughed. "You're right."

"It's deadly out the window of a combine. Pheasants, quail, coyotes—you name it."

"I bet."

"I'll take the next bird, what do you say?"

"That would be fine."

Emmert told me to leave the gun up front, between us on the bench seat. "Might as well pull those shells out of the glove box and lay them on the seat. Give me a few minutes and we'll see another one."

It was actually quite a little while before we found the next pheasant. We visited three more parcels of MNM's property. Two of the three had no farmhouses at all, just brand new metal grain silos erected on the cement or stone foundations from the departed houses. They were bright and shiny, and had steel fabricated pipes sticking left and right from the tops. "That's where they store the grain in the fall, and the seeds in the spring. Everyone buys seed from MNM, because they practically have the market cornered."

"Why's that?"

"Because if you don't buy the seed from them, you might end up in court."

"Come on, Emmert?"

"I'm serious. Ask the Everdeens in New English. They got real trouble. Have about ten kids, and four of them are handicapped. The two youngest really bad. They lived next to MNM, but they didn't buy their seed, because they really couldn't afford it. They just replant the same seed from the same plants over and over."

"What's the deal with the lawsuit?"

"MNM sued the Everdeens for patent infringement."

"How's that?"

"MNM owns the patent on the DNA of the corn that's resistant to weed killer."

"How do they do that?"

"It's like anything else, they just prove it."

"How did they know the Everdeens were using that brand of corn?"

"They tested it, and when the Everdeens failed to concede and buy their product, MNM sued them."

Emmert was driving again. To the meat packing plant.

"You wanna see what life is like for these migrants; wait 'til you see what's going on there. They busted up the union workers who earned eighteen bucks an hour. The Mexicans make eight-fifty and ship half of it back to the homeland. With the other half, they support their babies born here who are automatically U.S. citizens."

"Wait a second," I thought. "Why did you say the Everdeens kids were handicapped?"

"Because they were. They are."

"Why is that important?"

"There are some that say that MNM's corn causes birth defects and cancer."

"Why don't the Everdeens sue MNM if that's the case?"

Emmert nodded his head.

"You would think that, wouldn't you? But that's the thing, MNM is big business. They got unlimited resources, deep pockets that can outspend anybody around here. They would tie things up in court for decades. No lawyers around here would take on their case because they know that MNM would outspend them."

We were on the paved road that runs between What Cheer and Marshalltown. The right-of-ways on either side of the road were wide and grassy, and open to hunting. We drifted past a cut cornfield with a hundred signs in front of it. They were all in a row, as if they were planted there themselves, all advertising MNM's brand of seed.

"Here's more of their land. They advertise like crazy on busy roads like this, when there's a healthy crop of corn. If you scratch an Iowa farmer, they'll tell you that they'd rather grow corn than anything else. And MNM, they got the market... there's one."

Emmert slammed on the brakes, and tossed the truck to the edge of the road. An instant later, he had the truck door half open, the four-ten loaded and his gloves covering his chubby little hands. I watched him walk along the gravel shoulder, eyes peeling the ditch, gun armed and at the ready. Sixty yards later, he reached down for a handful of gravel and tossed it into the weeds beneath him. It worked. The noise, the commotion, scared them into flight. All of them. Emmert swung on each departing hen, but didn't shoot until the rooster he spotted from the road tried to get away. He sent it flailing into the barbed-wire fence, just a heartbeat away from the MNM's pronouncement,

"The seed that feeds." It was an amazing display of shooting. He didn't aim. He just fired from the hip. Dad would have been impressed. Anybody would have. It was incredible.

Emmert wasn't thrilled. In fact, when he walked up the sloped embankment, rooster dangling lifelessly from his hand, he had to catch his breath. The years, the weight he carried under his coveralls, were cursing him now. I thought about backing the truck to meet him, or fetching the bird myself, but it all seemed so easy. All he had to do was walk twenty yards to the fence, gather his bird, and walk up the small hill to the road.

Emmert was still huffing when he dropped the rooster in the bed of the pickup and opened the driver's side door.

"Whew," he said. "That was hard work."

His face was beet red and beads of sweat clung to his forehead like the dew on an August melon. I let him simmer there for a second. Emmert needed a break in the same way Dad's old Harley did when I drove it to the bank last summer. I complimented him on his shooting. I told him about Dad and the way he likes to pheasant hunt, too.

Emmert smiled and absorbed it all. He didn't try to shake it off, or dismiss the accomplishment. It was no big deal. That's how a lot of guys go after pheasants: drive around, jump out, shoot 'em dead.

It took several miles before Emmert's face regained a healthy color, and he was in the mood to talk.

"MNM is well connected," he said. "I remember that one of their researchers had to write a report for the Food and Drug Administration about the safety of growth hormones in our food."

Emmert pulled a red handkerchief from the top pocket of his overalls and blew his nose. He folded it in half and wiped it again.

A white and brown state police car approached us from the opposite direction. I noticed the wide brimmed hat and the sunglasses behind the steering wheel. Emmert didn't lift a finger, but he did raise an eyebrow to the sideview mirror. It kept going.

"The researcher did such an excellent job on the report that the FDA hired her. And here's where things get interesting. Her first task on the job was to approve the report that she wrote while she worked at MNM." Emmert laughed. "MNM never had any trouble with the FDA that's for certain."

"Nobody said anything?"

"No. The people who hired her at the FDA were well connected too."

"How do you know so much about this, Emmert? Was it your son-in-law that told you these things?"

"I can't say for sure, Derrick. You understand."

I nodded. "Of course, but why do you think it was the migrants who killed that truck driver?"

We were interrupted by my cell phone. It was Mom.

"Derrick, I thought you should know that your father has decided that we should have a garage sale."

I took a deep breath. "When did that come about?"

"This morning, after we went out for breakfast and he left the waitress a hundred-dollar tip."

"What?"

"I tried to tell him no, but he insisted. Now he's upstairs putting price tags on all the furniture."

"Mom!"

"I don't know what to do, Derrick. He wants to sell that grand piano that Allison wants. He wants to sell the antique bathtub too."

Emmert looked in my direction but the truck carried on. So did the conversation.

"He said he wants three dollars for the tub, two for the piano."

"Oh, Mom."

"He's losing it, Derrick." Her voice cracked. "I don't know what I should do. He's lost all track of money. What it's worth."

I sighed. "I don't know what you should do. What if you did have a garage sale? Nobody goes to those things in the winter."

"Derrick!"

"Mom, I think you need to really think about getting him some help. Like a nursing home or assisted living situation. Some medicine, maybe? At least look into it before he does something really wrong."

"Oh, God. Don't say that."

"Mom, you'd better look into it. *We'd* better look into it."

She didn't answer me right away, but asked when I would be home. "Soon, Mom, soon. Hang in there."

I hung up the phone and bowed my head. Dad's dementia was revealing itself in many different ways. He was confused. Confrontational. Something had to give. The guy lost all sense of what a dollar was worth. He forgot about giving the bathtub and the piano away to my sisters. He was on the verge of doing something bad, I could tell. And poor Mom, she was stuck in the middle. We all were.

"Sounds like you got a lot on your dance card," Emmert told me.

"You could say that. Ever have a parent with dementia?"

"No," he said. "My dad died suddenly. Heart attack, we think. And Mom had sugar. Had to have her feet amputated, and that was pretty much the beginning of the end. Her circulation was so bad, they kept coming back for more chunks." Emmert reached across my knee to the glove compartment and pulled out a bottle of corn husker's lotion.

"Want a slug?"

"No thanks, Emmert."

I watched him pour a teaspoonful into the palm of his hand, carefully screw the top back on, and reach across my knee again.

"I wish there was something I could do for you, Derrick," he said, as he worked the lotion into his hands. "It must be hard to see that happen."

"It is."

I turned my head to the scenery—to the rolling hills, the pleasing contours, the vast openness of Iowa. The more I see, the more I think of it as the perfect getaway. Dad would love it here. All that ground. All those crops and tractors, ripe for tinkering and puttering. He wouldn't have time to get confused, or so I hoped.

When Emmert pulled into a gas station on the outskirts of Marshalltown, I handed Emmert a twenty-dollar bill for fuel, then visited the men's room on the side of the building. The door was locked, so I waited patiently for several minutes outside. I could hear the conversation inside, but I couldn't understand it. Never was any good at Spanish. There were two of them, maybe three, not counting the children who were crying and babbling the way kids do. The adult voices were quick and rambled. Female. They had places to go, people to see. The important stuff.

I heard the toilet seats slam, and the blast of water. The voices moved to the sink, and I heard the hum from the automatic hand dryer, one at a time. All the while, the conversation buzzed along at a frenetic pace. They were getting closer and closer.

At last they opened the door. Senoras. All in their early twenties. All carrying navy blue jumpsuits draped over an arm, a baby or a toddler in the other. I smiled graciously, but didn't say anything. My eyes turned to the children, and how their coats were too small or too big. Some of them had spaces between the bottom of their sweatpants and the tops of their socks. But that all paled in comparison to the little kids' faces. Their smiles weren't smiles at all, but wide, mangled clefts.

Oh God, I thought. *How horrible.*

It almost took my breath away; the cutest kids, and the most ghastly deformities.

I hated to stare, but I couldn't pry myself away from the image. It was horrible. They opened the side doors of a van, and piled inside. No car seats. No seat belts. The smallest children sat on laps and became involuntary airbags for the adults. I had never seen anything like it. And hoped that I never would again.

Emmert was waiting for me at the pickup when I returned from the restroom.

"Where are we headed, Emmert?"

"You'll see," he said.

Three blocks later, he pulled into a meat packing plant. It was a long, barn-like structure, with sections of wooden fencing near several gangways that led inside. About a dozen pigs, oblivious to their impending fate, looked at us through the wooden slats as we exited Emmert's pickup and headed for the office door.

I tugged on his arm, "Emmert, what are we doing?"

"Just watch me. We're going to talk to them about custom butchering a pen-full of our hogs."

The pigs behind me must have overheard our conversation because they oinked and squealed as if they were trying to organize a jailbreak.

Emmert was quite the schmoozer. Before I knew it, he had the woman behind the counter talked into giving us a mini-tour of the plant. She was half-salesman, half-encyclopedia.

"Iowa slaughters more hogs than any other state of the union," she said, proudly.

The plant was loud and mechanized. Mexicans were everywhere—on forklift trucks and behind handcarts. I looked up and saw giant, stainless steel hooks on a chain conveyor. They rattled and bounced as if they were the carts on a roller coaster. But this wasn't a fun place. This was all business. When we turned the corner, the hooks on the conveyor were filled with pigs, hung by their chins, disemboweled. Where the conveyor met a stainless steel ramp, the hooks detracted and the pigs slid down the metal slide. Waiting there was a gang of Mexicans, in their dark blue jumpsuits, their head nets and their razor sharp knives.

"Most of the pork we handle goes right to the factories

that make hot dogs, lunchmeat, and other processed foods," she said.

The first team of Mexicans eased the pigs' legs into an enormous press, where it severed the hocks into a blue, plastic bin.

I couldn't watch.

Emmert seemed to relish the process. I thought he was going to jump right in, roll up his sleeves, and help separate the chops from the roasts.

I left. And waited in the truck.

Emmert was bound and determined to hang the murder of Charles Cigan on the migrant workers of Iowa. It was old-fashioned prejudice. The Mexicans were different than the other people in Iowa. They talked funny, and kept to themselves. And the uniforms set them apart from the others in the state. They were pawns of MNM, who owned the meatpacking plant. The Mexicans would work for eight-fifty an hour; the Iowans wouldn't do it for twice that amount. The migrants were blamed for the loss of jobs, and now they were getting blamed by Emmert for the murder of Charles Cigan.

Emmert wasn't buying the idea that there could be somebody other than the Mexicans responsible for Cigan's murder. On the way to Leon's farm that evening, he said that the Mexicans would use the gas in Cigan's tanker to run their vehicles for a year.

I told him it was something bigger than that. Some sort of cover up, some sort of revenge.

"Why else would they snip off his fingers?"

Emmert disagreed, and offered Leon's couch as the best spot for me to sleep.

"There are blankets in the linen closet. Turn up the heat if you want to. I'll come by and pick you up before eight tomorrow morning."

I walked Emmert out to his truck and thanked him for what he had done. Although the presidential caucuses were only twenty-four hours away, and his tour of central Iowa had nothing to do with it, he helped me to get a handle on what life is like in the little state that plays such a big part of American politics.

"Tomorrow we'll get after more of your story," he told me. "But if I were you, I'd clean your pheasant before the cats find it." He reached in the back of his truck and underhanded me his bird. It hit me in the breadbasket like a lateral in a football game.

"Thanks," I said, and waved goodbye.

Emmert waved back, and cranked the wheel. His old Ford whined in the radiance of Leon's mercury light. He honked the horn once for good measure and once for good luck. I waved back, Iowa-style.

I looked down at the rooster Emmert gave me. It was stiff and lifeless, but that was okay. They're still beautiful, with all those colors, all those feathers. I admired his spurs, nearly a quarter of an inch long and sharp as a tack. This bird was an old one. They don't get spurs like that in the first year. I held it up to the mercury light and guessed its weight at about three or four pounds. I thought for a second about getting it mounted, how much it would cost, and where I would keep it—at the newspaper or my house?

But then it hit me. This rooster wasn't a mounter after all. Between its eyes, on top of its head, Emmert's rooster had a strange growth. It was pea-sized, hard and callused, and the feathers were thin and pokey, as if the skin over the growth was stretched like a rubber band. I didn't want to touch it or, Lord forbid, eat it. I didn't want anything to do with it.

Emmert's account of the Everdeen's handicapped children came to mind.

So did the images of those poor Mexican children with their deformities.

And now a pheasant with a strange growth on its head.

There was more to the story.

There was more to discover.

I had to find out what it was.

Sixteen

I DIDN'T REALLY SLEEP very well that night at Leon's farmhouse. Strange sleeping quarters, and strange surroundings have a way of keeping me on edge. The upstairs creaked and groaned, and the furnace made a funny sound every time it kicked a blast of warm air. I kept waiting for my phone to ring, but it never did.

My gun was doomed. Lost forever, it seemed.

The twenty-four hour deadline I imposed on the ransom note would expire in the morning. And the more I thought about it, there's was no way that they would exchange my gun for my silence. After all, if whoever had my gun read the paper, or watched the news, they would know that it was only a matter of time before the police caught up with me, and the place where Cigan died would be revealed.

My gun was a lost cause. If Dad had it insured with Lloyd's of London, or registered with the Bureau of Alcohol, Tobacco and Firearms, I wouldn't know where to start the process of filing a claim.

Emmert laughed when he said that recovering my gun would be a "long shot."

Early the following morning he brought the morning newspaper with him. The headline on the front page said it all: "*Police narrow search for Michigan man, Cigan in Keokuk County.*"

"It looks like your cover is really blown now," Emmert laughed.

I shook my head, and laughed along with him.

"I think it's time that we go to the police, don't you?"

He nodded his head. "Mother sent over some bacon and eggs to fry up. Let's have a big Iowa breakfast and then you can go right to the state police post in Oskaloosa. We'll keep an eye after your dog, and if you cooperate with them, you just might make it back here for the caucus this evening."

I listened to him and his plan. The voice of reason and experience.

"What do you say?"

"I'll make some coffee."

"No, no. Sit down," he said. "I'll make the coffee. I'll make breakfast. You read the paper. It's all about you."

It was, too. They knew the motel where I slept the night before, where I bought my license, and some of the places where I hunted. Not only was my cover blown, but all my secret pheasant hunting honey holes too. The farmers never had a wanted man on their farm—and they seemed to relish the thought of telling everyone about it.

The Watsons were quoted as saying, *"Mr. Twitchell hunts our farm every fall, and brings us maple syrup from Michigan."*

I laughed at their sincerity, but almost cried when they said, *"We really don't care for the syrup, so we usually feed it to the pigs."*

The VanBuskirks were just as forthright.

"We met Mr. Twitchell last year, after his truck burned. We had an ad in the paper to sell our Suburban, and he ended up buying it."

I remembered the VanBuskirks. They were nice people and

apparently they remembered me, too. *"He was kind of forgetful, however. Locked the keys inside the vehicle after he took it for a test drive. We had to run all the way home to pick up another set."*

The article went on and on, about where I had been, where I had hunted, and the kind of person I was.

The Oxendales said, *"He's really a nice fellow. Very courteous, but I don't think he's a very good shot. Every time he hunts our place we hear a lot of shooting, but he hardly ever gets any birds."*

I rolled my eyes.

It was time to go to the police.

The gig was up.

Emmert was well into making breakfast when he said I should keep reading.

"It's towards the end of the story," he said.

> *Police got a tip late Monday afternoon from Angel's Pizza in Grinnell. The manager said he received a phone call regarding the missing truck driver.*
>
> *"The phone call was unusual in that the person calling said that they would exchange a misplaced firearm for the pizza parlor's silence in the Cigan matter," said State Police Detective Stanley Upah.*
>
> *"We interviewed all the employees and they have no knowledge about Mr. Cigan. Furthermore, none of them claim to have been missing a firearm. We're not sure if it was a prank call, but we traced the call to a pay phone nearby."*

I looked up at Emmert and the way he jammed his hand on his hip. One eyebrow was higher than the other, and I knew exactly what he was thinking, but I played dumb.

"What?" I asked him.

He picked up a piece of bacon with a fork, flipped it over, and shook his head. The pan sizzled at the notion of fresh meat.

"You didn't put your cell phone's area code on that ransom note, did you?"

My mind began to wander.

"Of course I did. Where's the phone book and I'll prove it to you?"

Emmert laughed.

"Don't bother. I already checked our caller I.D. and the phone book at home. Angel's Pizza has the same number as your cell phone. He rolled his eyes. "The only difference is the area codes."

I buried my head in my hands. "Oh, brother."

Emmert laughed even harder.

So did I. After a while.

"This thing is getting more and more crazy," he said.

"Thank goodness it's almost over," I conceded. "I mean, what else could possibly go wrong?"

Emmert cocked an eyebrow like he did a moment ago, the same way my father used to do when I was growing up.

"Maybe you shouldn't say that, Derrick. There's plenty that could go wrong."

Emmert and I spent the next twenty-five minutes talking about my gun and whether or not I would get it back. He seemed to think that the odds were pretty good. After all, if whoever killed Cigan were willing to negotiate with a pizza parlor, they certainly didn't care much about my missing shotgun.

And when it really came down to it, the gun didn't matter. I mean, it mattered, but not as much as my safety. Dad would rather trade a thousand guns for the safety of his only son. Despite his diminished mental capacity, I was certain of that.

But that's not to say that I really didn't want the gun back. I liked that old double barrel for a variety of reasons. It fit me like a glove and was light and quick, not to mention pretty as a picture. What's more, it carried with it the patina of three generations- both Twichells and Grandpa McSkimming.

As I made my way to Oskaloosa, Radio Iowa was abuzz with the impending caucuses. Iowa's three-term Democratic Governor Wilburn Levitt was expected back in his hometown of What Cheer to cast his vote. His posters were everywhere—on the shoulder of the paved roads, in yards of farmhouses and in the quaint towns that were nothing more than a whistle stop for the railroad companies that hauled Iowa's bounty to bigger and better markets.

Levitt spent most of the fall amassing a war chest of campaign contributions and courting voters in the other early primary states: New Hampshire, Nevada, and South Carolina. His message of smaller government, public accountability, and a get-out-of-Iraq foreign affairs policy was exactly what the nation wanted to hear. He echoed the need for independence from foreign oil, and wanted Iowa to be the first state in the union to have that distinction. Iowa loved him, compliments of the ethanol boom that increased the price of a bushel of corn from a dollar seventy a year ago to nearly four dollars this year. Most of Iowa's farmers are happy, and it shows. Many of them are now able to put away a few dollars if not invest it in new equipment.

But Governor Levitt really didn't have that "polish" that most presidential candidates possess. He could talk, but he couldn't rally the troops, so to speak. He wore nice suits, but they made him appear uncomfortable. There was no buzz about him. No sizzle. He didn't have that swagger, or the good looks that successful politicians need. On the surface, Levitt was squeaky clean. He hadn't had an affair with an intern, or any shady real estate dealings. Of course, he promoted ethanol on a nationwide scale because Iowa stood in line to reap the lion's share of the profits.

The Iowa State Police in Oskaloosa seemed to care less about the caucuses, even though they probably had half the department on overtime because of it. All they wanted to know was where Cigan's body was. When I told them, and drew them a map to the barn, the detective excused himself from the room, certainly giving coordinates to the troopers on the road. And after they let me ramble on and on about exactly what had happened, the interview turned into an interrogation. They wanted me to confess to Cigan's murder.

And I knew they would try that tactic. I had spent enough time at police stations over the years to know that they always are buddy-buddy at the beginning, but then change their tune when your cards are on the table. He accused me of killing Cigan just so I could further my reporting career. Then he accused me of covering up the crime scene with the tractor, the implements, the pigs. But I didn't back down.

"Sure, like I hauled a tractor and all those pigs in the back of my Suburban all the way from Michigan."

I told him about my missing shotgun, and how my cell phone number was the same as the pizza parlor's in Grinnell. I denied every accusation, and even volunteered for the lie detector test.

Round and round we went. He wanted a confession. I said that I wasn't that dumb. He said I was guilty. I said only of being in the wrong place at the wrong time.

Finally, I left. They had nothing on me. I had nothing left to say. There was work to be done, back in What Cheer. I didn't need to ask directions to where the caucuses were being held; the town was crawling with media. National media. Local media. The television stations from Des Moines, and Iowa City. They all gathered outside the county building with their gaudy trucks and their satellite beacons. What Cheer rolled out the red carpet, with a brand new county building compliments of a three-quarters-of-a-million dollar apportionment from Iowa's U.S. Senator the year before. The county building was the nicest and newest building in all of What Cheer. It was made from cinder blocks and trimmed in polished brass. Inside the front doors, an enormous statue of Chief Keokuk greeted the visitors.

For years, the Iowa caucuses were an interest to me, but I really had no idea what they were all about. It was akin to the election of a new pope, complete with the puff of white smoke from the chimney atop the Sistine Chapel. Even though the caucus was a really big deal in my eyes, media credentials weren't as hard to get as I thought they might be. I lined them up earlier in the fall, when I knew my trip would take place.

We occupied the largest room in the county building, which wasn't very big at all. The edge of the room was lined with digital television cameras, all on tripods, all pointed toward the podium. It seemed that half the town was there. Lots of Iowans. Most of them were older. White socks. Dark shoes. Seed caps and work pants. I recognized the fellow with the shrub of a hairline who sold me the hunting license. He recognized me, too, and called me "trouble." I sat in the back row, and watched everyone file inside to the coffee maker and the spread of anise cookies and fig bars that the local women's group baked. The Oxendales were there, and they waved half-heartedly in my direction. I winked, then raised an imaginary pistol in their direction. They got the message when I pulled the trigger and missed again.

I overheard the chairwoman say that they only had a hundred seats, but there were nearly sixty-five reporters. "We've never had a standing-room-only caucus," she said.

The rebuttal was just as plain.

"You've never hosted an Iowa governor who's running for president."

Gradually, the room filled with people, and the chitchat became a quiet roar of conversation. I saw Emmert smile as he told the story-of-stories involving me and the escapades with my shotgun. He had a small gathering around him who were glued to his every word. There was laughter and backslapping.

A young lady sat next to me, dressed in thick, waffle-like leggings under a faded denim skirt. Her camera bag was leather, boxy and looked like it could have been handed down from her beatnik parents. The camera she toted was a nice one, a Nikon, with a long, sleek lens and an impressive flash. I watched her fidget with the light meter, and dial the knobs accordingly. Her fingers reached for the reporter's pad and pen in her front pocket. I reached across her lap and introduced myself.

"Vivian Bruff, *The Times Observer*. Peoria."

"Nice to meet you, Vivian. What brings you to Iowa?"

"The same reason you're here. Governor Levitt and the Cigan matter." She pushed her small, dark glasses against the brow of her nose. No make up. Nearly black eyes.

"I know, but what's the story?" I asked.

"With Governor Levitt or the Cigan guy?"

"The governor," I said. "The guy seems squeaky clean. As clean as the…"

"Wind driven corn chaff?" she suggested.

"Something like that." I smiled. "There's no dirt on him. No mistresses. No shady dealings. A friend of the farmers and the environmentalists."

"What about his aide who committed suicide?" she asked me.

"Didn't hear about that." Vivian knew her stuff. She was more prepared than I was. Imagine that.

"Head of health services. Addicted to prescription drugs. Caught him filling prescriptions for himself."

She brushed her thin, black hair away from her face and I noticed the earrings, three of them in a row, like service buttons on a preacher's lapel.

"The guy just couldn't quit. He couldn't live without them."

"What happened?"

"Hung himself. From the foyer's railing at the capitol."

"Oh, God."

"Yeah. I'm surprised you didn't read about it. A group of a hundred sixth graders were having a field trip that morning, and when they saw his body dangling there, they misunderstood it for the tension between the political parties."

I laughed. "Happens all the time, right Vivian? Right after back-stabbing."

She laughed along with me and together we watched Mr. Levitt enter the caucus, flanked by a pair of Secret Service agents. The faces in the audience turned his way, and the conversations paused. He wore a blue blazer, a harmless checkered oxford and khaki trousers. No tie, and just enough makeup beneath his receding hairline to keep the glare of the lights from beaming off his forehead. He waved and smiled and pointed to faces in the crowd that he thought he recognized.

"Looks like he's been spending some of his campaign contributions," she offered. "Cover Girl paid him nearly fifty grand."

"They did?" I asked.

"Sure. They do testing on rabbits and animals."

"Don't forget the politicians."

She smiled. We were hitting it off, despite the difference in our ages.

"He's doing pretty well for himself. He's raised almost three million dollars." She reached to the inside pocket of her jacket, and whipped out a pamphlet from McNeel, Rothman.

"What's this?"

"It's one of Illinois' biggest lobbying firms. Got offices in D.C. too." A pack of chewing gum appeared out of nowhere. "Want a piece, Jarred?"

"It's Derrick. And no thanks."

"Sorry. You look like a Jarred I used to know. Went to college with him. " Her feet bounced on the chair in front of her, and she sent the gum wrapper skittering underneath. "McNeel Rothman is his biggest contributor. Got all kinds of clients with deep pockets and devious agendas."

Her jaw was moving non-stop. And then the gum cracking began. At every bite.

"Let me guess, MNM is one of their clients."

"Of course. They're huge in Illinois, the Midwest, everywhere. Why do you ask?"

"They're into everything," I said. "Who else are McNeel's clients?"

She didn't have the chance to answer. The caucus chairwoman was at the podium, welcoming the guests, the dignitaries, and all the members of the media.

"Here," Vivian whispered. "Here's a list of their clients. They have to register them all because of the Lobbying Disclosure Act."

Most of the names I didn't recognize. And there were a lot. There were abbreviations and acronyms for causes and political action committees that held very little meaning. Iowa's real estate developers had a huge presence: *Tigua-Con, The Grawburg Group, M&D Investments*. The farming, food, and products community didn't try to conceal anything. They laid it right out there: *John Deere, Swift Premium, Oscar Meyer, and Cover Girl*. There were oil and fertilizer companies, *Shell Oil Company, Exxon*, and a company I had never heard of: *Still Meadows LLC*. There were plenty of Native American tribes represented, too: *the Choctaw from Iowa and Illinois, the Coushatta in Wisconsin, Illinois, and Indiana, and the Odawa and Chippewa from Michigan*. MNM wasn't the only seed company represented.

As my finger passed down the list of others—*Darsch Seeds Inc., Hi-Bred, Great Plains*—Vivian stopped cracking her gum and whispered, "That missing truck driver from Peoria double-crossed the wrong people. That's why he was murdered."

The chairwoman was giving instructions to the delegates, "Township clerks, please pass out the ballots after our speakers..."

"I thought he was from Bettendorf? And how do you know he was murdered?" I asked her.

Vivian stopped chewing, momentarily.

"He *is* from Bettendorf, but the company he works for was in Peoria—one of the hangouts for the mob since the Shelton brothers kept Capone and his gang in Chicago during prohibition."

"And?"

She sat back in her chair and leaned in my direction.

"And anybody that's been gone for more than a week has got to be dead."

I caught a whiff of mint on Vivian's breath and it reminded me of Colleen, and the way she used to taste.

"Besides, from what I hear, Cigan had it coming." She was whispering softly now. "An extortion case gone bad."

"Keep going."

Vivian never looked in my direction. All she did was whisper and snap her gum. I was dialed into the sight, the sound, the smell. The words poured out of her.

"They bought a big block of property on the outskirts of Peoria. The pipeline had a right of way across the property, and the Cigans filled up their tankers before Peoria knew the gasoline was missing. Had a great little racket. Cigan had a number of clients on both sides of the Mississippi that he delivered bootleg gasoline to at a fraction of the cost at the pump."

She took a breath but I interrupted her with a question.

"Didn't Peoria come up short at the end of the day?"

"Heck no," she said. "One tanker is like a drop in the bucket. And besides, it's not like they did it every day. They only did it two or three times a week, in the middle of the night."

My mind was racing again. Her words were remotely familiar. The scheme was just like the one my dad told me about.

Before I had the chance to ask who "they" were, my cell phone rang. I answered it as quietly as I could.

"Morning, Son."

I knew the voice anywhere, the confused time of day.

"Hi Dad," I said. "This isn't really a good time to talk. Can

I call you back?"

"Tell me something." Dad's words were slow. It was almost unbearable. "My fly rod—the one in the static with the Menominee rod case—going to sell at the garage sale."

Dad messed up; his fly rod was in the *attic,* and it had a *mahogany* case.

"Fifty cents," I said, sensing that he wanted an idea of what was the correct price.

"Thanks, that's it."

"Yep. Split bamboo is a dime a dozen."

"Right, a dime for a dozen," he said. "Love you, Son."

I hung up the phone and smiled. There were no voices. No caucus or conversation. My mind was seven hours east on the family farm, with an old man and his diminished mental capacity. Dad was in my head. If he was willing to depart with a six hundred dollar fly rod for fifty cents, there was no telling what else he would do. Mom must have been a wreck. She could only stand so much. First he wanted to sell the Harley for ten dollars. Then the bathtub and the piano. His dementia made him obsessed, and for Dad, his obsession was the garage sale. He—his condition—was pressing, pushing, jabbing us all. Mom and I and everybody else in the family would have to come up with some creative ways to temporarily satisfy his obsession, without giving away the farm. It was like dealing with a child, and it was sad. It was time to think about having him admitted somewhere. Assisted living. A nursing home. Something before he hurt himself, or someone else.

"Everything okay?" Vivian asked me.

I nodded and asked, "How come you know so much about Cigan?"

She didn't miss a beat.

"Because they were always the family to watch in Peoria. They were bullies. The kind of people who would walk across the street just to say something mean to you."

She flipped a page in her note pad and continued scribbling notes. She was good at listening, writing and talking, which is not exactly my strong suit. I have a hard time chewing shoes and tying my gum.

"Charles Cigan pushed my uncle and his cello down the stairs once," she said. "And now that Cigan's gone missing, I've taken an extra special interest in the case."

Governor Levitt had the floor. He thanked everyone for attending and made a joke about the number of television cameras in attendance.

"They look like pigs at the trough, don't they folks? They're all lined up, ready to start eating our corn." Some of the people laughed, politely. Others smiled and looked at their neighbors.

I asked Vivian why she thought that Cigan was involved with extortion.

"It's not that," she said. "He had a nice little arrangement—selling stolen gasoline under the table."

"Was he the one making the money?"

"No, no," she said. "He was only the driver. His father was the one that set up the deals, kept everyone quiet, and made all the money." We both looked to the governor. He raised a hand, a fist, and rested his thumb on top of his index finger for emphasis. I'm not sure what the governor was talking about, because I was so intent on listening to Vivian's story.

"About two weeks ago," Vivian said, "young Charles tells one of the old man's customers that he wants a thousand dollar delivery fee for the gasoline, or else he's going to call the police. The next thing you know, Cigan is missing. He's dead."

The county building erupted in applause, although I'm not sure why.

"Who were his customers?"

Vivian whispered, "That's what and who is at the center of the investigation."

"Apparently the police picked up some dope from Michigan

who knows where Cigan is, but so far the police aren't saying if they found his body." She snapped her gum. "He looks a lot like you, believe it or not."

"You don't say?"

"Yup, saw his picture in the paper," she quipped.

More applause.

The governor was saying all the right things, whatever it was. He turned to the audience and asked, "Who else has a question?"

I never even batted an eye. My hand reached for the ceiling, and despite the blur of well-dressed reporters and their fancy cameras catching every nuance, the governor pointed his sleek, silver ink pen in my direction.

"Yes, you in the back row…in the golf shirt."

I smiled, and stood up proudly. Vivian looked up at me—in admiration, I was certain.

"Yes, Governor, Derrick Twitchell, from the *Alma Recorder*, in Michigan." I glanced down at Vivian, who was anything but impressed. "Thank you for fielding my question."

I felt the cameras pan my way, the eyes of the world upon me. I must have made a great impression, with my note pad, and a spare writing utensil tucked behind my ear.

"Can you tell me, Governor, what's being done to find Charles Cigan?"

The governor looked back at me as if I had just fallen off the turnip truck. He rolled his eyes and shook his head, then he turned to an aide who shrugged his shoulders.

"Anybody else?"

I sat back down to the sound of laughter, from the audience, the reporters, even the Secret Service men.

"What?" I asked Vivian. "He didn't even answer me."

She shook her head.

"If you were paying attention, you would have known he just answered that question. Nice going, Jarred."

Seventeen

The drive from Iowa back to Michigan was uneventful, although it seemed to take much longer than normal. I was torn between the family responsibilities that awaited me at home, and the unpleasantness of the trip that had just passed. It was a disappointing trip. And it all started when I crossed the boundary and trespassed onto Emmert's neighbor's property. If I had only stayed on his side of the line, I would have never found the body, or forgot my gun. I would never have seen the Mexicans and their birth defects, the pheasant with the tumor on his head or made an ass out of myself at the caucus. And what about the caucus? It was interesting, but it wasn't as earth-shattering as I thought it might have been. It was unassuming. It was laid back. Could I ever have expected anything else from dear, sweet Iowa?

I usually drive home from Iowa with a satisfied feeling in my heart. Despite the birds I may have missed, or the times that Synch might have flushed a bird out of range, I always leave Iowa with the notion that I tried my best. And there's something contentedly pleasing about doing your best. Whatever it is.

This year was different. I didn't get in enough pheasant hunting, enough long walks with my aging dog. I only killed two pheasants the first afternoon there, and I had some really bad luck. Some of the bad luck I deserved. Some of it I didn't. Next year, I'd have my way with Iowa that was for certain.

The closer I got to home, the more I dreaded the thought of what needed to be done. Dad needed help. Mom needed help with Dad. We all had to pitch in and make the tough decisions about his well-being. Since I wasn't really anxious to get home, and not really contented with the trip, I took my sweet time. In fact, I dawdled. When I made it to Peoria, I stopped for fuel and bought the last two days' worth of newspapers. Vivian's stories were everywhere. She was a good reporter, even on the pieces that had nothing to do with Cigan. She was very thorough. Detailed. And when it came to covering the Cigan matter, she was particularly motivated. I could see the extra effort she put into the story. I sensed the painstaking way she selected each word.

Her latest story quoted Governor Levitt:

> *"Charles Cigan's disappearance is a top priority in Iowa, and we are sparing no expense in the investigation. We had a tip yesterday (Tuesday) that Cigan and his truck were in Iowa, but his tanker was recovered in the evening at a truck stop in western Illinois."*
>
> *There appeared to be no sign of foul play, although authorities admit that the cab appeared to have been recently cleaned.*
>
> *Authorities found a pair of magnetic bound "Got Milk?" signs behind the rig's seat, which matched the dirt outline on the truck's doors. Police theorize that Cigan must have put the milk signs on the side of the rig anytime he wanted to create confusion as to the tanker's contents.*

> *Sam Garfield Cigan, father of Charles Cigan, owned property east of Peoria, where Shell Oil Company maintained a gasoline pipeline. Authorities obtained a search warrant and found the pipeline, stretched twenty-three feet over the Illinois River bottom. The pipeline was buried underground, except where it crossed the river. Police found a cast iron valve on the underside of the pipeline—adding credence to the theory that Charles Cigan was involved in some sort of black market, gasoline conspiracy.*

The governor merely regurgitated what Vivian told me at the caucus. Her theory then was still relevant now: whoever was buying gasoline from Cigan probably had an idea of why he was murdered. It had to be something big. I couldn't imagine that Cigan would be out hawking fifty gallons here or there as if it were ice cream bars on a warm, summer evening. No, it had to be something bigger. Something really big, like money laundering, or extortion. Cigan's customers were filling their gas tanks at a much cheaper price than what they'd pay at the pump. Cigan and his old man put the profits in their pockets, but must have kicked back some of the earnings to their customers in order to keep the whole collaboration quiet.

The whole thing was remotely familiar. If it could happen in Illinois, why couldn't it happen in Michigan? And if it happened in Michigan, could Dad be involved? It seemed horrible to think about, and a notion I hoped wouldn't be true.

When I made it to the outskirts of Grand Rapids, and the interchange between I-96 and 131, Colleen called. At first I thought it was just to chitchat. I told her a little about Iowa, the hunting, and how I squirmed my way out of the incident with the police. She wanted to know about Synch, and whether or not she found any birds. She sounded concerned when I told her that our baby was slowing down. She was getting old.

So was my dad.

I told her about his condition, and the garage sale he planned on having. She said that someone with the same phone number as ours had taken out an ad with the newspaper.

"We thought it was rather odd that someone would have a garage sale so close to Christmas," she said. "But then they said they wanted a display ad, so we couldn't really turn it down. I never realized that it was your folks until just now."

I explained how Dad had obsessed about it. And how he had no sense of money. What it was worth.

"I could pull the ad, Derrick, if you want me to."

I turned her down, but she knew the situation was bothering me.

She sighed, but then asked about Ira Kaminsky.

"What about him?"

"You interviewed him, didn't you?"

"Yeah, why?"

"I don't know. He won't say anything, to our reporters. About the disappearance of Max Hermes."

"Sounds like he got some good legal advice."

She made a sound with her teeth of resigned consolation.

"You're the last guy from our office to talk to him, Derrick. Come on, can't you give me something to go on."

All of a sudden I realized that she wasn't calling just to chit-chat. She was fishing for information about the man suspected in a thirty-year old mystery. She was working me. Trying to back-door her ex-husband. And it almost worked.

"Oh, Colleen," I said. "I always loved it when you begged."

"I am not begging."

"Okay, you're not begging, but you're still sexy."

"Derrick!"

"What?" I asked. "You don't like it that I got the inside track on Kaminsky?"

She didn't answer right away.

I lowered my voice, and in the sweetest tone I could deliver, said, "Or is it that you don't like to think of yourself as sexy?"

"Oh, Derrick."

"What?"

Silence.

It was killing me.

I looked at my phone to make sure we were still connected.

"What is it, Colleen?" I asked her.

"I gotta run."

She was gone. And I'm not sure if it's because she really had to run, or if it's because either one of my questions threw her for a loop. Maybe both of them. Maybe she didn't like the fact that I had one-upped the paper. Maybe she didn't like the fact that I was on to her ploy. In either case, it was fun to think about.

I rolled into the family farm late Wednesday evening and found Mom and Dad sprawled out in the living room on their respective recliners. A half-eaten bowl of popcorn rested on a TV tray between them, next to the empty glasses of sherry for her, a Rusty Nail for him. The television was blaring loud, but that didn't keep them from drifting off to sleep. It was like old times. The two of them were sleeping together, with their chins tucked into their throats, making the sounds of mating frogs in a spring marsh.

I turned down the television, covered them up with a blanket, and realized that maybe their problems weren't so bad after all. A garage sale wasn't going to be the end of the world. I could see it in their contented faces, hear it in their blissful snoring, and realize it in the wonderful years between them. Synch and I turned off the lights in the old farmhouse and went upstairs to the bedroom of my youth. I never slept so well.

The following morning I woke up early and wrote my pheasant-hunting story for *The Recorder.* It didn't really have a lot to do with pheasant hunting, but more about the good times that Iowa is enjoying. I had a quote or two from the Iowa Farm Bureau about the high price of corn and the booming ethanol industry. Good old Emmert was in the story and so were his comments about "we got birds now, but not like there used to be." His picture made the paper, with his little four-ten shotgun, and his pheasant with the bulb on its head. I didn't mention anything about birth defects, the dead body or anything else that was remotely controversial. It was just a nice little story about a quaint little state in the middle of America's heartland.

By early Friday afternoon, it seemed that half of Alma and most of Mt. Pleasant had read my story. And they really liked it.

When I stopped for a burger and a glass of beer at the local watering hole, Braveheart's Pub, the waitress said that the check was "all set," and that a couple who had just left "took care of it, but wanted me to tell you to keep up the good work."

That felt good.

It felt even better when I went to Dad's bank in Mt. Pleasant and the woman in charge of the safe deposit boxes said that she had read my story too, and it reminded her of life on the farm during her childhood.

"You have a way with words," she said. "You know how to make the reader feel like they are right there with you."

I smiled, and then joked, "Awe, you're just saying that because it's true."

We were laughing together.

And our laughter stayed with me until the seriousness of Dad's trust hit me right between the eyes. It was time to send out another letter, and he wanted them mailed with more regularity. With each letter, I was to take more and more money from the stack of bills. The stakes were getting higher and higher. But why?

So far, I had sent out one letter to the FBI and one to the U.S. Attorney's Office. Since then, the FBI reopened a thirty-year-old mystery, and a man delivering gasoline in Iowa was murdered. Was it a coincidence? I doubt it.

Happenstance? Hardly.

Dad was involved, but since his short-term memory had left him, there was no way to find out the details.

The *Evening Journal* had details about Max Hermes. Plenty of them. His body was found four feet underground. In the back of Shell Oil's Alma refinery. Gagged. Hands bound behind him. A single bullet hole in the back of his head that shattered his skull. He was murdered, mob style.

Dad? With the mob?

Chick Twitchell, mafia lawyer?

It was horrible. I languished there in the bank's privacy cubicle, not exactly sure what to do. I was Dad's trustee, in more ways than one. And now he wanted another letter sent out. His instructions were clear: ninety days after I mailed the first envelope, I was to send out the second. Thirty days after that, I was to mail the third.

The third envelope inside the manila envelope was just like all the others. Plain white, security-thick, with that peculiar name and post office box for a return address. But it was to whom the third letter was addressed that threw me for a loop. In a very plain font, I read, *Judge Deborah Noyes.*

I couldn't believe my eyes.

Judge Noyes was dead.

And had been for several months.

Now what?

I bet I sat there for fifteen minutes, thinking, thinking, thinking about my options. A trustee is serious business. Being your dad's trustee even more serious. Since Dad was still alive, it made me think even longer and harder about betraying his instructions, and the trust he had placed in me.

What business could he possibly have with Judge Noyes?

The anguish was crawling inside my head. It felt like an

episode of "Let's Make a Deal." Behind door number one was the option of opening the letter and reading it.

Door number two was the safest option: mailing the letter even though she was dead. It was just as Dad wanted.

I could read the letter, reseal the envelope and then mail it. Was that being nosey? I rolled my eyes and sighed the sighs of distress. Forgive me, Dad. I wouldn't really do that.

I could destroy it too. Judge Noyes was already dead. Any business he had with her was water under the bridge.

I cracked the door to my little cubicle and watched the bustle inside the bank lobby. People were cashing checks, and making deposits. Shuffling money here and there. The bank managers looked content and prosperous. And unstressed. Some of them had paunchy little guts, and big smiles, but none of them helped me decide what I should do.

I didn't know what to do.

The heartache was killing me.

What a quandary.

A catch twenty-two.

I closed the door and laid the envelope on the table. And then I counted the one hundred dollar bills – all one hundred sixteen of them. I thumbed the stock certificates printed on the pretty paper, and the leases upon leases from Warmouth Oil Company that Dad had stashed away. I noticed a key, the plain old key. What was it for?

I re-read some of the clippings from Grandpa's accident, and it made me wonder all over again if the accident was indeed an accident.

None of the information provided answers to the riddles that were swimming in my head.

I couldn't betray Dad's trust. I had to do the right thing. I couldn't hop the fence like I did in Iowa. There was only one thing to do: tell Dad that Judge Noyes was dead, and let him decide if I should mail the letter after all.

Eighteen

IT WAS A NICE DAY for a garage sale. Snow. Cold. Howling winds. What else would you expect from Michigan in the early months of winter?

Mom and Dad had a busy week. They hung plastic tarps from the ceiling in the garage so the customers wouldn't meddle with Dad's hand tools, trinkets, and gardening equipment that were stored along the walls. They moved the old Mustang from the third stall of the garage up the gangway of the barn's mow to make room for all the stuff they were going to sell. On a long table against the back wall, I saw used books and old blenders. Curling irons. Playing cards and board games. And clothes. Mom must have insulated the attic with the number of clothes she had for sale. They hung on hangers from a metal pipe that dangled from the rafters. They were laying around in square cardboard boxes the size of microwave ovens and cases of copy paper. She had an entire box of socks, "Three for a dollar." And shoes, "Fifty cents for tennis shoes. Seventy-five for dress shoes." It was almost unbelievable. I couldn't believe that someone would actually go through the trouble of saving all that stuff on the outside chance that they might in fact sell it.

But Mom's stash was nothing compared to what Dad had up his sleeve. He had dressers and chairs. His favorite recliner. His three sets of golf clubs. The hutch from the dining room. Of course, the piano. The brass bathtub. His trouser press. Rocking chairs and oak bar stools. That sweet fly rod in the nice case. The kitchen table and chairs. I looked for the kitchen sink, and was relieved. None of the stuff he wanted to sell cost more than a dollar; the prices written on pieces of masking tape stuck to the furniture in obvious places.

When I peeked through the back door of the farmhouse, Mom was up and skating around the kitchen just as she always does. She had the giant coffee maker from church perking in the corner, a tray of fresh crumb cakes and coffee cakes next to that. I smelled her ham hock lentil soup, and noticed the stack of plastic bowls, crackers and spoons, ready for lunch.

If she was going to have a garage sale, she was going to have a garage sale. A biggie. A whopper. The mother of all garage sales, where nobody went away hungry.

"Is that why you took out the ad in the newspaper, Mom?" I asked her.

She nodded her head. "Of course, Son. Your father wasn't about to let the garage sale thing go." She dried her hands on the dishtowel, and kissed me on the cheek. "So I figured that if we were going to have a garage sale, it might as well be a good one. Those used socks out there aren't going to sell themselves."

"I know, but you're going to have to sell a lot of socks just to pay for the ads in the newspaper."

"I don't care about the money, Son."

"What is it, then?"

"It's your father, Derrick. I just want to see him happy."

She bent at the waist, and pulled out a roll of clear plastic wrap from the cupboard. It made me think of Carolyn St. Peter, back in Iowa, and the way she did the same thing.

"If this garage sale costs us a few dollars, that's okay." She stretched the wrap over the tray and tore the edge.

"As long as it makes him happy." She turned from her duty, and smiled, gently. Motherly.

"The neighbors will haul the big stuff away, and your father will think that he had a successful garage sale. "

"So you and Judy Craigmyle set it all up?"

"Yes, she's coming over with her dad and his trailer to haul it away."

"So they're going to buy it and keep it at their house?" I asked.

"Yes, in their pole barn. They won't even take it off the trailer. We'll bring it back gradually. Dad won't catch on."

She looked towards the living room, for Dad, I presumed.

"Whose idea was that?" I asked her.

"Judy came up with the idea. I thought it was a good one."

"You're right. Is anybody else coming over?"

"Sure, some folks from church, the neighbors, your ex-wife."

"Colleen?"

Mom smiled. "How many ex-wives do you have, Derrick?"

"How do you know she'll be here?"

"She called. Said she wanted to stop by. Said she had an appointment in the neighborhood."

"Why didn't you tell me?" I asked. "I would have worn something else."

"Don't be silly, Derrick. You look perfectly handsome in that golf shirt." She smiled. "Now how about some bacon and eggs?"

I declined. Politely. It just didn't seem like the time or place for a giant meal.

That didn't stop Dad from thumbing his way into the crumb cakes. He stood at the counter and ate two or three before he realized I was seated at the card table behind him.

"Morning, Son." He gave me the crooked smile.

"Morning, Dad. All set for the garage sale?"

"Oh yeah. Going to be great."

"Great weather for it," I said, sarcastically.

"Should be worse."

Mom disappeared, upstairs to change her clothes, we figured. Dad looked out the kitchen window to the view of the barnyard.

"Fist customer is here. Brought a tailor."

I looked outside, expecting a man with a piece of chalk in one hand, a tape measure around his neck. It wasn't a tailor, but a trailer, pulled behind the neighbor's pickup.

"In a buying mood." He smiled. "See, going to be great."

"You're right, Dad." I paused for a second and fumbled with the right way to broach a thorny subject. "I wanted to talk to you, Dad, about the third letter in your trust."

He looked in my direction. "You nailed it, didn't you, Son?"

"I brought it with me, Dad."

"Why?"

"Because it's addressed to Judge Noyes, and she was murdered a couple months ago."

Silence.

"She was?"

He scratched his chin, and played with the patch of long whiskers on the side of his jaw.

"How?"

I told him all about Ernie Peffers and his motivation, but spared the details about his demise. "That's bad. She was a good fudge. Good person."

"Why would you send her a letter now?"

Dad drew a blank. "Don't know. Why don't you open it?" He headed for the back door, for his worn-thin coveralls. "Can't do jack about it now."

I followed him to the top of the stairs.

"Why did you use a strange name, and a post office box in Alma for a return address?"

It didn't register.

"Think I'll need a scarf?"

"Yes, you'll need a scarf. Are you sure you want me to read the letter, Dad?"

"Why not?"

I almost asked him about Kaminsky and Hermes, Cigan and the oil connection, but I knew it would be way over his head.

"I guess because it's your business, Dad, and I'm not so sure I want to know everything about it."

Dad wrapped the scarf around his neck two or three times. It was long and soft and one that my sisters knit for him many years ago. One end was green, the other brown. Separate, each scarf was too short; together, they were too long, but that's the way he wanted it. His coveralls looked like a snowsuit, complete with mittens that were attached to the sleeves by tiny alligator clips. With extra-large goulashes and cap, Dad looked like an oversized child—ready for a winter's day of sledding, laughing, and cups of hot chocolate.

"Open it, Son. It'll be fine."

And with that statement, Dad opened the back door to the garage sale of garage sales.

He left me in the kitchen, the letter still in my hands, the doubt still in my head. I watched him from the kitchen window. He shook his neighbor's hand and flashed that crooked smile. He laughed.

I looked to the refrigerator and noticed a small article from their local newspaper amongst the scattered photographs of grandkids. The clipping pictured a smiling young lady, clutching what looked to be a piece of currency in her hands. The caption said it all:

> *"Nice tip! Jenny's Diner employee, Charlotte Waugh, got this hundred-dollar tip this week from Chick Twitchell after he and his wife paid their breakfast check of eleven dollars. Waugh said she'll use the money to help pay for college tuition at Albion College."*

I smiled. It was all I could do. Dad had lost his good judgment, and there was no bringing him back. Mom was by his side, despite the way she voiced her concerns. She would always be near him. *In sickness and in health, in good times and bad.*

I tapped the envelope on the table, and ripped open the opposite edge. The paper was plain white, very fine. Almost transparent. The font was sleek and smooth, classy and yet powerful.

When the time is right there will come a day,
I'll call in some markers, your debt to pay.
Your career is impressive, I watch from afar,
I hold your future, your secrets ajar.
In a few short months you'll review a file
Our opponents contend an eyesore beguile.
I know you'll be prudent; this isn't a race
Approve the project, the condos, The Place.

Dad's letter certainly could have been a lot worse. I mean, with the thought of the other letters still reeling in my head, I was half expecting some sort of death threat. Through all the rhymes and innuendo, the message was clear: she had to approve his project, or he was going to spill the beans about something controversial. And whatever that was, it would embarrass Her Honor, if not ruin her career.

I folded the letter and put it in my pocket. Things were starting to happen outside. My sisters rolled up in their minivan, and I watched them shower Dad with affection. They were okay with the arrangement to have everything stored at the neighbors. It was nice to see everyone getting along. Mom stayed with me in the kitchen and watched it all with proud amusement.

Judy Craigmyle pulled up in her Durango, and, together with Xochitl, planted a big kiss on Dad's cheek. Dad patted Judy on the fanny, and we thought nothing of it. His dementia took many forms. Lack of inhibition was one of them.

Mom needed help moving the coffee pot and the tray of cakes to the garage. By then, a half-dozen other neighbors were there—sizing up Dad and his condition, I was certain. They helped themselves to the coffee, whispering about the way he looked and talked differently since the stroke.

I watched him. My Dad, the poet laureate. He didn't remember anybody's name, but tried to play matchmaker. It was embarrassing, but gradually I was getting used to it.

Despite the cold and snow, it felt like a garage sale. Don Craigmyle and another man were gently throwing furniture on the trailer and covering it all with wool blankets. Eventually, they would cinch it to the trailer with nylon straps. My sisters were catching up with their old pal, Judy. Two or three more cars pulled into the barnyard and parked in a line next to the others. People were coming and going. Mom sold a pair of socks, and a paperback. Everyone raved about her crumb cakes and a busybody from church "just had to have" the recipe.

All at once, my daydream was interrupted.

"Mr. Twitchell?"

I looked up, and saw a stocky-shaped man in front of me. His head was extremely round, and his hair cropped short. The bristles formed a horseshoe shape on the top of his forehead.

"One of them," I said.

"Can I talk to you?"

We were wedged into the corner of the garage. Much too close to the others. I hesitated, and his voice lowered.

"I'm with the state police."

I didn't second-guess him, and gestured with my head to the back door of the farmhouse. He followed me inside, and up the back stairs to the kitchen. We didn't shake hands or monkey around with small talk. He was all business, despite his off-duty apparel.

"I was there....Peffers' house Labor Day weekend."

I nodded. Before I could say, "I was there, too," he continued.

"The guy wasn't armed. I knew it. The other guys knew it. Christofis killed him."

"How do you know it was him?"

"I was there. Right next to him. He was the shooter. Ballistics couldn't say for sure it was his gun because the bullet shattered when it entered the back of Peffers' head."

"Why are you telling me?"

He hesitated. I watched a blush-red patch climb up the side of his neck like the vines of ivy on a brick wall.

"I heard that you were there, and you sent a letter to Lansing. They sent a couple guys in from the director's office to follow up on the shooting. It was investigated and ruled justifiable, but since your letter, they're not so sure."

"So you lied during the initial investigation?"

"Along with the others. They all like Christofis. I did, too."

"Why don't you tell Lansing what happened instead of me?"

"I did. I was the first to change my story, and they fired me."

"They did?" I asked.

"Said that it was a breach of duty."

"Why are you telling me now?"

He took a deep breath. "Because if you were there, you know that I'm not lying. The guy was unarmed."

"You want me to tell your story?"

"Yeah. Heck, yeah. These guys wrecked my career. I had eight years on the force. Now I'm tending bar and working on my private investigator's license."

"That's too bad," I said. "I've tried to tell the truth about Peffers for months, but nobody will listen."

I found my reporter's notepad, and a pen. My camera wasn't far. We sat down at the kitchen table, and he unzipped his leather jacket.

"Who are the others?"

He didn't even blink. "There's five: Jansma, Epple, Lebo, Slack, and Kyd."

I nodded and wrote as fast as I could.

"Most of them are young. They got kids and stuff. Bills to pay. They don't want to say anything, because they'll end up like me, on the outside, looking in."

I sensed that the stranger across the table from me was relieved. The stress of keeping a secret was lifted, and the more he talked, the more comfortable he became. I let him ramble, my ink pen flying across the pages. "Lieutenant Christofis told us to say that the gun we found in the car was in Peffers' hand and that's why we shot him." The blush on his neck retreated. "He recruited most of us. Hired us. Trained us."

"Christofis?"

"Yes, sir. We looked up to the man. We called him 'The Mustache' when we were at the academy."

I nodded. *It was a cool mustache*, I thought.

"Four of the six troops said that they put Christofis' story on their report. The two in back of Peffers' mobile home said that they couldn't see from their vantage point."

"Did they lie about finding the gun afterward?"

"It never came up, because the story was that he had it in his hand." He looked at me as if he was sizing me up. "*You were there*, weren't you?"

I nodded.

"I was the guy who found the gun in Peffers' car." He looked at me as if I were supposed to corroborate his story.

"Who shot the dog?"

He smiled—that tidbit confirmed my presence.

"Kyd. Melissa Kyd. She was in back of the mobile. Said

that Rottie was tough. Had to cap it twice with her nine mil."

The trooper seated across from me was more than cooperative. I took his photograph. A couple of them. There was no remorse or hesitation. He told me everything about the other troopers: how many kids they have, what kind of officers they were, what they liked to drink, their latest felony arrest.

He had some dirt, too. Slack was written up for careless driving after he backed his cruiser into an ice fisherman's snowmobile. Kyd was reprimanded for calling her boyfriend while she was supposed to be on patrol.

I asked him about Christofis and my former publisher, Mr. Potato Head, and what kind of relationship they might have had. He had no idea why Hovey would help cover for Christofis.

The interview lasted forty-five minutes or so. Mom interrupted us several times with her passing errands.

And just as I was about to call it a wrap, Colleen walked through the door. I couldn't help but blush. That blonde hair had me swimming in sunshine. Now I was the one with the burning ears.

"Colleen, this is..."

Through all the excitement, I didn't even ask his name, or how to spell it. As a reporter, that should have been the first thing I asked.

The trooper bailed me out. "Robert Buccleuch." He spelled it. Slowly. "Rhymes with wa-hoo."

Colleen didn't miss her opening. "I heard about you at the *Evening Journal.* That's where I work. You were with the state police up in Alma."

He nodded.

"Sorry about that," she said. "What a terrible story. And I apologize that it didn't fit our editorial needs."

"You two have met?" I asked.

"Not exactly," she said to both of us. "Mr. Buccleuch approached the paper about his story, but we had to turn him down."

He shrugged his shoulders and zipped his jacket. I thanked him for stopping by, and said I would call with any more questions I might have. He shook my hand. It was a manly shake.

As soon as he left, Colleen and I hugged. It was wonderful. I couldn't help but close my eyes and reel in the sensation. She was so warm and firm, a delicious embrace.

"What a nice surprise," I told her.

She backed out of my arms, slightly. "I know."

"How are you?"

"I'm okay. I'm well," she said, frankly. "Busy as ever, you could say."

I glanced at her, and her new hairstyle. It was nicer than I had ever seen it, and I told her so. She thanked me, but didn't dwell on the topic. She switched topics to Dad, and the way he looked so much different than what she remembered.

"Everybody says that," I told her. "They say that he's a shadow of his former self."

"I really need to keep him in my prayers."

"If you don't mind, that would be great. His dementia is a horrible thing."

"He called me Judy at first," she said. "But then he told me to go inside and meet you. Apparently you're in the market for a new wife? Is that the case, Derrick?"

"According to him, it's true."

"Any prospects?" She bit her lower lip.

I paused. "None. How about you?"

She sat down at the table and took a sip of her diet soda. "I think we should talk about something else."

I slid into the chair across from her. "Like what, Robert Buccleuch? Why don't you cover that? That's a big story, Colleen. I would have thought that it would have been right up your alley."

"It's too racy for the *Journal*, you know. Besides, I never got the chance to take part in the decision. Buccleuch spoke to one of the reporters, who talked to Byron."

"And he's the one who rejected it, right?"

"That's right. It's too racy, like I said."

"What are you going to do when my story stirs up more controversy?"

She raised her eyebrows. "I don't know. That will be up to Byron. I'm just biding my time till it's my turn at the helm."

"Don't you think there's a connection between Hovey and Christofis?"

"What are you getting at?"

"I can't say for sure, Colleen, but it just seems like Hovey is covering for Christofis. They've got something going on there."

She shook her head in disbelief. "That can't be."

"Do me a favor, then. Just keep your ears open. I think there's something rotten in Denmark."

She grinned. "Now it sounds like you need my help."

I watched her smile. It was devious, but inviting. And even better than the invitation was the acknowledgement that she was the one who was vulnerable only a few days previously.

"Is that the case, Derrick?"

I nodded. "I think that we make a much better team when we work together."

"Is that an invitation, then?" Her teeth glimmered.

"I'm in," I said, happily. "You help me with Hovey-Christofis, and I'll tell you what I know about Kaminsky."

She reached across the table. So did I. Our hands met at the center, over a crossword puzzle filled with numbers and ampersands and indiscernible scribble. Dad's handiwork.

"You've got a deal, Derrick."

"Where are you off to, anyway?" I asked.

She stood from her chair and headed for the back door. "We have a reporter on vacation, and I had nothing to do today," she said. I waited for more details. "So I figured that somebody's got to cover the news in her absence."

"Let me guess, you thought it would be newsworthy to cover the great Twitchell garage sale."

"Hardly. There's a group of investors down here that's been slamming us with press releases."

"Why is that news?"

"It's not, but the nature of the development is."

"I'm listening."

"It's a great big condo association on the Chippewa River up by Mt. Pleasant."

"And."

"And they're going to fill in a giant wetland. The opponents contend the marsh is one of the last remaining breeding grounds for the Eastern leopard frog."

"No."

She nodded, yes. "That's what they say. I'm going to interview the front man on the development, but the opponents have already begun to put up a squabble in front of the courthouse."

She didn't need to say anything else. I knew what was coming. "Judge Noyes' replacement will hear the case." We said it almost in unison.

"How did you know that?" she asked me.

It was an easy question, but it posed a difficult answer. Our pact to work together was only seconds old, and yet it was already up for its first excruciating test. I could have told her the truth. I could have lied. My response was somewhere in between.

"It makes sense, doesn't it?" I asked, sheepishly. "If they were protesting in front of the courthouse the project must have something to do with a court approval."

"You know something, don't you?" She was the one with the cute grin.

"I don't know much that's for certain, Colleen."

She wasn't buying it.

"When you think of something, let me know."

"One more thing, Colleen…"

She had one foot down the back stairs. Maybe two.

"What's that, Derrick?"

"What's the name of the development?"

"Petro Place Condominiums. Why?"

I smiled, *of course.*

"Just wondering, Colleen. Thanks."

Instead of shutting the door at the top of the stairs, Colleen left it open. I watched her skip down the steps, that scrumptious little bottom behind her.

Nineteen

THE EDITOR of the *Gratiot County Recorder*, Walter Claety, had a saying any time he thought someone was lying to him: "Don't piss down my back and tell me it's raining."

It wasn't an everyday utterance, but I heard it enough that it stuck in my craw. The way he said it was just as remarkable because he didn't have many teeth. "Piss," sounded like "pith."

"Don't pith down my back and tell me ith raining."

Most of the time he winked when he said it, as if it were some sort of novelty.

I always encouraged sudden outbursts of emotion from Walter because the more he said things like that, the better he would think he knew me. And the better he knew me, the more loyal the ties were between us.

After a few months at the *Recorder,* Walter and I were getting along famously. Ad revenue was up—way up—compliments of the sales I was making. We increased the number of pages in each issue of the newspaper from eight to twelve, and subscription revenue went up almost twenty percent. I talked Walter into raising the newsstand price per copy from fifty cents to a dollar fifty.

"It'll work, Walter," I told him. "Give a discount to subscribers."

It did work, and our bottom line kept getting better and better. We got a jumbo litter box for the cat, and the new cleaning lady we hired was in charge of attending to it on her weekly visits. I talked Walter into getting a price on having the leaks in the upstairs apartments fixed. He took the initiative, and had a contractor give him a price on giving the front of the building a facelift, too.

I felt as if I was really part of something great. As if I was on the ground floor of a major turnaround. I took pride in my work, my stories, my commitment to covering the news in the community.

And yes, my motivation was fueled by revenge. I had an overwhelming desire to get even with the *Evening Journal.* Colleen didn't have to tell me that they felt the pinch from the inroads I was making with their most loyal advertisers. It would be hard for her or anyone else to admit that they were getting "out-reported" by a one-man wrecking crew from the weekly paper down the street. But I was out-reporting them. I was out-working them. People enjoyed reading my work- both the newsy stuff and the fun pieces I wrote about hunting and fishing.

Somebody at the *Journal* realized that maybe there was a need for an outdoorsy column in the paper. After I left, they hired an elderly woman from five counties away with very little knowledge of either hunting or fishing. What's worse, she couldn't write, either. It's as if Byron Hovey told Colleen not to mess with her stories—just to prove that outdoor writers were a dime a dozen. Her columns were absolutely horrible, and it made me realize all the more that I was getting under the *Journal's* skin.

And then came Robert Buccleuch, and his incredible story of loyalty and betrayal. He was my ace-in-the-hole. He was the guy to spring my career, I just knew it. For months, the Ernie

Peffers matter was simmering. Since I had nobody to corroborate my presence at the murder scene, I really had no leverage, no angle for a story.

But now I did. And the story became a spoor. I felt like Synch when she first strikes the scent of a pheasant. My tail wagged. My instincts took over; I had to follow the story. I was a bird dog. I had to find out more. With Buccleuch in my hip pocket, I had all kinds of ammunition. I had an ally. Leverage. An angle. And the story took hold of me. I was relentless. As tenacious as Synch in a field full of game, the wind in her face.

The following weekend, my story featuring Robert Buccleuch made the front page of the *Gratiot County Recorder*, the *Detroit Free Press*, the *Flint Journal*, and the *Lansing Daily Press*. Here's how I put it together:

I described the setting of Peffers' murder, and had a photo of him backing down the driveway, arms extended over his head. I explained in great detail the anguish Buccleuch endured when he originally lied about the shooting. The anguish was magnified when he couldn't keep the lie a secret. Buccleuch was an honest cop, but he made a bad decision. Perhaps a couple of them.

His first mistake was believing that the detectives from the director's office who conducted the second wave of investigations were actually concerned with the truth, rather than the careers it would tarnish. I set up an appointment with both detectives at police headquarters in downtown Lansing. Initially, I was treated with a matter-of-fact professionalism. They offered me coffee. I declined the offer, but when the interview started, I said that I wanted to tape record everything. They looked at each other and agreed.

And I sang like a canary. I told them everything I saw. The unarmed man. The dead Rottweiler. The trooper who found Peffers' handgun. And Christofis. His informal meeting after the shooting. The way he pointed his finger at the ground, as if to say, "What took place here, stays here."

The two detectives didn't believe me until I showed them the photos from the crime scene. Even then, they were skeptical.

Then I turned the tables on them. I asked them for their badge numbers and the proper way to spell their names. I confirmed the chain of command, and where in the pecking order they ranked.

"We are on the record, gentlemen, and I am investigating the murder of Ernie Peffers."

Suddenly, they were the ones leaning back in their chairs, crossing their arms, and avoiding eye contact. They were showing the body language of a guilty person, and I told them so. I was the one with the swagger, the interviewer's moxie.

And then they became combative.

I told them that their attitude wasn't helping their case. Even a lawyer would tell them that.

It was so much fun—being in the bowels of police headquarters and creating an ulcer of contempt. I think they thought that I was going to buckle under the weight of an intimidating situation. They underestimated me.

"Tell me about Lieutenant Christofis," I fired at them. "Robert Buccleuch. Why was he terminated? Because he told the truth?"

The two detectives said that it was a matter for internal affairs. Then they asked me to leave. They said that they would throw me out if necessary.

"Why is that, detective? We're not finished here."

All they did was stand, and point to the door.

I left, but not without getting in a few jabs along the way. It probably wasn't very professional, but I felt as if I had to let off some steam. If I had still been working for the *Evening Journal,* I probably would have been fired for my conduct. But what the heck, instead of investigating the truth, the two detectives were pissing down my back and telling me it was raining. I believed Buccleuch. I believed in myself. I was there. They didn't want to believe that I was right, that there could be something more to the story.

And when I made it back to Alma, neither Lieutenant Christofis nor Commander Wieczorek returned any of my calls, despite the six messages I left for them that week. Jansma, Epple, Lebo, Slack and Kyd were just as unresponsive. As a gesture of my good will, I had a dozen pastries delivered from Alma's French bakery. In my best handwriting, I wrote a little inscription inside the box that read, "*Compliments of reporter Derrick Twitchell.*"

The ballistics department at the state police had no interest in speaking to me, and only reluctantly turned over their findings when I approached them with a request under the Freedom of Information Act. Bottom line: they couldn't say for sure who shot Ernie Peffers.

The police psychologist wasn't about to say anything, either. There was no way she'd break the HIPAA code just to contribute to my story. I knew that everyone involved with the shooting had to talk to her as a matter of departmental policy. What the troopers said during those sessions, and how many sessions they had, was confidential. I was fishing for information—anything she could tell me without betraying her patients' confidence.

Hovey was incredulous. He couldn't believe that I would actually march into his office and ask him why he covered for Lieutenant Christofis.

"Get the hell out of here!"

"Can I quote you, Mr. Hovey? And why wasn't Robert Buccleuch's story newsworthy?" I asked him.

He stood from behind his desk. "Get out of here!"

"Are you afraid, Byron?"

He waddled toward me, but I kept my distance. There was no way that he could catch me. I was much quicker than he was.

"Get your yellow ass out of my paper!"

He followed me into the hallway, past the row of cubicles, and Colleen's office. The blood rushed to his face, wonderfully.

I don't know what got into me. I was like a man possessed, flinging the insults, firing the questions. I was flushing pheasants like a dog.

"Do you resent being called Mr. Potato Head?"

Hovey charged me, but I slid through the foyer's double doors into the cold December air. I ran to my Suburban, started the motor and took several deep breaths. It was insane! Craziness! I shouldn't have done that. But it felt so good. I basked in the light of a proverbial burning bridge. It warmed my soul, it purged my core. All that frustration I was carrying since August was vanquished. It poured out of me. It gushed from my pores. And it felt absolutely incredible.

I was making enemies. Lots and lots of enemies. And they were impressive, too: the state police, my former publisher, and a man accused in a mob-style murder. If you're going to do something, you might as well go about it full steam ahead.

The story I wrote stirred up a firestorm of interest. The big-city television stations from Saginaw and Flint sent reporters and camera crews to the state police post in little old Alma. I was there. Schmoozing. Rubbing elbows. Telling them about Christofis, "The Mustache," and his disregard for the situation.

Robert Buccleuch was serious about telling his story. He had no problem going on live television and telling our part of the world about the Peffers matter. They pushed him from one reporter to the next, answering one question after another. He didn't wince under the glare of the lights, or cower from his former employer.

By the eleven o'clock news, the director of the state police released a statement that the Peffers matter was considered closed. They chose their words carefully where Buccleuch was concerned, but added, "We wish Mr. Buccleuch the best of luck with his future endeavors."

The *Evening Journal* had nothing. They continued their silence, and when I called Colleen on her cell phone to complain about it, she said that I wasn't the first.

"It's been crazy," she said. "I mean, our lead story today was the area unemployment rate. It's crazy what we're doing."

I laughed. "That will sell lots of papers. You guys are missing the boat."

"I know it, Derrick, but you don't have to rub it in."

"Why don't you cover it?"

She didn't answer.

"Colleen?"

"It's still Byron's paper, that's why."

"You really are loyal, aren't you?"

"Yes, I am." She hesitated. "You know that."

Her statement had me thinking. If we both showed more loyalty to each other, we might still be together. "Derrick, I'm sorry. "

"For what?"

"For not staying married to you."

"What brought that on?"

There was a long pause.

"I don't know," she said. "I miss you."

The pause was just as long on my end.

"You do?"

"Yes," she said. I sensed a sigh. "It took me a while to realize it after you left, and I hope you won't use it against me..."

I didn't know what to say. It's not as if I would, but I wasn't quite sure what I should do with it, either. Her vulnerability was unusual.

"Are you there?" she asked.

"Yes, I'm here."

"This is the part where you say, 'Oh Colleen, I would never do that.'"

"I would?"

"Derrick!"

"I do?" Man, was I tongue-tied. "I can."

The phone was silent.

"Colleen, are you there?"

She didn't answer right away.

"Yes, I'm here."

"Why don't we get back to business?" I asked. "Can we do that?"

"Sure, just as long as we don't talk about Byron Hovey, Christofis and Buccleuch."

She still liked to call the shots.

"Okay, then," I said. "I guess there's not much to talk about, is there?"

"What do you want to know?"

I couldn't believe that she backed down.

"Have you heard anything?"

"No. Nothing. Byron's at the other end of the hall. You know that."

"Sorry, I just thought that you might have…"

"What about you, Derrick?" she said. "Are you ready to tell me about Ira Kaminsky?"

I hesitated for a second. In my mind I raced through the list of stuff I could tell her, and what I couldn't. Some things Kaminsky told me were off the record, some of it was on the record. "What do you want to know?"

"What's his story?" She asked.

It took me a moment to summarize his life into as few sentences as possible.

"He was the grandson of a Russian immigrant. Grew up in Detroit, and his family was involved in the alcohol trade across the international border during prohibition. Married. Two daughters. Widowed. Spent most of his career in the oil business, but I guess you already knew that."

"Kaminsky worked for Warmouth Oil, right?"

"That's right, he started it," I told her.

"Max Hermes was in the oil business too?"

"Correct, only he worked for Shell."

"They found Hermes' body on Shell's property?" she asked.

"That's right. I read it in the *Journal.* Some hotshot reporter named Colleen Beyer wrote it."

"Derrick."

"I hear she's really attractive, too."

"Derrick."

"Poised. Sincere. And incredibly intelli-"

"Derrick! Would you like to come over for dinner tomorrow night?"

Her invitation lingered for a half-second. I didn't know what to say. She had made several veiled gestures my way that I declined. But now she really laid it out there. If I turned her down now, it may have been for good, and that would be a shame. I still cared for Colleen, always have. It wasn't my fault we couldn't conceive. Maybe it was, but it wasn't intentional. I mean, nobody intends to be infertile. Or partially infertile. Or whatever the case may be.

"Are you still there?" she asked. "Or should I send over a courier?"

"No, no, Colleen. I'll be there. Saturday. What time?"

"Six-ish?"

"What should I bring?"

"Our dog," she said. "I miss her, too."

Twenty

SHORTLY AFTER WE DIVORCED, Colleen bought an older, two-bedroom brick house in Mt. Pleasant, about twenty minutes north of Alma. Her house, along with all the others in the neighborhood, was squished together on a skinny lot trimmed in perennial flowers. It had a long back yard, a one-car attached garage, and a basement where she stored her basket-making materials. Her house was cute and well-maintained, a mirrored reflection of its owner.

Her neighbors were a collection of characters. On the day I helped her move into her new house, the man across the street said that he was incredibly lonely, and found comfort only in watching pornographic material.

The woman next door, Betty Harper, wore her hair in a permanent state of curliness, matching the coiled pelt of her beloved toy poodle, Spanky. Colleen quickly learned to adapt to Spanky's schedule. Mrs. Harper let her dog outside after the eleven o'clock news, and because Spanky was "so stubborn," Mrs. Harper had to yell at him before he would obey her commands. The trouble was that not everybody in the neighborhood went to bed at the same time as Mrs. Harper. The yelling kept everyone awake, especially in the summertime, when the windows were open and the neighborhood coveted a breath of fresh air.

"Spanky, get over here. Here! Spanky, here!"

Colleen said it was like Mrs. Harper played the role of a female toy poodle, and the yelling was some sort of canine courtship. Instead of standing outside with Spanky and convincing him that life indoors was more pleasant than outdoors, yelling seemed to be a way that Mrs. Harper could vent her pent-up emotions.

I was really looking forward to hearing Mrs. Harper yell, and seeing Colleen's reaction to it all.

I couldn't wait to be inside Colleen's house.

To rekindle the old flames, if it all worked out.

But, then again, I wasn't about to force things, either. If it happened, it happened. If it didn't, it didn't.

I've been burned before. And it stung.

I couldn't wait to see her again.

My thoughts kept swimming towards her, and there was nothing I could do about it. I was adrift in the sea of Colleen.

I woke up early on Saturday morning and gave Synch a bath. She had a way of pouting through it all, because a bath usually marked the unofficial end to pheasant hunting season. Even though Colleen would probably recognize a clean dog as extra effort on my part, it was entirely better than showing up with a dog that smelled like a dirty dog.

Before lunch, I went to the *Recorder*, if nothing more than to check the Internet and try to find out more about Lieutenant Christofis, Judge Deborah Noyes and Mr. Potato Head. Heck, even my dad. Who were these people? What was their story?

The Internet was helpful. I got their home addresses, and how many kids they had, but there was very little in the way of history. I reread my story from last August about the Noyes murder and saw the related pieces from the accompanying papers across the state. There was no juicy stuff. No sizzle.

The sizzle I'd have to dig up. I'd have to sniff out.

I switched gears and pulled out the ancient editions of the *Recorder*. I started in the late sixties—when Dad started his law practice in a city an hour south of Alma. When the oil business in our part of the state was really starting to perk.

I looked for anything with Christofis, Judge Noyes, or Hovey's name on it. I paid attention to the photos, the captions, the headlines. Lots of shots of politicians. Local fellows. Rising stars. Civil rights. Segregation. Vietnam. Our soldiers killed. Others decorated. What a crazy time that was.

When I made my way to nineteen sixty-nine, I got a hit.

The headline caught my attention: "*Local authorities crack down on Vietnam protesters.*"

The photo was an image of the state police confronting a group of long-haired students. Trooper Christofis was in the fray—his billy club cocked and ready to flail. I don't know who the photographer was, but he was right there with the cops, with the youths' cursing anarchy. Christofis had the same spear-like mustache; shades darker than it is now. By the expression on his face, Christofis relished the confrontation. He was into the legalized brutality.

After ninety minutes of scanning every page of every paper, I was getting frustrated with the progress I wasn't making. It was like finding a needle in a haystack. There was lots of news, for sure, but it had very little relevance when it came to what I was after. What was I after? I had no idea. All I knew was that there had to be some connection between my dad, the oil business and the cast of characters involved in Peffers' shooting, and Hermes' murder.

Alma and Mt. Pleasant are at the center of Michigan's oil business. There should have been lots of stories about the oil business, but then again, as Ira Kaminsky once told me, "Information is key in the oil business." Maybe that's why there wasn't much of anything. Nobody wanted to talk.

If that were the case, maybe those oilmen would rather have kept things under their hats. Maybe those oilmen weren't about to talk about things. They must have liked their anonymity. Get the leases, do the geology studies, apply for drilling permits. Hire people to punch a hole in the earth, and hope that it pays. Go about your business. Quietly. Under the radar. Stay clear of controversy and make a quiet living.

I called Richie Dawes—the oilman I wrote a story about five months ago. He was the guy who said that the thugs from Chicago paid his parents a visit after they invested in a dry well. Dawes remembered me, but I could tell that he really didn't want to talk. He knew Kaminsky and the trouble he was in. I asked him about Judge Deborah Noyes, and the only thing he would say is that it was a horrible shame what happened to her.

"Christofis is a state trooper," he said. "We talked to him about those goons from Chicago, but we decided to pay them off instead of making a formal complaint."

"If you think of anything, let me know," I told him.

By Saturday afternoon, I was in Mt. Pleasant at the library, the university's library—where they kept a huge collection of historical information about the state's oil business. I poured over the timelines, charts, and graphics. They had it all. Michigan's first well in Saginaw, nineteen twenty-five. Faces. Places. A coffee table book with a glossy, smooth finish. It offered a historical view of the oil business in our state. Mt. Pleasant and Alma were mentioned over and over.

The book had pictures from the nineteen thirties. Men in coveralls, coated in black sludge. The chains and pipes, heavy equipment in the background. Most were smiling, some clenching cigarettes in their lips. The booming oil business insulated many Michigan residents from the effects of the Great Depression. It helped energize the war effort in the forties, and fueled the gas-guzzling automobiles in the fifties. By the sixties, the oil business turned its attention from southern Michigan to the areas in the northern half of Michigan's Lower Peninsula. In the summer of nineteen seventy, the oil industry acknowledged its first bit of controversy.

And it all stemmed from a pristine area the naturalists held dear.

The environmentalists wanted to outlaw oil exploration in the Pigeon River State Forest, a state-owned area in the northern tip of the Lower Peninsula, where aspen-covered hills shake hands with one of the state's most treasured trout streams.

Of course, the oil companies wanted to proceed with oil exploration and considered it their entitlement since they leased the rights to it from the state of Michigan.

The environmentalists were pitted against the oilmen. Each had allies in Lansing. Some elected officials waffled. Sympathetic newspapermen from across the north country fanned the flames of controversy.

And then a photo caught my eye. It was Dad. Arms outstretched, hands embracing a man on either side. I recognized one of the men right away, a younger, slick-haired Ira Kaminsky. The other man was a baby-faced Jonathan Noyes—one of the new kids on the block, who worked for the environmental cause. The photo's caption said it all:

> *An Oil & Gas picnic hardly seems like a place to conduct a meeting, but C. 'Chick' Twitchell (center) plays makeshift mediator between Ira Kaminsky, of Warmouth Oil Company, and Pigeon River conservationist Jonathan Noyes.*

The collar on Dad's golf shirt was enormous. So was the width on his belt; it could have been used to keep a saddle on a horse. And sideburns—they were more like saddlebags. It was funny to see him that way. My age. Three kids at home. A wife. All that responsibility. And look at him now—not sure what day it is, not a care in the world.

And Kaminsky. His teeth weren't yellow or stained yet, but they did look to be too small for his head. They were like baby teeth. He smiled and held the cigarette smoldering between his fingers. All was well for Kaminsky, ten years prior to the disappearance of Max Hermes of the Shell Oil Company. The accompanying story near the photo said it all,

> *State government could not speak with one voice on the topic of oil exploration in the Pigeon River State Forest. Many elected officials throughout the north country supported the oil companies because of the jobs they created. Others suggested that the area should be protected because it was the "crown jewel" of Michigan's thriving tourism industry.*
>
> *The Michigan United Conservation Clubs did not support the environmentalists' stance of absolutely no exploration, but helped broker a deal that satisfied all parties involved. The oil companies agreed to pay the state a twelve percent royalty in addition to the cost of the mineral rights. The fees collected would be used for public recreation projects throughout the Great Lakes state.*

I shook my head, and thought, *so that's how it worked. One hand scratches the other in those back room deals.*

My eyes turned back to the photo of dear old Dad. He was one of the big shots in the oil business. And we never even knew it. It was the secret side of his life and hard to fathom. I couldn't picture him with Kaminsky and the other guys from the oil business. I couldn't imagine him getting cozy with all those men at the Oil & Gas picnics. Or the golf outings—sipping gin and tonics. Laughing. Telling jokes. It was as if I never even knew him.

And I couldn't wait to tell Colleen.

I stopped for a bottle of her favorite merlot, then the pastry shop for something blueberry. Familiarity isn't always a bad thing.

Colleen surely appreciated it. She gave me a peck on the cheek when Synch and I rapped on her front door. I could smell the spearmint gum, her perfumed aura, so nice.

"Come in, come in," she said, smiling. "Blueberry pie and my favorite wine, what a nice surprise."

"You're welcome," I said. "I knew you'd appreciate it."

"Can I pour you a glass, or do you want a beer? There's Budwei…"

"I'll have a glass of wine." I interrupted. "Sounds good for a change."

Before I knew it we were inside her house, in her quaint little kitchen. Synch was sniffing the cupboards and the crevice between the refrigerator and the closet. Colleen stooped on a knee, and held her close.

"What a nice dog," she said. "Remember me?"

I watched Synch and the way she licked Colleen's cheek. Of course she remembered. I could see it in the way she wagged her tail. I sensed Synch's forgiveness, too. A dog's loyalty knows no bounds.

Colleen's wine glasses weren't the frail, leggy variety, but they were rather sturdy and squat, the way I like them. I didn't have to tuck my nose inside, just to get a sip. The wine simply spilled out the side, and that was perfect.

But first we had to have a toast. Colleen was good at it. "To good times and bygones. Former bosses and renewed alliances."

"Cheers." I winked.

She pointed to the living room, and the tray of cheese and crackers.

"Have a seat, Derrick. I gotta tell you about what I found out today."

I followed her blonde wake. It smelled incredible.

"What is it?" I asked.

She sat on her flowered love seat. I sat on the matching

couch. A comfortable distance. Bonnie Rait played on the stereo; "*I can't make you love me.*" One of my favorites.

"You're not going to believe what I found out," she said.

She was keeping something juicy, I could tell.

"Judge Noyes' husband—her widower—Jonathan works for the state of Michigan. He's with the Department of Environmental Quality. And he's the one who approved the environmental impact study at the Petro Place Condo project I told you about."

"What do you mean?"

"You know that controversy about the Eastern leopard frog?"

"I remember."

"He's the one for the state that okayed the environmental study. Said that there are still plenty of frogs out there, and plenty of places for them to make tadpoles."

She rolled her gum between her fingers, and stuck it to the edge of her cocktail napkin.

"His wife had Petro Place Condos on her docket before she was murdered. Doesn't that sound like a conflict of interest?"

I picked up a piece of cheese, laid it on a cracker, and popped it into my mouth.

"I don't know, it's not like either one had an interest in it."

I took a sip of wine. It was warm and flavorful, just like the lyrics: "*lay down with me, tell me no lies. Just hold me close, don't patronize.*"

"It's not like she had to approve his report. Just the project, right?"

"Correct, but Noyes was also in charge of regulating the owners' other business." She took another sip. Her teeth stained a faint, merlot red.

"What do you mean?" I asked her.

"Petro Place? Think about it. The guys who want to develop the condos are the same guys who own Warmouth Oil Company."

Colleen gestured with her hands for emphasis. "Derrick, Noyes was in charge of overseeing how much oil came out of the ground. He regulated Warmouth, and now he's okayed their condo project."

She took a breath. A deep one. I found my opening.

"Colleen, I need to tell you something."

I wasn't exactly sure where to start.

"About this Warmouth Oil Company."

I hemmed and hawed. It was hard to say. "That's Dad's company."

She put her hand over her mouth.

"At least the company he worked for. I don't know his involvement, but I know that he did some legal work for them. I saw a picture of him at the library—he had his arm around Kaminsky and Jonathan Noyes. They were at an Oil & Gas picnic together back in nineteen seventy."

"Oh heavens, Derrick!" She gasped. "I had no idea."

"I know it, neither did I until..."

"Until today?" She was on the edge of her seat. So was I.

"Not exactly today, but recently."

"I don't know what to say." She took another cracker.

"It's not really a crime what Noyes has done. I mean what you've told me about him and the judge isn't anything wrong..."

"No, you're right," she said. "I just thought it was odd, and then to hear that your dad is involved with Warmouth..."

"How do you know so much about Noyes?" I asked her.

"It's simple. We always request the personnel files on governmental employees through the Freedom of Information Act." She was swilling her wine now, and enjoying it. "Didn't I teach you anything while you were at the *Journal*?"

Her hand batted mine, nonchalantly. I dismissed her advance.

"What made you choose Noyes? I mean he wasn't even in the picture until his wife was murdered."

She leaned back in her chair, holding a cracker in one hand, the empty glass in the other. I watched her take a bite.

"I ordered it last fall, Labor Day, after the shooting. Had it sitting in the office forever, but when I heard that he was the state's point man on the environmental thing for Petro Place, I started looking into him."

"When?"

Colleen gasped. On her cracker. She raised an open hand to her mouth and coughed.

"You get choked up about these things, don't you?"

I handed her my glass of wine, and she took several swallows.

"I'm sorry, Derrick," she said. "And no, I don't get choked up that easily."

"So when did you find out about Noyes?"

She took another sip. Maybe a gulp.

"I heard about him and Petro Place yesterday, but I haven't looked at his personnel file at all." She cleared her throat and tugged at her blouse, sending the crumbs further down her front and into her bosom. "I picked up his file on the way to the grocery store. It's sitting on the kitchen table, still in the envelope."

"Let's do it." I smiled.

She hesitated for an instant.

"Okay. I'll be right back. Want some more wine?"

"No, thanks," I said.

"Sit here and relax. I'll be right back."

I did try to relax. Despite the feminine décor and frilly ensemble, Colleen's house had a real hominess to it. It was warm and cozy, and smelled like the fragrant wisp of burning candles. The only thing out of place was Colleen's trophy on top of a stereo speaker. It was at least thirty inches tall, and featured a metallic figurine swinging a bat. The inscription on the plate beneath said it all: "Heavy hitter: Big Ten batting champion."

I smiled at the contrast—such a graceful, beautiful woman, capable of such orchestrated power.

Synch found a spot to rest between the living room and the kitchen, where she could see the coming and goings of everyone important in her life.

Colleen was more than a minute, but that was okay. I heard her tap-tap-tap the dishes. Dinner smelled wonderful.

It was a nice feeling. The domestic life. The dating life. The two of them combined. The two of us, combined as well.

I forget what song was playing on the stereo, but when Colleen rounded the corner from the kitchen, it was like the two of them were choreographed. Her buoyant steps, her smiling posture. She synchronized with the music, and the two of them together captured my heart.

"What is it?" she asked.

"I was just thinking what a nice little life you've carved out here."

"Thanks. I appreciate that."

She looked around the living room and told me about the remodeling she had recently completed. New carpet. Furniture. All that.

I was impressed. And I told her so.

She laid the envelope on my knee, and it wasn't a small envelope, either. It was big and brown and heavy.

It seemed that I had discovered a bit of ancient history where Jonathan Noyes was concerned. Colleen had the recent stuff involving Petro Place Condos.

The envelope would answer everything.

I opened the envelope, removed the stack of papers, and turned to the back of his file—way back to when Jonathan Noyes was hired with the department. As a new hire, they had all the particulars about his education, his grade point average, his accomplishments. I read:

> *"Jonathan Edward Noyes. Date of birth: September, 1946. Graduated St. Benedict Lutheran High School in Peoria, Illinois. June, 1963. Grade point average 3.99. Salutatorian. Lettered in baseball. Band. Student Council. Thespian Society."*

Colleen watched me.

"I ain't the best reader," I said.

She snickered, and folded one leg under the other.

> *"Double major in environmental science and microbiology, Michigan Technological University, December, 1968. Grade point average, 3.75. Minor, public administration. Marching band. Ski patrol at Mt. Ripley, Hancock, Michigan. Chapter president, Delta Sigma Phi fraternity. Resident Advisor. Volunteered with the Department of Natural Resources during the hunting seasons at deer check stations."*

Colleen let out a fake yawn, and my pace quickened.

> *"Hired: March, 1969. Top score at the civil service exam. Plenty of accolades. Letters of recommendation, Dean of Biology, Vice President, Student Affairs. Twenty-four years old. Passed physical despite a family history of cholesterol and diabetes. Hired as wildlife habitat biologist, Emmet County. Made the 90-day, new-hire waiting period. Added spouse Deborah E. Cigan to the department's health insurance register."*

The name hit me.

Like a ton of bricks.

"Holy cow, Colleen!"

I stood. Ranting. Raving. As if I were stung by a bee. A swarm of them.

"What is it?"

"He married a Cigan. She was a Cigan, before she married him!"

I raced to the kitchen. I was in the living room. Back and forth, like a pacing lion. Synch sensed the excitement and followed me back and forth.

"Oh, Colleen, this is not good."

"What? Who is Cigan? What's wrong with you?"

"This can't be good. This can't be good."

I grabbed her by the arms, both of them. I squeezed her. My head was shaking. Nodding. I raced back to the kitchen and opened the fridge. She said that the beer was in the back.

We sat at the kitchen table. I ran my fingers through my hair. In anguish.

"The deeper we get into this thing, the worse it gets," I told her. "Look at this! Look at this!" I said. "We just started, and see what's happening…"

Colleen took my hands. Her nails in mine.

"What is it, Derrick?"

"It's Cigan. It's Cigan. That truck driver that was murdered in Iowa. He was a Cigan. He and his dad were both Cigans, from Peoria, Illinois."

I pointed to the file in my hand.

"They were selling stolen gasoline to who knows who out there."

She squeezed my hands and leaned into me. We were only a foot apart.

"This isn't good, Colleen. I'm afraid to find out more."

She reached for my face. I felt her hand on my cheek.

"So you're saying that Judge Noyes was a Cigan, and that somehow she and her husband might be involved with what took place out in Iowa?"

"If there's smoke, there's fire, Colleen."

"That reminds me…" She stood, and walked towards the oven, "I've got to check on dinner."

"There's something else I need to tell you, Colleen."

I watched her open the oven door and pull out a casserole

dish. She sprinkled the top with French-fried onions. It had to be green bean casserole.

"What is it?"

"This is off the record, okay?"

She closed the oven door, and looked my way. "Of course."

"It's Dad. He appointed me as trustee of his trust. After his stroke. And now that he's been declared incompetent, I had to move on some of the things he wanted done."

Colleen stopped stirring the Italian round steak in the crockpot.

"Like what?"

"He's got these letters I'm supposed to send out. Like three months ago, I sent out a letter to the FBI. Last month, to the U.S. Attorney's Office. Last week, I was supposed to send one to Judge Noyes, herself."

"You did? Oh heavens, Derrick."

"That's just it, Colleen. I sent the letter to the FBI and they issue an indictment against Kaminsky..."

Colleen whispered, "The Hermes matter."

"That's right. I send out the second letter to the U.S. Attorney's Office and Cigan shows up missing."

She was right with me. "And Cigan was Her Honor's maiden name."

"Correct. Last week I got the chance to read the letter he wanted me to send to Judge Noyes."

"You did?"

"Yes," I said. "He told me to—just before the garage sale started."

"What did it say?"

"It was a poem. It was weird. Something about approving the Petro Place Condos."

"Heavens, no." She gasped.

"Yes, Colleen. There was a threat to it as well. Dad had

some info on her that he wasn't afraid to use against her, and I'm sure there will be some clues in his file."

"You know I found out some stuff on Her Honor just after she was murdered." Colleen propped her hand on her hip. "Stuff that never made it to print."

"Tell me."

"I'd rather show you, Derrick."

She walked to the couch, reached behind it and pulled out her case for the laptop. I watched her reach into the side flap, and pull out a stack of papers.

"Here it is." After several seconds of rummaging through the stack, she handed me a tiny article, dated January, seventy-one.

"When the governor was appointing Judge Noyes' replacement, I looked into her career. I found this in the archives at the *Journal*, but Byron said he didn't want it in the article."

The article had a small picture of Her Honor, complete with her funky hairdo.

> *Governor William Milliken appoints Deborah Noyes to Alma judge seat. Only a month after the passing of 84-year-old Judge William Mylar, 27-year old Deborah Noyes becomes the youngest judge ever appointed or elected in Michigan. Noyes attended DePaul University and the University of Chicago Law School. She passed the bar eighteen months ago and has practiced law in Cheboygan since that time. "We are very pleased to have her on the bench," said Williams. "She will make a fine judge and we're honored to have her serve."*

"Is this it?" I asked.

"What?" Colleen asked.

"Early seventy one. Her Honor was appointed because her husband caved in on the environmental impacts of drilling in the Pigeon River Forest."

She shook her head.

"Oh, Derrick. No wonder you're so upset. Come here." She came to me in a heartbeat. We hugged for a moment or two. It was incredible—the two of us clasped in harmony. The worry, the stress, the trouble with my dad seemed to wilt in her warmth. My burden was shared—she carried the load.

"Let's eat, Derrick," she said. "Let's give thanks for what we have."

I felt her hand on the back of my neck. She toyed with my hair and it drove me wild. It had been forever since she had done that.

"Tonight, we'll count our blessings."

In the subtlest of ways I felt her press against me—our belts, our hips, our loins.

"In the morning, we'll put our best foot forward."

I closed my eyes, and pressed her head against my chest. Her hair was soft and smooth, her perfume a fragrant sanction.

"What are you trying to say, Colleen?"

Her hands traced the small of my back, and her head drifted from my chest. I looked down, into those deep green eyes and was lost in the pleasing emotion of it all. The woman I had never stopped loving was in my grasp, making me feel like all the trouble in the world was a distant memory.

"Forgive me, Father," she said, a testament to her religious convictions, "but tonight I don't want to be alone." I smiled, and knew that she was reading my mind.

"And I think you don't want to be alone, either."

Twenty-One

COLLEEN GATHERED THE PILE of papers in Noyes' personnel file, stood them on end, and tapped them on the kitchen table. In no time at all, they were in a nice little stack. She put the stack in the envelope, and clasped the metal tabs over the envelope's lid.

"There," she said. "That takes care of that."

I looked up at her and confirmed her notion.

"Out of sight, out of mind."

"My sentiments, exactly," she said. "Are you ready to eat?"

"Yes, I'm starving."

"That's good. I made one of your favorites…"

"Italian round steak, I could smell it from Alma."

"You're right," she laughed. "Green bean casserole, and boiled potatoes."

"Wonderful. How about some help?"

"No, I got it."

I watched her and the way she moved around the kitchen. It was fun. Amusing. Her movements, her smooth femininity, were like the rekindled memory of a favorite song. I knew what was coming next. I knew each verse, every harmony, the endearing melody. It was comfortable, but not boring.

She sported a new set of fingernails, painted two-tone white and light pink. I wondered when she had the manicure, and whether or not she was having them done on account of me. In the subtlest of ways, she made me feel important. What's more, those little gestures made her all the more attractive.

The skin at her wrists was fair, without tan, and a far cry compared to summer, when she radiated a simmering sheen of gold. I remembered that wonderful day we spent on Hamlin Lake, and the way I smeared lotion all over her back. She had great skin. Silky smooth. Elastic. Pleasing in every way.

But as quickly as my fantasy started, it was interrupted by the most innocent of questions: "What do you think?"

She was crouched at the oven door, a cookie sheet of beautiful, round bread rolls in her hands. I noticed the food, but more importantly, the seductive curve of her back, and the wholesome goodness of her seat. It was mouth-watering.

"Nice," I said. "They're perfect."

She acknowledged my compliment, but misunderstood what I was complimenting.

"No they're not, but thank you for saying so."

She reached for a breadbasket from the overhead shelf, next to the row of trophies from her softball career. I heard her say, "They're kinda soft, I think, but thank you just the same."

I basked in the illusion of it all. Such appetizing reverie.

"That's just how I like them."

"I remember," she said, smiling. "You don't like 'em with a thick crust, do you?"

"That's right. I like something I can sink my teeth into."

She wrapped the bread in a cloth and put the cloth in the basket as if it were a litter of newborn puppies. I watched her set it aside, and turn her attention to the potatoes. With the help of her tongs, she plucked each one from the pot of scalding water, and dropped them into a cute serving dish. After that, she walked toward me at the table, basket and a bowl in hand.

"Maybe you could light the candles," she suggested. "I'll get you some matches."

"I can pour the water, too," I said. "Want some?"

"Sure," she said. "There's a gallon jug in the fridge."

She handed me a set of glassware, and a book of matches. In no time at all, I was inside her freezer, fumbling for the ice. I heard her steps behind me, and the tap-tap-tap of serving spoons. Her kitchen was small, and getting smaller by the second. As I crouched to peek in the fridge, we bumped rumps.

"Sorry," we said in unison.

When I spun to take the water to the table, I nearly sloshed each glass over the front of her.

"Sorry," we said together.

Finally, we had a seat, and I lit the candles. They were long and erect, a brilliant red.

Colleen adjusted the music—not too loud, not too soft.

We were all alone, a table full of food.

She offered the blessing, and a poignant question that took me almost the whole of dinner to answer: "What happened in Iowa?" she asked.

Boy, did we laugh.

At my expense. At my predicaments and forgetfulness.

"So where is your gun now?"

"I don't know," I said. "Somewhere out in Iowa. It's gone. It has to be."

"That's a bummer," she told me. "What will your dad say?"

"He would be disappointed, but I don't know how he'd ever find out."

"What are you going to do?"

"I'm not sure what I can do." I told her. "He had it insured and registered with the authorities, but I'm not sure I want to get into all that. The police know that my gun is missing, so does Emmert. It'll show up on the Internet, or in a pawnshop out there."

I wiped my lips with a napkin.

"Dinner was excellent. Thank you."

"You're welcome, Derrick." She said, pouring the last of the wine in her glass. "How long has it been?"

I hesitated, sensing the double entendre.

"How long have we been divorced?"

"Four years."

"Four years." I said. "Nobody makes Italian round steak like you do. How long were we married?"

"Seven years," she said. "And no children."

"What about Synch? She counts for something."

"How is she doing, anyway?"

"She's fine," I said. "She still is a pretty good little hunter despite her old age. She really made me proud the last time Dad and I went hunting."

"Tell me," she said.

It was a rather long story, but that was okay. Colleen leaned into her kitchen chair, and sprawled her feet beneath my legs. I felt her ease out of her shoes, and rub a toe under my pant leg. When my story came to the part about forgetting my gun under the beech tree at the back of the farm, Colleen slapped the back of my hand. When I told her about Dad and the way he nailed both roosters, she wiped a tear from the edge of her eyes. And when I told her about Synch and the way she brought both roosters proudly back to us, we both got a little misty at the thought of our little baby, all grown up.

Colleen and I had spent the majority of our thirties and part of our forties together.

She had the prime of my life; I had the best of hers. I shouldn't have walked out on her. I should have stuck it out with her through thick and thin. Of course there were going to be bad times. Giving up was relatively easy; a bigger man would have stayed the course and stood by her side, no matter how many tantrums she threw. I should have been a comforting partner regardless of how many times we were disappointed with the baby-making experience.

I had kicked myself over and over, but at the same time, it was nice working with her at the *Journal* after our divorce. It was like I got just enough of Colleen to satisfy my need to stay in her life, but not too much that we got sick of each other. When I left the *Journal,* that connection between us was finally severed. And for Colleen, it left a big hole in her life. It must have, why else would she come back to me the way she did?

I was so glad that she came back to me.

I missed her so much.

I missed the long, wistful dinners. The lingering conversations. The admissions—at least from me—that I really am an airhead. All those dumb moves that I make; they're entertaining to recount. It's not like I take pride in being a dope, but I certainly do dopey things. And it's not from being lazy, or stupid. I simply don't always think about what I'm supposed to be doing.

One thing about C. Derrick Twitchell, no matter how many times I get knocked down, spun around, or kicked in the groin by life's ups and downs, I always get back up. I keep trying. I keep battling. Over and over and over again. And that's a good thing.

Colleen knew that I was in line for a little good luck. I recognized it in the way she looked at me when the connection between Alma's Judge Noyes and Iowa's Charles Cigan was revealed. Good things and good luck happens to people who are out there hustling to get ahead.

It was a break that could benefit both of us. It was a great story, and we had the inside track on everybody else.

But I didn't dare bring up the story for the rest of the night. It was time to unwind. Just the two of us.

I helped her clear the table, rinse the dishes and put them in the dishwasher. She made a pot of coffee and served the ice cream, *a la mode.*

Or rather, the blueberry pie, *a la mode.*

Whatever.

It was something we laughed about. My silliness. The way I used words in all the wrong ways.

Colleen told me that it wasn't all wrong. She said that she received a ton of comments from the readers about my outdoor writing. They missed reading my hunting and fishing stories. So did she.

"I know, but you have a new outdoor writer," I said, referring to the elderly woman who took my place on the back page of the sports section.

"Not a very good one. She's boring. And her stories are painful to read."

"Then why have it at all? I mean, I'm sure she's a nice person and all that, but her writing is atrocious...."

"Don't remind me."

Colleen took a bite of blueberry pie and shook her head.

"I think Byron wanted to prove a point after you left."

"What's that?"

"That you weren't as important to the paper as you really were."

She rolled her eyes.

"He told me not to edit it. I can't even touch it."

"It's loaded with errors..."

"I know, I know."

"It's a poor reflection on the paper."

She sighed.

"Don't remind me. It's Byron's call. Totally. He can be bull-headed at times. A real stooge."

I laughed.

"I've never heard you bad-mouth someone like that."

"I know I shouldn't, it's just that I get so frustrated with what goes on there."

"Tell me about it."

Now it was Colleen's turn to vent. She told me all about the problems at the paper and how she would fix them if she were the publisher. She was fun to watch, fun to listen to, and I told her so. She had a great mind for business—the newspaper business—but at the same time a wonderful, compassionate way with people.

"Thank you, Derrick, for the compliment."

"You're welcome, Colleen."

I smiled in her direction and her eyes turned to the candle, now a four-inch shadow of its former self. Wax drizzled down the shaft, and piled at the base in quaint, stiff formations. When she slid it across the table, the flame riled slightly in the commotion. I felt my hand in hers, palm side up. Her face glowed in the candle's sultry balm, her expression a lustrous glance.

"What are you doing, Colleen?"

She dropped her chin, slightly, and wrinkled her eyebrows. I knew the look; she and the candle were concocting something mischievous. Now it was her turn to initiate the stare down. We were locked in a lover's trance that was so familiar, yet so buried in our past.

I never even flinched when the first spatter of wax stung the center of my palm. She tilted the candle sideways, and the drips came with more regularity. They were hot and rich, thick and steamy. We never blinked; we never strayed from our optical impasse.

She put the candle down, gracefully, and smeared her right hand into my left. The candle wax oozed between us, and traced a clear, red line down our wrists.

Colleen stood, in her poised little way, and asked me to dance.

I smiled, politely, and said that I would.

"I'd love to. The tango, my dear?"

"Mmm..." she purred. "Hardly."

Shania Twain beckoned from her living room: "*I give my hand to you with all my heart. Can't wait to live my life with you, can't wait to start.*"

My right hand found the small of her back, the ribbons of muscle on either side of her spine. She draped her forearm over my shoulder, and pulled me near. I watched her close her eyes, bury her face in my chest, her ears into the buttons of my golf shirt. It was such a wonderful sensation—the two of us as close as close can be. She wanted to lead; so did I. We were both leaders, both confident people.

"From this moment as long as I live, I will love you, I promise you this."

Several minutes later, when Shania stopped singing, and our bodies stopped swaying, Colleen pulled my head to hers. Our lips met, and melted like wax in the flames of desire. I heard her utter a gasp, a vote of confidence. Our kiss, our embrace, our heartfelt entanglement was just right with her. She took her hand—the one with all the wax- and led me past the linen closet and photos of her family, down the hall to her bedroom. I was flung, one-handed, across her queen-sized playpen, my hand still coated in the vulcanized remnants of dinner.

And dessert.

She stood over me. Hovering there for as long as it took to unbutton her blouse. I savored the view, the vulnerability, the complete surrender.

"Aren't you going to take off that shirt of yours?"

I moved toward her, to the edge of the bed, and obliged her request. She rewarded my obedience with one of those never-ending kisses on my lips, my earlobes, the brow of my neck. It was such a wonderful sensation, and I told her so. I returned the favor, plunging my tongue into hers, tasting her wine all over again. My lips moved to her chest and the guns she holstered proudly in her bra. They were so nice and round, a handsome handful. My nose traced the silky outline of her laced hammocks and the stiffening proof beneath that I was making all the right moves.

She pushed me backwards on the bed, landing on top of me. Our faces only an inch apart. Her blonde hair, draped around us, became a screen. It brushed against my ears, the side of my face, until I gathered it in my hands and felt it slide between my fingers. I pulled her lips to mine and we kissed the kiss of rekindled love.

It was so nice to hold her. To feel her pressed against me. To have her tread the balance beam of satisfying herself and pleasing me, too. I wanted more. I wanted to feel her bare chest against mine. I wanted to suckle her guns. Play with her triggers. Have fun. Lots and lots of fun.

And so, I fumbled with her bra, and the three or four hooks on the back. It was like old times; I never was any good at it.

Colleen snickered; she knew that I hadn't had much practice in that department in the last four years since our divorce.

"Allow me," she said.

And with that statement, she sat up and reached behind her, sending her black number wriggling down her arms. I don't know where she flung it, but I didn't care. My eyes were glued to the graceful slope of her breasts and the way they reached for me like the needy hands of a child.

"Come on, Derrick," she whispered, pulling my head to her.

I didn't know where to start. There was so much territory to cover, so much fun to be had. I felt her hands on my head, and the way she helped ease the stress on my neck. How nice. When my lips rounded the abundant playground south of her nipple, I looked up at her face. In the faint dim of the neighbor's flood light, Colleen was smiling proudly, the same way she did when I complimented her on a delicious dinner. It was as if my infatuation with her body made her feel accepted. And sexy. Complete.

We rolled over, but the exploration didn't stop. I was so into her. Her mouth, her arms and shoulders, round and taught. Her breasts—so creamy white, milky smooth. I tugged at the button of her corduroys, and it popped. The zipper—a mild obstacle. I scooted farther down her legs and tugged on the cuffs. She raised her hips and wiggled. Her pants came at me in bunches. In kicking, thrusting waves.

And now she sprawled before me in a set of black panties that climbed up the sides of her hips. I kissed her ankles, her knees, the top of her thighs. When I made it to the silken tangle of fabric, I kissed her over and over. I caught a whiff of her nectar. Nature's perfumed aphrodisiac.

I moved north, to her belly button. To her breasts, all over again. And finally, her face. I loved the whole of her. Everything about her. All that she was. All that she is. All that we could be together.

But we were just getting started. She rolled me over and went straight for my blue jeans. My belt, the button fly. I squirmed and wriggled and gave her everything I had. My jeans. My boxer shorts. Everything. And when I was free of my clothes, she pulled the snaps on either side of her underwear. They dropped to the floor, revealing a tawny blonde tuft of fur so adorably cute that I wondered if she could make it purr.

I knew exactly how to get Colleen ramped up, how to pull her to the edge of ecstasy. She was always one for receiving oral favors, and I took pride in delivering those goods. And that was the thing about pleasing her that way; there was no mistaking when I was on the right track. She pulled on my ears. She tugged at my scalp, my hair, everything. It was all I could do just to hang in there. She was into the rhythm of it all, and so was I.

An intimate encounter with Colleen was an adventure, a memorable experience. We combined two combustive ingredients—emotion and desire. She loved me. I loved her. We loved each other.

I surrendered to her.

And she into me.

She rolled me on my back, straddling me in the process. We were pressed together. Our faces, our bodies, the parts of us that made us woman and man.

She never stopped kissing me, never took her hands from the sides of my face. All she did was move her hips until I nosed my way inside her. And when I did, she raised herself to a sitting position. I was so inside her, pressing that special place where soul meets body. I gave her all that I could, every inch of my love. She closed her eyes and swayed her hips. Slowly. Gently. She wanted us to last in that moment forever. So did I.

I felt her breathing quicken, sensed her impending explosion. Her entire being was intent on that beautiful connection between us. She was lost in the swarming flurry of joy. So was I. I took mental snapshots of her face—pursed with the mist of perspiration. Her eyes, squinting and relaxing as she tread the tightrope of giving in and letting go. I held her by the hips and marveled at this stunning woman—mature, graceful, and beautiful—giving me everything she could.

It was all I could do to hold out, to hold back, to delay that final euphoric eruption.

I wanted the moment to last; I needed a distraction.

Something to take my mind off the loss of control that was looming inside me.

And miraculously, I got it.

In the form of Colleen's neighbor, Mrs. Harper.

Good old, Mrs. Harper.

The eleven o'clock news must have finished.

Through the storm windows, a brick wall, and the intensity boiling in Colleen's bedroom, I heard Mrs. Harper yell at her dog. And what she yelled couldn't have been more appropriate:

"Spanky, come! Spanky, come!"

Twenty-Two

COLLEEN AND I had a wonderful evening together. We didn't get a lot of sleep, but that was okay; we had four years since the divorce to make up for. We had so much love to give, so much love to share.

Synch wasn't impressed. It's not like she resented Colleen's involvement, but she was an old dog and set in her ways. She had a routine that suited her needs—a walk after dinner, a teaspoon of vanilla ice cream before bed, and a leisurely stroll through the backyard, first thing in the morning.

I had struck out on all three counts. Throw in a strange environment, like the unfamiliar smells of Colleen's house, and she was justifiably antsy first thing in the morning. I scratched her under the chin, and let her into Colleen's backyard, where I could barely detect the curved outlines of her perennial flowerbeds. It was a pleasant view of her garden, even in December when everything was covered in a fluffy-white blanket of snow.

My attention moved from the backyard to the kitchen; it was time for a little coffee and breakfast in bed. Colleen had a fresh pineapple on her countertop, a box of pancake mix in the pantry. The eggs and milk were in the fridge. I had all the ingredients for breakfast.

Cooking is much more fun when you're cooking for someone you love.

And if they appreciate it, it makes the effort all the more worthwhile.

I knew that Synch was appreciative. While she was outside snooping around the yard, I found a can of dog food in the glove box of my Suburban. When the pancakes were finished, I plopped a warm one on top of her bowl of food. She loved it. I could tell by the way she choked and gagged, but kept wagging her tail.

And Colleen was just as appreciative. When the bedroom door creaked open, I saw her curled up with a pillow, her eyes mere slits.

"Morning, Derrick."

"Good morning, Colleen," I said, holding the cookie sheet loaded with a plate, cup and saucer.

"Breakfast in bed. How nice." She yawned the yawns of early morning. "What did you make me?"

"Banana pancakes, pineapple, and coffee."

Colleen sat up in bed, and adjusted the silk teddie that slumped over her shoulder. I set the cookie sheet carefully on her lap, and kissed her forehead.

"Mmmm, thank you," she said.

"You're welcome."

Colleen took a sip of coffee and asked if I had been into the Noyes' file yet.

"Not yet," I said. "Wasn't sure if you wanted to look at it with me. "

"Go ahead, Derrick. I know you're dying to find out what's going on."

"Are you sure?"

"Of course. I'm going to get up and take a shower, and go to Mass." She gestured. "Want to go?"

"Today?"

"It is Sunday morning, Derrick."

"I didn't bring any decent clothes, or a razor."

"That's okay." She took a sip of coffee, and a bite of pancake. "I won't get dressed up, and I'll skip shaving my legs. We can be the hairy couple."

I smiled. She brought me so much joy. "I'll go."

She nodded back, and took a bite.

"These are good. I miss your banana pancakes."

I agreed with her. Breakfast in bed was one of my specialties while we were married, but she had a few of those fortes of her own. "I miss your Italian round steak."

We missed each other, in more ways than one, but neither one of us was certain about the future. The pressing need at the moment was Jonathan Noyes' personnel file. Colleen knew it. I knew it. We were on to something big. Really big. She still knew how to read my mind.

"Why don't you get started, Derrick? I'll be out there in a little while."

"Are you sure?"

"Yes, go ahead."

I brushed the little blonde bangs from her forehead, and kissed her once more. In a heartbeat I was gone, into the file of the man with a mysterious background. And it wasn't like we had to look for trouble where Jonathan Noyes was concerned. It hit me the night before on the opening page, when he married a Cigan. He was from Peoria. He had the experience and education to get a job with the DNR, but he had the connections to do almost anything he wanted.

And that was the thing. The start of his career, as well as the end, was rife with special treatment and brokered deals between Michigan's oil cartel and the state government. In the beginning, he helped negotiate the deal in the Pigeon River; at the end, he signed off on the Petro Place Condos. The territory between the beginning of his career and the end was a kaleidoscope of deceit, a labyrinth of complicity.

And it all came back to Dad.

Here's how it happened.

In the early nineteen seventies, a dairy farmer in southwest Michigan noticed that his herd of four hundred cows was lethargic, listless, and had decreased appetites. Their hair fell out in patches; their hooves abnormally long and grotesque. What's more, the herd quit producing milk, and the calves died after eating the same high-protein food pellets as the cows.

The farmer thought that there was something wrong with the food, and contacted the manufacturer, who denied his accusations. After several more cows died, the farmer made contact with the State Department of Agriculture, who performed a double-blind study on two sets of mice. To assure that the results of the test wouldn't be tainted by inter-departmental politics, they called in a second branch of government—the Department of Natural Resources, and its up-and-coming-star, Jonathan Noyes—to conduct the experiment. Both agencies fed the mice nothing but the food pellets provided by the farmer. The mice died. All of them.

By nineteen seventy-four, both agencies agreed that the problem was that the feed was laced with a fire retardant most commonly used in the manufacturing of plastics. An investigation revealed that between five hundred and a thousand pounds of PBB were accidentally mixed into thousands and thousands of bags of cattle feed. The cattle feed was distributed to scores of elevators and feed stores in southern Michigan. Poison in a bag, disguised as food. How horrid.

The aftermath was ghastly. Farms were tested and quarantined, and the cattle were hauled to Kalkaska County in northern Michigan. The state hired excavators to dig a giant pit in a secluded part of state land, where the chemicals in the cattle wouldn't enter the water supply. Truckload after truckload of cattle were dropped off and lured into the pit with freshly cut hay. There were thousands of cows, milling around on their deformed hooves, searching for something familiar in the grassless moonscape of gravel. And on a warm, sunny Saturday morning in August, nineteen seventy-four, the state police pulled out their lawn chairs and rifles and surrounded the gravel pit. When the commander in charge gave the order, the troopers opened fire with their rifles and their handguns. The commander told them to aim for the head; to make things as quick and humane as possible, and that was the most civilized way they could do it.

But some of the cattle escaped the gravel pit and had to be shot from airplanes or helicopters.

Farmers looked on with tears in their eyes. The sounds of their wailing cattle was more than a lot of them could take. It was their financial ruin, not to mention an emotionally exhausting experience. Farmers get attached to their cattle—to the husbandry and responsibility that keeping them requires.

Jonathan Noyes approved where the mass burial was to take place. He approved the depth of the pit and oversaw how it was to be covered up and planted with rows of white pine seedlings. When the civil suits came rolling in, he was subpoenaed to appear from Van Buren County on the shores of Lake Michigan to Lenawee in the Irish Hills. The farmers all had reasonable claims. They all had financial damages.

It was his job to look into Michigan's seed and feed industry—to investigate how cattle feed was produced, distributed and sent to market. He was supposed to do it with integrity and professionalism.

Nobody ever would have thought that Jonathan Noyes might have been paid to soft pedal the effects of PBB in humans. It was too early to tell that PBBs would eventually make the daughters exposed to it start menstruating before they were eight years old. Nobody knew that joint pain, liver failure, and immune system disorders could be linked to the chemicals stored in their tissues. Noyes became an advocate for the seed and feed industry and he did it with such subtle aplomb that his superiors hardly suspected a thing.

Almost.

His personnel file showed that he was written up in the spring of seventy-five for staying at the three-hundred-dollar-a-night La Samanna Resort on St. Martin Island in the Caribbean.

> *By staying at the property owned by those who may be affiliated with the case involving the contaminated feed, you have cast a bleak shadow on the integrity of the department and the principles it has worked so hard to cultivate.*

It was the same resort that I stayed at with my family when I was a child.

Noyes denied any wrongdoing. He claimed ignorance in his rebuttal:

> *I had no idea that the owners of the resort were somehow affiliated with the case. My wife and I planned our vacation based on a variety of factors, never thinking to investigate who owned the facilities.*

One of the defendants in all those PBB civil suits was the same company that owned the resort where Noyes and his wife stayed on their vacation: MNM Seed Company.

I almost choked on my morning coffee.

The guy was slick. This Noyes character. He was working both sides of the tragedy: getting paid by the DNR for his objectivity, while at the same time taking favors from one of the companies involved in the feed tragedy.

But before that blemish in seventy-five, he had a letter of commendation from December, seventy-four. And it stemmed from the way he handled the media.

> *Although we prefer that any future comments regarding the PBB situation be handled by the media liaison*

in Lansing, we applaud your professionalism during this extremely sensitive time.

Stapled to the letter was a newspaper clipping from the *Muskegon Chronicle*. The copy in Noyes' file was fresh, but I could tell that the newspaper clipping itself was old and tattered. I could see the faded color; almost feel the frailness of the paper.

Shock waves continue to haunt farming community.

The story's lead was just as poignant:

Even as scientists, health professionals, and government officials try to predict the long-term effects of what PBB will have on our community, short-term psychological troubles continue to plague local residents, those involved with cleaning up the mess.

Someone in the DNR highlighted Noyes' comments:

For generations we have grown accustomed to having safe food at our disposal. When you have to think twice about it, I can understand why some people would become upset.

The story went on to quote a familiar name;

Sergeant Brian Christofis with the state police in Benton Harbor said, "The staff psychologist has been extremely busy treating the officers involved in the disposal of those cattle. Behind the state police badge are people with emotions and feelings, just like the rest of us. You can't believe how horrible that scene was in Kalkaska County. It was the kind of thing that makes people have nightmares. The sound of those cows wailing in that pit stays with you."

It seemed odd. Christofis always struck me as a stiff, unemotional fellow. He must have known how to play the game;

how to come across as passionate when he knew the cameras were on him. Maybe that's why he got promoted.

> *"Even though we were four miles from the little town of South Boardman, the townspeople said they could hear our gunshots and the bawl from the dying cattle."*

The accompanying photograph was just as graphic. It showed a medium-sized bulldozer pushing a small mountain of dirt over a gravel cliff and onto the black-and-white-colored carcasses beneath. I could only imagine the smell, the flies, the sounds of wailing cows and crackle of gunfire. It was such a gruesome image, I had to look away.

The by-line pulled me back: It was Byron Hovey. Mr. Potato Head. The future head of the *Journal* was a staffer at the *Muskegon Chronicle* way back then.

The story illustrated the longevity of their involvement. Thirty-five years ago, Christofis and Hovey were acquaintances. Maybe more than that. You scratch mine, I'll scratch yours. No wonder Hovey took Christofis' side in the Ernie Peffers murder; they had a history together.

Things were beginning to make sense.

The story was coming together.

Hovey covered for Christofis in the Peffers matter.

Christofis murdered Judge Noyes' killer.

And Noyes' husband worked for the agency that helped Hovey sell so many papers.

I took a break from the tediousness of the situation. Colleen was in the shower. I could smell the balmy warmth of steam oozing under the bathroom door. I heard her incessant humming—a mix of country music and classic hymns. The coffee was past its prime but it still satisfied my yearning. I wanted to know more about the biggest scandals to hit mid-Michigan in fifty years, but at the same time I was a little leery, too. Dad was his own man, and deserved his privacy. There are some things you just don't want to know about your parents.

I was torn about what to do. The three letters Dad had me mail were weighing on my mind. The letter to the FBI landed Kaminsky in hot water. The second letter to the U.S. Attorney's Office paved the way for Cigan's disappearance. But the third letter—to Judge Noyes—made me think that perhaps there was something unsavory about her and her husband, too.

And it didn't take long for that element to be revealed.

By the end of the nineteen seventies, the federal government had price controls on a barrel of oil. It set the price so low that nobody wanted to drill new oil wells. When Ronald Reagan was elected in nineteen eighty, the first thing he did was lift the price controls. Within a few months, the price of oil nearly doubled—from twelve dollars a barrel in seventy-nine, to twenty-one in nineteen eighty. The result was that everyone wanted to get into the oil business, and Michigan became a hotbed of interest. Almost overnight, celebrities, guys with money to burn, and high-stakes gamblers wanted a venture in the modern-day gold rush. The trouble with that prospect is that there were more people who wanted to get into the oil business than wells to accommodate them.

About that same time, the environmentalists pushed for more regulation, and got it. They convinced authorities to develop an "environmental review" for every new oil-drilling project in the state. Jonathan Noyes was chairman of the review committee, which came up with over five hundred items to be considered—from the distance an oil rig should be from a stream, to the effect it might have on wildflowers in the area. His superiors commended him for developing such a comprehensive review—one that the environmentalists would approve of and the oilmen could live with.

Noyes got in the business of inspecting every new oil well project in his home territory of mid-Michigan. And there were plenty. The big boys—Shell, Exxon and Mobil—had a few projects on the table, and steamrolled Noyes and his little environmental review. They all had biologists and naturalists on staff who were one step ahead of the state when it came to environmental impacts of a new drilling project.

Noyes rubber-stamped the big boys' projects, but made some waves at the expense of the smaller companies that weren't as well connected. He had plenty of reports and recommendations for the smaller, start-up companies that came to life with the higher price of oil. He was a bully, it seemed. He denied their drilling permits. He made them jump through too many hoops.

Noyes' supervisor had written a comment in the border of his annual review:

Caution: Noyes with a nose.

Apparently they must have talked about his investigative skills, but never bothered to double-check his work. Rumors swirled about Shell's latest project—an extremely deep hole in mid-Michigan that tapped into a substantial oil field. Crewmen were sworn to secrecy. Service contractors kept their mouths shut because they liked the big bucks they could command. Armed security guards were hired and they installed a guard booth at the end of the access road. Credentials were issued to everyone who was allowed near the premises.

And there was an additional shroud of mystery that Shell could hide behind. State law required that all companies report the results of their project within six months. And it was during that six months that Shell's permitting agent, Max Hermes, must have put the word out that he could be bought. The stakes were high. The state of Michigan had planned a massive leasing auction, and everyone—from the small start-ups to Shell's chief rivals, Exxon and Mobil—wanted to know Shell's next move.

Alma's most famous oilman, Ira Kaminsky, must have been in the mix. I remembered his interview with me, and the words,

"In the oil business, information is key." Hermes had the information. And everyone wanted to know what it was.

If Shell's project was as good as it was rumored to be, they'd want to repeat it in a neighboring parcel, on lands the state was ready to lease. The whole industry wanted the same thing as Shell—a sure thing, a slam-dunk, a guarantee that their investment would pay handsome dividends.

It was just about then Hermes came up missing.

The police had hundreds of suspects, and almost all of them besides Hermes' wife were in the oil business. Without a body, it would be nearly impossible to prove who did it.

And that's where Jonathan Noyes, Ira Kaminsky, and the newly promoted Lieutenant Brian Christofis fit into the equation.

Hermes must have confessed to Kaminsky, who in turn locked up the preacher's land before the state's lease auction. The preacher never knew that the congregation's land could be worth so much, but if he had waited until after the auction, he probably could have negotiated three times the amount that Kaminsky's goon, Roger offered him. Then again, Roger must have strong armed him into signing the papers without much negotiation at all.

Shortly after the state's lease auction, Noyes approved the drilling permit for Kaminsky's Warmouth Oil Company in eastern Isabella County. I knew that because Noyes' signature was on the oil leases in Dad's safe deposit boxes. I kept the copies from the bank in the overhead visor in the Suburban. The leases agreed with what was in the Noyes' file. Warmouth Oil Company tapped into the covenant field of oil Dad told me about under that beech tree at the back of the family farm.

Christofis was in charge of the Hermes investigation, even though he had a one-sixty-fourth interest in Warmouth's wells. Kaminsky must have cut Christofis in on the well before the plot to snuff out Hermes was even hatched.

Then again, "Christofis Holdings, LLC" was all over Noyes'

personnel file. Every oil project Noyes approved was there in black and white, the stakeholders itemized in alphabetical order.

I shook my head and smiled. Dear old Dad, the country bumpkin lawyer with a list of clients that would make J. Edgar Hoover blush. Dad couldn't be implicated in all this mess. He wouldn't break the law; he wouldn't help others break it, either. If I knew anything about my dad, it was that he was a good man, an honest man with morals and convictions and a loyalty to his family, his faith, and his future. I wanted to believe that he didn't do anything illegal. He would have been smarter than that.

Even if he did do something wrong way back then, he was hardly one to be prosecuted now. His defense lawyers would put him on the stand with his dementia, and his mixed-up vocabulary, and his lack of memory. He would make a sympathetic witness. There wasn't a jury in the state that would send him away.

I knew it. Colleen knew it. Everybody did. But now that I knew this stuff about Dad and his involvement, what was I going to do with it?

It was going to make a great story. An unbelievable story. But what were the stakes? Did I really want to expose Mr. Potato Head because of the way he sold me down the river? Did I really want to prove to the world that Christofis killed Ernie Peffers?

"Heck, yes, you want to do that!" Colleen told me. "It's a journalist's dream story."

"I know, but just think of the lives I'll ruin."

"Derrick, please."

She was standing at the kitchen sink, the cookie sheet and breakfast dishes in her hand.

"You have to move on this thing. You just have to. I mean, this is the kind of stuff that careers are made of."

"What about Dad, though?"

"What about him?"

I noticed her terry-cloth bathrobe and the way it looked so soft and comfortable. She wasn't wearing socks, and I wondered momentarily what other undergarments she was missing.

"He hasn't done anything wrong, and don't forget, he was the one who wanted you to send out the letters."

I nodded my head and watched her stand at the counter, hand propped on her hip.

"It's like he wanted to come clean with something. His conscience? Himself?"

She waltzed in my direction, a brilliant white towel wrapped around her head like a turban.

"He wants you to get involved, to expose the corruption."

I wiggled back in my chair, and Colleen sat on my lap. I wrapped an arm around her back, another around her front until my hands met at her side. Her robe was soft and inviting. Comfortable. I noticed the way the slit in the front of her robe crept past her knee, past the bottom of her thigh. It was such a pleasant view, such a pleasing vision. Colleen leaned toward me and nibbled on my earlobe. It sent shivers down my spine. I closed my eyes and gathered the scent of her perfume mixed with the garnished fragrance of soap, whatever the brand.

"I think half the state's newspapers and every television channel within a hundred miles are waiting to hear from you, Derrick."

Her words were soft, and subtle. They blew through my head like satin curtains in an April breeze. We sat there for a moment and I kissed the nape of her neck, the brow of her collar. I stole another glance, down the valley of her chest. No bra. No barriers. Nothing, but the unfettered goodness of it all.

"I think you should go for it, Derrick."

Twenty-Three

MONDAY MORNING, I visited Dad's safe deposit box. It had been three weeks since the Judge Noyes correspondence, and two weeks before the Christmas holiday. Dad wanted another letter sent. At least those were his instructions.

And honestly, it was more than I wanted to deal with.

I had an array of conflicting emotions swirling inside me. On one hand, I was anxious to find out more about Dad. On the other hand, I was growing weary of what he had up his sleeve. It was one thing to follow his instructions; it was another matter to become mired in the mess that was Kaminsky, Hermes and Christofis. As much as I loved and respected my father, he was beginning to test my patience. I made a decision that I wasn't going to be a party to any more of Dad's ethereal planning. If his next round of letters had anything to do with the cops, the police, the authorities of any kind, I wasn't going to mail them. Enough was enough. It was time to let sleeping dogs lie.

I hesitated for the longest time inside the bank's little cubicle. The last of the manila envelopes was fatter than the others. There was something substantial inside, something with a heft to it. And when I opened the flap and peered inside, I realized that there was more than one envelope. There were several. Addressed to me. To my sisters and mom. And to Judy Craigmyle.

All the people that mattered in his world.

I laid the envelopes in front of me like the cards in a game of solitaire.

The letters weren't to be mailed; they were to be hand-delivered. There were no addresses on the outside of the envelopes, only our names in Dad's finest handwriting.

When I severed the end of my envelope, and knocked the contents from the end, a key slid onto the linoleum countertop. That didn't faze me. I picked up the letter, several pages long. It was handwritten, on Dad's classy letterhead.

> *To my dear son, Derrick,*
>
> *Isn't it strange how life throws us a curve? I never thought I'd be writing you a letter with the intent that you'd be reading it after I was gone. Guess you could say that I'm comfortable with my mortality, whenever that hour arrives. I've had a great life, and no regrets.*
>
> *It has been my greatest joy to be your father. I am so proud of the man you've become, the person you are, and the individual you will be. There was never any doubt that you should be my trustee, because I trust you, Son, implicitly. Thank you for seeing my plans through; I know it hasn't been easy on you.*

I took a deep breath. His letter was hard for me to read because it was so uncharacteristic of him. Dad never got very emotional. I mean, he was sure to pass out hugs at weddings and special occasions, but he hardly ever said, "I love you," even to Mom. But with that said, we always knew that Dad loved us. We always knew that he cared. To see his love in writing made me feel odd, and yet, I was curious about where he was going with it all.

> *The three previous letters you mailed for me had to do with some dealings I had in my law practice. I must confess, Son, that the people I dealt with weren't the most upstanding citizens, and they would do almost anything to get ahead. You should know the truth about what I did and didn't do because I'm sure you will be hearing some stories about my involvement. Rest assured, Derrick, I never broke the law, nor besmirched our name, our honor, our reputation in any way.*

I took a deep breath. Some of what he was going to tell me I would already know; some of it would be new and exciting. At last, the truth revealed.

> *When I was in law school, I met a man named Ira Kaminsky. We became friends, even though he eventually dropped out of school and went to work in the oil business. After I passed the bar, Kaminsky hired me to do some legal work for him and his company. All those overnight meetings I had while you were a boy took place up in Alma and Mt. Pleasant with Kaminsky and the other people in the oil business. They never were any good at paying my legal bills, but they always gave me a small percentage in the wells they were drilling. Some of the wells were productive; most were not. Over time, I took an interest in the business because of the financial stakes involved. Before I knew it, Son, I was in over my head. I couldn't walk away. I was in too deep.*

Dad was setting the stage for a big confession. He was justifying his actions. I could hear it in his voice—it was clear and concise—before the stroke robbed him of his ability to enunciate, or form complete sentences.

I started seeing things I really didn't like. Ira Kaminsky wasn't a very good businessman. He was reckless. He leveraged the income from his good wells against future drilling projects. He sold nine-eighths, ten-eighths or more shares in fictitious drilling projects, just to cover his expenses. The stakes became higher and higher, and Kaminsky took more and more risks. He brought in investors from Detroit, who were looking for creative ways to launder their illegal drug money. He hired a couple of thugs to intimidate landowners into leasing their mineral rights, and forced others into assigning their royalties to his company at a fraction of what they were worth. And then he went too far.

I was ready. This was the part where Dad said he knew about the murder of Max Hermes. I just knew it was coming. Lay it on me, Dad.

Kaminsky killed Grandpa.

I read it again.

Kaminsky killed Grandpa.

Dad?
How?
Why?

I know he did it, Son, but I could never prove it. It was one of those things that gnawed at my conscience. And it all started while you were a boy, back in the early seventies, when dozens of farms were contaminated with PBB. It was a horrible situation, Son. Words cannot describe what those farmers went through with their dead cattle and their sick families. It was a tragedy beyond your wildest dreams, and one that I tried to shelter from you and the rest of the family.

Back then, genetics weren't what they are today. It used to take an entire growing season for a scientists' theory to be proved, or not proved, instead of a few weeks like it is today. DNA couldn't be patented yet, either. In southwest Michigan, there was a group of farmers who formed a seed cooperative. They used some of their own seeds and some of the latest and greatest seeds on the market from a company called MNM Seed. In essence, the farmers were stealing the company's technology. Both sides hired lawyers, but it was clear that it would take years in court before DNA could be patented.

And that's when MNM Seed Company's third biggest petroleum supplier came to their rescue. It was Kaminsky who suggested an accident, a mishap, some sort of retribution to the co-op members. In exchange for a bigger stake in MNM's fertilizer production, Ira Kaminsky planned and coordinated the mix-up at the seed elevator. Kaminsky killed two birds with one stone for MNM. He helped eliminate one of MNM's biggest seed rivals while at the same time he delivered gruesome retribution to the co-op in southwest Michigan. Only that co-op in the southwest part of the state was supposed to get the tainted cattle food. Kaminsky set up the delivery with the teamsters from Detroit, but some of the feed made it to the Irish Hills. And that's where Grandpa McSkimming fit into the equation.

Dad was off on one of his tangents, but in a morbid kind of way, his little tale was entertaining. It felt as if I was on his knee at story time.

When some of the tainted feed was delivered to the Irish Hills, it was Grandpa who first contacted the company about his sick cattle. He threatened to call the authorities, to call the press, and to hire a lawyer if they didn't make it right. This was way before the farmers on the west side of the state got organized and did the same thing. I was the lawyer he was talking about, Derrick. Grandpa confided in me. Three days later, he was killed on the railroad tracks.

Kaminsky sent flowers and seemed sincere in his grief when he found out that it was my father-in-law who was killed. He may never have done that had he known it was my family member. That was in seventy-four, and like I said, I had no way to prove it. Even if the police had a motive, Grandpa's death still looked like an accident.

I kept silent, and Kaminsky rewarded me with more and more legal work. It was good work, too. MNM Seed Company was never indicted in the PBB scandal, and Kaminsky's Warmouth Oil Company became MNM's biggest petroleum supplier for their fertilizer production.

I spent my time wisely, Son. Kaminsky opened his books, his business to me. And I took advantage of it. I helped him set up several holding companies, a drilling company, three or four management firms and a consulting operation. Some companies would lose money, some would make money, but they all helped create avenues for Kaminsky to hide income. And lose track of it, too, Son. I created a scheme, a network of companies that had stakes and shares in other businesses. The income was impossible to keep track of, and that's exactly the way I wanted it.

I have enclosed a key for the post office box in Alma. There, you will find the fruits of my relationship with Ira Kaminsky and Warmouth Oil Company. Every-

thing is all set up. You and the family should be in the clear.

"In the clear?" It sounded intriguing. But so did his next statement.

And so am I, Derrick. I am in the clear, if I have passed. They can't find me here. They can't threaten me anymore. Kaminsky. His thugs. Roger Chinonis is his name and he's Kaminsky's hit man. I am in a better place, where there is no more high blood pressure, no health concerns. I want to play golf four days a week, take Sugar for long walks in the cool of autumn, and take long drives in the countryside with your mother every Sunday afternoon. That's what I want to do.

Thank you, Son.

Thank you, Derrick.

God bless you, and be well.

Twenty-Four

By lunchtime Monday, I was into Dad's post office box in Alma. It wasn't one of those little boxes, either, where a catalog and three or four normal-sized letters could feel cozy. No, Dad had one of the jumbo boxes that could have housed months and months of mail.

And it was a good thing, too.

There were months' worth of envelopes inside. Bank statements, credit card solicitations, catalogs, and holiday sales flyers. He had it all. I loaded up an armful and took it to my vehicle. Then I went back for seconds. It was almost embarrassing. I felt like Rip Van Winkle after he woke up from a long nap and stumbled to his mailbox.

I raced home as fast as I could and spread everything out on the kitchen table. Synch uttered a sigh of relief when she found her old quilted floor mat. She balled up in the wonders of sleep and seemed to dream the dreams of home sweet home.

But it was all so new and exciting for me. Dad and his treasure. All those financial institutions gathered in one place. He seemed to have the market covered when it came to financial institutions with numeric assortments in their names: First

Savings, Fifth-Third Bank. Of course, he had the old familiar names too: Isabella Bank and Trust, Charles Schwab, and Raymond James. I was looking for another letter from Dad, one that would explain what I was supposed to do. After several minutes, I found it in the bottom of the stack.

To my dear Son and trustee, Derrick,

There's an old saying in the accounting business that "pigs get fat, hogs get slaughtered." Take heed, Son. Please, use this money wisely. Don't flaunt it, Derrick; that's not our style. Be conservative, and don't make a fuss if the amount deposited each month fluctuates. That's the nature of the oil business, and the rationale behind the oilman's prayer, "Lord let there be another oil boom. I promise not to piss it all away this time."

I have stakes in thirty productive wells, some north, some south of a line that the authorities regulate how much oil per day can be pumped out of the ground. Several wells are producing at the state maximum and have for years; others can't be nursed that hard. We only take what the land will give, and what it gives fluctuates from month to month, from day to day. All told Son, at fifty dollars a barrel, my one sixty-fourth interest in those wells generates about a thousand dollars.

"A thousand dollars?" I thought. *What does that mean?* At *fifty dollars* a barrel? The last time I checked, oil was sixty. Dad kept me guessing, but I don't think that was his intent.

All the money is direct deposited, but there are some monthly deductions you should be aware of. The church gets its share, right off the top. That's the way I wanted it. I encourage you to do the same, as well as take out some life insurance. I took out a life insurance policy on myself years ago, after Grandpa's accident.

The face amount of the policy is a million dollars, and the policy is in the bottom left drawer of my rolltop desk. You, your sisters and Mom are the beneficiaries, equally. There's also a long-term care policy too, just in case I cannot care for myself. It's a good policy, Son; it'll pay a hundred and fifty dollars a day. Your mom has a similar policy, but I never told her about it or the life insurance.

As far as she's concerned, Derrick, we have enough money in our retirement accounts at home for whatever she wants. She's got more money than she could ever spend.

As trustee, I'd like you to send yourself and your two sisters four thousand dollars a month from my trust account at Isabella Bank and Trust.

It was hard to fathom. Four grand a month? Suddenly I was rich! At least comfortable. Quite comfortable. Dad didn't stop there.

Send Judy Craigmyle two thousand five hundred a month.

Nice. Dad was going to take care of an old friend. An old acquaintance. I thought it was a sweet gift, but a little odd. I kept reading.

When each grandchild graduates from high school, please give each of them a thousand dollars, and explain to them about the college funds I have started. Disburse the funds to whatever school they choose, but only if they maintain a decent grade point average. Those accounts are in the safe deposit box; their names on each one.

My head was still on the four grand a month. How awesome! It was going to be hard not to let it change my lifestyle.

There was so much I could do with it. There were so many doors it would open.

Dad corralled me.

> *There are some other financial things you should be aware of too, Son. It has to do with the business arrangements with Warmouth Oil Company and the partnerships I set up over the years. Please understand that when we discovered the covenant field, we really had no idea how long it would last. Some fields dry up before you can recoup your drilling investment. I suggested that we diversify our interests—that we invest in other opportunities while the getting was good.*
>
> *And Ira Kaminsky listened. He tried restaurants and real estate, but that bored him. He wanted to be in the oil business, plain and simple. He already had a tanker that hauled the oil to Lewiston, but then he invested in four or five new ones. In no time, Kaminsky's new venture was cutting into the business of more established companies in southern Michigan. He used his connections with the Teamsters to underbid his rivals and to vandalize their rigs.*
>
> *And his timing was perfect. After the initial uptick in the early eighties, oil prices eventually fell to half of what they were. That downturn lasted for most of the eighties and into the nineties, but the trucking operation flourished.*

Dad seemed to be wandering again, but I didn't care. It all had to do with the story I was covering. Or, at least the story I thought I was covering.

> *Over time, Kaminsky bought more tanker trucks, and took interests in trucking operations. One of the companies he invested in was the Parker Oil Company*

from Peoria, Illinois. He bought eighty acres and two or three tankers. Just as they did in Michigan and Indiana, the trucks hauled gasoline from the distribution centers to filling stations. The trucks also hauled oil to MNM Seed Company's fertilizer plant in Bettendorf.

Son, there's another account called "Still Meadows, LLC." While on the surface it appeared as if Parker Oil was a legitimate business, the reality was that it occasionally dealt in gasoline stolen from a pipeline on the company's eighty acres. Kaminsky and his partners were making money hand-over-fist, and MNM Seed Company was happy because they got their gasoline from the lowest bidder. MNM never realized that they were buying stolen gasoline without the dollar-a-gallon tax.

For years, Kaminsky had a nice little racket. MNM paid Parker Oil who, in turn, paid Still Meadows. Kaminsky used the money to ensure the company's existence. Contractors were hired to install a fence around the eighty acres and an enormous gate across the driveway. He hired an Illinois lobbying firm to look out for his best interests, and he got real cozy with the local authorities. Everything had to be secret, Derrick. Top secret. Kaminsky would do anything to keep it going.

I sensed what Dad was getting at. Kaminsky was about to have Charles Cigan murdered because he threatened to expose the whole ring.

They never thought that I would be the one to betray them. Their own lawyer. Kaminsky can't find me now, Son. I am out of the picture. The FBI has enough evidence against him that he will never see the light of day. Nor will any of his goons.

> *Be patient, Son. The Still Meadows account will be yours. God bless you, Son, and be well.*

That was it.

He offered no more direction.

"The Still Meadows account will be yours."

What does that mean, Dad? The balance will be mine, or control of the account?

I thumbed through the stack of envelopes and found three months' worth of Still Meadows bank statements. The most recent was only a few days old, and as I traced my finger down the list of deposits, I realized that these guys were handling substantial dollars: twelve thousand and change, nine thousand, eleven, thirteen. There were some checks written, too—to the lobby firm McNeel Rothman, a couple of banks, Woodbury Automotive Service in Mt. Pleasant, and the Democratic National Committee—but not nearly as many or as much as what was being deposited.

And then I found the balance.

Three hundred fifty nine thousand, two hundred seventeen dollars.

Almost forgot, fifty-two cents.

But who's counting?

It was a ton of money.

And all I had to do was be patient.

Yeah, right.

I pictured myself at the bank with a withdrawal slip in my hand.

"How would you like your three hundred thousand, sir? In big bills or small?"

There had to be a catch.

There had to be something else.

Help me, Dad.

Twenty-Five

I STILL REMEMBER the first time I had to deal with the FBI. It was regarding a federal judge from Midland who was being investigated for a variety of unsavory crimes, including bribery. The people doing the bribing were the Indian tribes, some of which were from our hometown. They had grand plans for a gaming facility. The agent I dealt with was from the Bay City office, and he was extremely cautious about giving me any information. It was as if we were sparring partners in a boxing ring: he'd jab me for information, and I'd counter with more and more questions.

The FBI is the investigating arm of the federal government. The results of their investigations are turned over to the United States Attorney's Office, which is the government's prosecutor. It's also the department that cuts the deals with key witnesses and informants. It gives informants immunity in exchange for their testimony.

Anyway, there is something different about the FBI. It's not as if the other law enforcement divisions aren't professional; it's just that the FBI agents are *so* professional. It just oozes out of their pores. It's as if they measure and calculate everything they say before they say it. Some would say they're cagey. Wiley. They want to catch you in a lie. They stuff your answers into little compartments inside their heads, distinguish fact from fiction, and hammer away at the fiction. You feel as if you're digging yourself a hole. A hole that gets deeper and deeper.

Six months after the federal judge's investigation began, the agent and I had a decent working relationship. And it was based on the building blocks of trust. He'd flip me a bone, with the promise that I wouldn't attribute it to him or the department. And so, I'd have to verify the tidbit through other means. Sometimes I could verify it, sometimes I couldn't. When I couldn't, I couldn't, but I never betrayed the agent's trust. Over time, he gradually opened up, and helped me cover the story.

And just when charges were to be leveled against the Midland judge, something bad happened. The Clinton administration caught wind of it, and ordered a brand new investigation. The agent had spent half-a-year on it and, just like that, his superiors pulled him off the case. All those interviews, all those wiretaps and surveillance details were to be thrown out. And now that the judge knew about it, there was no way that they'd ever get anything on him.

Understandably, the agent was upset. He was really upset. Furious. Three years shy of his retirement, the only agent I knew in the department turned in his badge. He quit.

That was newsy.

Especially since the gaming contingency from our hometown eventually got their casino.

But that happened in the early nineties. It was ancient history. Since then, I'm not sure what happened to the agent.

In other words, I was starting over with the FBI and didn't have the luxury of building a relationship with a new agent. And really, that was okay. The Kaminsky story was nearly written. I didn't really *need* the agent's information. My plan was to get a few quotations, a few sizzling tidbits that would draw the attention from the editors at newspapers across three states.

If I had the chance, I hoped to verify Dad's contention about Kaminsky being locked up for the rest of his life.

Once I was sure that was going to happen, only then would I feel comfortable handling the kind of money in the Still Meadows account.

If at all.

I mean, I had four thousand bucks coming my way every month, compliments of Dad's trust account. All I had to do was go to Isabella Bank and Trust and make it happen.

What would I do with three hundred thousand?

Plenty.

I could buy the *Recorder,* if Walter Claety would sell it. That would be great. I'd hire Colleen to run it all, if she would be interested. And we'd have daily editions instead of weekly. We'd give the *Journal* a run for its money. We'd bury them.

I'd take a trip with Colleen, too.

We should do that anyway. I never took her on a honeymoon. It was long overdue. Someplace warm and sunny. Carefree.

She was excited about the four thousand a month and she swore not to tell anyone about it. I didn't tell her about Still Meadows or Dad's involvement with Kaminsky.

Those were the thoughts that came to mind Tuesday morning as I made my way south by southeast to Detroit. The federal building.

It took an hour before I could even get in to see one of the superiors, a half-hour before I met with the agent who was handling Kaminsky's case. Just like all the other agents I had known, he was tall, fit, and handsome. All business. He was maybe thirty-five, and wore a gray, Harris tweed suit that had pant creases as sharp as a tack.

And just as I suspected, he was evasive when it came to an investigation. He had plenty of statements, but they all started with "we can neither confirm nor deny." He was jabbing me for information, and I counter punched with more questions. I came across as if I knew a lot about the case, but that I wasn't about to share any of the information unless he provided something quotable. Back and forth we went.

Finally, he gave me something.

"Mr. Kaminsky is facing some serious charges. His arraignment was last month. The judge refused bail because of the risk of flight, and the fear that he'd intimidate witnesses."

Off the record, the agent was more specific.

"This case almost landed in our laps. Someone well connected with Mr. Kaminsky handed us all the information we needed to build a strong case against him. They had a history together, because most of the financial stuff is untraceable...before the nine-eleven laws made it more difficult to hide money. We are looking for that person now."

I nodded my head, and asked another question.

"What can you tell me about her?"

The agent looked at me as if he was wearing x-ray glasses and we were playing a game of poker. He caught my bluff. "How do you know it's a her?"

"How do you know it's not?"

"How come you know so much about this case?" he asked.

"Is it a crime to cover a story for the newspaper?" I asked, smiling.

We were back to sparring, but I had everything I needed. The quotation I could use, and the assurance that Kaminsky would be incarcerated for a long time. Or, at the very least, involved in a long, drawn-out trial.

I wondered for a second who would be Kaminsky's lawyer, and considered the irony that it was his own attorney who put him away.

By late Tuesday, I was home again, banging out the story that would set my career on a fast track. It flowed from my head to my fingertips as if it were driven through a hose. My fingers were flying across the keyboard, across the paper, across the state's major newspapers. The Associated Press. And half the state's television stations. By the weekend, I was getting offers to be on newsmaker television shows from Saginaw, Lansing, Kalamazoo, and Detroit. Someone affiliated with the Polk Award left me a voicemail about submitting my story for consideration. Several universities called and wanted me to speak to their journalism classes. A professional recruiter contacted me and said that they had several newspapers interested in hiring me.

It was great. I felt important in so many ways.

My career was steamrolling along.

And I owed it all to Dad, and to Colleen and the quirky set of circumstances that occurred during my trip to Iowa.

By the following Wednesday, I was at Dad's bank, Isabella Bank and Trust. When I approached the teller with a withdrawal slip in the amount of fourteen thousand, five hundred dollars, she looked at me as if I were from Mars. Her eyes moved to the computer screen, then back to me. Apparently a middle-aged, slightly overweight reporter dressed in a golf shirt and a worn-out overcoat couldn't possibly be entitled to that kind of dough. She took the deposit slip to the manager, who looked at my identification and me over top of her half-moon shaped reading glasses. She was the same manager who okayed me to view Dad's safe deposit box.

Together, they came back, and the manager asked how I would like it distributed.

"Four different cashier's checks, please."

With that, I wrote everyone's names on a piece of paper. The teller walked to a typewriter behind her, while the manager asked if I would like to open an account.

"No, thank you. Just the checks will be fine."

"You should be aware that we offer a full range of financial services here." She opened her hand, extended her arm and directed me to a bank of offices near the front door. "Raymond James has offices here. Maybe you'd like to open an individual retirement account, or an annuity? We also have..."

The teller was back at our booth, a frustrated look on her face. She interrupted the manager's presentation.

"I can't read your writing, Mr. Twitchell." She gulped. "Is that Trudy or Judy?"

"Judy," I said, grimacing.

"Carol or Carla?"

"Carol." I winced. "And my other sister's name is Allison, with two Ls."

She turned away, and I turned my attention back to the bank manager who was trying her best to entice me. I cut her off with a simple statement.

"Just the balance, is all I need."

"Yes, Mr. Twitchell. That would be fine."

She smiled, disingenuously, as her attention turned to the monitor on the countertop in front of her.

The teller returned a moment later and handed me all four cashiers' checks.

"It's two-fifty a check, Mr. Twitchell," she said, politely. "Would you like me to take it out of the account, or would you like to pay cash?"

I hesitated for a second, recounting the fact that I had paid for my morning coffee and a lottery ticket with the last ten dollar bill in my wallet. I probably could have coughed up ten dollars in singles, coins, and a few pop bottles in my vehicle but, then again, there was probably enough in the trust account if there was fourteen thousand.

"Why don't you just take it out of the account?" I said confidently. "I'm sure there's enough in there to cover ten dollars."

The manager almost laughed.

"Here's your balance, Mr. Twitchell, after today's eleven

hundred dollar deposit and your withdrawal. Have a nice day."

I tucked the checks in my coat pocket, and headed for the door.

So that's what Dad was talking about, I thought. *His stakes in the oil wells generate a thousand dollars a day, not a year or a month.*

About halfway to the door, my knees got a little wobbly. My heart thumped inside my chest. I couldn't believe what the manager wrote on the piece of paper. The numbers were clear and round and there were plenty of them, in a seven-digit row. Four million, seven hundred fifty three thousand, nine hundred twenty one.

Almost forgot.

Sixteen cents.

Twenty-Six

By late Wednesday afternoon, I was headed back to the family farm. The story I had written almost a week prior had legs, as other reporters from across the state picked up on different angles and worked it into their local papers.

The *Evening Journal* was noticeably quiet, as Mr. Potato Head, a.k.a. Byron Hovey, was in the middle of the controversy. Colleen said that he spent a lot of time in his office with the shades closed and his door shut. They didn't talk the entire week, and Colleen didn't say a thing to anybody about the rekindled love in her life.

Someone sent a copy of my story to the *Journal's* corporate headquarters in Connecticut. Oh, what the heck, I admit it. I sent it to them, just to get even.

The Ernie Peffers angle in my story ruffled some feathers within the ranks of the state police, too. Lieutenant Brian Christofis took an early retirement, even though he was old enough to do it anyway. Post commander Stephan Wieczorek was transferred to the end of the earth—the west end of the Upper Peninsula. Melissa Kyd was the first of the remaining troopers to break rank and confess to what really happened to Ernie

Peffers. When she did, the others caved, too, and begged for their jobs. Kyd kept hers, but everyone else was terminated.

Somehow though, I knew that there would be repercussions. I was sailing along, not getting poisoned, or shot at, or blown up in fiery car crashes. I had a sense that trouble was on its way.

For a hundred dollars, I went to the pawnshop and bought a blunt-nosed, thirty-eight caliber handgun. It was the same kind of weapon Ernie Peffers used on the judge. If nothing else, I figured it was a nice little insurance policy just in case trouble came knocking on my door. When I took it to the range with a fresh box of shells, however, I realized how inaccurate it was. Inside of fifteen feet I could generally hit a pie plate. At thirty feet, I was lucky to hit the bale of straw behind it. At fifty feet, even the mound of sand behind the bale of straw was safe.

In any case, I never wanted to use it.

I wanted to ride off into the sunset with my four thousand dollars a month. I'd do some writing and make big plans with Colleen. She was all I ever wanted in a woman.

That whole picnic fantasy thing with Judy Craigmyle was exactly that—a lustful passing. Colleen was the woman I never stopped loving. She was the one who had my heart for all these years. I couldn't wait to see her again, to take a warm, holiday vacation. She loved the idea when I called her from the road. She said she'd be ready to go the day after Christmas, at the end of the week.

All I had to do was make the arrangements.

Not exactly my strong suit.

I'd lose the plane tickets, or the name of the hotel, our passports and luggage. It was just one of those things that I've come to expect about myself.

Those were the doubts that ran through my mind as I pulled into the driveway and noticed Judy Craigmyle's Durango parked near the back door. I remembered what Mom said—Judy visited Dad on late Wednesday afternoons. Judy's visit gave Mom the chance to have her hair done and run a few errands. *This is good*, I thought. *I can deliver Dad's letter to her as well as her first twenty-five-hundred-dollar check. Won't she be surprised.*

But I was the one who was surprised.

Or maybe 'shocked' would be a better term for the emotions that ran through my head.

When I rounded the corner of the old farmhouse and climbed the stairs near Mom's dormant snapdragons, I noticed Dad seated at one of our old kitchen chairs—the ones that were sold at the garage sale. He wasn't wearing a shirt, and Judy was behind him, her left hand on his shoulder, her right hand clutching a straight razor. She had on a Santa hat—to go along with her brilliant red sweater. They were giggling. And making small talk, whatever it was. Ray Charles played in the background, and must have helped cover the sound of my approaching vehicle. I could hear it plain as day.

She was shaving him. But she wasn't just shaving him; she was *seductively* shaving him. She was too close to him. Her breasts rubbed against the back of his head. Her hands were all over him—in the curls of his hair, the curve of his chest.

Judy Craigmyle was Dad's mistress! I could see it in the way she smiled at him, the way he absorbed it all. She wasn't helping a friend of the family with his hygiene; it was her way to show him that she really cared.

I watched her take a swipe at his chin, and swish the razor in the large bowl of hot water on his lap. She was careful. Joyful. Like she was feeding her baby a spoonful of Cream of Wheat cereal. It was a tender thing for her to do. A tender moment. It made me smile. The two of them, together.

I only watched them for a minute. Probably a few seconds. Just long enough to absorb the scenario, witness the spectacle. They looked so cute together. So happy.

I wondered how long it had been going on. Since Dad handled her divorce? Since the day she broke her arm in the car accident, way back when?

Judy must have fallen in love with the man we all remembered; loved to care for the person he had become.

I backed down the stairs to my vehicle, and a hasty getaway. I didn't know what to think or how to react. I wanted to deny what I had seen, but I couldn't. The image of Dad and Judy together was warmly innocent but decidedly wrong. And how could Dad keep it all together? How could he be the devoted husband for all these years while at the same time entertain a woman on the side?

And Mom—if she ever found out about it she would be crushed—I was certain. Or would she? I had no idea what my parents' relationship was. Or wasn't.

I drove to the library, where I could forget about Mom, Dad, and Judy, whatever their relationship was.

I went to the Internet, where I could find a place to take Colleen on a holiday vacation. I thought about going back to St. Augustine, where we went while we were dating. Might be fun. Might bring back memories. It was definitely warm and sunny, and full of interesting tours, but not necessarily the most romantic of destinations. I had to make a decision. And quick.

An hour or two later, I called home. Dad answered with an "Ola," and I'm not entirely sure where he learned to say that. When I told him that I would be there in a few minutes, it made him happy. "You'll have to meet Judy," he said with a bit of laughter.

"Is she there, Dad?"

"Yes. Nice girl."

He hung up without saying goodbye. *I'm sure she is, Dad.*

Dad had me smiling again. His dementia may have been a curse, but it certainly wasn't the end of the world.

In the few minutes it took me to get to the farm, I imagined all sorts of awkward situations involving Judy and whether or not she saw me at the farm a few hours before. I hoped that she didn't see me pull out of the driveway. Or standing at the door, watching the two of them carry on like lovers.

It was really none of my business. The two of them. Nobody was getting hurt. And if Judy could care for him in his state, it showed that she really did care for him. She adored for the man that he was, regardless of his mental capabilities.

And really, my previous visit to the farm was no big deal. At least for the two of them. For me, it was a little confusing. I was certain that Dad loved Mom, and I was happy for it. But at the same time, he obviously cared for Judy in a romantic way. I didn't know what to think. As long as everyone was happy, and nobody got hurt, I guess I was okay with the whole arrangement. Maybe they weren't lovers after all, but just really close, special friends.

She and Dad had just finished dinner when I marched up the stairs and into the kitchen. Ray Charles was gone. So was the red Santa hat, and all the frivolity that went with it. Judy was just an old family friend with a soft spot for a trusted neighbor.

Dad was happy as a lark. Naturally. When he wrapped his arms around me for a hug, I smelled his aftershave. Lots and lots of aftershave. I wondered if it was part of their ritual, part of their playful courtship.

Judy pulled her coat off the hooks near the back door, and said her goodbyes. She kissed Dad on the forehead and wiped the smear of lipstick with her thumb. He smiled, and patted her on the back of her hand. It was such a pleasant farewell, such an innocent adieu. They both kept such wonderful secrets, had such splendid memories. I could see it in their smiling eyes.

When Judy opened the back door, I told Dad that I would be back in a minute. Judy paused momentarily as if she really didn't want me to tag along. It was as if she had been caught in a lie.

In a way, she had.

But I wasn't going to give it away.

I broke the tension with a comment about her plans for the holidays, and what cold weather we had been having. She was all small talk when she opened the car door, reached inside, and started the engine. I watched her pull on her black leather gloves and the way the brown stitching snaked its way up the sides. It had been lightly snowing since I drove to the farm, and now her car was coated with a frosty dusting. She brushed the snow from the driver's side of her vehicle with the aid of a bristled snow scraper. When she made it to the passenger side of the hood, I took the scraper from her hand.

"Thanks, Derrick," she said.

"You're welcome, Judy," I said. "I wanted to talk to you about Dad while he was inside."

She paused again, at the front of her car. My open-ended comment left room for multiple topics. Judy countered with an attempt to keep the conversation harmless.

"He's doing well, I think."

I could see her breath in the evening chill.

"You're right," I said. "He could be a lot worse."

I was into the task at hand, flinging the snow from around the doors, the side windows. Judy took the opening to jump inside her vehicle. A few seconds later, I joined her.

"Thank you," she said as she wiggled in her seat and turned the dial to defrost. We were greeted with a shroud of miniature snowflakes that had fallen into the engine's compartment.

"I want to be up front with you, Judy."

All at once she got a concerned look on her face.

"What is it, Derrick?"

I told her all about Dad's trust and the way he appointed me as his trustee. She listened intently, almost teary-eyed, when I handed her the envelope with her name on it.

"He wanted you to have this."

"Oh my God, Derrick. How awesome!"

"There's more, Judy." I reached into my overcoat and pulled out a check. "He wanted to take care of you financially, too. You'll get one of these every month."

She unfolded the paper, looked at the amount, and the tears welled up inside her. They pooled in the bottom of her eyelids.

"I can't believe he would do this." She reached into the glove compartment for a tissue. "Every month?"

"Every month."

"This is incredible. I never knew he had this kind of money." Tears poured down her cheeks in torrents. She was not ashamed. "I can't wait to thank him."

"I know it."

"Thank you, Derrick." She sniffled. "I think he made a good choice in a trustee."

Our hands met at the console and she gave my hand a squeeze.

"Your dad always took care of the people he loved. He always took care of me."

"What do you mean?"

She wiped a tear from her eye, and composed herself, slightly.

"He had such a big heart. A generous way about him. He never charged me a thing for my divorce, or the restraining order against my ex."

I nodded in agreement, but the way she talked about him was if he had already passed.

"And when I got into the mortgage business, Chick helped me set up the corporate papers. He even reviewed the lease agreement at my office. And then he sent me clients—people who were interested in buying new homes or refinancing their existing places."

I was smiling. Her stories never surprised me. Dad's generosity was endless.

"Over time, he sent me commercial stuff, too, that really set my career in motion. The banks and mortgage companies I represented loved me. I won trips to all sorts of wonderful places…"

She hesitated. I sensed that maybe she didn't want to say anything else about it. Like maybe Dad joined her on some of those trips. I changed gears.

"What kind of commercial business?"

The tears were gone now.

"Back in the eighties, it was restaurants and real estate. Apartments. Hotels. Stuff like that. Then it was trucking. Gasoline trucks. Oil trucks. I financed a lot of rigs."

The wheels were spinning in my head. I remembered Dad's letters and the way he outlined Kaminsky's career.

"And then last summer we were working on a condo project up in Isabella County."

I nodded my head in agreement.

"Petro Place condos, right?"

"That's right. It was almost all set to go when Chick had his stroke. That would have been a nice one."

"It still can be, can't it?"

"I don't know about that. The guy who set up all those projects is in jail. Ira Kaminsky. He was the guy in your newspaper article."

"I know."

"This check sure helps. They all will."

She clenched the check in her hands and held it to her lips. It was almost as if she smelled the peace of mind each dollar brought to her.

"I can't wait to read what's in the letter."

"That," I said, "you can do in private."

She nodded and put her car in gear. It was time for me to go.

"Good luck, Judy, and thanks for looking after Dad." I reached for her hand. She gave it a squeeze.

"Bye, Derrick."

I exited her vehicle, closed the door, and listened to the snow as it crunched under her tires. When she backed into the turnaround, I saw her raise a hand and wave. When I waved back, she beeped her horn. Her car disappeared onto M-21, past the Christmas lights in the yard, and the skiff of snow, and the rows of spruce from my youth.

Dad was still in the kitchen when I came in from the cold. He had a section of newspaper folded in front of him and was busily working at a crossword puzzle. I looked over his shoulder and got another glimpse of what was going on inside his head. He had symbols and numerals and all sorts of nonsense scribbled in the boxes. I patted him on the back, and asked him if he was having a good time.

"Sure," he said.

"That's good, Dad. What did Judy make you for dinner?" Dad looked at me as if he couldn't remember either—dinner or Judy. I moved to the refrigerator and looked inside the plastic containers. One had roast beef and potatoes. Another lasagna. In no time at all, I had a plateful heating in the microwave.

I asked Dad if he wanted a beer.

"No thanks, Son. Going to have a drink before bed." His speech wasn't any better—it was slow and deliberate.

"Rusty Nail?"

"That's right, Son. Two triggers of scotch, a jigger of Drambuie and a fist of lemon."

"You used to have crème de menthe once and a while, too, didn't you?"

"Not in a Rusty Nail, Son"

I laughed. "That's right, Dad. That wouldn't taste very good."

The microwave chimed, and I took my plate to the table. It smelled wonderful.

Dad was back to his crossword puzzle, as I opened a beer and spread my napkin on my lap.

"Five-letter word for blessing," he said, almost as if it were a question.

"Grace."

"Right."

"Would you like to say it, Dad?" I smiled in his direction.

He smiled. It was lopsided. Of course he would. He bowed his head, and started in. His delivery was very slow, and purposeful.

"Father in heavenly heaven. We thank you for this veal."

He almost had me smiling. We were so much alike. He had an excuse for being mentally challenged; I've been that way my entire life.

"Let it be used to flourish our bodies, and thus our service."

He paused for a second or two, and I thought the prayer was over. I said, "Amen," but Dad kept praying.

"Thank you for the seal," he said.

"Amen."

I was hungry, very hungry, so I picked up my fork and started after the lasagna. Mom always puts Italian sausage and a bit of feta cheese in hers. And the roast beef was so tender she must have put it in the crockpot early that morning. I could practically cut it with a fork.

"This roast beef is excellent."

"Thank you, Lord for traveling mercenaries…"

He didn't mean to confuse "mercies" with "mercenaries," and confuse "seal" with "meal." It was a reminder of what was wrong with him and it made me sad. All of a sudden I regretted asking him if he wanted to say the blessing. Or the five-letter word for it.

I picked up the newspaper and looked at Dad's crossword puzzle again. There was no such mention- in the "down" column or the "across"- for "five-letter word for blessing." I shook my head and looked across the table at my father, his fingers still clasped at his belly, his chin still lowered in prayer. He was mumbling, but that was okay. Prayer is a good thing.

I unfolded the section of newspaper. The crossword puzzle was on the back page of the first section—the only section—in Owosso's weekly newspaper. I recognized the headline, the story, when I turned to the front page. It was all mine: "*Suspect in murder case linked to PBB, state police scandal.*" I smiled. The little paper in Owosso plucked my story off the wire, complete with the photos of Ira Kaminsky.

"Did you read this story, Dad?"

He looked up from his prayer and raised an eyebrow.

"Do you remember Ira Kaminsky, Dad?"

He nodded.

"Of course you do," I said.

"Is your story in paper, Son?"

"It is."

"I'm proud. It's good."

"Thanks." I wiped my lips with a napkin. "I couldn't have done it without your help."

He nodded, but I was certain he didn't know why I thought he was helping.

"How did you get so much money in those accounts? Are you really making a thousand bucks a day off those oil wells?"

He stared in my direction.

"I think it's wonderful that you want to give it to us kids and Judy. It's really nice. Even the grandkids."

"What am I going to do with it?" he laughed. "There's no U-haul behind the hearse."

"That's right, but I want to thank you for the check every month. That's really, really nice."

I wanted that point to be clear, but at the same time, there was more to discover.

"What's the deal with the Still Meadows account? You told me I should be patient. What do you mean?"

He folded his arms and traced the outline of his chin. The wheels inside his head were spinning, but they were spinning in quicksand. He was drawing a blank.

I finished my dinner, my beer, my inquiry for the day.

Our conversation was interrupted by the sound of the garage door opening. Mom was home.

I got up from the table and put my dishes in the dishwasher. Dad refolded the newspaper and returned to his puzzle.

Mom opened the back door and said that she was surprised to see me. Then she asked where Judy was.

"I relieved her about a half-hour ago," I said. "Would you like me to give you a hand with the groceries?"

"Sure, Son." She leaned towards me and gave me a kiss on the cheek. "I'll stay here and put everything away."

As I put my coat on, I heard her say that Dad smelled good.

"She must really pile on the aftershave, Chick."

Dad smiled and dabbed the pencil to his tongue.

About thirty minutes later, the groceries were put away, and I heard the latest gossip from Mom's trip to the beauty parlor. They were talking about Kaminsky, and about my story in the paper. Mom bragged about what a great reporter I was. It felt great to hear those things.

By then it was almost nine o'clock and Mom suggested a bowl of popcorn and a nightcap.

"Dad likes to look at television before bed, but I can't just sit there. Too many commercials, too many advertisements. I have to knit, or talk on the phone. Dad has a drink while he relaxes—a Rusty Nail. Would you like me to make you one, too?"

"Sure, Mom. Dad and I can have a drink together."

I looked in his direction. He wasn't working on the puzzles anymore.

"What do you think?" I asked him.

"Great," he said. "Make mine a double."

"He always says that," she snickered, quietly. "I usually add some ginger ale to his," she whispered. "The doctor said that alcohol isn't the best thing to have with his medication."

Mom reached for a couple of old-fashioned style glasses from the cupboard, and placed them next to the freezer. She reached inside and grabbed a handful of cubes, and with her other hand whacked the ice with a meat tenderizer. They splintered and shattered, but that was the way she had always done it. We didn't want to interrupt her routine. I sat at the table with Dad, and watched her parade around the kitchen. She was in her glory. Juggling tasks. Taking extra care of the men in her life. The ginger ale and popcorn. Easy on the salt. No butter.

"Why don't we go to the living room?" she suggested. "It's more comfortable there."

I took our drinks and together we walked through the dining room. Mom had the giant oak table covered in her knitting stuff. Needles and yarns. A brown-and-yellow sweater, missing an arm. A Christmas stocking the size of a boot, ready for someone's name to be knitted onto the rim along the top. All her grandkids got their own stockings. So did I, way back when.

I noticed a package amidst the clutter. It was wrapped in plain brown paper, taped at the corners and both ends. It was the size of a flat, long birthday cake. Dad's name and address were written on the front in simple, nondescript handwriting.

"When did this arrive?" Mom asked.

Dad stopped for a second. The three of us looked at the package with the same amusement as if it were a newborn calf. Dad picked it up and we noticed the mail underneath.

"It's the mail, Chick. There wasn't anything in the mailbox. The postman must have brought it up to the house."

Using both hands, Dad carried the box to the living room. There was something heavy inside.

All of a sudden, the popcorn and Rusty Nails weren't all that important.

Mom had a running commentary.

"Who could this be from? Did you order something? Is it an early Christmas present?"

Dad sat in his lazy chair, the box across his lap. He reached into his pocket for his jackknife.

For a fleeting second, I thought that it might have been a bomb of some sort.

We watched him slice the tape at both ends, and slide the paper wrapper from the cardboard box. He placed the paper on the floor, and turned his attention to the box. At last, the box sprung open, the lid blocking my view.

"It's a gun!" Mom cried. "Did you buy another gun, Chick?"

Her voice was loud and demanding, but she wasn't upset.

I stood up and looked inside. It was a gun all right. Encased in bubble wrap. In two pieces—the stock and the barrels. A double barrel.

Dad was awfully quiet.

So was I.

I had forgotten all about the gun I left in Iowa. The gun I *forgot* in Iowa. I wanted to run away. I wanted to tuck my tail between my legs and scramble for the door.

This couldn't be it.

There was no way.

Dad unwrapped the stock. Walnut. Exquisitely engraved. English. Dual triggers. They all matched Grandpa's relic.

By the time he unwrapped the barrels, I was composing the alibis inside my head. How upset I was to see Cigan's body inside that tanker truck. How I forgot the gun at the scene of the murder. How it was gone when I went back for it the next morning. Apologize, Derrick. Be thankful. Tell him it'll never happen again.

My face was burning hot. My ears on fire. Dad never looked in my direction. That made it worse. He was giving me the opening to say something—to come clean with my confession.

Mom continued her line of rhetorical questions.

"You have a gun like that, don't you Chick? That looks like Dad's shotgun!"

Dad didn't answer. He guided the barrels into the receiver and snapped them together as if he had done it a thousand times.

"Didn't you give that gun to Derrick?"

She looked at me, and I shrugged my shoulders.

Dad flicked a piece of tape from the barrel, then raised the gun to his shoulder as if he were shooting an imaginary clay pigeon. I recognized the shape, the effortless way it came up to Dad's shoulder. It was Grandpa's gun. It was Dad's gun. It was mine.

And it was back where it belonged.

On the family farm.

But how?

And who?

"Dad, there's something I need to tell you."

I looked at Mom. "Could you give us a minute?"

"Sure, Derrick." She got up from her chair and left the room. I felt bad for asking her that, but I really didn't want to have to explain everything, either. I closed the door and sat in the lazy chair next to him. I placed his cocktail on a coaster, next to mine. His drink was much clearer than mine. It bubbled.

I started right in with what happened at Emmert's farm in Iowa and how I panicked when I saw Cigan's dead body. I told him about the golden opportunity the story was, and how I took a chance by emailing the photos to the the *DesMoines Register*. I struggled with what to do that night when I knew the gun was missing. And then I confessed to a dumb move when I left the ransom note without my phone's area code.

Dad watched me. And listened without judgment. I'm not sure how much he absorbed; how much he took in.

"I was going to tell you about it, Dad. But when I started reading all your stuff in the trust and in your safe deposit box, I forgot about it, to be quite honest with you."

He took a sip of his drink, and wiped his lips with his free hand.

"I never had a clue that you were involved in all that," I said. The silence was killing me. I disappointed him again, I could just tell.

Finally, he spoke. "It's okay, Son."

I sighed. A sigh of relief.

"Maybe we should just keep Grandpa's gun here from now on, until I get a gun safe of my own."

He shrugged his shoulders.

"It's yours, Son. It's your gun."

He handed it to me, and I thanked him again.

"You know where the safe is."

I stood next to the lazy chair, but I really wanted to give him a hug. I wanted him to tell me that he forgave me for being so forgetful. Instead, I changed topics, and told him the story about pheasant hunting in Iowa.

"Did I tell you I got a double on pheasants while I was out there?" I laughed.

He looked at me and smiled, approvingly.

"Ten minutes before I found Cigan's body."

I raised the gun to my shoulder, and swung it left, then right, at the far corners of the living room. The mad cackler of a pheasant on the back of Emmert's farm erupted out of those thick weeds and I folded him like a house of cards all over again. It was great reliving the moment, recanting the adventure. Dad was right there with me, or so it seemed by the expression on his face.

I pushed the lever at the back of the receiver and the barrels swiveled away from the stock. The old double barrel was hinged in the middle. I peered down the barrels and noticed a small obstruction near the end of the left barrel. I wondered what it was.

Instead of saying something to Dad about it, I told him that I would go downstairs and give the old gun a proper cleaning.

Dad agreed.

I walked past the dining room, and into the kitchen, where I smelled Mom's cookies baking in the oven. "Everything okay, Derrick?"

"Everything's great, Mom. I'll try a cookie in a few minutes."

It was still a mystery as to who sent Dad the gun. Nobody ever looked to see the return address on the outside of the package. I almost ran down the stairs to the workbench. The wooden dowel Dad used to clean the barrel was right there, in plain sight. I pushed it down the left tube of steel, and a rolled up piece of paper unfurled on the bench.

I carefully set the gun down and opened the piece of paper. Across the top were the words, *United States Attorney's Office.*

Holy hell!

Even the mention of those four words made my heart thump inside my chest.

The return address was Detroit, the Federal Building.

The very place that I visited the previous week.

Dear Mr. Twitchell,

Thank you for your assistance in the matter of United States of America v. Ira Kaminsky. In exchange for the information you provided us, we have seized the assets of Still Meadows LLC and have placed the funds into the account you proposed. Confirmation of that wire transfer is attached.

Your gun was traced to you via the Bureau of Alcohol, Firearms and Tobacco and was held up in processing.

That was it.

No signature.

No name.

Or person.

Nothing.

That was it.

My dear old dad was an FBI informant, a key witness for the federal government against Ira Kaminsky. Whatever documents Dad mailed them were good enough to spring the trap.

The funds in the Still Meadows account were mine. The second piece of paper was a receipt all right; the funds transfer. The three hundred thousand was off shore in the French Virgin Islands. It was the island where our family vacationed occasionally, where Jonathan and Judge Deborah Noyes sipped rum punch in the shade of swaying palm trees. It was St. Martin Island, home of the banking community where 'discreet' is a way of life, and laundering money is considered an art form.

All of a sudden I figured out where Colleen and I should go on our vacation.

And I couldn't wait to get there.

We were going to have a great time.

We were going to be rich.

If it all came together.

Twenty-Seven

CHRISTMAS AT THE TWITCHELL FARM was a memorable one. A very, merry holiday. My sisters brought their families in from out of town. Their husbands were pleasant, and their children polite, if not full of stories from their adventures at high school. They played "spoons" at the dining room table, even though their parents had spent hundreds of dollars on brand new electronic video games. The men donned worn out snowmobile suits from the closet downstairs and wandered out to the barn to feed the cats and Leroy, who was losing his calf-like appearance.

Dad suggested a snowmobile ride, but he couldn't remember where he left it. He looked in the garage and the barn before he eventually found it in the drive shed. The grandkids took turns doing laps around the yard, and pulling each other on a plastic sled.

Judy Craigmyle and Xochilt stopped by for a visit, Christmas day, just after the big meal of the day was finished and the kitchen cleaned up. She and my sisters barely had the chance to speak since the end of last summer, when Dad had his stroke.

Together with Mom, they sat at the kitchen table and drank tea most of the afternoon. By the sounds of their cackling laughter, it was an excellent reunion.

When the leftovers were served for supper, Judy and company headed for home, but not without hugs all around. Dad got an extra long one, an extra squeeze.

She missed out on the family game night, including a no-stakes poker tournament that was organized by one of the grandsons. He brought a traveling poker kit, complete with the different colored chips and several decks of playing cards. All three grandsons played, a brother-in-law, my dad, and me. Texas Hold 'em.

The grandsons were way too aggressive. They lacked patience. We cleaned them out of their chips in three or four hands. Dad was great, even though he folded when he was only one card away from having a straight. It was almost as if he forgot what a sequence was good for. He took forever when it was his turn, but he bluffed two of the grandkids into folding, and goaded the third into gradually raising his bets until he was nearly out of chips. Even in his diminished state, Dad knew how to work a room, work a table of adversaries. But that was the thing; he didn't rub their noses in his victory or vanquish the defeated, he taught them the virtues of patience without pandering to their insecurities. It worked. His grandsons didn't huff away from the table, sore losers; they stayed right there and watched us finish the game. They wanted to learn. And learn they did.

My brother-in-law learned how to eat crow a hand or two later. And it came with his sons at each elbow, looking on.

Ouch.

Then it came down to Dad and me. And I must admit that Dad was incredibly intimidating. His face never faltered, whether he was sitting on a good hand or bad. He just stared. The stroke may have stolen his ability for facial expressions, but it certainly helped him conceal what was going on with his hand of poker. Dad made one mistake when he showed his fourteen-year-old grandson his hand. Even though Grandpa made a gesture to keep his lips together, the grandson's eyes couldn't keep a secret. They were happy. Way too happy. I folded. Dad had a good hand.

I pictured Dad at some high stakes poker tables, where the antes were life and death. Where bluffing, nerves of steel, and incredible guts not only paid enormous dividends, but saved your life. It was a poker table where Kaminsky and Roger were breathing down his neck on everything from the way he set up the different businesses, to the reason why the stream of income didn't always add up to what was in their accounts. I conjured up images of Dad at the Federal Building, negotiating the deal that would land Kaminsky behind bars, his only son in the money. He'd be cool and calculating. He'd use the alias for a name, a post office box in Alma for his address. And yes, dear old Dad, with the stone-face way he could stay happily married to Mom while at the same time entertain a woman on the side. He was the master of keeping his facial expressions in check, at bluffing others into thinking that he was telling the truth.

Back on the farm, however, it was a cute scenario. The old man and two generations of boys. Playing cards. Card playing. It was the stuff that the grandsons would always remember.

So would I.

Of course, Dad won the poker tournament. But not without a little drama. I took several hands from him, and for a while I had the upper hand in chips, too. But he quickly turned the tables on me with a good hand, an excellent bluff, and an "all in" that sealed my fate.

The grandsons cheered him on and slapped him on the back. They admired him.

He laughed. He was still the man. And it felt good.

Everybody loved him. Despite the secrets he kept from us and the bad things that he was involved with, he insulated the family from it all. He kept our best interests at heart, in the front of his mind, at the core of his soul.

And when it was all said and done, Dad led me to the story that turned my floundering career into a huge success. I was so thankful, so blessed to have such a wonderful father. He meant the world to me, and to my sisters, who could hardly contain themselves when I presented them with their handwritten letters. They both cried when I handed them their checks, and said that there would be more every month.

They sat on his lap as if they were ten years old again. They called him "Daddy" and showered him with affection. It was Christmas in more ways that one. The gifts, the presents, and whatever he said in their letters made him almost immortal.

Even Mom got a little choked up when she read his letter and my sisters told her about what he had done.

It was a great Christmas, full of many pleasant memories, but by noon the following day, I had to be at the airport in Detroit, about ninety minutes' drive from the farm. My plan was to meet Colleen in Chicago. She had flown to her folk's house in Wisconsin for Christmas. Together, we'd make our way to San Juan, Puerto Rico and eventually the Queen Juliana Airport on the Dutch half of St. Martin Island. I booked the same hotel, *La Samanna,* where we stayed when I was a kid. It was the same resort where Jonathan Noyes and his wife, Her Honor, stayed, too. I really didn't care if MNM Seed Company or their subsidiaries were still the owners; it was water under the bridge as far as I was concerned. The only thing I wanted to do was kick back and relax.

I needed to get to Alexandria Bancorp to pick up the money.

Mom and Dad said that they'd keep an eye on Synch while I was gone.

Dad volunteered to take me to the airport.

"We'll take the Harley," he said, only half-joking, I was certain.

And when it came right down to it, I didn't mind driving all by myself. I looked forward to the time alone in the old Suburban. It would give me a chance to unwind. It would help me get geared up for the week ahead in a remote location. What were we going to do for five days? Horseback ride? Parasail? Ride bikes, go fishing, read a book? I could brush up my resume, and email it to the recruiter who said that she had a few job opportunities for me to consider.

It really didn't matter what we did, as long as Colleen and I were together. I pictured the two of us gently baking in the warmth of a powerful sun. I envisioned carefree breakfasts, leisurely lunches, candlelight dinners of fresh fish, exotic rice, and tropical fruits, served by waiters and waitresses who spoke with heavy French accents. I hoped that the weather was toasty hot and the service was as good as I remembered.

I was optimistic that the magic Colleen and I shared two weeks before would boil over into our trip together. There would be lots of hand-holding, plenty of quality time, and limitless intimate possibilities. I always wanted to curl up in a hammock, where the only places we could keep our hands, our lips, our minds was on each other.

By the time I made it to Chicago, I was really anxious to see Colleen. I never told her exactly why I chose St. Martin Island, other than I had been there before. She really didn't need to know about Dad's three hundred thousand. After all, it wasn't mine yet, and I learned a long time ago that you don't count your chickens before they're hatched. Besides, I've been known to mess up the simplest of tasks, the gift baskets of life, and if I let her down, I didn't want it to turn into one of those stinging expressions of "See? I told you so."

No, I wasn't going to tip my hand. I was only going to tell her exactly what she needed to know. We were going to have a great time. We were going to spend my checks that I made off the Kaminsky story, plus some of Dad's four thousand. Our belated honeymoon had benefited from compounding interest. We would enjoy it in the lap of luxury.

If I managed to walk away with the three hundred thousand, it would be an unbelievable surprise.

And it would make for some interesting conversations.

"What are we going to do with all that money?" I'd ask her.

"Buy Walter Claety's newspaper?" I'd suggest.

"Invest in the Petro Place condo project?"

"A new Suburban?"

I knew that she'd suggest giving it to the church, or to charity. She'd remind me that from God, all good things come. We would banter back and forth that the return on God's investment in Walter Claety's paper could pay much better dividends over the long haul.

Those were the scenarios I imagined as I exited the airplane and headed for my connecting flight at the other end of O'Hare Airport. I love to fly. It's fun. And exciting, for some strange reason. It must be all that jet power, all that freedom wrapped into an enormous hunk of metal. And the airports. So hectic. So many people coming and going. Where do they go? What do they do? They all have a story to tell. They all have their own little lives, their own little worries. Their kids must worry them. Their parents, too. They're sandwiched between them all.

Just like me.

Only my sandwich is open-faced.

I only have to worry about my mom and dad.

The vacation would help clear my mind, if only for a few days. And I couldn't help but smile about the prospect when I spotted my girl waiting for me near the gate of a giant American Airlines jumbo jet.

"Is this seat taken?" I asked her.

"It is now," she said.

I kissed her on the lips, and asked her about Christmas.

"It was wonderful. Midnight Mass was very moving. The music, the singing."

"Excellent. Everybody's fine?" I asked.

"Everybody's great. And healthy. I promised my nephews some souvenirs. They take after my heart and want to play softball."

"They do?" I asked.

"My older nephew is almost six, and he takes batting practice in the basement."

"Seriously?"

"Plastic baseballs, but I want to get him a wooden bat instead of a plastic one."

"Like a big heavy bat?"

"No, no, Derrick," she said. "One of those mini-bats, about that long." Her hands were stretched about shoulder's width.

"Good. He will like that."

I watched her dig into her purse for the envelope that held her boarding passes.

"I got a call from the home office."

"Oh?"

"They're coming out next week, just after New Year's. It's about Byron Hovey and the story you wrote."

"No kidding."

"Yeah, they said that there may be some shake ups at the paper. Apparently they've conducted some sort of investigations into the relationship between Hovey and the guys in your story."

I laughed.

"No kidding."

"They think that he wasn't reporting everything that he should have been." She tore the corner off the envelope, rolled her chewing gum between her fingers and deposited it into the paper. "They say that there's some history there. Hovey wasn't reporting all that he could about those guys."

"Does that mean that you're going to be publisher now?"

"Who knows, Derrick? I don't even want to think about it now. I want to get away from the office."

I nodded my head in agreement, and countered, "Are you ready to have some fun?"

Of course she was ready. Of course I was, too. We were going to have a ball.

And not even a long, turbulent plane ride south could dampen our enthusiasm. The jump from San Juan to St. Martin Island took less than an hour in a little sixty-five-passenger turbo jet. We held hands and marveled at the rich, blue water beneath us.

I had made arrangements to rent a car once we got to the airport. Thank goodness they drive on the right side of the road.

By seven o'clock that evening, we were in the hotel lobby. Even though it had been years since my last visit to St. Martin, I still recognized the sleek marble countertop and the massive potted plants that framed the entryway. I was in high school the last time I was here, but it hadn't changed a bit. The heat was a welcome friend. It tugged at my senses like a guilty conscience. Only this was better. I was cheating Michigan's winter, where it's anything but warm.

Colleen wasn't one to wait around. Before the woman behind the counter could check us in, Colleen drifted off to the bank of brochures tucked around the corner. I could see the wheels spinning inside her head, as she picked up each brochure and looked at the photos. We were going to have a great time with whatever she was cooking up.

When the woman behind the counter rang the bell, it pulled Colleen out of her daydream. She turned to the commotion, and followed the bellhop out the front door again, to a four-passenger golf cart. The young man loaded our luggage onto the back and, together, we made our way across the paved trail to a quaint bungalow not far from the beach, the ocean, and an adorable eatery, candles flickering on each table.

When the last of our luggage was brought inside, and the garment bags hung in the closet, I tipped the bellhop just like Dad used to do. It made me feel important. No sooner had the door closed when Colleen planted a big, wet kiss on my lips. It made me feel loved. She suggested a bite to eat, after a quick shower. I took her drink order—cranberry juice—and headed off to the restaurant not far away to make reservations for two.

Dinner wasn't an elaborate undertaking, but it did have that French appeal. Lots of sauces and *pate de foie gras,* Pinot chocolate, and sorbet. We practiced our people-watching skills, but the pickings were rather slim. It seemed that all the beautiful people in the world had already eaten and were on to doing whatever beautiful people do after dinner.

After we left the restaurant, Colleen and I went for a leisurely walk on a darkened beach. The water lapped at our ankles and dampened our pant legs beneath our knees. She kicked water in my direction, then ran away, half-heartedly. I chased after her, and caught her by the elbows. She spun around and we kissed each other in the dim of the Caribbean moonlight. I kicked her feet out from under her, and she fell, still in my arms, to the sandy mattress beneath us. There was not a soul around, but I didn't want to rush things. I wanted to tempt her. Tease her. Fan the flames of desire, not jump head long into the fire. There would be plenty of time for that.

I guess it worked. After a long, throaty kiss on the beach, Colleen talked dirty to me—one of her specialties, and one that I missed for all those years.

"Let's go back to our room," she said while she kissed my earlobes, my cheeks, my neck, "and light some candles."

I felt her nibble my skin, my fingers, my wrist.

"And open all the windows."

She pawed at my shoulders, my biceps, my hair.

"I want to hear the sound of the sea, the Caribbean at night, and the noise of two people making mad passionate love," she whispered.

It was music to my ears, so I sat up, slightly. She pulled me back.

"Are you up for that kind of evening, Mr. Twitchell?"

Her words poured from her heart; they were taunting me, challenging my manhood. "Can I count on you to give me your all?"

"I'm there, Colleen," I said. "I didn't come all this way just to lie on the beach."

"Let's go, then."

I don't know who was in more of a rush to get back to the bungalow, Colleen or me. We barely made it inside the door before she kissed me, and I kissed her. She pulled me to the windows, and threw them open. The drapes waved softly in the warm breeze. And so did the water. It lapped on the shore as if it were keeping rhythm. I followed her to the nightstand, the petite box of wooden matches. I was behind her, watching her every move. When she pulled a match, I held it between her fingers. Together, we slid the head across the striker, and the flame erupted. It was so right, so fitting. We held it to the wick, and the candle came to life. Together, we made it happen.

And we made love as if it was our last day on Earth.

And as it turns out, it very well could have been.

The following morning, I got up early and went for a walk, all by myself. Dawn in the Caribbean had a peaceful busyness to it. A host of unfamiliar birds sang their hearts out—an early morning tradition, no matter what the setting. A couple of Americans jogged past me, the sweat dampened her Rutgers University t-shirt. The restaurant where we had dinner the night before was abuzz with activity, as the staff tended to the buffet line, and the patrons sipped their morning coffee.

I took the moment of tranquility to check my voice mail.

It had been more than twenty-four hours since I had checked it, and when I did I knew within seconds that there was something wrong. Horribly wrong. I had seventeen voice mails, which was about sixteen more than usual. My neighbors called. And friends. The fire department. And my employer, good old Walter Claety.

"Your house burned down last night, Derrick. And if it wasn't for me being here, they would have burned the paper down, too."

The news nearly took my breath away. It was awful. I was devastated. I didn't know where to start, so I called Walter as fast as I could.

"My house burned down?"

"It did. I'm sorry, Derrick."

The news hit me as if I had lost an old friend. A confidant. Someone I shared my life with.

"What do you mean the paper almost burned, too?"

"I was here, downstairs, late Thursday night. Cutting the negatives for the paper, when I heard a crash upstairs. I mean it was bad. Glass everywhere."

"What was it, Walter?"

"It was a fire bomb. A bottle full of explosives. Something." Walter stuttered. "I kicked it outside, then called the police. Called nine-one-one, but they were already at your house, battling the fire. I knew we shouldn't have run that story, Derrick. Don't know why I listen to you."

"You're okay, aren't you?"

"I'm fine, but I did get a little smoke damage in here."

"That's the most important thing."

"No, it's not."

"What is it, then?" I asked him.

"It's that I'm too afraid to run a follow-up story."

"What did the cops say?"

"They got nothing."

Walter's grammar was brutal.

"They can't prove who done it."

"That's just great, Walter. No witnesses, right?"

"That's right."

I finished with Walter and called the fire department. They said that my house was a total loss, completely gutted. It made me sick to my stomach. Fires emit a horrible smell, and one that I was way too familiar with after covering them all those years for the paper. The smell from a house fire stays with you. It's the smell of tragedy, and it stings your nose, singes your psyche. I could see the plume of smoke from the Caribbean, smell it two thousand miles away.

I didn't need to tell the fire department who might have started the fire. The police had already issued a bulletin for Ira Kaminsky's right hand man, Roger Chinonis. The authorities read the paper, too, and sensed that there might be trouble coming in one form or another.

Trouble was after me.

I could feel it.

I sensed it.

They were on my trail.

I felt like a rooster pheasant when a group of hunters stop their truck at a field's front door. I sensed the danger. I heard the truck doors slam, and the loading of the hunters' guns. I felt that sense of panic when their dogs traced my steps. Every pheasant faces that ultimate quandary when pursued by persistent danger—keep running away from it, or try to hide and hope that it walks past. I didn't know what to do, but I knew that the evil in Ira Kaminsky and Roger Chinonis were after me.

The hunted were chasing the hunter.

And I didn't know whether to run or hide.

I had to think fast.

I had to call home and make sure everything was okay. I

had to ask Judy Craigmyle to look in on the farm. And call the police in Owosso.

But just as important, I had to get to the bank. I had to get the money. Dad's money. Kaminsky's money. The loot. The prize.

After that, I could hide.

And wait for them to flush me out.

Colleen didn't know the urgency of the situation. She took forever in the bathroom, and when I said I was going to town, she said that she wanted to tag along.

"I'll be right back," I told her.

"No really," she said. "I want to go with you. There's something I need to tell you."

I protested mildly. "Can it wait till I get back?"

"No it can't, Derrick." She erupted from the bathroom, hair still wet, her smile as wide as Lake Michigan.

"Let's go, Colleen. You can tell me on the way."

"Where are we going?" she asked.

"To the bank. I want to get there as soon as it opens."

"Why?" she asked, a hairbrush in her hand.

"Come on, Colleen. I'll tell you on the way."

I took her by the hand, and quickly we walked to the rental car. By the time I started the engine and headed out of the resort's sprawling complex, I was into the finer points of Dad's trust. I told her about Grandpa McSkimming and the PBB scandal. And then there was the Still Meadows account, and how the money was waiting for me. All three hundred thousand. Tax free.

For a woman of many words, she was almost speechless. Almost.

"What are we going to do with all that money?"

"We?" I asked.

"Give it to the church? Or charity?"

She had me smiling at such an urgent time. Her commitment to doing the right thing was ingrained in her head. I didn't have the heart to tell her about the fire at home and the immediate threat to my life. We were nearly to the bank, six or seven blocks away from the resort.

"Let me out here." She pointed to the pharmacy, a block away from the bank. "I'm almost out of toothpaste, and I want to look at the souvenirs. Something for my nephew." she said.

"Okay. I'll meet you down the street at the bank."

I squeezed her hand and dropped her off. Alexandria Bancorp Ltd. wasn't as impressive as I thought it might be. It was like a normal bank, with a Caribbean flavor. All was quiet. They only had two or three tellers, all of whom were at their stations, counting the contents of their drawers. I looked up, past the cameras to the ceiling, covered in a tin veneer. Instead of ceiling fans, the bank had giant, brass-looking leaves swaying back and forth. They were all connected to a metal rod that pumped back and forth like the arm of an old-fashioned locomotive. I felt a gentle puff of air.

One of the tellers asked if she could help me.

What an understatement.

"Of course you can."

I gave her the account number, and handed her my identification. And then, I gave her directions on how I wanted the money. Five thousand in euros. Twenty thousand in U.S. dollars. Pre-paid credit cards. Two cashier's checks and a wire transfer back to my savings account in Alma.

When she handed me the twenty thousand, I visited one of their little booths and slid the stash into my secret belt with the zipper on the inside, my pockets, and my extra long tube socks. It was a wad, I admit, but I didn't know how else to carry it back to the states. I've never done anything like that.

I must have been in the bank for fifteen minutes. No other customers came or went. The manager paraded by me wearing a seersucker suit and a preppy yellow tie. He never asked why I was pulling most of the proceeds out of his establishment; it was just another ho-hum transaction. I figured that maybe Colleen would be along at any second. She's not one to spend a lot of time shopping.

At last, I was finished with my business. I breathed a sigh of relief. I had the dough.

Halfway to the car, halfway to my getaway, the world stopped. It was Roger. The goon. He grabbed my arm, and jammed the barrel of a gun into my side. It was hard and lifeless—the perfect device for getting his point across. I didn't have time to fight. Or fly like a pheasant. He shoved me into my rental car. I was at the wheel.

"Drive," he ordered.

"Which way?"

I started the engine and backed up. He waved his gun left, as if he was swishing a fly.

"Where are we going?" I asked him.

He didn't answer. Roger looked in the sideview mirror, then behind us. His sunglasses were one-way mirrors. His cologne barely masked the smell of his morning coffee. St. Martin's capital city of Marigot was going about its business. Nobody was in a rush. They never are in the Caribbean.

We came to a stop sign and I asked for direction.

He swished his gun and we were headed towards the resort.

"Keep going," he said. "And pick it up a little."

I stepped on the gas and we zoomed along, past the villagers on their way to the market. There were others on little scooters. Motorized bicycles.

"What do you want?" I asked him. "You want some money? I got money."

He didn't say a thing.

His silence was killing me.

I felt my nose run. The same way it did when I nearly got in a fight with Byron Hovey. It was the adrenalin, coursing through my veins, racing through my senses. With each second that passed, I was losing out on the opportunity to escape. I should have plowed into a building, a post, an abandoned bicycle. Anything. We passed the entrance to the resort and kept going. There weren't as many people. No more distractions. No more chances for escape. I was doomed.

"What is it, Roger?" I was getting the nerve. "Tell me what you want!"

"Shut up."

I kept driving. Nobody behind us. Nobody in front. The nice, paved road was eclipsed by the rain forest on both sides. It formed a canopy of green over the road. I guessed we were a mile or two from the resort.

"What do you want, an apology?" I said. "I'm sorry, Roger. It won't happen again."

"Pull over."

"Where?"

The road barely had a shoulder. I didn't know where or how.

"Up ahead. On the right. This side of that path."

I pulled over and noticed the rear end of a Lexus parked down the path. It was small and black, Roger's getaway car. This was not good.

My nose was running furiously. I sniffled. And wiped the end with my hand. I was in the hands of a professional killer. I was out of time. I thought about Colleen. Mom and Dad. My family. Dear Synch and all those pheasants we killed together in her career. What a wonderful life.

"Pop the hood, and put your wallet on the seat," he said. He was gruff, all business.

I reached for the lever for the hood, then into my back pocket. I laid my wallet on the console between us. "Hands on the wheel."

My heart pounding.

My lungs racing.

I wanted to believe that it was all a dream.

A bad dream.

I prayed that the fire wasn't true.

I looked at him and the way there was no emotion. No pent-up aggression, or heart-racing fury coursing through his veins. He was so cool. So professional.

"Missed a good cookout last night, Twitchell," he said. "Your house went up in a ball of fire." He was rubbing my nose in it. "Too bad you're not going to be there to cover it."

I didn't know what to say. He could take my house, but I was still alive. And I clung to that hope.

"Tell me something, Twitchell," he said. "Who's going to write your obituary?"

My execution was just a minor speed bump. I thought for a second about smacking him in the face, but then he would have pulled the trigger on the gun and smattered me all over the inside of the vehicle. He read my mind, and cocked his gun. It was just like mine—the one I left at home—with the snub nose and the squat profile.

"Hands on the wheel!" He raised his voice, and I did what he said.

He reached in his pocket, and pulled out a small roll of duct tape.

"Tape your left hand to the wheel." He handed me the roll and I did what he said.

"Leave your fingers exposed."

Oh God, I thought. *This is what he did to Charles Cigan! He's going to snip off my fingers!*

It was the most brutal thought I could imagine.

And I started to cry.

Like a fool.

How am I going to type my stories with nubs for fingers?

How am I going to pull the trigger on Grandpa's gun next fall in Iowa?

"I'll tell you whatever you want, Roger! Don't kill me."

I pleaded with the man, but he didn't say a thing. He wrapped the tape around my right hand, much tighter than my left. He reached across the wheel and wrapped my left even harder than the right. I was stuck. Trapped. At his mercy. I said another prayer. I asked for forgiveness.

"Take the money, Roger. There's five grand in my wallet. The rest I sent home. I'll give it to you, I swear, as soon as we get back."

He didn't even flinch.

"Who's we?"

I hesitated. The guy thought I was alone. He must have checked the itinerary from Detroit, not Chicago, and didn't realize that I had company.

I looked in the rearview mirror, and saw a native coming at us, riding a motorized bicycle. It was my one shot for freedom.

"There's four or five of us," I said, trying to pull off the bluff of all bluffs.

"Bullshit."

The bike came closer and closer. Roger looked behind us, and saw it coming. I had lost the element of surprise.

"Here comes one of them, now."

He got out of the car and opened the hood all the way. The native stopped the motorcycle on the opposite side of the street, and set down her bag of rations.

"*Bonjour*. Can I call you a taxi, sir?"

I recognized the intonation, the voice, it was Colleen. I squirmed in my seat. I wanted to yell at her to run. Or call for help.

Roger took control of the scene and I bit my tongue.

"I think the alternator has gone bad," he said. "We just called the garage. They're on the way. Don't need any help."

"That's great," she said. "I've got lots of experience," her accent as thick and potent as the *foie gras* from the night before. I watched her pick up her bag and walk across the street. I noticed the bat handle, as plain as day. It was child-sized. Wooden. Small. She was so cool. So collected. And convincing. It was as if she were walking to the plate with the bases loaded and two outs in the ninth.

Roger never suspected that she was with me. I couldn't watch. Only hear what was taking place.

"Is your alternator on the port or starboard?" she asked.

Nice touch, Colleen. I thought.

"Not exactly sure…"

I lowered my head, and looked beneath the open hood. He reached across the engine compartment and Colleen had her opening. I watched her pull the bat from her bag. She was at the plate, a fastball right down the middle.

Roger saw the distraction, too, but it was too late. He backed up, quickly, his feet shuffling the pavement. He reached for the gun in his sport coat, but she caught him with a thunderous blow to the side of his skull. It snapped backward as if it were hit with a shotgun blast. *That*, I did see. But more importantly, I *heard* what took place. She hammered him. It was a *thwack* I'll never forget.

Roger Chinonis crumpled in a heap, next to my door. He didn't wince in pain, or moan. The big man with a thick neck was awfully still. Blood poured from his mouth and his ear; it pooled onto the pavement in a small trickle.

We panicked.

"Come on, Derrick!" she yelled at me. "Let's go!"

She tossed her bag into the back seat and jumped inside.

We were shouting.

"I can't!" I yelled at her. "Help me!"

My hands were taped to the steering wheel and I couldn't turn the key in the ignition.

She rammed the key forward and put the car in gear.

"Go, man, go!" She was yelling even louder.

I squealed the tires and cranked the wheel as hard as I could.

We almost wound up in the ditch on the other side of the road.

"Reverse! Reverse! Reverse!" I yelled.

"Oh, cripes, Derrick!"

We left Roger lying in a heap.

Nobody saw us.

The car was zooming along, my hands still taped to the wheel.

"Is this your idea of a honeymoon!?" She was yelling at me.

"What?"

"I saw you go whizzing right past me. And you've got this guy with you!"

"What?" I asked. "Like I really planned that!"

"How about a little appreciation!"

She had lost her French accent, but she was still riled up. We both were.

"Thank you, thank you! A thousand times, thank you!" I was huffing with adrenalin. "I couldn't believe you actually did that! He could have killed us both."

The rainforest was gone now, and we were entering town. I was flying. The driving was okay, just as long as the road was relatively straight. I dreaded the thought of turning a corner, where I might dislocate my elbows in the process.

"How did you come up with the scooter?"

"I stole it," she said. "Had to. I told the guy to call the police."

"I think we should go there right now. We're going to go right down there and make a police report. I learned my lesson in Iowa."

"Step on it, will you?" she demanded. "It's downtown."

"Where?"

"Three blocks from the bank. But there's something really important I need to tell you."

I looked at her and the expression on her face.

It was something significant, I could tell.

"You mean after all this stuff with Kaminsky and Roger, the PBB nightmare, the recovery of my prized family shotgun, and Dad's three hundred thousand you have something important to tell me?"

My tone was half-joking, half serious. Of all the crazy things I had been through, I seemed to have forgotten about the most important person in my life.

She was smiling, now. Joyfully. Tears rushed down her face. There really was something important. Really important.

I approached the intersection of Main Street but couldn't crank the wheel far enough. I ran out of space. And time. I slammed on the brakes, and the wheels on my little rental car screeched to a halt. Colleen had to brace herself with the handle. I couldn't reach for anything; my hands were still taped to the wheel.

We sighed in unison.

"What is it, Colleen?"

A group of cars and passers-by looked in at us, and the way we were blocking traffic. She placed her hand softly on my cheek, her face mere inches from mine. I felt the warmth of her skin, the fire boiling inside her. She was suddenly crying. Tears of joy. The mother of all emotions.

"Derrick, I'm pregnant. We're going to have a baby."

Her words were so incredible.

I had waited my entire adult life to hear them.

And finally it happened.

And I didn't know what to say.

Now I was the one with tears in my eyes, a loss for words.

"Oh, sweetheart. Oh, Colleen. You've made me so happy."

She laughed.

I laughed.

We cried.

Together.

She brushed a tear from my cheek, and pushed her nose against mine.

It was a tender, special moment.

The crowd outside the car window looked in at us as if we had lost our marbles.

I didn't care about them or anything else in the world.

Everything in my universe was right here beside me, an arm's length away.

She saved my life.

In more ways than one.

I was so grateful.

So honored.

So much in love.

At long last, I was going to be a dad.

"Colleen?" I sniffled.

"Yes," she said, still beaming with pride. "What is it, Derrick?"

I wiggled my fingers, now turning an unpleasant shade of blue.

"Could you help me get rid of this duct tape so I can give you a hug?"